CONDEMNED

CONDEMNED

by Paul Kuttner

Dawnwood Press
NEW YORK

Copyright © 1983 by Paul Kuttner

All rights reserved. No part of this book may be reproduced in any form or by any electronic or mechanical means including information storage and retrieval systems without permission in writing from the publisher, except by a reviewer who may quote brief passages in a review.

Library of Congress Cataloging in Publication Data

Kuttner, Paul.
    Condemned.

    I. Title.
PS3561.U797C6   1983   823'.914   83-1872
ISBN 0-911025-02-2

Published in the United States by Dawnwood Press, Suite 2650,
c/o Sterling Publishing Company, Inc., Two Park Avenue,
New York, N.Y. 10016.
FIRST EDITION 1983
Designed by Dennis Critchlow
Printed in the United States of America

What the Critics say about
Paul Kuttner's first novel
THE MAN WHO LOST EVERYTHING

"The ultimate nightmare of the city dweller in the 1970's"
———*San Francisco Examiner*

"The most diabolical sequence of events. An exceptional novel."
———*The Sun*, Colorado Springs

"Will keep you wanting to turn the page. It would be unfair to reveal the ending—one you would not expect."
———*Norwich Bulletin*, Conn.

"Not simply a tale of suspense but an honest picture of beautiful, tender and often frightening love."
———*Herald American*, Palm Springs

"A chilling, thrilling, endlessly suspenseful story . . . I recommend it most enthusiastically to all who want to get deeply into crime novels well-structured."
———*Manhattan Cable TV*

"Absolutely hooked from page one . . . I simply could not put down Kuttner's passionately suspenseful novel."
———*The Midwest Book Review*

"Sustains a suspense from the first to the last. Kuttner has something to tell us, something that perhaps we'd rather not hear."
———*Tampa Tribune-Times*, Fla.

"All lovingly described."
———*Library Journal*

"A suspenseful thriller."
———*American Library Association Booklist*

"A spellbinding plot . . . Takes a hard look at what happens to an average guy when the pressure is on."
———*Cedar Rapids Gazette*, Iowa

"Author Kuttner has managed to weave tenderness, passion and terror into a suspenseful plot with a surprise ending."
———*Copley News Service*

"The reader is carried along on the roller coaster of terror to the finish."
———*News Sentinel*, Ft. Wayne, Ind.

ABOUT THE AUTHOR

Paul Kuttner, at 16, became the youngest foreign correspondent in London, writing political, economic and cultural reports for a Swiss weekly. Later he worked in Hollywood and on Broadway as a columnist for *What's On In London*, the London counterpart of *Cue* magazine. As a publicity director with a New York publishing house, he helped to make the *Guinness Book of World Records* the best-selling annual in the world. He has translated about ten books into English and is the author of the American novel *The Man Who Lost Everything*—just translated into Spanish and now a best seller in Spain and South America.

*Dedicated
to the memory of
Margarete and Paul, my parents, and Annemarie, my sister,
and also to
Stephen, my son.*

When in disgrace with fortune and men's eyes,
I all alone beweep my outcast state,
And trouble deaf heaven with my bootless cries. . . .

From a sonnet by Shakespeare

Whoever battles with monsters had better see that it does not turn him into a monster.

Nietzsche
BEYOND GOOD AND EVIL

PART ONE: RECOGNITION

1

Paul Hammer had not been in the air-conditioned waiting room more than five minutes when the door to his son's office flew open and slammed into the wall. Hammer instinctively leaped to his feet and bumped into an enamel-dial bracket clock on the mantelpiece behind him just as a young man in rumpled brown slacks and a pea-green T-shirt with the boldface lettering "Don't Eat The Yellow Snow!" charged out of Dr. Jesse Hammer's study.

The young man stood still for a moment, eyes wild and twitching maniacally in a gray, haggard face. The next instant he bolted across the waiting room; but no sooner had he reached its farthest corner when Jesse Hammer came dashing out after him, followed a few steps behind by the patient's distraught parents. At their approach, the young man—already cowering in the corner—slowly began to slide down. He whined and whimpered infantilely, begging not to be beaten.

Jesse Hammer yanked a noisy beeper from his white smock, swiftly flicked off the high-pitched call signal with his thumb and stashed the device away in his pants pocket. He bent toward his patient and spoke to him calmly. His soothing, reassuring voice had an immediate effect. The whimpering subsided and the deranged man allowed his parents to pull him back to his feet. Jesse continued his soft murmur as he guided the invalid by his elbow out of the waiting room. The unhappy mother exchanged anxious words with her husband, and both meekly followed the doctor into the hallway.

Stunned by the unexpected little drama, Paul Hammer did not move an inch. He heard a spitfire barrage of agitated words from the corridor. An outer door closed firmly, then silence.

A minute later Jesse returned, visibly preoccupied, and strode energetically toward his office.

"Hello, Jess."

Jesse spun around, his hand already reaching for the door to his study.

"Dad!" A few brisk steps and he had reached his father. Their hands tightened in a firm, warm clasp. "You're early. I hope you didn't have to wait long. It's been a hectic morning."

"So I notice."

"Oh, that scene just now." Jesse chuckled. "You should've seen Ernie when he first came here, a couple of months ago." He opened the door for his father and glanced at his watch. "It's almost one, Dad. Let's have some lunch and talk. Did you have a good flight?"

"Very good, thanks . . . Hey—look at that!"

They had entered Dr. Hammer's spacious office. Even with the two immense, paper-strewn desks and the masses of flowers in vases, it was dominated by two morning-glory-crested bay windows looking out on a sprawling green lawn surrounded by ancient oaks and beeches. Half a dozen sheep were grazing in this peaceful, rustic setting alongside the shady grove.

"Some place you have here!" His father appreciatively scanned the sun-flooded study.

"Glad you like it," Jesse said, washing his hands. "Certainly makes work more pleasant for me."

"So it should. Especially if you've got to deal with those loonies all day long."

"Dad, they're *not* loonies." Jesse was drying his hands, then hung up his white smock and slipped into a gabardine jacket. "Most of them are bright people, faced with conditions they couldn't handle on the outside, that's all." He closed both windows. "And with my new mind control method here, they learn how to cope again. Ready?"

They left the administrative wing of the red-brick recuperation complex, uncomfortably conscious of the sweltering summer heat on their cool skin while crossing the private parking lot in front of the

Neurological Rehabilitation Center.

"Any air pockets on your way over this time?" Jesse asked as they headed for his old Volvo.

The elder Hammer shook his head. "No air pockets. Slept almost all the way from London. . . . Are we going to your place?"

"Yes. I've got a nice surprise for you when we get home."

"Oh?" They settled into the sun-baked leather seats of the car and fastened their seat belts. As they sped down the deserted country road, Hammer gazed admiringly at the huge fields of yellow corn, stalks standing stiff as an army of Prussian tin soldiers.

"I love this part of the country," he mused as Jesse swung onto Route 17B. White ashes, firs and lush elms lining the highway at irregular intervals in densely wooded copses flashed by, shading bits of the hot, dusty rural road on which they traveled, but the midday heat was so intense that the bleached tips of the trees stood frozen, like mosques and minarets, in the still summer air.

They were already well past the sleepy villages of Callicoon and Hortonville when, out of the blue, a merciful gust of wind suddenly blew across the sun-shimmering fields, the meadows sprinkled with wanton cloudbursts of daisies, right into their car, so that even the green, sylvan curtain of conifers and saplings seemed to sway and nod in grateful response. Hammer breathed deeply, letting the warm breeze wash over his face and feeling completely at ease, tranquil— as one could only in the serene habitat of nature—and he filled his lungs thirstily with the fragrance of verdant cow pastures.

"It's always such a nice break from city life to visit you here." He turned back to his son. "I still don't understand, though, why you sent me a First Class ticket this time. Your old man isn't so broke that his son's got to provide him with plane tickets, least of all First Class."

"Why shouldn't I treat you right, Dad? After what you've been through you deserve the best. Besides, I figured that unless I sent you the ticket, you'd never get back over here to your adopted country."

"Hell, I'm not complaining, Jess. But why First Class?"

Jesse shrugged. "Just felt that it was time you tasted some of the finer things in life. After all, you *are* important . . .sort of." He aimed a quick, boyish grin at his father. "Always intrigued me, your title! Director of Creative Management."

"Big deal! Fancy name for 'illustrator' . . . Hey, look out, Jess! You're driving like a madman." The car had swerved around a dead chipmunk, almost sideswiping a telephone pole.

"Come on, Dad, calm down!" Jesse furrowed his brows and slowed down considerably. "I don't know how you ever lived through those years in the camps if you were that jumpy."

"Well, maybe my nerves *are* shot to hell. I'm not getting any younger, you know."

"No, you're doing fine. But don't turn into a grumpy old man now and start knocking your title. You're head of the art department of one of the most prestigious U.S. ad agencies in London."

"I know, I'm a certified genius. Still, don't imagine that the title means much to me. Teaching the limeys how to put the American touch on ads for underarm deodorants, toilet paper and sanitary napkins isn't my idea of art."

"But how many people can say that they're secure in their jobs with all this unemployment today *and* make their living doing what they know best?"

"I know, I know. It's just that I've set my heart on painting; you know, painting landscapes, oils, watercolors. By the weekends, though, I'm so bushed I've got barely enough energy to pack the easel into my Morris."

"Then why not chuck your job and spend the rest of your life painting?"

"Are you crazy? I've still got eight more years to go. You don't want me to give up my pension, do you? Forty thousand dollars is nothing to laugh at."

"Forget about that pension, Dad!" Jesse stopped briefly at a flashing red light at an intersection, then turned right on Highway 52. "Give up your job and settle here with me. We'll have enough money to. . . ."

"Hold it! Hold it!" the father broke in. "I'm not going to 'settle down' with anybody. I'm much too young to have my son taking care of me, Jess. I'm only fifty-eight."

"I'm not asking you to give up your independence. I want you to relax, go anywhere you want, paint. You know yourself that you're talented; maybe you can make a living selling your work."

"Stop it, Jess. That's unrealistic. I know you mean well, and I appreciate it, but. . . ."

"Dad, listen to me!" Jesse's pleading voice became more urgent. "I feel I owe you something. You raised me single-handedly after Mom died. You spent a fortune putting me through school. Now I want to pay back every penny of it."

"Oh no, you don't!" Hammer turned again to his son, resolutely determined not to let anyone divert him from his set ways. "You have *your* life; I have mine. I'm proud of you, your success—let's leave it at that." He faced front once more, squinted against the bright sun and seemed momentarily blinded. Then his face brightened. "Well—I see the old cottage still looks the same."

The Volvo had swung into a driveway and stopped between two burly rhododendron bushes. To the right of one of them, and set well back from the road, was the gray-shingled cottage with its fistfuls of marigolds peeking out of green window boxes. Towering pine trees and ashes shaded the house, their drooping branches brushing the roof lazily in the summer breeze.

Father and son climbed out of the car and stretched their legs in the weed-choked driveway, then walked into the house.

"Looks like I'll have my work cut out for a week. Damn dandelions all over the place."

"I want you to take it easy, Dad. It's your vacation. Where's your luggage anyway?"

"Jeffersonville. I got a room in a hotel there."

"That's silly. You know I've got plenty of room. We'll pick it up tonight. Come on, let's grab a bite to eat."

Jesse opened the kitchen windows to let out the musty smell of wood paneling and took a deep breath of the fresh pine-scented summer air wafting in. At last the two men sat down to a lunch of beef tartar and bagels, with hefty mugs of the local wood-pressed apple cider, and for a few minutes enjoyed the food in appreciative silence.

"You know, Jess, about my savings," Paul Hammer reflected. "I've really gotten back on my feet again. I've managed to scrape together close to thirty-five thousand dollars since you went into practice. Eight more years, and I may be able to double it, if I invest it right. Now add my pension to that and I'll be sitting pretty with about hundred-ten grand. Together with Social Security I could live quite well on the interest. So you see, you don't have to worry about your old man's finances. Besides, you're no millionaire yourself, son."

"Wrong, Dad, I am. Or rather I will be."

"Sure, you have a nice office, a good position, and probably make a decent salary, right?"

"Right."

"I've never pried into your finances, Jess, and I'm not going to start now. But don't tell me you're making a million."

"I make eight hundred a week."

"Not bad! I'm really glad for you, son. Forty grand a year is a good start."

13

"I could make two, three times that much in private practice if I chose to."

"Why don't you?"

"I told you, I don't choose to. Come on, dig in, there's plenty more food in the fridge."

"Thanks, I will. Why *don't* you start your own practice?"

"Because I've never been so happy in my life. My new psychological theories are accepted here by the staff for gospel. I've started a new concept for an institution of psychic disorders. Honestly, I live for it day and night."

"As long as you don't end up getting sick yourself."

"I won't. In fact, that mind control method is showing the rewards of my labors already. Last month they made me Assistant to the Director of the Psychiatric Wing. And when he retires in a couple of years, I'll take over his job. We're talking seventy-five thousand dollars."

"That sounds wonderful, Jess." Hammer gestured enthusiastically with his fork. "But that doesn't mean I would ever take a penny from you, even if you made ten times that. So, let's drop the subject. Got any more of this cider?"

"Sure, in the icebox."

"Tell me, son, " Hammer said, helping himself to another bottle, "what are you doing about your love life? Do you really expect to find a wife among all those nuts in the clinic?"

"For the thousandth time now, they're not nuts. Sick, yes, like any patient in a hospital. But many of them are completely cured, I assure you. And we don't take any criminally insane, violent patients."

"Okay, forget it! Just that I'm so damn worried about you sometimes. You're thirty, Jess, and you dedicate all your energies to these . . . well, these patients. You're more than a hundred miles from New York City; from a decent Martini, for heaven's sake."

"Stop worrying so much, Dad. You take life much too seriously." A sad little smile creased his face. "I've hardly ever seen you smile since Mom died."

"Let's not go through that again. I've gone through enough to turn anyone a little bit sour. And your beloved psychiatry can't claim that's an abnormal reaction."

"Of course not; I wasn't criticizing you. I know what the war did to you. But can't you understand, now that I'm in good shape I'd like to bring a smile to your face—and get to *see* that face once in a while?"

"I know, son. And your offer to help me out does make me happy. But if you ask me, what you need around here isn't your grumpy, quick-tempered old father, but a woman. Someone to share your happiness with, the money."

"Dad, remember I told you I'd have a surprise for you when we get home? Well, I *have* found someone, a beautiful girl who was. . . ."

"What! *Now* you're telling me?"

"Okay, simmer down! Just let me get the worst out of the way first—she *was* one of my patients, right here at the Sullivan County Neurological Rehabilitation Center."

"Oh oh!" The father's shoulders slumped with a long-suffering sigh and his mug rattled noisily on the table. "I should have known."

"Come on now, don't judge her before you know the whole story. This girl is *not* a nut. She's brilliant and hopes to be a concert pianist. But she's gone through some rough times. Suffered several really traumatic experiences."

"So have I. Probably worse than anybody you can point your finger at. But nobody ever had to lock me up on a funny farm."

"You're a strong person, Dad. Bear in mind that the camps in your youth became your definition of suffering. All pain after that, you simply shrug off. Still, people do react differently to life's problems. Some survive, some go under."

"Meaning that she *can't* take it. You're stuck with a weakling."

"For God's sake, don't twist my words around! She's not weak. Far from it. She bounced back magnificently. She's fully recovered and eager to meet you."

"I only hope your diagnosis is accurate, Dr. Hammer." Paul helped his son clear the dishes off the table and place them in the sink. Next, Jesse put up water for coffee and took a Sara Lee pound cake out of the refrigerator.

"To be honest," Hammer said, cutting the cake, "I have a mental image of a whimpering female in my mind, cringing and sucking her thumb."

"Nothing of the sort. She's spunky, all backbone, and has a bit of an Irish temper."

"And she's not likely to bounce back to . . . well, into the booby hatch?"

"It's *not* a booby hatch. For the last time!"

"Okay, okay, I'm sorry. Just that that place you work in brings back horrible memories. Incarceration. The camps. It's about the last place in the world *I'd* like to end up in."

"Now don't get paranoid, Dad. We're not talking about you, the horrors *you* went through, but the young lady I'm engaged to."

"Yeah. As you were saying: a spunky girl and all backbone."

"Right. And there's no reason for her to go back to the Center . . . provided there are no unforeseen circumstances."

"So there *is* a catch!"

"For crying out loud, cut it out! She's as sane as you and I. *Anybody* can land in the clinic. But there's no need to test her and shock her just to see how well she'll react to tension."

"So you've landed the perfect woman," Hammer said cynically, pushing the dessert from him.

"Yes . . . No, not perfect, but fine for me, even with her temper."

"Oh yes, that Irish temper."

"I'm afraid you're getting the wrong idea again. It's not that she's always angry at the world. But she hates to see anything that's unfair. If she thinks that someone is being treated unjustly, she gets furious, vicious—she's very tough that way—completely uncompromising when she takes a stand in the matter of justice. And in the past, that temper did lead her to some pretty explosive acts. That's how she wound up in the clinic."

"Well, well." Hammer nodded gloomfully. "Nice prospects!"

"But she's not mad," Jesse emphasized each word with great deliberation. "Okay, I grant you she *is* vulnerable after what she's gone through, but she's exquisitely beautiful, very bright, she trusts me with absolutely everything and is remarkably cheerful considering. . . ."

". . . . considering she ends up with a catch like you. After all, in a couple of years you'll make seventy-five grand and that should certainly help to set up a household and pay for her shrink and her piano lessons."

"Okay, I'll choose to ignore this little dig."

"Why, Jesse? Why is it a dig? How many girls can say that their bridegrooms are as successful as you are?"

"No question about it, you're absolutely right. But now be honest with me and tell me how many bridegrooms can say that they'll be marrying into two or three million dollars?"

"Two or three *what*?"

"Dad, the girl I'm going to marry at the end of the year is the granddaughter of Louis Luckstone."

Hammer raised a skeptical eyebrow. "And who, if I may ask, is Louis Luckstone?"

"You honestly don't recognize the name Luckstone?"

"Pardon my ignorance, but for the last seven years or so I've been out of the country. And London is not buzzing with the name

Louis . . . whatever his name is."

"Luckstone. Then again, why should you know? He's not mentioned in *Ad Age* very often. Come on, let's sit in the sun for a few minutes. I'll do the dishes later. And you better prepare yourself for a little shock."

2

They walked out into the back. Two lounge chairs, their aluminum supports warm from the late summer sun, stood in a meadow yellow with daisies and buttercups.

"Jesse, this place is a mess," Hammer observed, casting a baleful eye on the unkempt lawn, the thistles, the crabgrass. "Haven't you used a lawn mower since I was here last?"

"I'm busy, Dad, and help's not easy to come by around here. Plenty of unemployed but not too dependable."

They stretched out on the chairs and for a while let the sun bake them in silence. Bees were humming in the grass, flies kept buzzing against the windowpanes and screens behind them, starlings fluttered in frenzied flight from sycamore to appletree and back again.

"Now then, who is. . . ." Hammer dropped the soft inquiry as a loud roar filled the nearby woods. Hammer jerked his head toward his son. "What's that sound?" Somewhere, not far away, the screech of a chain saw jolted the calm of the lazy September afternoon.

Jesse sat up. "One of the neighbors cutting wood for the winter. Lots of that around with money being so tight."

"Uh-huh . . . Okay, what about Luckstone? Who is he?"

Jesse grinned at his father. "One of the richest men in America. Head of a multinational conglomerate and one of the President's closest friends and economic advisers."

Hammer stared at his son for a long time, then shook his head incredulously. "And you're going to marry his daughter?"

"His granddaughter. And she brings two or three million bucks into the marriage. Not that I'm marrying her for the money—in fact, she's the one who proposed—but maybe *now* you'll understand why I told you to forget about your pension. Because Nicole wants. . . ."

"Nicole?"

"That's her name. Nicole. Nicole Luckstone. When I told her about you, all your suffering, and showed her your paintings in the cottage, she said she'd be thrilled if you'd accept ten percent of her wealth. Because. . . ."

"Ten percent of two mill . . . She really *is* nuts."

"Wait, Dad. She says it's due to *you* that she got to know me at the clinic; all those sacrifices you made bringing me up alone, spending your life's savings so I could study psychology."

"But, Jess, that's crazy. Ten percent of two or three million. She doesn't even know me."

Jesse simply shrugged. "At least two hundred grand, Dad, after we get married. And the wedding's set for Christmas week."

Hammer let down his feet in the tall grass and sat up straight. "You're not pulling my leg, Jess?"

"I've never been more serious in my life. Besides, she can always write it off as a donation or get the money back from her grandfather. She even said so. I ask you now: why wait eight more years when you can have twice as much next year?"

"I'm . . . Really, I'm speechless."

"About time you quieted down."

"It's like a fairytale. The happy ending of a 1930s movie. You with a good job, a pretty wife, wealth. And me. . . . I just can't believe it."

"It's true, though."

"And her grandfather won't mind?"

"It's her money and she can do with it as she pleases."

"What about her parents?"

"Dead. Both of them. She's been an orphan since she was ten. Just like Mom died when I was ten. That's one of the things we have in common. You raised me since I was ten, and her grandfather raised her since she was ten. That's why she wants to meet you so badly."

"You mean to compare notes?"

"To see the man who raised a magnificent specimen like me."

Hammer shook his head. "I can't get over it . . . I suppose losing both parents was one of those traumatic experiences she went through?"

"I'm afraid so."

"And that drove her crazy?"

"Of course not. How can I explain it to you? Look, let's start at the beginning. She worshipped her parents. One day she was seeing them off at Kennedy Airport. The plane took off for Paris, reached about five hundred feet, and crashed. You could almost say she saw them burn to death right in front of her."

"Jesus! That *is* rough. And only ten."

"So she was left with Eric in Louis Luckstone's care."

"Who is Eric?"

"Her twin brother. I guess I forgot to mention him before. They were always together. He witnessed the plane accident too. If they were inseparable before, after their parents' death they were almost like Siamese twins. They went to the same classes, the same summer camps, they did their homework together, and shared the same bedroom."

"Sounds a little too close, doesn't it?"

"Without him, she would have gone to pieces; of that I'm convinced. Her grandfather recognized the importance of that tie, the strength they gave each other. He was only too happy to see how their closeness helped them overcoming the obstacles that teenagers from troubled homes often face. But it wasn't meant to last. Tragedy struck again."

"Oh?"

"Three years ago, when she and Eric were seventeen. Both of them were in Mexico vacationing while LL had some business to attend to in Guadalajara."

"LL? Who's. . . ."

"Everybody calls Louis Luckstone 'LL'. In any case, the two kids had rented a Ferrari and were racing along the coast toward Acapulco when they collided with another car. Eric was killed instantly. Almost half the bones in Nicole's body were broken. For five months she was in the hospital, in a cast, recovering from multiple fractures."

"Awful!"

"But these fractures were nothing compared to the psychological wounds inflicted by her brother's death. He had meant everything to her, and his sudden disappearance left a gaping hole in her life. Worst of all, however, were the nights when she woke up screaming, unable to stop, sometimes for hours on end. You see, Dad, in the automobile accident Eric was decapitated. She remembered seeing her brother at the wheel, a bloody stump on his shoulders, with no head. His head was catapulted out of the car onto the road. That's how she last saw the 17-year-old boy she adored."

"Oh my God!"

"Now, for the first time she was absolutely alone in the world."

"What about her grandparents?"

"Oh—LL divorced his wife decades ago. And the other grandparents died years before. Anyway, LL became the most loving, doting guardian imaginable, I'm told. He took her along everywhere, even on business trips, and she in turn came to depend more and more on him. The old man was badly shaken up himself by this latest loss, of course. In fact, Nicole often had to reverse roles and comfort LL."

"And she did bounce back, as you say, eventually."

"Took about a year, but she made it. And then one day she went out again, for the first time since Eric was killed, with Dave Shadow, the son of LL's closest associate. Dave and Nicole had known each other since childhood, but there was never anything serious between them. Fact is there was never anyone before in her life romantically, while Eric was alive. Anyhow, gradually she joined David's social set. They started going to parties together, much to the delight of her grandfather, who was overjoyed to watch her blossom into a beautiful and much sought-after young woman.

"Of course, the inevitable happened. The two fell in love, became an item in the society columns, and everything would have been okay if it hadn't been for the fact that Dave was a playboy—a regular Don Juan. What LL didn't know, at least not at first, was that the parties often turned into orgies, with lots of sex, booze, hash, coke—you name it. Finally LL got wind of what was going on, when Nicole dropped the bombshell and announced that she was pregnant. The wedding with Dave was set for last summer, much to the displeasure of LL, who suddenly didn't think much of his prospective grandson-in-law. But Nicole insisted and Dave seemed quite content with the idea of marrying into really big money."

For a few moments Jesse stopped, listening when the sound of ax blows joined the drone of the chain saw as another neighbor prepared a wood pile for winter.

Then, with obvious reluctance, he resumed his tale. "Dave's father—remember? LL's aide—had cut off his son financially months earlier because of his wild behavior, so David saw the marriage as a marvelous means of continuing the luxurious lifestyle to which he had become accustomed. The two got married. But there was one thing wrong with the marriage from the outset. While she still loved him—he didn't love her any more. After the wedding ceremony he simply vanished. Twelve hours later she found him at a friend's house, in a bathtub filled with Burgundy . . . and two naked girls."

"Christ!"

"She quickly realized the truth, that he only married her for her money, but he promised he'd change his ways, and she always gave him another chance, hoping he'd fall in love with her again. Remember, she still loved the guy. Of course, everybody guessed, which wasn't difficult, considering how brazenly he carried on his extramarital affairs, because soon he disappeared again with other women, sometimes for two, three nights at a clip."

"Why didn't she leave him?"

"She did, after a few weeks. Of course, there were the most awful rows and reconciliations in-between, but what really brought it to a boil was when, in one of his drunken scenes, he accused her in front of a huge party of having had incestuous relations with her twin brother. Dave was dead drunk, pointing at her and yelling to the crowd that Eric was killed in the car on their way to an abortionist. That she was pregnant with her brother's child."

"Jesus! Some husband! But . . . how did he get that idea? Was there any truth to it? I mean *was* she. . . ."

"Absolutely not! The hospital records never showed anything of the sort, I was assured."

"Assured by whom?"

"Nicole herself. She trusts me with *everything*. And by LL. But she blamed herself for Eric's death nevertheless."

"Jesse, if she felt guilty over her brother's death, isn't there the remote possibility she really *was* pregnant by him? You did say they were strangely close at the time."

Jesse shot his father a long, steel-hard look. "Nicole confides her most intimate secrets to me. And she swore that she had never lied to me."

"Women have been known to keep secrets even from the men they profess to love . . . just *because* they don't want to lose them."

"But not Nicki. Besides, I was her psychiatrist long before I was her fiancé, and she *did* offer to send for a copy of the hospital records."

Suddenly Jesse jerked his head back. A bluebottle fly had landed on his nose, another on the chair, the next second they buzzed around in circles again.

"Flies all over the damn place this summer!" he remonstrated. "Anyway, when Dave Shadow ridiculed her with this monstrous lie in front of that crowd of friends and total strangers, she went berserk with humiliation, with the fear that news of the scene might trickle back to her grandfather. Worst of all, it opened an old wound she thought had healed. She literally went mad with grief hearing the memory of her brother smeared that way, then hearing the snickers of the guests she considered her friends. More importantly, what little she still felt for Dave had finally been dealt the *coup de grâce*."

For an instant Jesse took a breather. He tried to swat one of the flies on his pants but missed. Three more immediately took its place.

"Nicki was like a woman possessed," he went on. "She grabbed a carving knife from the sideboard and attacked him then and there. They fought like wildcats, people told me. It took half a dozen men to tear her from him. Later that night she hemorrhaged and lost her baby. After that she left him. By this time he had gambled away most of the money she brought into the marriage. She filed for divorce on the grounds of adultery. He couldn't contest it—there were too many witnesses to testify in her favor."

"What about her grandfather?"

"Nicki returned to him, and he was relieved that it was all over between them. It also gave him the chance to look after her again. To prove how much he still loved her, he immediately placed almost three million dollars at her disposal."

"Isn't that rather foolish?" Hammer shook his head skeptically. "I mean, after he saw how easily a man could part his granddaughter from her money?"

"I'm not so sure, Dad. Just keep in mind she's his only living relative; he dotes on her and was so overwhelmed by the loss of the baby that he couldn't do enough for her. He felt she had learned her lesson and that it was the only way he could reconfirm his trust in Nicole, instill new confidence in her. And it worked, Dad. Now it was her grandfather she loved more than anybody else. He was the only human being who had never let her down. She began to worship him. At the same time, though, she was scared. She believed that everything she touched, everyone she loved, was doomed. She lived in constant fear that any display of affection was bound to end in death. She began to withdraw more and more from the few people who still befriended her and felt responsible somehow for the death of her parents and her brother, and for the horrible character of her husband."

"And that's when she was admitted to your clinic?"

"Not even then yet. You see, two months after their breakup, Dave came to see her again, acting contrite and looking run down, almost destitute. He was a sick person, an alcoholic, a drug addict, and he asked her forgiveness, promising he'd give up booze, drugs, his women. She didn't even have to love him in return, only to give him another chance to prove that he *could* make her happy if she gave him that chance. But the magic of love was gone. It just didn't work any more.

"In fact, her love had not turned to indifference but implacable hatred. She let him know in no uncertain terms that nothing could change her mind. She just was no longer interested in him. But he was equally adamant. He threatened to kill her and himself if she didn't take him back. This time, though, she stood firm, and he could do nothing but stalk out, cursing her and vowing revenge. He registered at a nearby motel. Next morning the maid found him dead. An overdose of heroin." Jesse pulled out his handkerchief and briefly mopped his brow.

"When that news was relayed to Nicole, she collapsed. It came so unexpectedly and was more than she could bear. She actually blamed herself for the death of her estranged husband now. Again she had proved to herself that all those she had loved died a terrible death. Even LL could no longer pull her out of her depression, her total withdrawal from everybody, everything, and as a last resort he asked us to have her committed to our Center, probably because it is close to his estate and he could keep an eye on her." For a moment Jesse stopped as his eyes followed the erratic flight of a Monarch butterfly. Then he continued.

"I spoke to LL myself—the Clinic's Director was away at a convention in Europe—and I promised him that we'd do our best to help her. Even with the federal and state funds and the in-patient payments we still operated on a deficit. I told him that we were desperately short of equipment, nurses, doctors, needed countless repairs, and so on. Without blinking an eye, LL promised an endowment of two million dollars, insisting that we have the facilities to give the best treatment available to medical science. He said that he'd send up his own construction crews to do the repair work, and—behold!—within three months the place was humming with activity, with a new spirit. We had the resources to pay the best doctors, get the nurses, set up the most up-to-date medical facilities—the works. And for the next five years he has donated a cool million per annum to keep it running efficiently."

"Must be some guy."

"All he asked was that we name a wing in the new complex after Eric, and that we bring a semblance of normality back to Nicole."

"And you did, of course."

"It was touch and go for a while. She got the finest treatment, but even so it took about five months to snap her out of it. After going through so many traumatic experiences in her young life, some of the doctors felt she might never completely recover."

"And you think she has?"

"Look, there's always the chance she may be pushed back over the brink if she encounters a situation in life with which she just can*not* cope. At the same time, you could argue that applies to anyone. As for Nicole, she is enormously self-disciplined, has an iron will and a great capacity for optimism now—a true rejuvenation of the spirit."

"Sounds almost as if you're in love with the girl," Hammer commented without cracking a smile.

"You'll meet her and then you can see for yourself. But not even her grandfather knows that there was a period in the beginning when, for a few days, she completely withdrew from everyone, even the staff; she just stared sullenly through the barred windows on the lawn outside while we tried to activate her ego, to have her verbalize her inner feelings."

"To let it all hang out, as you youngsters like to say."

"Exactly. But my staff and I might as well have been talking to a wall. We made no progress. She had grown inward to the point where no outside stimuli penetrated her consciousness."

"Is that what you call autism?"

"Pretty close to it—yes."

"But didn't you say she improved again?"

"Two unexpected things happened. One Sunday evening one of the orderlies made a pass at her. He probably figured that since she was so withdrawn from life, she'd hardly be aware of what he was doing to her. Well, he forced himself on her in her private room while most of the inmates and staff were watching a movie. Then, suddenly she erupted. All the pent-up rage broke through, like a dam bursting. Her outrage at being violated once more was savage, diabolical. She almost killed the orderly, a burly two hundred pounder. Her wild screams after being stripped of her clothes attracted members of the staff, and just like during that last party with Dave Shadow, it took several men to pry her hands off the orderly's throat."

"But Jesse, Jesse my boy." Hammer literally tried to rub the worried expression off his face with both hands. "With those murderous instincts, how can you even entertain the idea of spending your life with this woman?"

"Dad, the man was trying to rape her. Besides, how would you, how would *any*body respond to those outrageous events in their life? Most people would have grown up totally neurotic, full of hostility, suspicion, despair, alienation. And, remember, even you have a pretty short fuse. But Nicole's psyche worked it out differently."

"How?"

"Instead of driving her further into autism—the more common alternative—she went the other route. She became verbally aggressive during therapy sessions, afterwards insisted that God had singled her out for punishment, for an unending series of tragedies. Remember, she was only nineteen. She railed against God, but she soon realized that He was inaccessible, untouchable, forever silent, so she denied Him altogether. But she needed someone to hate, to blame all her ill fortune on. And she chose the human race. People. She simply went through a phase of hating everybody. I can still see her, Dad, pounding her fist on the table, wishing that there was some human being she could get revenge on for all that had been done to her."

"I think I begin to understand her at last." Hammer was visibly moved. He sat up, wiping his brow, then rose cumbersomely out of his chair and dragged it through the tall grass.

"What's the matter? Where're you going?"

"Into the shade. The sun's too hot for me." He sighed and stretched out on the lounge chair under an apple tree. "Well now . . . what happened next?"

"Okay . . . First, after several weeks of that phase, the fires of hate gradually cooled down. Then, one day, she lost her way on the grounds and entered a large building, our Hall of the Performing Arts. There, in front of her, on the stage, stood a grand piano. A Baldwin. Music had always been her great passion. Later I learned that whenever she felt on top of the world or was depressed she'd retire to the Music Salon at LL's and fill the house with music. There was nobody in the building that morning except for her, and she started playing. It was only ten o'clock, a warm sunny day and the windows were open. By noon the auditorium was packed with inmates, doctors, orderlies, nurses, maintenance men. Dad, get this: Nicki played without sheet music for *seven* long hours. She has a fabulous memory and knows most of the classical solo works by heart. At first she concentrated for the most part on military music, marches; later polonaises, then Wagner transcriptions, Bach, Beethoven, and when she finally stopped at five, drenched in sweat, the audience leaped to its feet and gave her a rousing ovation. Until that moment she wasn't even aware that anybody was in the hall with her. But hearing this initial sign of appreciation, a genuine expression of love for something she had done, something she could control, brought the first smile in months to her face. It struck home through the hard crust she had built up around herself. Every day after that Nicki retired to the recital hall and played the piano for six or seven hours. Always different pieces."

"Jesus! She must know some repertoire, the girl."

"She does. Over the weeks she drove herself mercilessly, but the point is that she succeeded in defusing her anger, her unspeakable frustration. Slowly she began to introduce a more delicate element into her forceful music—études, waltzes, sonatas, even minuettes, Scarlatti, Mozart, Vivaldi, Boccherini. Her playing became markedly more restrained, softer, she smiled to herself more frequently. Her music had managed to pierce the armor, and that in turn made her early morning therapy sessions with me, my staff, that much more pleasant, a matter of cooperation. As I explained to her, she always had her music to fall back on in case someone caused her pain in the future."

"In other words, that's when she started bouncing back again."

"Exactly. Whenever she didn't play piano, she, like other progressing patients in the convalescent wing, would seek out the therapists to discuss personal problems with them. Mostly, though, she'd join me while I was taking walks on our beautiful grounds and talk about the contempt she earlier felt for herself. Nothing at the clinic had actually escaped her, despite her apparent autism. But best of all, she started worrying about the future."

"And being around one another most of the time, you two fell in love."

"*After* the therapy. So it's not just a matter of countertransference, where the therapist falls in love with a patient; it's all aboveboard. Anyway, she'll continue with her studies at home. LL has hired one of the finest piano teachers for her, and for a wedding gift he is building a house for us nearby."

"Unbelievable! Like a dream, son, it's all like a dream. Even with that temper of hers." Two deep furrows appeared on Hammer's brow. "Jesse, what do you think is the cause of it—that strong feeling for absolute justice you mentioned earlier?"

"Well . . . she told me once—but keep this under wraps, Dad—that it's sort of a defiance, a challenge to the blows nature has dealt her. More like an affirmation of her own worthiness, and at the same time an angry reply to destiny, God—whatever. But all this is a matter of the past. Once we're married, there'll be little reason for such outbursts."

Paul Hammer nodded, only partly appeased and deeply in thought. "Let's hope so . . . In any event, that's it, I suppose."

"Of course, LL had to make sure that Nicki wouldn't go through the same nightmare with me as she did with Dave, so he had someone run a check on me."

"A check?" Hammer regarded his son with some concern.

"About my character, what sort of family I come from and...."

"Hey that would involve me too. Did he ever say what he came up with?"

"Sure did. You may not believe this, Dad, but you're actually one of his employees."

"What are you talking about? He doesn't run Elwin, Boyd & Cohn."

"Do you remember about ten years ago when E.B.&C. became part of the Tristate Corporation?"

"Of course. So what?"

"Tristate is one of the companies owned by LL's Eastern Seaboard multinational conglomerate."

Hammer's eyes grew wide with surprise. "Good Lord! You mean I'm one of his worker ants?"

"And he had no difficulty getting a dossier on you; financial, loyalty, work efficiency, police records, you name it, and how you supported me through school. He told me he liked you, sight unseen, and couldn't be happier with Nicki's choice for a new husband."

"Well, whaddya know! You and me both working for the same boss."

"We could both do a lot worse, believe me. In fact, these last few years, since Eric's death, he's become the most generous person in the world. A tough businessman, but very human. And humane."

"I can see that. A million here, two million there."

"It's not just that, Dad. That was mostly for his family. Nicki's all taken care of, money-wise. He himself is reputed to be worth between one and two billion dollars. But the millions he does not plow back into his uncountable enterprises, he's using for philanthropic purposes. That's what put him on the cover of *TIME* a couple of months ago."

"No kidding!"

"Of course, he's always mentioned in *Fortune*, *The Wall Street Journal*, but what brought him to the public's attention here were the two philanthropic projects he's heading. One's a local development that will just about eliminate unemployment in this county, and...."

"Sounds like he is his own government."

"He almost is. And the other project is world-wide, to eliminate cancer by setting up Interferon Labs everywhere."

"Oh *now* I remember! The interferon project is bringing it all back to me. That's why his name sounded vaguely familiar. But I must confess, Jesse, I never bothered to read anything about his life."

"The fact is he's been staking out this part of the country. It's only a couple of hours' drive from New York City, and as you know thousands of people are settling down here because the land is still relatively inexpensive. It's turning into a sort of bedroom and weekend community for the middle and upper classes, so LL is working now on this huge complex of stores, apartment buildings, hotels, hospitals, schools, sports facilities and art centers. It's not far from here—between Bethel, where I attended the Woodstock Festival—and Fosterdale. He'll sink more than a hundred million dollars into it. That by itself, with the construction and the maintenance, should absorb most of the unemployed in Sullivan County, especially among the minorities. And of course, this is strictly family info—the fact that LL donated five million dollars to the next Presidential campaign, or rather his many companies have, to make it legal—didn't hurt in that area. By the way, with regard to the local project, the Zoning Commission has suggested to name the new enterprise Luckstone City, in his honor. And the icing on the cake is that yesterday they received the President's blessing—he'll be here in the fall for the opening ceremonies of the construction site."

"All that, and the Interferon Labs too?"

"Something he's heading on a world-wide scale with a dozen other captains of industry. A crash program to discover how to isolate, purify and synthesize interferon in huge quantities to win the battle against cancer. They're hiring the greatest scientific minds in the world and providing them with all the financial resources and equipment they need."

"Terrific! But you know, Jess, it seems to me I read somewhere that interferon isn't quite the wonder drug it was cracked up to be, and that in some forms of cancer there have been no cures at all or even remissions treating patients with it."

"What you've read is correct, of course. But keep in mind that interferon can be therapeutically useful in the treatment of other ailments besides cancer, like in burns and infection and helping the body's immunological defense mechanism. At present it's so scarce and impure, though, for experimental purposes—sixty-five thousand pints of blood are needed to produce one tenth of a gram of interferon—that its full biomedical research can't be measured until it can be made available in large quantities, and that's where LL's labs come in. Of course, there's much more involved in it, like genetic engineering, for example, and scientists specializing in cancer viruses that contain cancer-causing genes, oncogenes. But when all is said and done, he told me he'll shun every kind of publicity and monetary reward from the results of the research. All he wants is to help cancer victims everywhere, as he's helping my clinic."

"Incredible! Makes you really proud to have *him* for a friend."

"Even the President is said to be impressed by the old man. After all, it's good public relations for him, too, to be so closely allied to a man with such mass public appeal."

"It's just too much, Jess." Paul Hammer could not help but shake his head in amazement. "I still like to meet Nicole first, though. But . . .well, you're old enough to know best . . . getting married into this fairy tale family."

"It's no fairy tale, rest assured. And Nicole wants you to come over this afternoon and get acquainted with her; that is, if you're not too tired."

"Not at all. I stayed a day in New York getting over the jet lag. Tell her I'll be delighted to meet my son's future wife. Does she still live with her grandfather?"

"Oh yes. At least till our house is finished. Which should be in time for the wedding."

"Again, it's like a dream, Jess, almost like first coming to this country with your mother."

"I'm glad you feel that way, Dad. I'll show you the new house when I drop you off at Nicki's." He glanced at his watch. "I've got to get back to the Center. I'll see you at Rosedale when I'm off duty—at seven."

Paul Hammer rose from the garden chair. "Rosedale?"

"LL's estate."

"What about him? Won't he be there too?"

"He's expected back later this afternoon. He and The Shadow are away at some Board of Directors meeting in the city."

"The Shadow? Who's that?"

"Everybody calls him The Shadow. John Shadow. LL's closest aide. He's the father of Dave, Nicki's first husband. And that proves something too, doesn't it?" Jesse said, leading the way into the house. "I mean, LL could have gotten rid of The Shadow after what his son did to Nicki. But The Shadow stayed, despite his son. That's how LL commands respect. He's an overpowering personality." Jesse held the door open for his father. "Incidentally, LL wants to meet you tonight too, to take a close look at you."

3

As Jesse was driving his father to Rosedale, Paul Hammer could not help but express some apprehension about meeting his future daughter-in-law. Jesse tried his best to put his father at ease, reassuring him that Nicole had completely recovered and was the happiest, most level-headed person in the world.

When they reached their destination, Hammer could well understand that anybody living in Rosedale would be content with life. Parisian lampposts from the gaslit era flanked a gigantic wrought-iron portal on a rarely traveled road and it was opened by a uniformed gatekeeper. On each side of the gate stretched a ten-foot high brick wall crested by bales of barbed wire. Jesse and the guard exchanged greetings like old friends, with the son introducing his father briefly; then the car rolled onward on the broad sweep of a black-topped private drive, under the green canopy of stately blue spruces, beeches, oaks and maples, under gargantuan boughs nodding drowsily in the afternoon breeze. Hammer had never been to a millionaire's, let alone billionaire's, estate in his life. The verdant growth, a thick carpet of pine needles and leaves, the opulence and serenity of acres of the cool woodlands—with an occasional ray of sunlight stabbing the dense foliage—left him speechless as he craned his neck to soak up all the magnificence, like a child for the first time in a cathedral whose grandeur summons up awe and reverence.

When Jesse finally rounded a corner of the vaulted, serpentine road, a breath-taking sight burst upon them: bright sunshine, a cobalt-blue sky and, beneath it, an enormous expanse of lawn perfectly manicured and velvety as an emerald-green rug.

"My God!" Hammer exclaimed. "How gorgeous!"

Long neat beds of yellow-flamed tulips and blood-red American Beauty roses lined the edge of the lawn—a cornucopia of vegetation that extended for a hundred yards toward some tennis courts, a fabulous, aquamarine-tiled swimming pool, a couple of immense hothouses, and a complex of buildings. Some of these were built like old English Tudor mansions, others like Swiss chalets, and one sprawled across the green as a solid gray castle, stupendous in size and complete with parapets of turrets, belltowers of masonry, merlons, crenels and machicolations. High overhead, a trio of hawks was circling majestically in the cloudless summer sky.

Jesse halted his Volvo in front of the largest of the Tudor houses on the grounds. He turned off the engine and grinned triumphantly at his father. A Mozart sonata, clearly audible through one of the open bay windows, sprinkled its jewel-like notes upon the sunny kaleidoscope of garden colors.

Jesse honked the horn only once, and the piano music in the manor house stopped instantly. The moment father and son had clambered out of the car, the front door of the house flew open and a striking young woman stepped out into the sunshine.

In as long as it takes to register the appearance of an object on the beholder's consciousness, it took for Paul Hammer to realize that his son must be considered one of the more fortunate human beings on this planet. All his fears, apprehensions and suspicions dissolved in a second. Here was a woman of such radiant beauty that for a moment Hammer just stood rooted to the ground, staring. Nicole's fall of blond hair gleamed in the sunlight like waves of silk, and her face revealed a loveliness so stunning, so childlike in innocence, that all he could do was to stand transfixed by the open car door, as though facing a fashion illustrator's dream come to life. Her figure was sheer poetry—ethereal, svelte, made to contemplate; it was hugged by a pair of tight-fitting white Gucci slacks and a turquoise silk blouse. She rushed into Jesse's arms and their lingering kiss excluded everything and everyone around them. Jesse whispered into her ear and she drew back at once. With a guileless smile she approached Paul Hammer and, taking both of his hands in hers, kissed his cheek demurely.

"I'm so happy to meet you." Her eyes sparkled with such undisguised joy at meeting her fiancé's father that Hammer did not know how to respond and continued feasting his eyes on her, still tongue-tied. "You don't mind if I call you Paul, do you? Jesse has told me so much about you that I feel I've known you for years."

"Hey, Nick," Jesse called from the car. "I've got to run or I'll be late."

"You go ahead, darling. Your father and I will have a wonderful afternoon together, won't we? See you tomorrow." She slung her arm through Hammer's and guided him into the manor house, nudging the door shut with her foot as Jesse drove off.

Hammer was instantly captivated by her charm, the sincerity of each of her gestures and words. Hard as he tried, he could not detect the faintest hint of the consequences of the tragic events that had hounded her young life. She was entrancing, uninhibited, a madonna with a Sunday morning face. Even the sitting room seemed to reverberate with the sunny gracefulness that her personality exuded.

The room was a symphony of pastel walls and peach-colored, fluted drapes which set off the dark warmth of the lacquered rosewood furniture among the floral-printed sofas and deep, soft armchairs. Sunlight streamed through the open windows. Large bouquets of fire-red roses and sprays of lilac scented the air with a springtime fragrance that seemed unreal to Hammer, almost fairy tale-like. A vase bursting with lilacs graced the Baldwin on which she had played Mozart as he arrived.

Hammer's eyes drank in the beauty of the room. An exalted new world opened before him—magical, all creamy petals, with a Princess Charming—the stuff of children's stories.

"Lilacs!" he marveled. "At this time of year?"

"Gramps had them imported from his greenhouses in Turkey. Like the tulips outside. How about some coffee and cake?"

"No thank you, Miss Luckstone. Jess and I just had lunch."

"Nicole. Paul, please call me Nicole, okay? Come on, sit down!"

"Thanks." Hammer dropped into the exquisite softness of an armchair while Nicole faced him sedately on the sofa, buttressed by a flock of Oriental pillows.

"You sure I'm not disturbing you?" he asked.

"Not at all. I've practiced since eight this morning. Do you like Mozart?"

"His Requiem."

"That *is* deep. What about Beethoven?"

"His last quartets and the *Missa Solemnis*. And when I'm really upset his *Moonlight Sonata*."

"Me too. When I'm in a deep funk I always play the *Moonlight Sonata* on the piano. But you seem only to go in for tragic compositions. I bet you wallow in Brahms and Bruckner as well."

"Right. And Mahler and Sibelius."

"Paul." Nicole shifted forward to the edge of the sofa and impulsively grabbed Hammer's hands. "Jesse has told me so much about you, about the tragic part of your life when you were a teenager. I can understand why you're tuned in to these melancholy or simply deep compositions, but don't you think Jess and I would prefer to see you happy, enjoying the more cheerful side of life? Living a life of minuets, Vivaldi's *Four Seasons*, *Don Giovanni*?"

"I don't know what to say, Miss Luck . . . Nicole. You're very sweet. And I am sure that you and Jesse will be happy together."

"You can't possibly know how happy you make me by *giving* him to me. I'll be frank with you, Paul. I cannot imagine another relationship as deep as Jesse's and mine, no matter how much passion other couples may feel for each other. I'm like a different being—you know, I think of nothing and nobody but him most of the day. Even when I wake in the middle of the night sometimes my first thoughts are of him and I wonder if he's asleep or also thinking of me."

"Seems to me I've heard words to this effect earlier today."

"You have?"

"When Jesse told me about you."

"He did?" The room rang with her golden laughter. "You must tell me later exactly what he said, what he thinks of me."

"I will. All I can say for the moment is that he's very much in love with you, and I'm truly happy about it."

"Good, that makes two of us here who are happy. But happiness must be reinforced by the right music, Paul. So, what do you say? Is it a promise?" She wagged a maternal finger at her prospective father-in-law and grinned at him mischievously. "Haydn's minuets and *Don Giovanni* from now on?"

A tiny smile crept onto Hammer's tight lips. He nodded. "Minuets and *Don Giovanni*."

"Great." She released his hands and flopped back into the bank of pillows. "Then you'll also agree to the gift."

"The gift?"

"Didn't Jess tell you? About the money?"

"Oh! Look, Nicole, I do appreciate the . . . well, the gesture, but honestly, I can't accept it, just like this, a huge amount from a stranger."

Nicole said nothing for a brief, awkward moment, then folded her hands on her lap.

"Is the father of my husband going to be a stranger? I thought our two families were going to team up."

"Of course, they are, child." Genuinely moved by the unpretentious offer of her friendship, another sad little smile softened Hammer's tense face. "But a largess of two hundred thousand dollars—it's an awesome responsibility. I'd always feel indebted to you."

"You shouldn't. It's a gift of joy, of gratitude. No strings attached. You have given me something a thousand times more valuable—the man I love."

"Nicole." Hammer struggled for words. He knew that rejecting such a sincere, magnanimous gift might hurt her deeply, affect their future relationship, even harm her attitude toward his son.

He regarded her pensively, wondering how best to decline the money diplomatically when one of the lilac branches drooping heavily over her left shoulder shed a fat, green caterpillar on the sleeve of her turquoise-blue blouse. Nicole also noticed the larva and an expression of loathing shuddered across her face. Hammer thought she would shake the furry animal off her sleeve or brush it off, but instead she seized the caterpillar with two fingers and squashed its fat body between them, then scraped its crushed, pulpy remains on the rim of the glazed, red Venetian glass ashtray on the travertine cocktail table. For an instant Paul Hammer closed his eyes, trying to block out this gratuitously sadistic spectacle. He recalled Jesse's assertion that below the surface of her beautiful exterior ran a river of fiery violence. Her carelessly, needlessly ugly squashing of the larva brought that other side of her character momentarily to the forefront and stopped Paul Hammer's thoughts abruptly.

"You were saying?"

Hammer opened his eyes, startled, and took a deep breath.

"Yes . . . look, child: to accept this money at this stage, much as I'd love to have it, would be wrong. Your grandfather I'm sure would agree with me. As a businessman he'd. . . ."

"But I did ask him, don't you understand?"

"You did? And what did he say?"

"Anybody who, like you, survived Auschwitz, then immigrated here, put his son through college and heads a department of one of grandfather's agencies in Europe deserves a good nest to rest in."

For a second Hammer seemed to be caught by surprise. "I had no idea he knew about my years in those death camps."

"Of course he did. Jesse told him."

"Funny, Jess doesn't usually bring that topic up when he tells people about me."

"Then you don't know about gramps himself, before *his* arrival in the States."

"His arrival! You mean he wasn't born here?"

"Then you *don't* know. Jess probably didn't want to stir up old memories. I'm sorry if I. . . ."

"No, please go ahead! That's all forty years ago. I'm not that thin-skinned."

"Well, grandfather was also born in Europe. And like all the other Jews, he too was sent to a concentration camp."

"Jews! You're Jewish?"

A slash of a frown put an anxious dent between her hazel eyes. "You wouldn't object to Jesse and me getting married, would you?" Anguish tightened her voice; her fingers suddenly were desperately entwined. "Because I do know that you're not Jewish."

"For God's sake, child, of course not! What do you take me for?"

"Mind you I'm not the least bit religious. Naturally, I always root for Israel, but I want the Palestinians to have their homeland too."

"I couldn't care less, Nicole, even if you were religious. And you know, Jesse doesn't care about a person's faith or race either. As a matter of fact, Linda, my late wife, and I named our son Jesse after that black athlete Jesse Owens, and the way even Hitler waved his hand at him. I saw it with my own eyes. In Berlin, during the 1936 Olympics."

"Yes, Jesse told me; although he was a bit vague about your stay in Auschwitz. That's what I meant to ask you: isn't there a chance that you and gramps know each other from Oświęcim—Auschwitz?"

"Good Lord! You mean he was there too?" She nodded. "What a coincidence! But you've got to realize that Auschwitz-Birkenau covered thirty square miles—the two camps were separated by several kilometers of fields and factories—and there were times when about a hundred thousand inmates crowded the thirty-nine camp sections there, as many people as in all of Trenton, New Jersey. Of course, most of them were gassed or perished some other way and were replaced immediately by new arrivals. So I would say there's little chance your grandfather and I met there."

"But tell me, why you? I mean, you weren't even Jewish; you were only a child when they arrested you."

"I was fifteen then . . . well, actually fourteen to be precise, in February 1943. You see, my parents were members of the White Rose anti-Nazi organization, which was headed by the university students Hans and Sophie Scholl and Professor Huber in Munich. On the 19th of February I was caught by the Gestapo, carrying a bundle of anti-Hitler leaflets from the printers to my parents' apartment. We were arrested, like the young students, the Scholls and Propst and Graf and Schmorell, and a few days later their Professor Kurt Huber. They were beheaded after a short trial."

"How dreadful!" exclaimed Nicole. "What about your family?"

"No trial. For some reason my parents and I were sent in a convoy with thousands of German Jews to Treblinka. My parents were killed in that extermination camp."

"Did you say Treblinka?"

"Yes."

"Jesse never mentioned that. He only said you were in Auschwitz."

"I was sent there, and to Sobibor, after Treblinka was shut down."

"Gramps was a prisoner there too."

"In Treblinka?" This time Hammer sat up straight and clasped his hands tightly around his knees. The blood drained out of his face.

"Anything the matter?" Concern darkened Nicole's voice. "You look kind of peaked suddenly."

"Are you certain he was in Treblinka?"

"Of course I am."

"Nicole, then there really is a chance that your grandfather and I know one another. Because if he *was* there, then—apart from those who escaped—he and I are among the thirty-nine survivors of the million or so prisoners who *were* exterminated in that camp."

"Paul, that's incredible! We've just *got* to ask gramps."

"That name, though. Luckstone sounds so English, and I don't recall anybody by that name."

"Oh, he anglicized it once he became a U.S. citizen in '53. Before that he, I mean his family, was known as Glückstein. His full name was Ludwig Glückstein."

"Glückstein. You know, that name rings a bell. It's quite possible that he and I met. Of course, I was quite young and have forgotten most of the prisoners' names. Besides, in many cases we addressed each other only by our nicknames. But . . . does he ever discuss the years in captivity with you?"

"Never. I know nothing about them. He point-blank refuses to mention them. He says it's too gruesome and he doesn't want to be reminded of those horrible years. All I know is that he was in Treblinka and Auschwitz. Of course, in his position nobody dares question him. He'd simply cut you dead. Not talking about it, he claims, is the only way he can put the past out of his mind. You see, his entire family was put to death there. He himself was horribly tortured, that much I know. He just sees no point in unburying all the old corpses of the past."

"I understand only too well what he means. I feel the same way about it."

"Of course, when he sees you he may recognize you and talk about old times."

"I doubt he'll recognize me. I'm close to sixty now and there's nothing left of the looks I had when I was fourteen."

"Well, perhaps you can tell him that you were there and he may

36

remember you."

"It's possible. Or I may remember him."

"You referred to Treblinka as an extermination camp as opposed to a concentration camp. Weren't prisoners killed in every camp?"

"Indeed they were. But in Treblinka, in Birkenau and some other camps they were gassed immediately upon their arrival. For the most part, in Treblinka, they were literally whipped out of the cattle cars and chased between the rows of barbed wire—the *Himmelfahrts Strasse*, or The Tube—to the undressing barracks, thousands of them, after the roll call was taken. From there they were marched to the 'Shower Baths' and gassed. Most trainloads were dead two hours after arriving in Treblinka."

"How horrible! That went on throughout the war?"

"Treblinka existed only in 1942 and 1943. Fourteen months altogether. On the average there were three transports every twenty-four hours, of about fifteen hundred captives per train, mostly Jews. Day and night. But some days as many as twenty thousand arrivals were killed. It was all quite efficient—the smoothest death operation in history."

"Ghastly! And to think that your family wasn't even Jewish. Did they turn against Hitler when they realized that the war was lost?"

"Not at all! Much earlier than that! The White Rose movement existed way back when Hitler owned all of Europe and most of industrialized Russia. As a matter of fact, my parents always were Social Democrats, but they seriously started turning against Hitler because of something I witnessed, just a few months after he came to power."

"In 1933? My God, you could only have been . . ."

"Five. Five years old."

"I don't understand, Paul."

"Well, here's how it happened: I had come home from my *Volksschule*—elementary school—the first grade, around lunchtime one day, and I was walking up the staircase of our apartment house when I noticed two men ringing the bell of the apartment directly under ours. They were the tallest men I'd ever seen and were wearing black uniforms. SS men. Being curious, like all children, I walked past them and sat down on the top step of the staircase to find out why they had come to visit the Friedländers, friends we had known for years. All I knew was that I hadn't seen Herr Friedländer for some months, either in the house or at the store."

"The store?"

"He was a salesman at the clothing store where my mother always

37

bought suits and shirts for me. Anyway, when Frau Friedländer opened the door the two SS officers saluted her with a resounding 'Heil Hitler,' then told her that they had brought her husband back from Oranienburg."

"From where?"

"Oranienburg, the second Nazi concentration camp, not far from Berlin. Frau Friedländer burst into tears, thanking the two men and praising God for bringing her husband back home to her. She asked where he was and one of the SS men pulled a small tin box out of his tunic. He handed it to her and said, 'He's inside this can!' Both SS men clicked their heels together, shouted 'Heil Hitler' and marched downstairs." Nicole pinched her eyes tight-shut for a long moment and gasped audibly. "I just sat there, unable to understand how a grown-up man could fit into a container no larger than a can of vegetables. Frau Friedländer kept staring at the can, and the tears were streaming down her face, and then she started to tremble and quietly shut the door. When I told my mother about the incident she started to cry, told me to have my lunch and went down to Frau Friedländer."

"But why had they killed him?"

"Because they *thought* he was Jewish. He wasn't. His crime, already in 1933, was that he had a Jewish name, my mother told me years later. The Nazis had cremated him and returned the ashes to the unsuspecting wife. It was then that my parents first turned against Hitler."

Tears were brimming in Nicole's eyes. Suddenly she stood up and leaned forward, planting a dry little kiss on Hammer's forehead, and once more slumped back on the sofa.

"I salute your parents," she whispered. "Dead or alive. What noble people they must have been!"

"My mother was the dearest person in my entire life. I'll never forget how she was killed."

"She should have clubbed their skulls to mush!" Nicole's eyes flashed wildly, rebelliously. "I know *I* would have. I never compromise, Paul. *Never!* Not with evil. I would have fought the SS way back in '33, in the camps, no matter what!"

There it was again, what Jesse had hinted at earlier. Her totally unyielding, uncompromising attitude—although this time Hammer readily concurred in her homicidal reaction, her determination to mete out punishment.

But he smiled sadly. "Nicole, one day I'll tell you why it took the free world twelve monstrous years to finish off the evil of Hitlerism."

"Well, perhaps you're right." She sighed. "Still, I wonder how gramps managed to survive that death camp. And you too."

"Luck, I suppose. Only luck and perseverance could save a handful out of millions to be gassed."

Nicole turned away from Hammer and looked out the window. Tears were running down her face again and she wiped them away with the tips of her long fingers. The next moment she bunched her hands into fists and banged them hard on her knees. It was at this point that Paul Hammer fully opened his heart to his future daughter-in-law.

4

Looking out across the field of late-flowering parrot tulips from Turkey and the deserted tennis courts, Paul Hammer thought that the rose-tinted sky and the dusky, mauve gardenscape were strangely reminiscent of one of Maxfield Parrish's twilight paintings.

In the distance, just visible behind a row of blue Douglas firs, he barely made out the helicopter pad on which, an hour ago, Louis Luckstone and his retinue had landed in one of his noisy flying machines.

Earlier in the evening Jesse had arrived to pick up his father, but Nicole had persuaded LL to live up to his promise and have a brief meeting with her prospective father-in-law, and now both Paul and Jesse Hammer were waiting in the enormous baronial entrance hall of the main administrative building at Rosedale for LL to make his entrance and get acquainted.

Nicole herself had another engagement planned for the evening and was compelled to miss what she called the "historic meeting of two of the few Treblinka survivors." She was scheduled to give a piano recital of classical music at the well-known Sullivan County vacation resort, the beautiful Recreation Farm, in nearby Fosterdale, and could not cancel it at the last minute, no matter how tempting it might be.

While Hammer and Jesse had been supping at the immense, mirror-polished mahogany table in the dining room, complete with solid gold candelabras, Wedgewood plates and fine fluted Steuben champagne crystalware, they could not help but overhear, through the open door, a trio of voices. Jesse identified them as belonging to LL, John Shadow, his right-hand man and constant companion, and Josh Hamilton, the financial director of the President's Re-election Campaign Committee and assistant to the White House Chief of Staff. While these three men discussed security arrangements for the President's visit to LL in late fall for the groundbreaking ceremony for Luckstone City telephones were ringing, telex machines kept clicking, and messages arrived from Kuwait, Johannesburg, Santiago, Paris and Jerusalem. Another came in from Washington informing Luckstone that the Federal Trade Commission and the Assistant Secretaries for Mineral Resources and Public Land had approved LL's purchase of a field of coal mines in West Virginia.

As the wheels of commerce whirred quietly, Paul and Jesse Hammer helped themselves to the culinary treats a liveried butler with a dead-pan Adenauer face had wordlessly placed on the oak side table: quail eggs stuffed with Beluga caviar, roast pheasant, wild rice with water chestnuts, salmagundi salad and Brie, and two chilled bottles of vintage Dom Perignon.

Once during the dinner, Jesse could not help smiling to himself and murmuring, "Ah, this is the life!" His more ascetic father, on the other hand, only tasted a few meager forkfuls of the vegetable and some cheese, wondering aloud how the impoverished masses of the Third World would look upon such a sumptuous offering.

After the meal, Hammer and his son thought it appropriate to retire to the lobby where the mullion-barred windows and the front door stood ajar to let the sweet fragrance of the dusk's honeysuckle and Rose of Sharon invade the gigantic greystone cave of LL's administration center. Half a dozen 16th century full-plated suits of armor, complete with helmet, visor, breast plate, lance, gauntlet and cuisse guarded the marble-floored hall with its precious collection of paintings. Here, in solemn splendor, were works by Tintoretto, Rembrandt, Hals, Gainsborough and a few fading, delicately preserved medieval tapestries. A large oak-carved staircase, branching off halfway to the left and the right, was protected by a regiment of antlers and big game, shot in various parts of the world. Tigers, lions, rhinoceroses and two huge elephant tusks hung menacingly overhead. The massive bronze portal itself was flanked by four ancient cloisonné Chinese vases, two of which served as receptacles for plume-like feathery jute plants while the other two held a couple of unbecoming umbrellas in them.

"I'm sorry to keep you waiting so long," boomed a stentorian voice.

It nearly stopped Hammer's heart. He turned slowly to find a portly six-and-a-half footer in a stunningly tailored black suit bearing down on him, both arms outstretched in a welcoming gesture.

LL's two companions followed, a deferential three or four steps in his wake. Hammer had not bargained for the size, the impersonal, tidal force of the man who was vigorously pumping his hands now and beaming from ear to ear behind thick horn-rimmed glasses. Looking up at the huge man, Hammer felt dwarfed. Here then was a personality of immense power, one of the richest and most influential men in the world, a billionaire, who dealt casually with heads of state, kings, sheiks, industrialists and world celebrities, who owned a fleet of planes, tankers and corporations in a dozen countries, and dispensed millions like others buy groceries.

Through a heart-pounding haze of nervousness and intimidation, Hammer heard LL introduce the aloof John Shadow to him and the granite-faced Josh Hamilton of the White House.

Hammer was glad that LL did all the talking, filling the hall with his colossal voice as he proclaimed his happiness at making the acquaintance of Nicole's father-in-law-to-be. Paul Hammer would always be welcome at Rosedale and need never make a prior arrangement for a visit here.

If he played tennis, he most certainly should take advantage of the tennis courts and bring his pals along. LL's staff would always be at their service. Josh Hamilton interrupted with a strained, artificial laugh at that point, remarking that he envied Mr. Hammer, because after knowing LL for more than ten years, he still had to announce his arrival at Rosedale well in advance. For that matter, so did the President.

Amidst smiles all around, LL explained that the "Prez" and Josh were only friends, while Mr. Hammer was family now.

Hammer stood transfixed. He stared up at the face, at the imposing bald pate fringed with a halo of white fluffy hair, as the hall again filled with the tycoon's roar of laughter. For an instant he thought that unless he could hold on to something he was going to collapse. His legs buckled, the bones seemed to have been sucked out of them. The man he was facing, this "LL," billionaire, friend of kings and presidents, the grandfather of the woman his son was going to marry, was indeed one of the Treblinka survivors who had been indelibly etched into Paul Hammer's memory for the last forty years. Hard as he had tried to forget him and the whole grisly experience of his youth, he could never expunge those images from his mind.

5

Seconds ticked away with an unnerving sluggishness.

"Don't you feel well, Mr. Hammer?"

Louis Luckstone's voice drilled through the miasma of old rotten memories. Hammer steadied himself on the tulipwood game table behind him. Louis Luckstone! What had Nicole said her grandfather's last name was in Europe? "Ludwig Glückstein." The perfect translation!

Clumsily, in movements noticeably erratic and shaky, Hammer removed his English tweed jacket.

"What are you doing, Dad?"

Hammer detected the note of apprehension in his son's voice as he rolled up the left sleeve of his shirt and twisted his arm outward so that Luckstone could readily see the tattoo of his Auschwitz prisoner number.

Luckstone gazed at it for a second, nodded meaningfully, and without further ado took off his own jacket, draped it over his left shoulder and likewise displayed the Auschwitz number tattooed on *his* arm.

"Mr. Hammer," the billionaire intoned darkly, "we are both victims of the Holocaust, not only a Holocaust of the Jews and gypsies, but of the decent men and women who fought the evil of Nazism, like you and your family. You and I are like brothers, more or less." And with both hands he grasped Hammer's hands and cupped them firmly in his. "You have lost your family in that hell, and I've lost mine. But we must look to the future and not let the past rule our present. We must prevent it from happening again by taking things as they come—and here I speak for myself—not only by reminding others about it but by changing the future by using the potentials God was good enough to bestow on me."

All eyes converged on a speechless Paul Hammer. He opened his mouth, but no words would come out.

Luckstone released his guest's hands, and a grim smile cracked the hard exterior of his face.

"I don't think we ever met in Auschwitz. When were you there?"

Hammer swallowed hard. "In 1944. In Birkenau."

"So was I. Well. . . ."

"What about Treblinka?" The words finally fell from Hammer's lips.
A deep, worried frown wrinkled Luckstone's rotund forehead.
"You were in Treblinka?"
"Yes."
"Where? In Camp One or Camp Two?"
Hammer knew only too well the meaning of those two camp sections. Number One constituted the arrival stage, the workshops, barracks, storage depots of confiscated goods. Number Two meant the death facilities, the undressing barracks, the thirteen gas chambers and the human incinerators.
"Number One most of the time."
A lightning-quick twitch raced through Luckstone's features as he turned briefly from his troublesome guest to put on his jacket.
"We may have met. Mostly I was in Camp Two. Although prisoners from those two camps rarely met." He took a deep breath and now started addressing his entourage as well. "Gentlemen, as you know I never discuss these terrible years. But my duty in Camp Two was to pull the corpses out of the gas chambers, throw them on a truck and take them to the makeshift crematoria."
"You forget one thing, Herr Glückstein," Hammer said. He had fully recovered his voice, which suddenly revealed an irrepressible hint of hostility. "You. . . ."
Luckstone spun around to his guest. "Please, sir, don't call me by my old name. The reason I changed my name to Luckstone was to cut the umbilical cord with the past. It's dead, done with. For four decades. We are the slaves of fate, and fate has been kind to me since the war. So it's no good harping on the horrendous past."
"Some were not slaves of fate, Mr. Luckstone." Hammer's expression was hard and severe. "They used their will, their talent to survive."
"But even their will, their talent were at the mercy of fate. In that hell we did not control events; events forged us. It's a sad, unavoidable fact, tolerating no contradiction." His shoulders drooped and he gave a deep sigh. "All right, my friend," he said with a forgiving smile, "what is it I forgot to mention?"
"Before you sent the corpses to one of the crematoria, wasn't it your job to yank out their gold fillings with a pair of pliers and tear the rings and necklaces and watches off their bodies?"
The smile on the tycoon's face had turned morbid and broadened, yet the eyes failed to disclose any semblance of amiability.
"How did you find that out?"

"Because I was one of the goldsmiths in the workshop in Camp One. My job was to melt the gold and design new jewelry from the stuff you gathered. Later the guards sold most of it on the black market."

"Yes, some of them became quite wealthy."

Hammer did not take his eyes off his host as he said, "And some of them managed to smuggle the gold out to Switzerland."

Jesse and the two other men exchanged puzzled glances. No one had ever heard LL discuss this forbidden period of his life, yet here was a man who did not simply reminisce with him about long-forgotten scenes of horror which both had managed to survive, but who almost brazenly challenged and taunted LL about some mysterious financial chicanery.

"Switzerland! Where did you hear that?"

"From Küttner, " said Hammer, and slipped back into his jacket.

"The SS guard the prisoners called Kiwe?"

"Yes. One day he came back from an outing with Franz Wagner, drunk, into the workshop. He was celebrating the safe arrival of about a hundred thousand marks worth of gold and diamonds in Switzerland. All of it for him."

Relief loosened the iron-tense muscles of Luckstone's cannon ball head. "Take it with a pinch of salt, my friend. You have no proof of it. Besides, Kiwe could never take advantage of the gold. Like Max Bielas, another SS guard, he was killed later by a Jewish inmate."

"But do you know how Kiwe succeeded in getting the jewelry out?"

"That's more than forty years ago, and I'm not interested in the SS. They were career murderers. Thousands got away with it. Klaus Barbie, the Butcher of Lyons, for example, lived for decades in a mansion in La Paz, and Franz Wagner later committted suicide in Brazil. Many of them even live here in the States, some with the blessing of the State Department and the FBI. But who said that life is fair?" LL shrugged fatalistically. "Just look at a mass murderer like Dr. Mengele. He ended up with millions from his brother's agricultural concern in Bavaria."

"Everybody knows about *him*. But we're talking about the *Treblinka* SS."

"No, sir, we're not any longer!" When Luckstone spoke again, in a harsh tone brooking no counterargument, his voice suddenly echoed menacingly in the cavernous entrance hall. "I told you: the past lies behind me, and I'm telling you now this conversation is at an end. If you want to go on living in the 1940s, go right ahead. But not in my presence. Save me your traumas, your phobias, your. . . ."

"All I. . . ."

"Don't interrupt me, *ever!*" Luckstone icily cut off Hammer. "I'm an activist, not a dweller in the past. Now I *can* control events. I couldn't operate my fleet of supertankers and cargo ships, run my global enterprises, my banks, hotel chains and oil refineries by harping on events that may make fine literature and movies but are beginning to get on the nerves of most people, who're fed up with this hashed-over history. So 'lighten up,' Mr. Hammer, as my granddaughter would say. These are the mid-1980s, not the early 1940s. You're always welcome here, but you won't ever bring up this subject again, at least not when I'm around. Is this clearly understood?"

The stern words filled the huge space, then silence descended heavily. Even accusations were preferable to the embarrassing hush that followed LL's unconditional demand. The billionaire did not glance at the other guests; his eyes were riveted imperiously on his former fellow prisoner, and Hammer was aware only of his heart pounding mercilessly inside his rib cage.

Finally, Jesse's subdued, apologetic voice broke the steel grip of tension. "Dad doesn't mean any harm, LL. But both his parents were murdered in Treblinka, and he just can't seem to get over it."

"Exactly. My parents, too." Luckstone turned to Jesse. "That's my point. Memories can play havoc with your life, destroy you. . . . Gentlemen!" He had regained his command and composure with the steady grace of one used to the feeling of power. "I am tired. You will be staying with your son for your vacation, won't you, Mr. Hammer?"

"I don't think so."

"Father!"

"I think it's best if I return to England tomorrow."

"What are you talking about, Father?" Jesse was visibly upset, bewildered. "You told me that . . ."

"A pity, Mr. Hammer. I'm sure Nicole would have liked to get to know you better. You're aware, of course, that she intends to give you ten percent of her wealth."

"I have already rejected the offer, Mr. Luckstone."

The billionaire's hands curled into white-knuckled fists. "You are an arrogant . . . well, no, perhaps just a proud man. And not overly gracious, if I may say so."

"My father is tired, LL." Jesse quickly tried to make amends for Hammer's faux pas. "He hasn't had a vacation in over a year."

"I like men who work hard," Luckstone said in a tone of reconciliation as if to wipe a sponge over their earlier bitter exchange. "Mr.

Hammer, you're welcome to stay at Rosedale as my guest. Any time."

Instead of answering Luckstone, Hammer traded harsh glances with Josh Hamilton and John Shadow, who remained at a respectful distance behind the billionaire, their eyes coldly fixed at the dramatic confrontation unfolding before them. At last Hammer turned from his host and walked toward the front door. Here he grabbed the handle and once more faced Luckstone.

"I have no intention, sir, of ever setting foot in this house again."

"How dare you!" Jesse's angry exclamation reverberated wildly through the large hall. "Now you're being deliberately rude. What the hell's gotten into you?"

"Jesse, your father is a mature person and knows what he wants," Luckstone said in a remarkably calm voice.

"No, I insist that he apologize to you, LL."

"Don't you dare tell your father who to apologize to," Hammer raised his voice angrily. "I'm getting out of here."

"John, show him out!" Luckstone's face twisted with ill-concealed hurt as he swung around to his right-hand man and again took off his jacket. "I've got to check the telex."

"Sir." John Shadow rushed forward to help Luckstone with his jacket.

"Don't fuss!" Luckstone dismissed his aide irritably. He strode across the hall and eyed the White House assistant with a frown as he reached the bottom of the stairs. "I'll see you in the morning, Josh. John will show you to your room. Good night."

"Good night, LL," Hamilton, Shadow and Jesse chanted, nearly in unison.

The moment the billionaire had vanished around the corner on the second floor landing, Paul Hammer pulled open the heavy bronze door all the way and hurried out into the garden.

6

Dusk had turned to evening, and the two enormous Rose of Sharon bushes on either side of the door burned a bright purple under the brilliant spotlights that illuminated them from above.

"What the hell is the matter with you?" Jesse's white fury stopped his father abruptly as he walked away from the billionaire's doorstep. "One of the richest men in the world offers his friendship and hospitality to you, and you virtually spit in his face."

The floodlights above the door held Hammer immobile in their glare as Jesse and the other two men who had followed his father out of the house clustered about him like moths.

"I don't like butting into a family quarrel, Mr. Hammer," John Shadow observed solemnly, "but I think you were extraordinarily rude. I've served LL for over thirty-five years and I can't imagine an excuse for your behavior toward him. Just who do you think you are?"

Hammer wheeled around, infuriated, and barked at his new inquisitor, "Go screw yourself!"

With that he turned and was about to stalk off into the night, toward Jesse's car, when Shadow stepped forward and held the offending guest back by his elbow, starting to say that he demanded an answer. As if stung by a bee, Hammer spun around and without warning smashed his fist into Shadow's face. The man's head snapped back and a stream of blood began to run from his nose. Shadow bent forward, doubling up in pain. He whipped out his handkerchief and dabbed wildly at his nose. When he straightened up he could only stare in shock at the enraged guest, who shouted at him, "You touch me once more, you son of a bitch, and I'll break every bone in your damn body."

"Have you lost your mind?" Jesse blew up. He was beside himself, so far without a clue to understanding his father's bizarre behavior, the suddenness of it. He had never seen him behave so irrationally. His voice was trembling with emotion, with dismay and confusion. "You're behaving like a madman, a lunatic. Do you hear?"

"Leave me alone!"

"No, you're going to listen to me!" Jesse raged. "And you'll apologize to John Shadow. This is an outrage. He hasn't done you any harm. Just this morning you said that only weak people crack and end up in loony bins. Well, let me tell you that if you go on behaving like this, in no time you'll be an A-One candidate for the Center."

"I'm in perfect control of myself," Hammer said, breathing heavily. "I just don't like being grabbed like a common criminal. Treblinka and Auschwitz were enough."

"Well, don't act out your frustrations around here. Because I'm not letting you convince LL that I come from a family of lunatics."

"Ah! That's why you're sticking up for the man in there."

"I'm not sticking up for anybody. I'm just furious at the way you're acting." Jesse whirled round to Shadow who was glaring intently at his bloodstained handkerchief. "You okay, Mr. Shadow?"

Shadow only scowled at father and son in response, and said nothing.

"See what you've done?" Jesse spat out. "A good thing Nicole didn't see you raving like a mad dog."

"That's another thing," Hammer snapped. "You better get this straight right now: You're not going to marry that woman."

"Like hell I'm not! Who the devil do you think you are telling me who I can marry?"

"You're my son, remember?"

"And you remember that I am over twenty-one and don't need your permission to do whatever I damn well please. What in God's name has gotten into you, anyway?"

Shadow stuffed the soiled handkerchief into his pocket. "I think you'd better leave now, Mr. Hammer."

"Don't you start in with me again unless you're looking for another belt, Mister."

"I'm going to ask you just once more, Mr. Hammer, to leave peacefully. If you don't I will have to get Grasser."

"You'll get what?"

"Grasser. Mr Luckstone's bodyguard. He'll bounce you out on your ear in no time."

"Then let me tell you, Mr. Shadow, that Luckstone's Nazi goons don't frighten me. And I have no intention of staying any. . . ."

"Sir!"

The single word hissed through the night like the swish of a whiplash. Josh Hamilton had grabbed a branch of the althea shrub and broken it off. It whistled through the air and smacked against the granite portico. The three men turned to meet the calm, arrogant face of the figure in the white turtleneck sweater.

"Sir," he repeated, addressing Hammer, "you won't mind if I ask you a question or two, will you?"

Hammer narrowed his eyes suspiciously. "You're the guy from the White House, aren't you?"

"Correct. LL is a close friend of the President."

"That doesn't impress me a bit."

"Let me assure you, Mr. Hammer, their friendship was not designed to impress you. But perhaps you'll tell us why you're suddenly so opposed to your son marrying LL's granddaughter."

Paul Hammer stepped away from his son and slumped on the bench beside one of the Rose of Sharon bushes. The three men exchanged glances, then focused their attention on the man who appeared to have literally caved in on the bench, staring at the fists bunched up in his lap. Only the pizzicato orchestra of crickets and the answering chorus of cicadas broke the stillness of the balmy summer night. At last Hammer looked up and unflinchingly met the three pitiless, accusing faces. His eyes seemed glazed and uncommonly large.

"Because," he said calmly, "in 1943 Louis Luckstone murdered my mother."

The three men stared in bewilderment at the pathetic figure on the bench, not quite sure that they had heard correctly. John Shadow's hiccup of a nervous laugh disrupted the silence.

"I beg your pardon?"

"Father, you're not well. Please let me take you home!"

"No!" Hammer grabbed the back support of the bench as if to gather strength from the cool wooden plank and sat up straight. The utter seriousness of his accusation was etched on his face. The calm of his voice was betrayed only by the white knuckles as he gripped the bench. "Mr. Hamilton wanted to know why I'm so opposed to my son marrying the granddaugther of a man posing as the world's Number One philanthropist. Okay, I'll tell you: LL and I were inmates of Treblinka."

"We heard that," Hamilton said impatiently, his arm tightly crossed against his chest. "In different parts of the camp."

"For a time. But not when my family and I first arrived there. I remember every detail like it was yesterday."

Suddenly the lingering bloody images of forty-odd years ago leeched into the sweetly perfumed night, splashed over the moonlit swimming pool and ghostly tennis courts, the mallow shrub and honeysuckle, as Paul Hammer glared up at the stolid faces of the three men surrounding him and began to tell his story.

7

Of course, there's nothing left of Treblinka today. The Nazis were smart enough not to leave behind any trace of the wartime functions of the extermination camp. They obliterated every vestige of it in the fall of 1943, planting trees, bushes and pines where watchtowers, tank traps, barracks, thirteen gas chambers and the cement pillars for burning a million corpses used to stand. Only the railroad station is left.

But when I arrived in February 1943, the place was humming with activity. In fact, for the sixty days following my arrival, an average of six thousand people were gassed and cremated each and every day. Those were the "perfect days," as Camp Commandant Franz Stangl used to say. That very same year, in August, there was a revolt by a thousand prisoners in the camp, and Himmler ordered it razed to the ground a month or so later.

And forget about rebellion among the new arrivals, Hammer told his three spellbound listeners. It was humanly impossible for them to have offered so much as a blow of resistance to the guards awaiting the transports.

Like all the other prisoners, my family and I arrived in a state of total exhaustion. Five days earlier, the Nazis had packed us into cattle cars in Munich, about 140 men, women and children to a car. Even cripples. There was a terrified elderly lady on the station platform behind me, I remember, completely paralyzed, in a wheelchair. One of her legs stuck out from under her blanket, horizontally, rigid—nothing was left of it but shinbone and skin. An SS man stormed over to her, heaved her out of the wheelchair and hurled her into the freight car.

"Better this chair goes to one of our soldiers," he yelled, "than to filthy Jew scum like you." Then he slammed the doors shut on us and bolted them on the outside.

We were crushed together like sardines. There was no room to sit, let alone lie down. It was horrible. Those five days, let me tell you, felt like five centuries.

I remember standing between my parents, their bodies warming me. It was a bitterly cold winter day, and as the freight train started moving east with about 3,000 Jews, anti-Nazis and other so-called undesirables, the icy wind howled between the slats and through the cracks in the cars and cut into our faces. There was no food, no water. Sometimes the train moved, sometimes it was shunted to a railroad siding where it stopped for I don't know how many hours.

Even if we stood on our toes we still couldn't reach the open slits near the top and look through them to see where we were. Soon, though, young children around me started to cry, and by evening old people passed out from hunger or lack of medication, but there was no room for them to fall on the floor—we were too tightly packed.

After the first day, those nearest the walls of the car started banging their fists against the slats, shouting for food, for something to drink, anything, but of course nobody heard us; the world was completely indifferent to our fate. They were dead to the rumpus we made inside those box cars.

There was exactly one pail in the car, and if you were strong enough to push your way through the crowd you could pull your pants down and squat on it while the others around you closed their eyes and turned their faces away. But the mass of excrement and the urine in the bucket was slopping back and forth with the jars and jolts of the train, and the stench became so nauseating that people fainted, collapsing against their neighbors. By the middle of the second day, the contents of the pail had reached the brim and spilled on the floor, on the feet of those closest to it. People with diarrhea squatted in a corner of the car because there was a small hole in the floor, and when they were finished defecating they shoved the excrement with their shoes through the hole, only to come back a few minutes later and repeat their watery droppings. Even the strongest among us started vomiting. The stink became unbearable.

On the evening of the second day, the diarrhea-hole in the floor had stopped up. The human waste had frozen solid and clogged it. It must have been twenty degrees below zero. There was no way to empty your bowels now but to void where you were standing. You excreted and urinated in your pants, your underwear. All this was carefully thought up and premeditated by the Nazis, so we'd cause no trouble once we reached our final destination. We had to be thoroughly exhausted, dehumanized, our spirit broken. Everybody grew weaker by the hour, sicker, the stench more abominable, the cold more intense as the train rolled east.

Then it happened. On Day Number Three. Somebody at the other end of the car suddenly went hysterical, maybe from want of medication, or because of hunger, thirst, pain, I don't know. Soon others joined in. Some went into shock, convulsions that made them puke, others struggled for breath. The waggon became an absolute madhouse.

And then someone shouted that an old woman had died. The bitter cold and rigor mortis were turning her frozen body literally into a pillar of flesh. Of course, she wasn't the only one.

By midday there were as many as fifteen corpses standing stiffly erect among the living, their eyeballs bulging, glazing over, then cracking with the cold. If you stood near one of those corpses it felt like your skin was touching a tower of ice, with the cold going through you, literally chilling the marrow of your bone. Worse even, those dead, bulging, reproachful eyes on this column of glacial ice were staring at you day and night, unblinking. Their lids had frozen to the eyeballs; they could not be closed.

But then the real horror started. It was late afternoon on the third day. Somehow a gigantic rat had managed to sneak through a crack between two boards as the train passed through a tunnel. It probably was as starved as we were, besides being scared out of its wits seeing itself cornered in a freight car jam-packed with over a hundred screaming, ravenously hungry lunatics. It couldn't find its way out again and was forced to go on the offensive: it attacked people. Maddened itself by lack of nourishment, it scurried across the filth-infested floor and lunged at the exposed calves of the women—an easy and luscious, tender target—then sunk its sharp, yellow teeth into their legs and tore away at their flesh, gorging itself at the same time on their blood.

In no time the air filled with the most horrendous animalistic shrieks imaginable. The women could not even defend themselves because, tightly packed as we were, there was no way for them to bend down and strike at the rodent that skipped and scudded around like a crazed mongrel. All they could do was to jump up and down, trying to shake the monstrous animal off their legs, or to stomp on it—but to no avail. The whole car was in an uproar; everybody was scared to death that it would be their turn next to be attacked by the rabid beast.

God knows how, but all of a sudden two men had gotten hold of the rat. This time the noxious animal evidently had miscalculated its victim as it leaped up at the hand of one of the men and plunged its teeth into his thumb. It clung to it with a tenacity as if it could no longer unlock its ferocious jaws, and even though the victim was in agony and screamed bloody murder the man next to him at once grabbed the giant rodent with both hands and jerked it back and forth with such force that the thumb became detached from the hand—but still remained firmly locked between the pincer-like jaws of the rat. The man immediately smashed the rat's head into the wooden slats of the box car, over and over and over again. Even so, above the screams of the terrified onlookers, the rodent could be heard squealing, louder than a spiked pig. It was horrifying. That went on for an eternity, but it was no use: the rat simply wouldn't die. The repulsive animal was covered with blood, its own, the mushy thumb's, and that of the legs it had bitten. Finally, though, after an hour or so, we heard a loud splintering crack. The man had at long last broken its neck.

But instead of throwing the odious beast on the floor the man merely laughed, then sank his teeth into the warm, gorged body of the rat and tore out its disgusting meat, a mouthful of the rodent's squirming intestines. It was the most revolting sight I'd ever seen. In no time someone yelled that he shouldn't be allowed to hog the meal and wolf it down all by himself, and the next second arms flailed the air and people actually started fighting for the worm-infested rat, trying to snatch it from the man who had killed it.

But this was only the beginning of the nightmare. Earlier in the day, a man with gangrenous sores in his face had accidentally dropped his spectacles in the bucket of shit and then retrieved them and put them back on. Now his whole face had broken out in large blisters; the boils around his mouth were running with pus, yellow-greenish cankers, and he was already in a delirium; but suddenly he screamed that there was only one way to survive, and that was by eating those who were already dead. A pocket knife flashed in his hand and it sprang open and his wild, festering eyes lit upon the baby that had died that morning and was still bundled in swaddling clothes in its mother's arms.

This mother had been standing near me all day long, gazing at the blueish skin of her dead child and she seemed completely unaware of the bedlam, the manic, ranting horror around her. But when the hallucinating madman brandished the open knife and announced that the only way to survive this ride of murder and mutilation was cannibalism and she saw the glint of insane hunger piercing those shit-encrusted, thick lenses—well, it seemed like a raging storm—no! more like electric jolts had shot right through her. All the grief of a mother whose child had just been murdered by the legal apparatus of the State and watched over by the dumb indifference of destiny—all that grief, the senselessness of the crime, erupted in one volcanic moment, and she spun around on the man with the pocket knife and plunged the spoon with which she had first fed her child into his face. His right lens shattered and jabbed a sharp splinter into his eye, simultaneously causing the glasses to fly through the air. But the mother's unspeakable fury remained unappeased, and she drove the weapon once more into the lunatic, this time his infested eye, and she twisted the spoon, maniacally, and scooped out *the eye as if it were the pit of a peach, letting it drop to the floor. The man howled deliriously! All hell broke loose then and there! Wild, bestial screeches of terror, of chaos, a storm of horrific shrieks, like a menagerie of monkeys gone berserk, but regardless of everything and still not mollified by the depravity of her foul deed, she now closed her hands around the instigator's neck and, tightening them, lightning-quick, choked the last desperate breath out of him. A bone-chilling scream blasted out of her skull; she had at long last found an enemy on whom to wreak havoc, to vent her vengeance, to inflict wounds, mortal wounds, for the diabolical act of injustice perpetrated against her newborn.*

But as she snuffed the last remaining vestige of life out of the starving psychotic, someone nearby grabbed hold of his pen knife while another snatched the dead baby from the frenzied, insane mother. The swaddling clothes unreeled swiftly, like a hospital bandage from a putrified limb, and the knife plunged into the tiny thigh of the unprotesting corpse. Blood trickled down the rickety matchstick legs of the baby and a slice of flesh was carved quickly from its bone and vanished in the mouth of the assailant. At once, the infant was swooped upon by a spider-like pinwheel of arms and hands from all sides and seized from the erstwhile attacker, its hacked body skipping and leaping in a danse macabre *over the heads of the famished prisoners.*

The deranged mother immediately released the throat of the man she had strangled and screamed that they should take pity and return her child to her, but she was only one of the maddened women wailing and crying out against the injustice, the unfairness of a clunking, moronic clod of fate that allowed this iniquity to happen. And as night fell, the demented mob tore the child limb from limb and gnawed at its meager bones, its tender young body, to still its own shuddering pangs and convulsions of hunger.

But neither night nor daylight brought us any solace, and we kept on riding in this unhinged, grisly snake pit—my parents and I—for five days and nights. Only when it was pitch-black and nobody could see us did I risk nibbling at the few buttered rolls my darling mother had cleverly hidden away in her coat pockets before leaving Munich, and even though I pleaded with her she would not touch the food, leaving it all to me, except for a few crumbs.

After traveling for four days, locomotives were changed. Our convoy moved more slowly now. By this time about fifty people in our car must have died. My father's jaws were frozen, the tears on his face had turned to ice in his stubble. He couldn't speak any more. He must have had lockjaw, tetanus. My mother massaged his face, but he couldn't get a word out. She started to cry and I felt so helpless, so desperate, all I could do was to bury my face in her rabbit collar and sob. I was only fourteen and wanted to die.

On the fifth day we heard a station announcer outside shouting Polish words, probably the name of the station. Again the train came to a halt. We waited for an hour, two hours, three hours, heard voices, distant shouting, gun shots. This time nobody in our car uttered a sound.

Finally, the train began to move again, very slowly, but only for a few minutes—I'll never forget the mournful hiss of the locomotive—then braked to a dead stop. Outside the bolts were turned with a screeching sound and the sliding doors pulled open.

8

Daylight and a blast of wintery fresh air slapped our faces. We took a deep breath. It almost intoxicated us, weak as we were. The next second a hail of iron rods rained down on us with such brute force that those still strong enough to stand upright near the doors were literally clubbed out of the car. Long horse whips lashed the skin of the living and the dead alike.

Screams of "Raus!" and "Schnell! Schnell!" could be heard all along the station platform. Anybody left alive pushed frantically past the corpses, which dropped like felled trees into the heaps of feces and lost pieces of clothing.

Guards in battle-gray uniform were running about everywhere. They were yelling at us in guttural accents to line up while their clubs kept slugging anybody not moving fast enough, regardless of how tired, starved or frozen we were. Everybody had to carry his own suitcase. Mine was covered with shit. All I wanted was to save my drawing paraphernalia and get rid of the filthy suitcase. My charcoal and sketch pad, thank God, weren't dirtied, so I took them out, tossed my luggage away and quickly followed my mother to the other side of the ramp, a square I was to learn later was called the **Sortierungsplatz**.

Even I had difficulty moving. My feet were numb from the cold, but I kept up with my mother and asked her where dad was. We looked around but couldn't see him anywhere. She called his name a couple of times, and the next thing we knew one of the SS guards came rushing toward her, his hand already on his holster. He yelled at her to keep her fat Jew-mouth shut while his German shepherd kept snapping at her swollen ankles. I got scared for my mother and put my arms protectively around her. As quickly as I could I pulled her away from the SS man but in doing so bumped into a Polish guard who was just then raving at a pregnant girl to hurry up and get back into line. To make her move faster, he grabbed his rifle by the barrel and swung out, striking the back of the girl's head with such force that the rifle stock broke. She toppled forward, without so much as a sound, and lay dead at my feet. I remember wondering whether the baby inside her had also died instantly.

But all this only amused the guards. They were laughing and shouting to each other, either in broken German or in Polish and Lithuanian and Ukrainian. It was only then I realized that the guards tormenting us weren't German but East Europeans.

Suddenly names were being called out. Prisoners shouted "Here!", and that was my first roll call. Some no longer had the strength to reply but only lifted their hands feebly. I heard my father's name being shouted and spotted a hand being raised weakly, far away.

My mother, too, had noticed. She whispered to me that we should join him and began dragging me behind her. But she didn't get far. Because a moment later a horse whip lashed across her face and a river of blood spilled down her cheeks. A Ukrainian guard yanked her back to the spot where we had been standing before and yelled something at her in Russian. I started to cry and hugged my mother. I kissed the deep cut in her face, and her blood; I tasted her blood as my tears mingled with it, and I pleaded with her to keep quiet and stop irritating the guards. Because now it was our turn. We were ordered to move on.

With one hand I held on to my mother, with the other I clutched my sketch book and charcoal. We were ordered to remove our money from our clothing and throw it on the ground. Behind us, some of the Ukrainian and Lithuanian guards immediately shoveled the money into large canvas bags. But about a hundred yards away, near the station house, a number of them were busy gripping the arms and legs of a young Jewish woman lying on the pavement. She had been in our box car. One of the guards kept jumping up and down on her abdomen. She was eight months pregnant. Little doubt in my mind about that *baby's fate.*

After about ten minutes, half of our convoy had disappeared. All I remember was seeing them being chased down a side street and around a corner. My father was among them.

Suddenly the guards yelled at the rest of us to stop. We came to a halt and stood there like zombies, in front of the railroad station, not knowing what to expect next. The station squatted in the gloomy landscape, with a clock devoid of hands in the tower and green bushes planted around the structure. The sign over the entrance read *"Treblinka."* I had never heard of the place. A few SS men now stepped out of this building and slowly walked past us, studying our faces like housewives inspecting stale bread at the local bakery shop. Even the Ukrainian, Polish and Lithuanian guards stood at attention when these officers passed. The SS men were talking to each other in very low voices; still, I could barely make out that they were addressing each other in German. The Master Race. But they too suddenly came to a halt, then clicked their heels and gave the Hitler salute. A man in a snow-white jacket came stomping down the street in which the other half of the transport had vanished. This officer stopped in the middle of the gigantic square now, well away from everyone, slapping a riding crop against the side of his black pants and jackboots.

"Frank!" he shouted. His voice resembled Hitler's.

One of the German SS men immediately detached himself from his comrades and marched toward him. He saluted smartly. "Herr Kommandant."

For a few minutes the two officers discussed something in an agitated whisper under the asbestos-grey sky. Unexpectedly, a shaft of sunlight broke through the dark clouds. To my trained artist's eyes, it looked even at a time like this much like a carefully planned movie scene: two officers standing alone in the spotlight of the bright sunshine on the huge cobblestoned square while the rest of us were trembling with fear, with hunger, cold, illness in the desolate, wintery dark. As macabre a picture as the one I remembered of an S.A. man setting fire to a synagogue in the Bavarian Alps one Christmas Day.

In the distance, behind the two whispering SS officers, half a dozen black-white striped, pajama-clad prisoners now appeared—the only six inmates in the entire history of Treblinka to wear this uniform, I learned later. Each of them wielded a wooden club. The tallest and strongest looking among them carried what looked like a piano leg.

The whole picture was imbued with evil, steeped in such ironic beauty that even in this hour of desperation I couldn't help being fascinated by it. Ever since I was seven years old I had been a fanatic about painting, and my young artist's eyes had sighted something I couldn't resist. I raised my sketchbook and in quick feverish strokes transferred the two officers in the circle of sunshine—one in battle-grey, the other in white—on to the paper, enshrouding them in dark ominous clouds, with the sinister group of prisoners in their zebra-striped garb lurking in the shadows. In less than five minutes the sketch was completed. As I was putting my finishing touches to it, the white-uniformed Commandant glanced up and started to address us when he noticed me in the front row. He interrupted his speech and uttered an order to his adjutant.

Frank swung around and strode toward me, grabbed me by the ear and pulled me to the Commandant, all the while yelling that a Jew-pig like me was supposed to obey the rules instead of painting filthy pictures.

He tore the sketch pad out of my hand and handed it to the Commandant. As the latter scrutinized my sketch, not a soul on the square stirred. There was no sound, only the wind howling in the trees and the barbed wire surrounding Treblinka. Finally Kommandant Stangl looked up and nodded. He ripped off the top sheet, held it behind his back and returned the pad to me.

"Do one of me I can hang in my house!" he ordered with an Austrian accent not unlike Hitler's own. "I give you ninety seconds."

Ninety seconds to sketch a masterpiece! But it had to be done. If I do well, I told myself, perhaps he'll spare my parents' lives and my own. His accent gave me an idea. As fast as I could I made a sketch of the Commandant in his white jacket and Adolf Hitler shaking hands. The Führer, *whom I could draw blindfolded in twenty seconds, had an expression of gratitude and pride on his face as he clutched Stangl's hands in both of his. For a background I chose a balcony's balustrade, with a mountain range in the distance—Berchtesgaden.*

"Time is up!" the Commandant barked, glancing up from his watch.

I tore off the top sheet and handed it to him. He stared at it as if in a trance. Not a muscle in his face moved. He kept gazing at it for what seemed like an eternity. His adjutant and I exchanged glances. Frank obviously wanted to see my work too but couldn't until given permission. After about three minutes the Commandant handed him the drawing.

"You'll agree," Stangl said to his aide, "that even the Führer would be proud to hang this in his office."

Frank nodded and looked up. "With your permission, Herr Kommandant, *can the prisoner draw a picture of me now?"*

The Commandant pulled the sketch out of Frank's hands and turned to me. "You have sixty seconds."

Again as fast as I was able to I made a sketch, this time of the towering *aide, whose indescribably ugly features and cold, contemptuous eyes I had been studying for the last two minutes, having him shake the hands of* Reichsführer Himmler, *complete in black uniform and rimless glasses. Over the years I had drawn the entire Nazi hierarchy dozens of times for our schoolrooms in Munich.*

"Sixty seconds are up!" snapped the adjutant and ripped the pad from me. Since I was given only a minute to finish this assignment, I had not been able to insert a background of mountains.

Immediately on sighting the picture, a wide grin spread across Frank's hardened visage, but a second later his expression darkened and he roared at me, "The mountains—you did not give me any mountains!"

"Because you gave me only sixty seconds!" I shouted back, deeply offended that this ignoramus should have the effrontery to criticize my sixty-second creation. "Give me thirty seconds more and I'll draw you the Alps." And with that I pulled the pad from him and started to add a mountain range and some cumulus clouds, with an eagle circling overhead.

I never got to finish it, though. Because a few moments later I heard my mother's voice behind me.

"Behave yourself, Paul!" she reprimanded me. "Apologize to the officer at once for your outburst."

I looked around. My mother had stepped out of the ranks of prisoners to approach me.

At that instant a voice unlike any I'd ever heard before roared over the Sortierungsplatz. *Everybody, including Frank and the* Kommandant, *whirled around. The biggest of the pajama-clad guards came rushing forward, toward my mother, swinging the piano leg in his right hand.*

"You miserable Jew-sow!" His shouting voice echoed back and forth over the square. "When the Kommandant *speaks with his aide you keep your Jew-yap shut. Or we'll send you up the chimney."*

My mother froze to the spot where she was standing, staring in horror at the menacing guard swooping down on her. He was swinging the bulking piano leg over his head now. I glanced around at the Commandant, wondering how he could allow a prisoner to interrupt him in his conversation with his adjutant. Neither of them did anything. Not a murmur of restraint. No reprimand. My head spun back to the immense guard. I heard him bellowing, "Back into your group!" and saw him strike the back of my mother's neck with the maximum force he could muster.

There was an audible crack that seemed to fill the large square, like the sound of a bat thumping against a watermelon, splitting it. My mother spilled forward, face down, on to the frozen ground, not five yards away from me, and lay motionless. I knew at once she was dead. The sketch with Himmler slipped out of my hands and I hurled myself on my mother, screaming I don't know what. I turned her around. Her head snapped back lifelessly.

Her eyes stared up at me terrified, unblinking. The last thing on earth she had witnessed was her assailant towering over her with the piano leg set to strike her down, and that terrified look froze on her face when she departed this earth and entered life in the next world. I looked up at the murderer, standing over me, the piano leg still clenched in his muscular fist. I always had a temper, but never in my life before or since had I been possessed by such an insane rage, such an urge to kill, to strangle and mutilate, as at that moment. Like a wild animal I leapt to my feet and flung myself on this brute, fastening my hands around his neck and tightening the grip, intent on choking him to death, pressing the last breath of life out of him before they'd get to me. I didn't care any more. Without my mother I didn't want to live.

The huge prisoner dropped the piano leg and tried to pry my fingers from his throat . . . in vain . . . I was like a demon possessed . . . when suddenly I felt the cold muzzle of a gun on my temple and heard the click of the safety catch being released. But I no longer minded dying. My mother had meant everything to me. I loved her more than anybody in my life and I wanted her vicious killer to burn in hell that very day.

But then, above the din of uproar on the square, I heard the Commandant's bark: "Stop!"

I thought he meant me and I didn't care. Let them kill me, I thought.

But he meant his adjutant. Frank lowered his revolver and Stangl stepped forward and with some grunting and groaning yanked my hands from the prisoner's throat. The striped guard doubled up, panting and struggling for breath, his face a mask of purple and twisted muscle.

"We aren't even Jewish," I yelled at the Kommandant. "We're Aryan and he killed my mother."

"Kapo!" Stangl snapped.

The pajama-clad prisoner had regained his breath and was massaging his throat. He straightened up. "Herr Kommandant," he croaked.

"You will not touch this boy! Now or in the future. Is this clear?"

"Jawohl, Herr Kommandant."

"Frank, I want a report on this boy and his mother. Why they're here. By noontime."

"Jawohl, Herr Kommandant."

"And my father also," I piped up. "He's here too."
"Your father? He isn't Jewish either?"
"No."
"You will address me as Herr Kommandant. Is this understood?"
But the tears were flowing now. I stared at the still figure of my mother gazing up at me with her petrified glazed eyes.
"Where is he?"
I gaped at the Commandant. "Who?"
"Your father."
"They marched up this way," I said, motioning with my head toward the street where Stangl had first appeared.
Stangl and his aide nodded to each other, knowingly. Frank replaced his gun in his holster with a satisfied smile, and I picked up the sketch book and charcoal.
"Well," Frank said with a smirk, "if he was with the group that went up this street, then he has already taken The Shower."
I stared at Frank and his master. Many times at home I had heard what it meant to take "The Shower" in a Nazi concentration camp. The sad truth was that while I was making that sketch of the smiling Adolf Hitler, they were actually gassing my father. My eyes fell on the lifeless body of my mother and I started to cry again, to sob helplessly this time. I dropped to my knees and the tears streamed down my cheeks on the likeness of Himmler I had drawn. I was all alone in the world. Alone at fourteen in an extermination camp.

9

Pearls of cold sweat cruised down the time-worn but still handsome features of the man who was once more living through the sewer of his youth. Even the arrogance stamped on Josh Hamilton's face could not completely mask the discomfort he felt at listening to the older man's emotional outpouring of his personal traumas. John Shadow simply bowed his head and stared at his shoes, burying both hands in his pants pockets.

Only Jesse had tears in his eyes. He wiped them in a furtive little movement as if concerned that his display of bereavement could be mistaken for a sign of weakness or a softening of his stand with Shadow and Hamilton.

The White House assistant stood in the doorframe, legs apart, the mallow branch behind his back like a riding crop.

"Those zebra-striped prisoners," he asked, tilting back and forth on the balls of his feet. "Who were they?"

"Kapos. Camp police."

"And the kapos, then, were they Jews for the most part?"

"Some of them were," Hammer explained, somewhat calmer now. "But there were others, too. In every concentration camp. Christians, political prisoners, murderers, Communists, homosexuals, gypsies. They all had to prove their worth. Several were as cruel as the most sadistic SS guards. They thought that would keep them from going up the chimney in smoke. Most of them did in the end, though."

"But, Mr. Hammer," Hamilton objected, "that was more than forty years ago. LL was about thirty; he's over seventy now. People change in four decades. You could have mistaken him for someone else."

"Oh, I know he's almost bald now. His face has changed and he has more wrinkles. But I'll never forget his features and, more important, his voice. And something else. I didn't pay attention to it twenty minutes ago. But I can tell you that the tip of the thumb on the left hand of my mother's killer was missing. In camp he once told me that as a child he used to help the family cook cut the meat with a cleaver—and one day had chopped off part of his thumb in the process. All right, gentlemen," he addressed the trio of listeners in a tone of utmost sincerity, his face set and grave. "You know him far better than I do. Tell me if Luckstone has a damaged left thumb. If he hasn't, I stand corrected and will apologize to you, Mr. Shadow, and certainly to Mr. Luckstone for my rudeness."

Hammer's eyes surveyed the scene before him in one sweeping gaze, from John Shadow who again glared at the gravel path to Josh Hamilton who this time lost his last remnants of swagger and nervously stretched the top of his tight turtleneck sweater. The silence was broken only by the mournful sounds of a grandfather clock chiming deep within the bowels of the executive fortress.

"Father," Jesse's voice now sounded gentler, more contrite, as if to soften the blow of their realization that Luckstone indeed had killed Paul Hammer's mother, his own grandmother. "Whatever you may think of LL, you have no reason to punish his granddaughter by refusing to let me marry her. Nicole can't be held responsible for what happened before she was born. And you're *not* going to tell her anything about your suspicions!"

"They're not suspicions, as you probably *will* concede now. They're facts."

"Still, you won't tell her anything about LL in Treblinka."

"We called him Baldwin, mostly."

"You what?"

"We called him Baldwin, because he always walked around with the leg of a Baldwin grand piano, using it to club the prisoners."

"Well, whatever you called him, you keep all this to yourself. I already told you about her. If she's faced with a new tragedy, she may really go over the brink. Just keep that in mind, Dad. I certainly wouldn't want *you* to be responsible for any harm to her which might occur if she hears about all this."

"Mr. Hammer." Even the timbre of Josh Hamilton's voice had lost some of its metallic edge. "Tell me, what exactly *do* you intend to do? I mean legally speaking. Even if what you say is true."

"That's absurd, Josh," Shadow cut in testily. "Legally speaking he wouldn't have a leg to stand on."

"Wrong, Mr. Shadow," Hammer replied forcefully. "I was an eye-witness. I can. . . ."

"Excuse me for interrupting, Mr. Hammer." The White House aide once more had recovered enough to project some of his self-assurance. "But if you don't mind my saying so, your word wouldn't amount to a hill of beans in court. It's no secret that LL was a prisoner in two of the most notorious concentration camps in Poland. Relatively few inmates survived these camps, and in order to survive I suppose some prisoners were inclined to overstep the bounds of legality, even of morality at times. If they hadn't, as you yourself pointed out, they'd have ended up in the ovens. Besides, LL is on no war criminal list. Moreover, the clandestine Nazi aid organization *Die Spinne* wouldn't touch him with a barge pole; after all, he was and is Jewish, *and* his entire family was wiped out in Treblinka. Most important, though, sir, Mr. Luckstone must be aware of all these ramifications. Or he'd have been more upset over your sudden emergence as a fellow prisoner."

The old pompousness was once more fully evident in Josh Hamilton's voice as he developed his argument. Judging from their expressions, Shadow and Jesse also seemed convinced that this legal opinion was so ironclad that Paul Hammer could not, in fact, do any harm to their benefactor. Hammer silently glowered at the conspiratorial trio, realizing his own folly in imagining he stood a chance of bringing the murderer of his mother to justice. Tears, tears of hopelessness, futility, helplessness, filled his eyes when he realized that a lifelong obsession, a dream on the verge of coming true, was being crushed with such legalistic condescension, such inhuman indifference.

"Mr. Hamilton." Hammer cleared the lump in his throat. "Are you married?"

"Yes."

"Do you have children?"

"A girl of seven."

"And you love her?"

"Of course."

"More than your wife?"

"That's a ridiculous question. I don't measure the love for the various members of my family by degrees."

"But you love them more, your daughter, your wife, than anyone else."

"That's a fair assumption. What exactly are you driving at?"

"Mr. Hamilton, if you saw someone pick up a steel pipe, or the leg of a piano, and in your presence smash the skull of your wife, then batter the head of your little girl, if you saw their skulls splitting open like raw eggs, wouldn't you want to hunt down the killer and, when you found him, no matter how many years later, bring him to justice?"

This time everybody waited in silence for the President's assistant to find the defense which would defuse Hammer's disturbing argument. For a minute Hamilton's demeanor revealed that he was searching for an appropriate reply, but then his eyes met Hammer's again squarely, resolutely.

"You have a point, Mr. Hammer," he said at last. "But again the situation is different, almost without precedent. A mugger, a dope addict, a common criminal killing today to obtain your week's salary is one thing, and a Jewish kapo scared out of his wits by the horrendous fate that may await him at the hand of the SS if he doesn't toe the line and kill his daily quota of prisoners is an entirely different matter altogether. And let me remind you of the indisputable fact that perhaps fifty minutes later your mother, like your father, would have been gassed anyhow."

Once more, Hamilton's cold logic routed the armies of emotion which Hammer had marshalled. The older man stood up slowly, holding on to the the bench for support, and nodded grimly.

"I see. What you're saying is that I should drop the whole thing, that it was just one more unfortunate incident. After all," he shrugged, "who needs a mother? You'd just leave her when you grow up, anyway."

"Come now, Mr. Hammer, don't put words into my mouth. I'm quite prepared to admit that what you went through was a gruesome experience, something none of us who hasn't lived through that nightmare can ever fully comprehend. But we're not achieving anything by harboring this bitterness, by prolonging this hatred. Millions lost members of their families in battles throughout. . . ."

"Now please, don't put words into *my* mouth, Mr. Hamilton!" Hammer started getting agitated again. "I'm not talking about a loved one being lost on the battlefield, but a defenseless woman, a civilian, being murdered on a station platform. And by somebody who was not in uniform, but who simply killed because he had nothing better to do."

"But, Mr. Hammer, pursuing this ridiculous policy of hatred ad nauseam. . . ."

"Damn you! How the hell would *you* feel if all of a sudden, out of the blue, *you* came face to face with the man who murdered your mother?"

"Just bear in mind that you have no absolute proof it was LL."

"Yes, I do! Not only do I *know* it was LL, but the proof is that part of the killer's left thumb had been chopped off."

"No court of law would give this case a hearing, Mr. Hammer. It's your word against LL's. All he'd have to do is to deny your allegation that he was the one who killed your mother, thumb or no thumb."

"And what would *you* say, Mr. Hamilton, if I told you that I may be in a position to secure more witnesses who'd bear out that what I'm saying is true?"

The three men regarded each other dumbfounded. Hammer's last statement, his sense of positiveness, came so unexpectedly, that the three were completely taken off guard and did not know at first how best to rebut the defiant elderly man. But only for a short time.

It was Jesse who first saw the cracks of illogic in his father's unmistakable threat.

"Dad, I know how unhappy you are, but please, *please* don't ruin your whole life by becoming fixated on revenge," he beseeched him. "Where in the name of heaven do you expect to find witnesses when virtually everybody from Treblinka is dead? Only a handful of inmates survived that camp, you told me. You can't possibly know where they are today, even if some of them still *are* alive. In Israel? Poland? Nicaragua? Where are you going to look? And if you *do* find someone, how do you know he'll remember seeing your mother killed? With thousands of prisoners being tortured and brutalized, do you honestly expect to find someone who remembers witnessing this *particular* atrocity?"

Hammer stared at his son coldly as if Jesse had deliberately thrown up an obstacle to prevent him from pursuing the revenge which had haunted him since childhood.

"Mr. Hammer?"

Hammer's gaze strayed from his son's tortured face to the disdainful features of Josh Hamilton.

"What?"

"Suppose you *do* find some witness. Do you really imagine for one minute that there's a lawyer, let alone a court in the land, who'd adjudicate such a flimsy case? With the defendant a Jew in a concentration camp thousands of miles away, more than four decades ago? And don't you realize that the statute of limitations for war criminals not previously named expired some time ago?"

"Mr. Hamilton, I think I should warn you that I know where one eyewitness lives, and perhaps even two."

Hamilton was silent for a long moment, exchanging glances with a very worried looking John Shadow.

"What do you expect *them* to do about it?" Hamilton asked in a tight voice.

"I assume help me to expose LL."

Josh Hamilton raised his eyebrows skeptically, yet his voice was tempered with a trace of apprehension. "Really? How?"

"Can't you figure that out for yourself?" Hammer's voice for the first time revealed a foretaste of triumph. "If the courts are closed to us we can always go to the press. I'm sure there'd be plenty of newspapers that'd be only too willing to carry the disclosure that one of the President's closest associates and strongest supporters was a murderer, a mass murderer. This could turn out to be the greatest scandal since Watergate."

"Father, please! You're going too far with all this!"

"Why? Just tell me why? Or do you think that LL didn't go to extremes when he clubbed your grandmother to death?"

"But you'll ruin him just to gratify your spiteful, peevish hatred."

"Hatred, yes, damn you!" Hammer flared up. "But it's not spiteful."

"Mr. Hammer," John Shadow said, keeping a healthy distance from his erstwhile assaulter. "I can't speak for what LL allegedly did in the extermination camp, but I can tell you that by hurting him today you might very well succeed in destroying all the worthwhile projects he has built up since the end of the war. I'm sure Jesse has told you that he's building a new town, not far from here, and that one of its consequences will be the elimination of unemployment in this county. Tens of thousands of people, including many minority groups will benefit. But more important, as head of the Luckstone Foundation, he is probably *the* leading fighter in the battle against cancer today. By ruining LL, you'd force him to withdraw his hundred-million-dollar contribution, and we'd lose his guidance in defeating this killer disease."

"Mr. Shadow is right, father," Jesse said softly, resting a foot on the bench. "Bringing LL to justice, even if it *would* be just to punish the man, won't solve a thing. And besides, it might very well destroy Nicole. If you yield to your urge to avenge your mother, you'd almost certainly cause Nicki to have another relapse, from which she might never recover."

Hammer glared at his son and shook his head in abject misery. "Even you, Jesse. Now *you're* turning against me."

"I'm *not* turning against you, Dad. But I feel you're mistaken in this."

"What is it you want me to do? Shrug it off as an unfortunate incident, as Mr. Hamilton would have me do? And dine at the table of my mother's killer? Or should I find some professional who'll take twenty or thirty thousand dollars to kill that bastard in there?"

"Hold it right there, Mr. Hammer!" Hamilton said sharply and stepped forward into the floodlights. "If you do that I'll see to it personally that you're prosecuted on charges of soliciting the murder."

"I apologize for my father, gentlemen." Jesse was visibly shaken. He approached his father and gingerly put a hand on his arm. "We'll be leaving now," he said, still addressing Luckstone's men. "I'll come see LL tomorrow and apologize to him on my father's behalf."

"Don't you dare!" Hammer flared again. "You make me want to puke. Fawning before your grandmother's murderer! Christ—what a son *you* turned out to be!"

"Come on, let's go!"

Jesse sounded tired, hurt. In the course of an hour or two he'd seen his promising future slip away, possibly his life's dream, his career, his upcoming marriage, all go down the drain—because of the stubborn, uncompromising hatred that drove his father to confront the very man who held the key to all that was right in his life.

"It'll be a pleasure," Paul Hammer snapped.

"I'll drop you at your hotel. Maybe you'd better go home on the first plane tomorrow, as you suggested. All I can hope is that when I see you again you will have come to your senses."

10

Maples, ashes and oak trees hurtled forward and whooshed past the dark windows as Jesse's Volvo hastened through the night. Only the beams of the two headlights pierced the pitch-blackness, stretching their white fingers a good hundred yards ahead on the deserted country road. Inside the car, father and son sat rigidly side by side, in stony silence. They were aware of the nearness of one another, although Jesse concentrated on the leathery smell of the seats and the cool, leafy country air rushing through the slightly open windows; his father focused instead on the tragic fact that they had both come to a divide on their lives' path from which there appeared to be no turning back. Too many harsh words involving his mother had fallen.

Above the hum of the car's engine, Jesse's thoughts gradually began to float in clouds of self-loathing. He knew he had hurt his father but did not know quite how to forgive him for dissolving the rich contentment in his own life. He gave his father a furtive glance, convinced that he would never want to lay eyes on him again; nonetheless, against his better judgment his consciousness made a subliminal effort to memorize the older man's once-loved features.

Minutes went by; the white centerline slipped dizzyingly under the speeding automobile as fierce, bitter thoughts raced through their minds.

"Do you realize what you're doing?" Jesse asked suddenly, opening a narrow lane through which Hammer could find contact with his son. Still, the father's pain at hearing what he believed to be Jesse's self-serving amorality kept him from showing any enthusiasm for discussion.

"I don't want to talk about it," Hammer said sullenly, hoping that Jesse would sense the weakness in his reply and persist.

"Well, I do," Jesse said with unusual force, steering the car onto Highway 52. "It's my life you're interfering with."

"What do you mean *I'm* interfering? You said you'd marry Nicole anyway, regardless of my wishes."

"It may not have occurred to you that now it is no longer up to Nicki and me alone if we can marry."

"What's that supposed to mean?"

"The Shadow rep . . . John Shadow reports everything he hears to LL. If LL gets wind of what went on just now in the garden, that you threatened to go to the press and expose him as the killer of your mother, that will tend to put me in a less than favorable light with him too, won't it?"

Hammer stared glumly through the windshield, at the beams of light dancing with myriad dust particles and nocturnal insects. Suddenly the car slowed down, then pulled over to the side of the road, directly under the low-hanging branches of a white ash. Jesse cut off the motor, leaving only the front and rear lights blinking in a regular tic-toc rhythm.

"What are you stopping for?" Hammer demanded. "We're miles from the hotel."

Jesse rolled down his window to let some of the cool night air enter the automobile and twisted in the driver's seat to confront his father.

"Because I'm upset. Because you don't seem to realize what you're doing to me, to my future. Not only have you probably ruined my chances of marrying Nicole, but. . . ."

"I don't see why. She's almost twenty-one."

"She worships her grandfather. She'd never do anything to hurt him. If he asked her not to see me any more, she probably wouldn't."

"You can't be sure of that."

"I'd hate to see him put it to a test. But that's not all. What about my position at the Center? In two years I'd have been promoted to head of the clinic. I have plans, Dad, ambitious plans for revolutionizing the operations of the clinic, especially with my mind control technique. I can make it a showcase for modern methods for dealing with psychiatric dysfunctions. I know I can. It's a once-in-a-lifetime opportunity that most men in my position wouldn't even dare dream about. Yet LL and the board have given me the go-ahead with almost unlimited financial resources to back me up. And then you come and smash it all, all my dreams, with a sledgehammer."

"You're young yet, Jesse, you'll find another place."

"For God's sake!" Jesse's infuriated shout filled the cramped confines of the Volvo. "Why don't you listen? I just got through telling you that this is the sort of chance that is *never* repeated. Maybe with luck when you're in your sixties and worn out, disillusioned. But I was going to be offered one of the top positions in the state, with no strings attached and plenty of funds, at an age when I'm still strong enough to fulfill my dreams and enjoy my success. And you've shattered all that."

"Look, Jesse, I'm sorry, but we've all got to make sacrifices."

"But why, when I'm so close to my goal?" Jesse's voice now was less angry, more plaintive—he sounded younger and more vulnerable. "Father, I love you. I understand how you feel about your mother's death. . . ."

"No, you don't! Or you wouldn't object to my anger. You wouldn't *want* to forgive the killer of your grandmother."

"It has nothing to do with forgiveness. To be honest, I'm not that deeply concerned about the unemployment that would result if the Luckstone City project collapses, or the loss to cancer research if LL withdraws his money from the Interferon Labs. I wish I were bighearted enough to care. But you must believe me, Dad, how much I'm torn between your desire to bring my grandmother's murderer to justice and the goals of my own life. You've read the books and articles about the children of the Holocaust, about how we're trying to understand what our relatives went through in the death camps. But most of us can't, Dad. We simply can't."

Hammer released a sibilant sigh in the dark. "I see. In other words, you're just out for yourself."

"That isn't fair and you know it. I *feel* with you because I think I'd be as vengeful toward *your* killer, if—God forbid—you met with such a horrible death as you with your mother's. . . . But I'm also asking myself what would I hope to achieve if I were in your shoes today. Dad, tell me, if you do ruin LL, do you really believe that your mother's death will be avenged somehow, or her soul put to rest? Do you think that, in fact, this is what she'd want you to do? To sacrifice my happiness, her own grandson's plans to help countless thousands of sick people? Or that she would want a lovely young woman who has suffered one ordeal after another to come to further harm? And suppose you really *do* succeed in getting LL's kapo activities into the press—what then? Will that convince you that you've exacted satisfaction from fate for her death? Will you then finally smile and say that justice has triumphed?"

Even in the dark of the Volvo Jesse could see the white of his father's eyes, large and bright with pain as they fixed on his son.

"If you only knew, Jesse," he said hoarsely, "what you're asking of me, what it would do to me . . . abandoning my mother."

"You're not abandoning her, Dad. Nobody's asking you to forsake your memory of her, or shut off your love for her. Christ, you're not giving up your mother, only the hatred you associated with her death."

"Tell me quite frankly," Hammer spoke up more forcefully, "whether you'd ask the same sacrifice of me, to drop all charges against the killer, if he was a simple laborer, and not a billionaire like Luckstone? If his arrest wouldn't affect your career or your fiancée's life. If it wouldn't be front page news."

"Father," Jesse was almost visibly groping for words, "what you're asking of me isn't fair. It. . . ."

"But I suppose what you ask of me *is*."

"Now please don't expect me to go into a long-winded speech about principles and Dostoevskian theories of guilt and punishment."

"No speeches are needed. I thought my question touched the very core of the problem."

"Well . . . all right. Yes, I *would* ask you to have the guy arrested if he was a nobody, but. . . ."

"That's disgusting!" exclaimed Hammer. "It's crass opportunism. You make me sick!"

"All right, so I make you sick," Jesse snapped back, angered himself now. "But you didn't give me a chance to explain. The nobody I'd want to pay for his crimes is someone like the hundreds of war criminals in this country and abroad who never gave a damn about the atrocities they committed. The ones who feel no pangs of conscience or guilt. They hide away behind their religious services and patriotic flags, watering their gardens and attending town meetings, making like model citizens while secretly gloating over the good old days when they could kill off their daily quota of defenseless victims with impunity. Those killers deserve to rot in jail or be executed. But LL is different. He is doing his penance. There's no doubt in my mind that he's trying to help all these people, the unemployed, the minorities and the cancer victims, as a sort of atonement for the lives he helped to snuff out in the camps. And he's helped them for decades already. But if you blow the whistle on his past, Dad, he may be forced to cut off his charitable work—something for which you'd be responsible—because nobody in the public eye would want to be tarnished with a murderer's money, and in the end nothing would be solved by it."

"Yeah." Hammer gripped the dashboard with both hands and stared glumly into the night. "I suppose you're right," he said after a long span of silence. "Maybe it's for the best, after all . . . if I don't go through with it."

Hammer tremulously gulped a lungful of air, the next second felt his son's hand on his own. He turned to look at him and saw the dark contours of Jesse's face. For a long time, father and son did not utter a word, hearing only the rhythmic click of the red emergency light, and—in the distance—the burp of frogs in the damp grass.

"Thanks," Jesse whispered at last. He cleared his throat and his voice was soft and low. "Thanks, Dad . . . I can guess how hard it must be for you to . . . well, to do what is right."

"No, you can't. Because I don't know if I can ever quite forgive myself for backing out of this."

"Dad, you'd make life much easier for everyone if you went back with me now, to Rosedale, and apologized to LL for your be. . . ."

"No, Jesse! That I won't do! Crawl back and say I'm sorry to the man who murdered my mother? Never!" He snatched his hand out of his son's. "I'll give up whatever scheme I may have hatched against LL—for *you*!—but that's as far as I'll go, and never mind the good deeds and millions he's spending. They're not bringing back a single one of his victims. So don't ask any more favors to butter up your benefactor, because I won't do it. Do you understand?"

"Okay, okay, take it easy! It was just a suggestion."

"What *you* want to do about it is up to you. For all I care you can apologize for me, give him any cockamamy story you want, but don't expect *me* to play footsy with him. That clear?"

"All right." Jesse nodded vigorously in the dark. "It may be better if I do it, anyway. I can soften him up better than you can. He *is* a tough customer. He has to be or he'd go under in the business world. He certainly has the power to be vindictive, and the inclination too, if you can believe what the papers say about his gobbling up competitors."

"You mean corporate competitors?"

"Yes. Of course, a guy like that *could* get rid of an individual, I guess, if he realized that somebody might be dangerous to him personally."

"In other words, he could have *me* rubbed out. Not only my mother, but me too now, if I revealed the charade he's been playing for the last forty years. Is that what you're trying to say?"

"I guess so . . . Though I don't believe for a moment there'd be a contract out to hit you, like in the movies. LL would go at it more subtly I suppose . . . if you ever went through with your scheme."

"Oh Jesse, Jesse." Hammer shook his head. "How did you ever find a father-in-law like him?"

"Grandfather-in-law." Jesse had regained his composure. Starting the engine again, he cautiously pulled off the highway's shoulder onto the road. "What about you now? Do you feel like staying with me for a while now that we've come to an agreement of sorts? Or do you want to go back to England?"

"No, Jess, with that man so nearby, I don't want to hang around here."

"But your return ticket is made out for three weeks from now."

"I'll just have Grace change it." He scrutinized his son's profile briefly in the dark. "You remember her, don't you? That gorgeous South American travel agent in Jackson Heights."

"Sure. She'll do it. But when will I see you again?"

Paul Hammer puckered his lips. "Who knows?" He let an audible sigh deflate his chest, then slumped back into his seat. "Hopefully when you get married . . . provided, of course, Luckstone is still prepared to have me as a guest at the wedding reception."

"Don't worry about that. I'll put in a good word for you. It's a shame, though—I mean you coming here for your first vacation in years and then going back to London to spend it all by yourself."

"It isn't as bad as that. I won't be alone very much."

"Sure, you've got friends, but. . . ."

"No—there's a woman I see occasionally."

"Dad!" For an instant Jesse took his eyes off the road to glance at his father. "Since when? Is it anything serious?"

"Well. . . ." Hammer shrugged, but hesitated long enough for his son to prod him.

"Aw come on! Is she your age?"

"Fourteen years younger—a divorcee. Otherwise she has no family. We were both lonely people, and now we enjoy each other's company. You know, going to concerts together, or on weekends into the country."

"What's she do for a living?"

"Computer programming. She worked on one of our computers; that's how we met. I really think she'll be pleased seeing me come back early, unannounced. I tell you, she cried when I mentioned to her I'd be away for three weeks."

"No kiddin'. Sounds *really* promising for you, Dad. Not that that surprises me, with your Paul Newman looks. What's her name?"

"Danielle. Danielle Brulle. I call her Danny."

"Has a French ring to it, doesn't it? Her name."

"I thought so too. But her family's been British for generations. Her father was in the R.A.F. during the war. Bomber navigator. Coming back one day from a raid over Schweinfurt, she told me, his plane's undercarriage wouldn't come down for the landing. He volunteered to fix it in midair, but his efforts proved futile. He couldn't lower the wheels. When he tried to get back into the plane, a huge steel plate from the bomb bay had come loose and blocked his way. It couldn't be budged by him or the men inside the bomber. He was trapped on the outside. Pinned under the fuselage where the stuck wheels were. There was nothing the crew could do but make a belly landing. Right on top of Danny's father. The plane didn't blow up, thank God, but the runway was smeared for a whole mile with his blood. His bones and his head were ground to a fine powder."

"How horrible!"

"Danny was only a child when it happened. But she still remembers him. She's so brave, Jesse, and so honest." Hammer sighed. "God knows, what a beautiful woman like her sees in an old sourpuss like me."

"Well, looks to me like she's serious about you. Maybe she'll convert you from a sourpuss into a happier sort of character. By the way, will you tell her about tonight's incident?"

"No reason not to. She's the first woman I trust with everything since your mother died, and it feels good, I'll tell you."

"Sounds better and better. I'm really glad you've found someone you care about, Dad. Look, what d'you say we have a drink in Monticello and toast Danielle?"

"Didn't you say you were going back to LL? To apologize for me?"

"Tomorrow. It's too late now. Besides, he said he was going to sleep when we were leaving. Plenty of time to do it tomorrow night when I see Nicki, just about the time you're flying back to London."

11

"Josh, give me a smoke."
John Shadow sat on the wooden bench under a bough of purple-petaled Rose of Sharon and accepted the Kent which Josh Hamilton

offered him from a sterling silver cigarette case. The White House aide then lit one up for himself. "Can you imagine what would happen if LL saw us now, smoking on the sly, like two schoolboys after their father has gone to bed?"

"Probably give us hell for smoking without his permission. Not that I'd blame him tonight. The way that clown treated him. What a violent outburst! And such ingratitude! I've never seen anything like it."

"Yeah. Strange that Jesse never mentioned what kind of a nut he has for a father."

"How could he? Even Jesse didn't know about. . . ." Shadow's hard stare fixed on Hamilton's face. "Josh, do you believe what Hammer said? About LL killing his mother in Auschwitz?"

"In Treblinka. Hammer didn't say he recalled seeing LL in Auschwitz . . . But. . . ." Hamilton shrugged his shoulders. "That bit about LL's thumb. It looks pretty grim . . . if he does go through with reporting it to the media."

"Jesus, I've known the man for about thirty-five years. Sure, he's aggressive. He can be rude, throw tantrums, all the rest you'd expect from someone wielding such immense power. But this! God!" The cigarette dangled listlessly out of Shadow's mouth. He looked off grimly into the night as his hands kneaded the blood-stained handkerchief. "I don't know *what* to do, Josh. With all his flaws, LL has been my whole life. This really threw me for a loop. If what Hammer says is true, it'd kill me, I think."

"I think you're overreacting, John." Hamilton took a long, pensive pull on his Kent and watched the smoke meander off into the cool dark. "He's no war criminal."

"That's not the issue here, feller. The case is more complex. A prisoner, a Jew moreover, murdering for the Nazis. That picture of LL really stunned me. And I'm not even Jewish—any more than Hammer's mother was. But here's a man I've idolized—even though he doesn't recognize all I've done for him—capable of such vicious crimes. It's just too much."

"Come on now!"

"Look, if any of this gets out, if Hammer succeeds in proving it, we're all finished."

"Well, it mustn't get out!" Hamilton flung back decisively. "I'll depend for that on you, John. The repercussions would be catastrophic. Anyway, I think I'd better get back to Washington tonight."

"But LL said you should stay overnight."

"Just make some excuse. Say I was called back by the Chief. Besides, the papers for the election campaign are already drawn up, so LL won't really need me tomorrow. And the security arrangements are settled too. For the groundbreaking ceremony."

"Josh." Shadow flicked the ashes from his cigarette on the gravel path and pondered briefly how to broach the next topic. "Those papers, the five-million-dollar contribution in escrow."

"What about them?"

Shadow's blue eyes shone ice-cold in the still night air. "Suppose LL is exposed?"

"What d'you mean?"

"Suppose that madman goes through with his plan, comes up with one, maybe two witnesses, and they blab about that incident in Treblinka to the press. Now imagine the *60 Minutes* crew getting hold of it. It'd mean Watergate all over."

The White House aide crushed the stub of his Kent under his heel. "It could be even worse. If this hits the front pages, the administration is as good as dead. LL and the President are too tightly linked in the public's mind. Christ, what a smear this could become! They'd throw the book at the Prez. Some people might even say that he's the friend of a Jew who has killed a good upstanding Christian woman."

"He may have killed Jews too."

"But Hammer will show up with witnesses claiming that they saw LL kill only his mother. John, it'd be the greatest lynching party since Reconstruction."

"Hell!" John Shadow nodded morosely. "And LL would be forced to withdraw the contribution of all his corporations—five million bucks worth. Or your people in the White House would have to make the first move and decline it. Five million dollars of campaign funds going down the drain."

"The question is how to prevent this nightmare from becoming a reality." Hamilton stroked his chin and stared across the lawn at the moonlit silver phosphorescence of the water in the swimming pool. "Even if the Treblinka incident can't be proved legally, Hammer can still make enough waves to throw a monkey wrench into the campaign."

"Right into the White House. And you know, Josh, *I* might get it in the neck as well."

"You?" Hamilton looked up at his friend in surprise.

"I've been with LL for over three decades. If his empire is rocked by these accusations, what happens to my career? And worse, what about

Luckstone City? And the world-wide chain of Interferon Labs? Forget it! It'd be the end of that dream too."

"Shit! The whole house of cards collapsing because of that s.o.b. Hammer."

"But what can *we* do, Josh?"

Shadow flicked the glowing cigarette stub into the damp grass, watching glumly as the red glimmer gradually faded from view.

"Nothing. . . . Unless. . ."

"What?"

"Quiet! Let me think a minute!"

Sheer concentration converted the government official's face into a block of moonlit marble. His eyes peered, unseeing, into the distant dark. Far away, the nocturnal hoot of an owl echoed ominously in the forest.

Slowly the White House aide turned back to John Shadow. "What we can do," he said in a soft voice, his facial muscles relaxing again, "is to stop him."

"What? Hammer?" Luckstone's chief lieutenant glowered skeptically at his friend. "He's probably on his way back to Europe already to get the two witnesses."

"True enough." Hamilton withdrew a monogrammed handkerchief from his pocket and slowly rubbed the sweat from his palms. "But suppose, John, just suppose he doesn't find them."

"What're you talking about? I'm sure he knows where they are."

"And we know *him*."

"So?"

"So we stop *him* from finding them."

John Shadow stared at the man beside him, unwilling himself to digest the threat implicit in Hamilton's remark, yet not completely averse to the as yet unspoken solution to their problem.

"Now let's not be hasty!" Shadow observed with an uncommon lack of conviction. "I don't know what's on your mind, but . . . don't you think Washington has played cloak-and-dagger enough in the last decade or two? You know, the Bay of Pigs, Allende, Watergate."

"Yeah, sure, sure . . . But then look at it from our angle. If Hammer goes through with his threat, it'll be curtains for LL, probably even for the President. I told you he's been associated publicly with LL too long to dismiss that factor. And five million dollars lost for the upcoming campaign."

"Look, Josh, I know all this. But I won't be party to any foul play!"

"Use your brain, John. You. . . ."

"I mean it, Josh." A seizure of twitches zigzagged across the skin underneath Shadow's eyes. "You know how shook up I am about all this. But I'm not going to be involved in anything that may rebound and ruin my own good name."

"What *is* the matter with you, John? I've never known you to be like this. Don't tell me you're too chicken-hearted to. . . ."

"I resent that remark," Shadow bridled. "I've had enough flak from Hammer tonight, and from LL this afternoon in the city, to take *your* guff. It's bad enough never getting any credit for what I do for the old buzzard—things you don't even know about, and never will—but I certainly don't need your two-bit insults!" Another nervous tic twisted his ruddy cheeks momentarily and he averted his eyes. "For your information, about being chicken-hearted. let me tell you I fought on the Normandy beaches on D-Day and they didn't pick cowards for that action. And I've been fighting ever since. I've clawed my way to the top with LL, to the very top, and I won't let your covert shenanigans ruin the life I've built up for myself. Not because of some lunatic like Hammer."

"Looking out for Número Uno, huh?" A cynical smirk broadened Hamilton's features into a smug grin.

"Right. Call me a coward, an opportunist, whatever, but I certainly don't want to lose my position in life at this stage of the game."

"Well, well, well. Poor John doesn't want to lose his cushy job, not while he's in the company of the world's most powerful men—even if nobody hears how hard he works for the old buzzard. But it's nice to bask in the limelight, isn't it, John, and to. . . ."

Shadow's eyes darted back venomously and fastened on Hamilton's gloating face.

"Don't give me that crap about *my* basking in the limelight, when you're the world's number one expert at it. I've seen you smile and nod in agreement when LL told some bigshot or other that wielding power is the world's greatest aphrodisiac. You certainly know about the feel of power. And you're the last person who has the right to cast aspersions on someone like me—you with your Oval Office!"

The smirk on Hamilton's face gradually melted and was replaced by a whisper-thin stretch of his lips, which in turn lengthened into a comradely smile.

"I'm not denying any of this, my friend," Hamilton said in a tone denoting conciliation and good-fellowship. "As long as we both know where we stand."

"Right. What you do is your affair. Just leave me out of it. I've got to keep my hands clean, and so does LL. You got that?"

"Okay, just cool it, will you?" Hamilton's voice was downright patronizing now. "Nothing's going to go wrong. And you'll be left out of it, I promise. LL won't suspect a thing. Whatever may happen to Hammer will look like an accident. He has no relatives except Jesse—as you well know from LL's report—so his disappearance won't be noticed by anybody except his employer. And they'll find a replacement for him. So that's all settled."

"Cut it out, Josh!" Shadow stamped his foot like a child. "I don't want to know the details. What your office instructs Langley is none of my concern, do you hear?" His voice had reached a high pitch of excitement bordering on hysteria; his rosy cheeks were turning crimson. "We don't want to read what happened to Hammer. He's your baby, Langley's; not ours. We know nothing about what goes on behind the scenes. Capiche?"

"All right, John, all right. Don't get all hopped up!" The White House aide spoke in a subdued tone of voice, trying to calm down his unwilling conspirator. "You and LL will be out of the picture altogether. And very soon, I can assure you, so will Paul Hammer!"

PART TWO: ON THE RUN

12

Sparkling Burgundy gurgled out of the narrow green bottleneck into two styrofoam cups, spilling a few red drops on the checkered, waxed table cloth Danielle Brulle had spread on the grass. Broiled chicken wings and potato salad sat beside paper plates heaped with bananas and grapes, making an appetizing rustic still life. Nearby, through a clearing in the wood, a herd of black-and-white Holsteins could be seen grazing and chewing their cuds in a dewy meadow of buttercups, cornflowers and larkspurs. Coin-speckled sunlight flecked the veined, yellowing September foliage of chestnuts and beeches and formed a background motif reminiscent of the idyllic, pastoral picnic scenes of Renoir or Monet.

Paul Hammer sipped his cold wine, watching the attractive woman opposite him over the rim of his cup.

"Happy?"

Danielle lowered her cup and granted him one of her devastating smiles. "I haven't been this happy in years."

"Do you *really* mean this, Danny?"

The radiant smile vanished from Danielle's face and her large green eyes betrayed a glint of hurt, which she quickly diverted by smoothing the wrinkles in her fishbone-patterned tweed skirt.

"As if you didn't know the answer, darling." The faintest trace of a smile reappeared in her face, revealing the indescribable joy she had no intention of hiding from him. "What made me happiest, though, is that, with all your trouble in the States, you came back so soon, Paul. To be with me. Because here you *are* safe . . . Silly, isn't it? I mean, seeing you so unexpectedly this morning was almost as if you had proposed to me."

Hammer reached across a platter of raspberry tarts to clasp her hands in his own. They were slender hands, bony, the skin pale and mottled from the chill in the air. He rubbed her hands briskly between both of his to warm them and inhaled deeply, sucking in the green leafy fragrance of the English fall.

"You know that I love you too, Danny," he said in a low voice.

"But not enough to marry me."

A long fatalistic sigh issued from deep inside him. "Your hands are frozen."

"Well, you know what these English autumns are." She smiled, then got hold of a pear and bit into it to cover up the pain at his unspoken rebuff. "There *is* a nip in the air today. You. . . ."

The crack of a gunshot nearby cut her sentence in half, the explosion echoing among the trees, on the other side of the clearing. Clouds of birds fluttered erratically to and fro over the forest. Startled, Danielle pulled her hand out of Hammer's.

"God, how I hate this shooting!" she said through clenched teeth. Still holding the fruit, she grasped her elbows in a vain attempt to fend off the shiver that ran through her. "I'll never understand why you'd want to bring that rifle along and kill these defenseless animals when you. . . ."

"Danny, please!" Hammer knelt back defensively, like someone trying to gain distance from an unwanted argument. "There are thousands of rabbits and hares around here. They'd just starve to death in winter."

"But why you, Paul? Let the other dumb hunters kill them. *You* certainly shouldn't take any pleasure in murdering defenseless creatures."

"I know, darling, I know it's a moral contradiction," he said, his face grave and broody. "God knows why, but I think shooting is a safety valve with me, sort of an escape hatch for being unable to kill those goddam camp guards who murdered millions just for the fun of it. And to cap it, I don't eat rabbit. You know that except for steak tartar I don't touch any meat. I won't even drink milk."

Danielle put down the pear; she shifted from where she was sitting, wiping her hand on a paper napkin, and hugged her lover. Hammer placed his arms protectively around her slender figure, and she nestled her head into the crook of his neck.

"I know you don't, love," she said softly.

"Not after being shipped like cattle in those awful box cars to. . . ."

"Pssssh." She planted the tips of her fingers over his mouth and gazed up into his eyes. "I love you," she whispered.

Hammer peered down into Danielle's face, feeling the tempo of his pulse quicken. With a sense of amazement he realized that her loveliness surprised him even now. The wide green eyes, her full-bodied generous mouth, that was slightly parted, moist, and waiting for him. Gently, he put his lips over hers and sensed her arms come up and wind around his neck, drawing him close as her tender kiss grew into one of passion probing the inside of his mouth.

The swish of wings overhead pulled the lovers apart as their eyes darted upward and found a flock of starlings against the sapphire-blue sky circling over the tree tops, in anticipation of the migratory flight to come soon. How free they were, starlings, wrens, warblers, bluejays, Hammer thought bitterly, and the old sadness invaded his heart.

"Don't cry," Danielle whispered.

"You're the only one who understands me, Danny," he said dismally. "Not even my son does. Even he wants me to forget about Luckstone."

"I know, darling, you already told me. But I think he's right."

"I just don't know, Danny," he said, quite miserable.

"You don't want to avenge your mother, darling, not really. You want to see him suffer. But, Paul, I could have done the same thing, tried to revenge myself ten years ago, when they caught Jim."

"Your husband attacked you. He didn't kill you."

"He would have if the neighbors hadn't dragged him away from me. The way he took my head and slammed it against the roof of of his car! God, he nearly broke my neck then and there, and then slammed his fists over and over into my face and battered my breasts and. . . ."

"Honey, please!" Hammer held her close to him, hugging her as tightly as he could. He could feel the hammerblows of her heart under her tweed jacket beating against his chest. "You must forget that terrible day."

She drew away from him, but only far enough to look into his eyes. Their lips were almost touching as they spoke. "I will, I will, darling," she said fiercely, "if you promise to forget about yours. But it's hard for me, too, Paul. Even the doctor said that those blows against my breasts may have triggered the cancer, the mastectomy."

"Sweetheart."

"I love you, Paul. Of all the men you're the only one who didn't mind seeing me this way, to kiss that scar where my breast used to be, the only. . . ."

"Of course not. You are you, Danny, more lovable than any woman I've ever met."

"Jim wouldn't even look at me after the operation. He was so disgusted. You know, I've often wondered whether somehow I drove him to hate me."

"That's ridiculous. He was a madman, Danny. He tried to kill you. And he had taken out a new life insurance policy on you just a few months before attacking you. You should have had him sent away for life."

"But I didn't, Paul. He would have gotten out in ten years, or twenty, more embittered than ever, and killed me for sure. I left him, that was enough. And I thought I could never trust a man again. I wanted to kill him, Paul, I really did. I could never forgive Jim for what he did to my body, to my feelings for men. But revenge is only sweet for a moment, my darling. It can have terrible consequences. That's why I say your son is right. You're much better off forgetting about Luckstone and . . . Paul! What's the matter?"

Hammer's gaze had swerved from the woman in his arms and was fixed on a row of wild gooseberry bushes about a hundred yards away, at the far end of the wood's clearing.

"Could have sworn I saw a rabbit. Over there. I distinctly saw something move."

"What're you going to do, love?"

His rifle lay by his side, loaded. He extricated himself from Danielle and stood up, lifting the weapon at the same time.

"It's right in that shrubbery," he said in a whisper. "Should be easy as pie."

"As long as you can kill it with one shot and don't let it suffer."

"Course not. Come on, Danny, cover up your ears. It'll all be over in a second."

Standing against the trunk of a beech, on its knobby roots, Hammer took careful aim, fixing his sight on the piece of fur visible among the shrubs and hedges bordering the dense growth of forest. Danielle kept a wary eye on her lover and was about to raise her hands to her ears to block out the explosion when the crack of a shot rang through the forest. A bullet smashed into the beech, right above Hammer's head, tearing out a huge piece of the trunk. Danielle let out a shriek. Hammer whirled around, shaken, tossed the gun into the nearest bush and hurled himself on the ground, hands clasped over the back of his head.

"Oh my God!"

Danielle's eyes swept the glade. There was no sign of life anywhere. She glanced at the splintered tree trunk, then again around the clearing in the forest. Far away, in the pasture, cows were trotting away, lowing nervously. Frightened, she turned back to Hammer. He was sitting up, his lower jaw quivering with fear.

"What happened?" she asked breathlessly.

He stared in horror at the whitish splinter above, and shuddered.

"Someone was taking a pot shot at me," he said in a hoarse whisper.

"What? At you?"

"The perfect ambush." A suspicious frown crept onto his brow. "Like someone was really after me."

"Don't be silly, darling! Who'd want to kill *you* of all people?"

For an answer Hammer merely stared at Danielle, long and hard. He surveyed the glade, then got to his feet, retrieved the gun, and turned back to her. "Luckstone," he said.

"Luckstone!" Danielle abruptly rose from the ground and dusted off her skirt. "What on earth makes you say such a thing?"

"C'mon, let's get out of here!" Hammer was already gathering the food from the bucolic spread and threw it pell-mell into the two picnic baskets. "That guy's after me, Danny. I know too much for my own good."

"Aw Paul, now I really think you're getting potty. You have absolutely no evidence to back this up."

"No evidence!" he exclaimed. "What do you call being shot at? Come on, give me a hand—grab the Burgundy over there! Besides, it's too cold to stay. You said yourself there's a nip in the air."

"Paul, listen to me! Do you imagine for one second Luckstone would follow you here to kill you? That's bloody daft!" She picked up the bottle and handed it to him. "This isn't Saturday night in Harlem. We're near the Vale of Aylesbury, in the Cotswolds, with pastures and churches. He wouldn't. . . ."

"Not by himself. He has executioners do the dirty work for him. Even Jesse hinted he did. Hurry, please, dear!"

"Look, Paul, if he wants to finish you off, why not have another shot at you? He certainly has the chance to—there's nobody else around."

Hammer stopped halfway through folding the checkered cloth and glanced once more around the clearing. There was nobody in sight. The only motion visible anywhere was the spiraling descent of the crusty, russet autumn leaves from the trees and the flitting about of robins. The mid-September sunlight was fading fast as clouds began to sail swiftly across the darkening sky.

"I suppose you're right," he muttered grudgingly.

"Of course, I am, love. There have been so many reports of hunters being killed lately. Just a fortnight ago one was killed in this very forest. They never caught the person who shot him."

They faced each other over the two closed baskets, like boxers about to square off for a big fight. A sheepish grin passed over Hammer's face. He stepped over one of the baskets and embraced Danielle tenderly. Her green eyes crinkled into a mischievous smile.

"You silly man! Don't tell me after that you don't need *some*one to look after you."

Hammer's countenance at once reverted to its customary seriousness. "Danny, I'm fourteen years older than you. It isn't fair to you."

Danielle merely shrugged. "Well, no harm in trying. Come on, it's getting chilly. Let's go!"

On their way back to London on the A 34 route, Hammer was uncommonly quiet, answering Danielle's questions only in monosyllables, so that she finally decided to keep silent herself and let him deal with his own thoughts. She could see at a glance that he was deeply troubled by something as he steered his old Morris under a slate-grey sky. They drove on in silence, past woodlands and fields of barley and green meadows where flocks of sheep were grazing between dry-stone walls built of local rock.

Around four o'clock, when they were still a good hour's drive from his London flat, he suggested that they have something hot to drink in one of the quaint little tea shops just outside the Chiltern Hills. They swerved onto A 40, one of the main roads converging on Oxford, and took the M 40 to a village near High Wycombe where they stopped at the edge of a thicket of poplars in front of a limestone farm house that had been converted into a tea room. He did not really feel like having a big meal so soon after their picnic, but there was something very important he meant to tell her, he said.

13

Just as it began to drizzle outside they entered the cozy establishment called "Auntie Maude's" and to their delight found a blazing fire in the hearth opposite their window table. The sap in the firewood was spitting and showers of sparks flew up the chimney as the old, humpbacked, yet ever-smiling proprietress added new logs to the fire and then took their order. In no time, their table was festooned with bone china dishes heaped with rum-buttered scones and finger sandwiches stuffed with pork, watercress and cucumber. For the sweeter tooth, Auntie Maude provided platters crammed with Cumberland tarts bursting with dates and crystallized ginger and Bakewell pastries thick with apricot and almond jam.

The two guests helped themselves sparingly to the delicious goodies and held hands under a large bouquet of pansies that hung in a macraméd net from the large oaken ceiling beam. They were the only guests, this being a weekday, and Auntie Maude was only too happy to offer them the choice of her assortment of specially blended teas.

Hammer waited until the old hostess finally retired to her kitchen before venturing to verbalize the thoughts which had been occupying his mind during the ride back to London. As a preamble he said that Danielle should make a point of remembering Auntie Maude's tea room in Chorleywood for the rest of her life.

Danielle put down her cup of freshly brewed China-Darjeeling tea delicately flavored with oil of bergamot, and eyed him quizzically.

"Why?"

Hammer lowered a spoonful of applesauce cake topped with whipped Devonshire cream and gazed into her eyes.

"Because it's here, over applesauce cake and tea, that I'm proposing to you. Danny, will you marry me?"

In an instant Danielle's eyes brimmed over with tears. The drops rolled down her cheeks unashamedly, and for a long time she said nothing. She couldn't. Then she stood up, leaned across the table, accidently bumping into the net of pansies, and kissed him gently on his lips.

"You've known the answer for a long time, haven't you, love?" she said simply.

She sat down again, her eyes sparkling like emeralds by the flickering light of the fire. They could discuss all the details at home later, he suggested, and make their plans for the future. Perhaps even invite Jesse and Nicole for their wedding, he added as a magnanimous and conciliatory afterthought.

14

After departing from the tea room, Hammer decided to treat Danielle to her favorite dish for a late supper—roast venison. He would even have one bite of the meat himself as a favor to her. Fortunately he knew a butcher some distance from his apartment who stocked the finest deer in the hunting season.

They stopped just outside London and bought all the culinary extras, such as mushrooms with pinenuts, eggplants, asparagus, artichokes and the ingredients for dumplings, figuring that Danielle would start preparing the vegetables while he went on to the butcher to pick up the venison. He had also given some thought to buying the records recommended by Nicole on his way back home, especially in view of the happy occasion of his proposal to Danielle: some Haydn minuets, Vivaldi's *Four Seasons*, and Mozart's *Don Giovanni*—his record collection was notably lacking in festive selections.

As the elevator of Hammer's high rise arrived to carry Danielle upstairs and Hammer handed her the keys to his three-room flat before leaving for the butcher, the commissionaire of the building stepped out of the lift and immediately addressed Hammer.

Jorgens, the hardworking caretaker of the apartment complex, was always on friendly terms with Hammer, but now seemed a bit miffed. Hammer had failed to report the gas leak in his kitchen to Jorgens in the morning before leaving for his trip into the country.

Hammer was puzzled and would not release Danielle's hand. "What are you talking about? Which gas leak?"

"The leak you reported to the gas company this morning," Jorgens explained. "You should have told me about. . . ."

"Wait a second, Mr. Jorgens. I haven't smelled any gas in my place.

Never."

"Well, all I know is that a couple of chaps turned up at noon to fix the leak."

"There must be some misunderstanding. I didn't call anybody."

"There was no mistake, Mr. Hammer. Usually tenants tell me if I have to let people into their flats. Maybe you forgot, I figured, so I let 'em in. Of course, I didn't let 'em out o' my sight. Stayed jolly well with them a good half hour, and believe me after a few minutes I could smell if for certain. Something awful."

"Was it that bad?"

"Bloody awful. Enough to suffocate you."

"You know what I think? It must have been one of the neighbors, the Beedens or Mr. Earl, that called the gas company after I'd left. But you're sure it's all right now?"

"As good as new, they said. Took 'em a few minutes to find the blinking leak I guess, but God knows why they needed two blokes to fix it. Damn union regulations I expect. The one in the red woolen cap did all the work while the other chap just talked a blue streak. Kept me in stitches, he did. A bit dippy, of course, but I've never seen such a comedian. Really first class! I told him he should be at the Palladium."

"Splendid. But I think I ought to go along and see that everything is all right."

"Don't be silly, darling," Danielle protested. "You heard what Mr. Jorgens said. It's all fixed."

"Even so, I'd feel better," Hammer said and stepped into the lift.

"No, it's all right, Mr. Hammer," Jorgens reassured his tenant. "The repairman showed me himself. He turned on one of the jets. It's safe again and working well."

"So there!" Danielle smiled. "You better hurry, angel, or the butcher shop will close. I'll manage."

"Well, all right." With a sigh of resignation Hammer stepped reluctantly out of the elevator. "You sure you won't need me around, Danny?"

"You'd only be in the way, love. Give us a kiss." Danielle pecked his cheek with a dry little kiss. "Go ahead now, sweetie. I'll get everything started."

With that she stepped into the elevator and, absurdly happy, shut the sliding doors with a mischievous wink.

"Thanks anyway, Mr. Jorgens, for letting the crew in. I'll thank the Beedens and Mr. Earl when I get back. Here, I hope a quid will cover your time upstairs with the repairmen."

"Aw, you shouldn't, gov'nor, really," Jorgens said, grinning, and pocketed the proffered pound note. "Not to worry. That's what I'm here for. Ta anyways. Cheerio, sir."

What a day, Hammer mused, climbing into his Morris and starting out for the butcher shop at the other end of town. First his surprise return from the States, with Danielle happily tearful to greet him, then the picnic on the outskirts of the Cotswolds, the unknown hunter's shot that went astray, his proposal at "Auntie Maude's," and now the peculiar gas leak. Good thing, his neighbors had noticed it, he reflected.

He had to wait about half an hour at the butcher's until it was his turn to have the meat cut and packed. On the way back, he stopped off for a few minutes at a music store to buy the Haydn, Mozart and Vivaldi records, then took off for home with an ever-increasing longing for Danielle. Only by concentrating on ways to sort out his thoughts, getting some sort of handle on how they should plan their future, could he calm himself down.

Her apartment was larger by far than his own, so that it might be a better idea for him to move in with her, rather than the other way round. Also, he'd leave it entirely up to her whether she'd want to continue working as a computer programmer or let him support her. Neither of them had any immediate family left, except for Jesse 3,000 miles away, and he was better off in every imaginable way than either of them, so there really should be no financial hitch anywhere as far as their forthcoming union was concerned.

True, it bothered Hammer, possibly more than it worried Danielle, that her cancer might start up again. But she hadn't had a recurrence of a carcinomatous symptom in years, so that a state of permanent remission was a strong possibility. No, they could and now *should* put their past problems behind them. They had both gone through hell and come out victorious—good, strong survivors.

Hammer was convinced that by now Jesse had apologized to Luckstone for his rude behavior at Rosedale a couple of nights ago and laid to rest the worst of the antipathy "LL" must have harbored in his heart for the ungracious future-father-in-law of his granddaughter Nicole.

Things really were looking up as long as he and Danielle did not focus their attention on the past, he felt. They could move forward, together. They enjoyed an active, most satisfactory sex life and, best of all, for the first time since his wife's death, Hammer did not think he was betraying her memory by loving another woman.

Having to cross London and getting caught at the height of the evening rush hour, Hammer could make only little headway in the heavy traffic. He became more and more impatient and hoped with all his heart that Danny would not worry unnecessarily about what might have happened to him, or perhaps think that he'd been involved in an accident or, worse still, that he had gotten cold feet and entertained second thoughts about marrying her. Nothing could be further from the truth. But even the telephone booths he passed were busy. All Paul Hammer wanted right now was to be with Danielle, desperately, to hold her in his arms, to plan their new lives together.

The more Hammer thought about the future, the more he became convinced that he wanted to share the rest of his life with no one but Danielle. Like a teenager, he found himself thinking about her at the most unexpected moments lately, and every time his pulse quickened and nothing else mattered very much. He knew he had not made a mistake in asking this extraordinary woman to become his wife.

The very second Hammer's car turned into his street, Clavin Avenue, he realized that something was wrong, terribly wrong. Clanking fire engines jammed the entire street. Hammer was forced to make a hasty U-turn and find a parking place in one of the adjoining side streets, Morgenstern Lane. He dashed back to Clavin Avenue, carrying the cut of venison and the three LPs under his arm. An ambulance had just come hooting around the corner from Ernest Bevin Boulevard and was stopping in front of his apartment building. The police had already cordoned off the entire block. Bobbies were all over the place, directing traffic, while four police patrol cars with their square blue lights blazing disgorged officers and plainclothesmen at breakneck speed. Everywhere, firemen in their black uniforms shouted instructions to each other and hastily disassembled the paraphernalia from their red engines.

Hammer was puzzled that he could not make out where the fire actually was doing its damage. There was no trace of smoke anywhere. Slowly he made some progress, threading his way through the mob of onlookers thronging the sidewalk. As he inched forward he came to the sickening realization that the hub of activity was centered on the house where he lived.

His heart began to pound wildly. Again he glanced up at his windows on the top floor but saw nothing out of the ordinary. No fire, no smoke. Nothing that would lead him to suspect that his flat was aflame.

Anyway, he reassured himself, Danielle was in the back, in the kitchen, and probably not even aware of the drama being played out in front. Oddly enough, no rescue ladders were leaning against the building's façade; instead, the firemen in their helmets, gas masks and hatchets were running through the open front door into the lobby. Hammer concluded the fire must be in the back somewhere, on the ground floor. There, as everywhere else, endless lines of canvas hose lay tangled, in knots, like battling snakes.

One of the firemen blocked all civilian access to the front door. Hammer had to explain repeatedly to him that he lived in the building, but without success. Did he have any proof that he lived here? It was then that Hammer remembered that he carried the monthly telephone bill on his person. He had found it in the mail box before going to see Danielle in the morning, and this invoice finally confirmed his address. Without further ado, a constable directed him to Jorgens who was talking animatedly to one of the firemen near the ambulance. Hammer hastened to the building's commissionaire to assure himself that everything was all right in his flat. But even before Hammer had a chance to open his mouth, Jorgens drew him aside. He pulled him over to the front of the ambulance, its rooftop light rotating rapidly and sweeping the fiery red beam around in jerky, insane patterns.

"There's been a beastly accident, Mr. Hammer," Jorgens said breathlessly. "It must have. . . ."

"So I see. The bobbies won't let me in the building and I wanted to make sure my flat's okay."

"I don't rightly know what to say, Mr. Hammer. But it really looks bad, dreadfully bad, I'm afraid."

"What are you talking about? What does?"

"Your place. Your flat."

"What!"

The package containing the cut of deer slipped from beneath Hammer's arm and landed on the road. He picked it up at once and for the umpteenth time glanced up the façade of the high rise, still searching in vain for some sign of smoke or fire.

"You must be mistaken, Mr. Jorgens. There's no fire anywhere up there."

"It's in the back, sir. There was a terrible explosion about ten minutes after you left. It literally blew the roof off the building. Demolished your entire kitchen, and the bedroom in the back."

"Oh my God!" For an instant Hammer's legs buckled. He held on to the hood of the ambulance. He wanted to ask about Danielle; however, the words would not come out. He opened his mouth, but his mind had gone numb, his tongue leaden.

"You mean your friend?" he heard Jorgens' voice among the shouts of the firemen and the dull thud of blood in his ears.

Hammer nodded.

"I'm frightfully sorry. . . ." Jorgens shook his head. Words were redundant. "You better come along with me, gov'nor. If I tell 'em who you are, they'll let you through."

Hammer walked as if in a trance. Although he was the central character, he felt like an onlooker watching a drama that was playing itself out around him. Jorgens led the way up the steps into the lobby, warning Hammer not to trip over the innumerable hoses and cables and other fire equipment. The electric power had just been turned on again, and when the two men reached the twelfth floor and emerged from the elevator, the smell of gas and smoke slapped into their faces. Hammer's apartment was crawling with firemen, ambulance orderlies and police, some in uniform and others apparently plainclothesmen. He saw Jorgens whisper to a man in a grimy raincoat, a Detective Inspector Friendly, who turned to a young rosy-cheeked assistant by his side and mumbled a few words in a subdued voice. Seemingly by magic, a glass of whisky was produced. Friendly urged Hammer to drink it down and relax on a chair in his foyer for a few seconds.

In a complete daze, Hammer placed the package of meat and the records on the telephone table and sat. Inexplicably, he was perfectly calm. He peered into the kitchen, already knowing the answer, yet dreading to confront the inescapably ghoulish details or to hear them confirmed by the police. Obediently, with trembling hands, he returned the empty tumbler, one of his own crystal glasses, to the Inspector's assistant, and heard Friendly ask him if he was ready to identify the victim.

The victim! The unspeakable was confirmed with bureaucratic indifference. Three hours earlier, tears swam in her eyes, tears of happiness as she reached across the table at "Auntie Maude's" to accept his proposal of marriage. Ninety minutes ago, her eyes had given him an unabashedly mischievous wink in the elevator. And now Danielle, his beautiful, compassionate Danny, was dead.

Icily benumbed, Hammer was led into his kitchen—or what was left of it. Where there was a ceiling in the morning after breakfast, only jagged rafters pointed toward a dark, starry sky. His stove and refrigerator were twisted steel and misshapen plastic. The wall to his bedroom was missing, a gargantuan hole replacing it, with bricks and mortar crumbled all over the kitchen linoleum and the rug in the next room. The splintered bed, table and chairs, the dresser and its contents, the pictures and shattered windowpanes, lay scattered in a shambles on the floor or draped over the rafters. The unmistakable smell of gas hung in the air, much stronger than in the hallway outside.

"Sir?" Inspector Friendly trained his grey eyes on Hammer.

That's what the blitz must have been like, thought Hammer. "Yes?"

"I'm afraid I'll have to ask you to pull yourself together when identifying Mrs. Hammer. She's lying behind the fridge."

"Behind the. . . ." Hammer glanced up, blankly. "Not Mrs. Hammer." The words came out in bits and spurts, shaky. "A friend . . . we were getting married."

"I'm sorry, sir," Friendly said in a soft, adenoidal tone. Ill at ease, he began twirling a loose button which dangled from his soiled mackintosh. "After you have calmed down a bit, I'd appreciate your answering a few questions—that is, if you don't mind."

Again someone grasped the traumatized Hammer by the elbow and steered him past a number of laborers working on the gas pipe and a police photographer snapping pictures everywhere. The exploding strobe lights of the cameraman added flashes of lightening and slashed the nightmarish scene like the glint of daggers.

Hammer clutched at the door tilting half-unhinged off the refrigerator, but even so he had to be held up by Friendly and his assistant when his eyes fell on the unthinkable horror that lay in a huddle, mutilated almost beyond recognition, behind the icebox.

One of Danielle's eyes had been torn out of its socket and hung from the optic nerve—like a piece of string—over her hair on the floor. Her jaw was dislocated. Much of her clothing had been blown off by the explosive force and hung in tatters and shreds from the rafters above, like indecipherable articles of laundry out to dry. Her left arm was missing. A trickle of blood gurgled out of a gaping hole where her cancerous breast had been removed. Paul Hammer collapsed.

At the police station he was given a sedative, but it had little effect on Hammer. Bureaucratic words sounded garbled to him, like sounds under water. He lived in his own world of misery—in complete inner loneliness. Someone apologized that Hammer had had to see his fiancée so grotesquely mangled. If he had not shown up in his flat at the moment he did, the authorities would have had the time to clean her up a bit and have him identify her later at the morgue.

A police officer told him that the insurance company probably would take care of the damage done to his flat and reimburse him for everything in a month or two. Did he have any other place to stay meanwhile? In a stupor, Hammer shook his head.

15

Hammer spent the remainder of the night with Friendly and his apple-cheeked assistant at New Scotland Yard, giving a full accounting of himself, his past, his present job, his friends and family, his relationship with Danielle Brulle. The detectives were particularly interested in anything that might have aroused Hammer's suspicions and could be used as a clue to solve this case. Would he give them a full description of the last few days? Was there anything that might shed some light on this mystery?

All Hammer knew, however, was that he loved Danielle, and that was all that mattered. He was still in such a state of shock that he considered himself in no condition, at this juncture, to give details about his trip to the United States.

"The United States?" Inspector Friendly cocked a surprised eyebrow. "You mean you've just returned from America?"

"Yes, the night before last."

"Was it a business trip?"

Hammer shook his head, "I'd gone there for a vacation to see my son. I told you I'm an American, naturalized. Jesse, that's my son, works as a psychiatrist in a hospital there."

"And your holiday is over?"

"No, I have about two more weeks to go. I came back to spend the rest with Danny . . . Miss Brulle."

"I see. And do you remember anything suspicious during your trip? Anything that might have led to this apparent attempt on your life?"

Hammer stared at his interrogator, slowly grasping the full impact of his question. In a flash, the incident in the Cotswolds rushed to the fore, and with it the soothing words of his beloved that this was just a careless hunter's bullet gone wild. For a moment, he considered mentioning this to the Inspector, but hesitated and relented.

Instead, Hammer shook his head. "Nothing. Why should there be? I have no enemies."

"Well," Friendly passed a tired hand over his eyes, "then how do you explain that thing in your kitchen tonight?"

"I don't know." Hammer slumped forward, wrestling with his hands. "Jorgens . . . the caretaker of the high rise I live in, he told me there was a gas leak this morning. The gas company sent down two repairmen to fix it while I was out, but apparently they botched the job . . . Oh God—God, Danny!"

"Here, come on, swallow this!" Friendly swiftly handed Hammer a glass of water and another capsule, obviously a tranquilizer. Hammer righted himself and downed it dutifully.

"We questioned Mr. Jorgens about the leak you reported and he. . . ."

"I didn't. I never knew there was a leak."

"Precisely, my dear fellow. That's what he told us. And evidently neither did your neighbors."

Hammer focused hard on the Inspector. "They didn't? Then how. . . ."

"That's what we wanted to find out—how did the bloomin' gas company learn there was a leak if nobody called them? So we made some inquiries ourselves, phoned the night-emergency repair service of your gas company a little while ago and discovered that they have no record of any crew visiting your flat. Ever!"

"But that's impossible. Mr. Jorgens himself let them in."

"He let two men in *posing* as repairmen, Mr. Hammer."

"Posing! But why. . . ."

"If you remember, Mr. Jorgens also recalled that he didn't smell any gas until some time *after* he let the men into your kitchen."

A troubled frown crossed Hammer's brow. "I see." As if by magic, his mind cleared of some of its enervating sluggishness. "I think I'm beginning to understand."

"While Mr. Jorgens was entertained by one of those chaps, his mate simply opened the jets without lighting them and let the gas escape. Then, under the pretense of fixing the gas leak, they had a free hand to plant a bomb in the gas range. Our explosives expert discovered that they connected the pipes leading from the ring burners to the stove with an explosive device, which was triggered by turning on two of the jet switches. Apparently it was powerful enough to blow most of your flat to smithereens, let alone anybody standing within a radius of a yard or two."

Hammer could not trust himself to utter a word for fear he would stammer or bring forth nothing but a clucking throaty sound. An explosive device had been planted inside the stove! His breath came in short little gasps and tears welled up in his eyes.

He glanced around the table, helplessly, and saw the silent faces, the poached eyes of the Scotland Yard men scrutinizing him as he started to sob again. Danny had been killed by a bomb meant for him, just as the shot in the Cotswold Hills palpably was intended to silence him. And he knew for certain now that LL was indeed out to get him. Obviously, Hammer knew too much. Danny had already paid with her life. It was only a matter of time before LL's henchmen would learn they had failed in killing him and strike again. The next time they would almost certainly succeed!

No! Never! Paul Hammer made a silent vow: *I will simply not let them! Never! Not satisfied with killing my mother forty years ago, he has murdered Danny now too. This time, though, I won't give him a third chance. Somebody finally has to stand up to him! Damnit! Damnit! Damnit! I want to live, God!*

Hammer knew that this was one fight he'd have to pursue on his own, even if it took the remainder of his life. No outside help. Even New Scotland Yard was useless in a struggle against a man with Luckstone's power. With his connections, he'd probably have friends there too, ready to protect him at all costs.

". . . . reach you?"

Hammer started. How long had Friendly been talking to him while the unspoken declaration of war raged in his mind and shaped the first steppingstones to his new strategy for revenge?

"I beg your pardon?" He wiped his wet face with the Kleenex they offered him.

"Perhaps you can tell us where you'll be staying so we'll know where to reach you."

"Oh. I'll take a room somewhere . . . and then look for another flat."

"Your son's address, perhaps you wouldn't mind letting me have it too, just in case."

There it was—"just in case." In case anything happened to him, they'd need the name of his next-of-kin. And he gave them Jesse's name, address and telephone number.

"Now, sir, will you be returning to the States to contact your son?"

Hammer shrugged. "I haven't been able to think of anything . . . anything concerning my future. I just feel numb."

Nevertheless the questions continued throughout most of the night. Had Hammer taken out a life insurance policy on Miss Brulle? No. Was she independently wealthy? Far from it. Did he stand to gain anything from her death? Nothing but grief. Hammer finally expressed his shock that the police were actually trying to implicate him in Danny's murder.

Scotland Yard did not suspect him, Inspector Friendly assured the broken man. They had Jorgens' statement that Hammer at first insisted on convincing himself that everything in the kitchen was safe. If Mr. Hammer had really gone up with her, he too would have perished in the kitchen.

Paul Hammer could hardly contain his rage when Detective Inspector Friendly asked him not to leave town, so that he would be available for further questioning. All this, while 3,000 miles away the real killer was free to enjoy the baronial splendor of his wealth, surrounded by orchids and flunkies, sipping his '48 Dom Perignon and smugly enjoying his power to order life or death for lesser mortals.

Well, not for long, Kapo Glückstein, thought Hammer. *This is not Treblinka or Auschwitz. I'm a free man now and I'm going to use my freedom to defend my life—and finish yours!*

16

Paul Hammer had a plan. A foolproof plan, hopefully. But he had to work fast, before the assassins converged on him and found their true target.

His single room in the rear of the Savoy overlooking the Thames afforded him the privacy he needed to make a transatlantic call just about the time he expected Jesse to leave the Neurological Rehabilitation Center for lunch. The few belongings he had hastily packed from his demolished apartment would have to last him for the next week or two. Except for his razor and pajamas, he did not even bother to unpack at the Savoy, since he had decided to leave London as soon as he had phoned his son. He would seek out the only two or three people alive who could substantiate and corroborate his description of LL's wartime atrocities to the press.

When Hammer finally heard Jesse's voice, it sounded so faint and far away that he had to shout into the receiver.

"What a surprise, Dad!" Jesse hollered back, overjoyed. "I was just going out the door. You all right?"

"I'm fine. Still a bit tired. Jet lag, I assume. Did you get a chance to speak to LL, to apologize for me?"

"Sure did."

"What did he say?"

"Well, he didn't latch on much, seemed rather cool I'd say, even indifferent to the way you felt about him. I tried my best, though, but he's got his hands full all day long, lining up big brass meetings at Rosedale for the next three weeks or so before leaving for the Mideast. Business calls without a break. I think there must have been half a dozen interruptions while I was talking to him. Looked as if he'd lost all interest, although he did say that he wished you had come and spoken up for yourself, face-to-face."

"You two were alone?"

"No, The Shadow was with him. He didn't utter a word, though—just listened. But what *could* he say? I bet he's still smarting from the belt you gave him that night."

"I suppose so . . . Jesse, do you remember what you said in the car after we left Rosedale, about men like LL being so vindictive, if they felt they were cornered, that they wouldn't think twice about getting rid of anybody crossing their paths? Those were your own words!"

"Well, Dad, he didn't strike me as regarding you exactly as one of his enemies. I don't think you ingratiated yourself with him, but not bad enough to be put on a hit list," he chuckled.

Hammer lay back on his hotel bed and for an instant held his breath before taking the plunge.

"Then prepare yourself for a shock, Jess. He *has* sent his hitmen over here. To get rid of me, rub me out."

Static crackled in the line for a while. No words emanated from the other end. Hammer sat up again, momentarily uncertain if they had been disconnected.

"You still there, Jesse?"

"Of course. But what are you talking about?" His son's voice at last came through with astonishing clarity. "Hitmen rubbing you out! You're alive, talking to me, aren't you?"

"Yeah, by a lucky break. Twice, Jesse, twice they tried to kill me yesterday. First in the Cotswolds, with a hunter's rifle, and then. . . ."

"For Chrissakes, stop it, Dad! Let's not hash that over again! Is that your schizophrenia talking now, or are you suffering from a persecution complex?"

"I'm calm, Jesse. I've never been calmer in my life. But bitter, angry as hell and scared to death."

"Just calm down now! I thought we had all this settled in the car. I even apologized for you to LL and now you . . . Look, Dad, why don't you talk this over with that lady friend of yours? What's her name again?"

"Danielle."

"Right. Maybe she can talk some sense into you."

"No, she *can't*, Jesse. Last night your lily-white Mr. Luckstone had her killed?"

"What! Dad, is there something wrong with the line? What was it you said?"

At this point Hammer revealed everything about the event that had taken Danielle's life and when he was through, Jesse was finally convinced that his father was a hunted man.

"God, I don't know what to say, Dad. I'm sorry."

"Yeah, so am I. I loved her more than I let you know. In fact, on our way back from the Cotswolds, I proposed to her. And she accepted."

"Dad . . . God, how I wish I could be with you right now! But see here, isn't there a chance that the explosion was an accident?"

"No way, Jess—the Scotland Yard bomb squad found the remains of the device. And there's nobody in the world who'd have an assassin track me down, nobody who hates me enough to get me out of the way, except Louis Luckstone. He *knows* I know too much about him. But if he can play rough, so can I. First it was your grandmother, and now Danny. Next time they may really get me. But I won't let him, Jess, I swear I won't. I did not survive the death camps to have him hunt me down forty years later. I won't let him kill me, Jess, and I won't let him get away with the other murders."

"But, Dad . . . Forgive me, I can hardly speak. It's like a nightmare. Look . . . can't you and I meet somewhere? I'd take a leave of absence. With me around you'd be safe, I promise."

Hammer picked up the phone and began pacing restlessly up and down in the hotel room.

"I appreciate your offer, son, but I can't accept it, endanger your life too. You know perfectly well I was willing to let bygones by bygones, hard as it was. But that bastard is trying to kill me now."

"But you have no absolute proof, father, only conjecture, and conjecture does not stand up in court."

"Jesse, we're not *in* court. This is outside the law, entirely, as Mr. Hamilton pointed out. And this time I'm going through with it. If I have to die, Jesse, at least let me die fighting, not like those exhausted, terrified inmates tumbling out of cattle cars waiting obediently to be gassed."

"Christ, do you have to keep reliving those years in the camps? Dad, listen! Why won't you let me be with you?" The pain in Jesse's voice stung Hammer's heart. "Just letting me talk to you will. . . ."

"I've got to handle this by myself, Jess," his father said tremulously. "After all, he's after *me*! You can certainly take care of yourself. I wish you all the luck with Nicole. I hope she'll understand. If she is the woman I hope she is—for your sake—she *will* understand. She has her own money—she doesn't depend on her grandfather for support, so she *can* marry you. As far as I can see it, both of you are well taken care of. But let *me* be now and tend to my business."

"Dad, please hear me out! Why not give it another chance? Listen, where are you calling from, anyway?"

Although 3,000 miles of ocean separated father and son, Jesse could distinctly hear the click as Hammer hung up. He slumped back in his swivel chair and dropped the receiver on the telephone, barely aware of the hot sunlight slanting through the bay windows behind him and stinging his back. Suddenly he was no longer hungry. It was useless getting in touch with his father, talking him out of his mad scheme, whatever it was. Jesse did not even know where he was staying, where he was headed, what new plan he was hatching. Perhaps his father was really going insane; perhaps he was imagining everything. And to add to the calamity, there was no one around to whom Jesse himself could turn and confide. None of his colleagues, that much was sure. *They* couldn't offer him any protection. There was not one among them that could be counted on to risk his or her cosy job at the Center which Luckstone's money was subsidizing. And the FBI? The cops? Unless he could come up with some hard material evidence, they'd dismiss him, and his father, as kooks, paranoiacs. Moreover, word of it was bound to seep back to the Center, maybe even to LL himself, jeopardizing Jesse's position there just when everything started to really look up for him.

Certainly, he could not confront Luckstone in person with his father's suspicions and lay the source, the blame for them, at the billionaire's door. That'd be suicide. And telling Nicole about all of this would be madness—perhaps literally madness, if her carefully built-up psychological defenses couldn't protect her from this enormous emotional blow. Her lifelong love a mass murderer!

It had been hard enough to explain to her the sudden departure of his father the night before. The bitter irony was that he had lied to Nicole, saying that his father had to return to England in a hurry to attend the funeral of a very close friend who had unexpectedly passed away.

17

London's *Daily Express* reported that Danielle Brulle was fatally injured in an accident the previous afternoon. There was no mention of any other victims. Hammer knew that the men who hunted him would not rest until they succeeded in eradicating him, and now they would know their bomb had failed to do the job.

LL was not likely to hire men who would accept defeat this easily—there would be further attempts—and soon!

Yet one thing puzzled Hammer. Shortly after arriving on the Continent, he had placed a long-distance call to Gustafson, the branch manager of his office in London, ostensibly to check on a piece of advertising copy that one of Hammer's associates was supposed to have finished by a certain date. Gustafson assured him that the assignment had gone out in time and mentioned in passing that new projects were piling up on Hammer's desk. Hammer would certainly have his work cut out for him after returning from his holidays.

So LL had not passed the word to have him fired. Gustafson had supplied Hammer with the answer to his unasked question. It seemed strange, though, that he was still with Elwin, Boyd & Cohn, when it would have been the easiest task in the world for Luckstone to terminate his employment and thus deprive him of his livelihood and his large pension. Hammer could not understand why a man like Luckstone would not take advantage of that simple option, meting out instant punishment with a simple nod to a subordinate.

Perplexed as Hammer was about this omission, he had more important matters to settle now. And the key to his next steps lay in the remnants of past horrors: finding the two witnesses who had actually observed Glückstein kill his mother.

18

Jesse was still of the opinion that it would serve his interest best not to discuss the attempts on his father's life with anyone, but the growing fury welling within left him no peace. The evidence pointed too overwhelmingly at the fact that LL was out to kill his father. Jesse had spent weary hours fighting this conclusion—being at first of two minds about his father's sanity—but to no avail. LL *was* guilty. And yet, here he sat, at the lavish table at Rosedale, dining with his fiancée, her grandfather and John Shadow.

Nicole could sense that something was amiss today with the man she loved. He had hardly touched the goulash on his plate, or the carrots and peas.

Her hand reached out to touch his as he toyed with his knife among the vegetables. "Not hungry?" she whispered.

"He's upset, Nicki," LL's forceful voice boomed through the large dining room. "That'll be all, Brewster," he turned to the butler. "We'll let you know when to serve the dessert."

The mastiff-faced butler nodded gravely, mumbling, "As you wish, sir," and backed out of the room into the kitchen.

Nicole was plainly baffled and grasped her fiancée's forearm as she peered inquiringly into his eyes. "What about it, hon? Anything wrong at the hospital?"

"I. . . ."

"Switch the damn thing off, John!" LL ordered, nodding in the direction of the telephone console next to John Shadow's plate. It had lit up repeatedly during supper, and both Shadow and Luckstone had used it to bark out orders to business operatives near and far. "Family's together for once and none of the damn riffraff around—those ass-kissing so-called tycoons and the political s.o.b.'s, so let's. . . ."

"Not on my account, please, LL," Jesse objected.

"Nonsense. See? Shadow cut it off already."

The faces of the quartet crowding around one end of the huge mahogany table were reflected in its lacquered surface. Jesse's nervous and angry; Nicole's lovely, yet puzzled; Luckstone's imperious, amused, but also apprehensive; Shadow's eyes cast down and merely uncommunicative.

"Sorry, Nick. Guess I'm just not hungry."

"Still worried about the brush-off your father gave me?" LL laughed between mouthfuls.

Nicole's expression turned milky-white. "What brush-off?"

A loud clatter drew Jesse's and the Luckstones' attention to the perennially subdued John Shadow. He had almost upset his glass, spilling a few drops of wine on to his plate. A deep flush darkened his cheeks. "Excuse me," he muttered without glancing up.

"Nervous today, aren't we, John Shadow?" observed Luckstone chidingly.

"What brush-off, Gramps?" insisted his granddaughter.

LL turned from his taciturn aide and chortled good-humoredly, "That's nothing for little girls to stick their noses in."

"Don't be patronizing, Grandfather!" Nicole bunched up her damask lace napkin and dumped it unceremoniously beside her plate. "I hate it when you call me a little girl." Her angry eyes swerved back to Jesse. "What's this all about, Jess?"

Instead of replying, Jesse rose from his chair, letting his napkin slide to the floor, and walked over to the buffet where he turned his back on the trio and made a great show of selecting a fruit from the platter of oranges, plums, apples and grapes.

"Well, Nicki," LL diverted the increasingly perplexed girl from her fiancé, "brush-off probably was the wrong word. I know that Jesse's dad had to leave suddenly for his friend's funeral, but he never said two words to me before he left. And after I was so friendly to him and invited him to use this house like his own, I thought his neglecting me was a sort of a rebuff. Wouldn't you say so?"

"Aw Jess, really!" Her grandfather's explanation had sufficed to clear up the matter of Hammer's alleged "brush-off" and put her back in the best of spirits. "You know my grandfather—how touchy he is where hospitality is concerned—he doesn't mean anything by it. Come on, sweetie, please sit down. The meat's getting all cold."

Jesse whirled around, no longer able to restrain the tension within that had been building to a breaking point. "Damn it, that's not why I'm depressed," he blurted out. "I had a call from my father this afternoon. Since he's been back in England, two attempts have been made on his life. That's why I can't eat."

The words left a deafening silence in their wake in the festive night air. For the first time, Shadow looked up from his plate, his eyes for an instant meeting Jesse's, before casting them down again.

"*What* did you say?" demanded Luckstone, a stern frown twisting his fleshy forehead into furrows of deep-set dismay.

"You heard right, LL. Somebody tried to kill my father a couple of days ago. Twice."

Nicole got up from her seat and strode across the room to her lover. She encircled his waist with her arms and leaned her cheek against his chest, then gazed up at him.

"Why, Jesse? What did he say?"

In a few words, he recited the grim story, recounting whatever he had learned earlier on the phone from his father. A deathly hush again settled on the interrupted dinner party; even Shadow had stopped eating and stared hard at his master.

Luckstone pushed his plate away and got up.

"I lost my appetite too," he announced. "Now you two sit down! Come on, Jess, Nicki!" His voice resounded commandingly through the large room, and the two compliantly took their seats again, hand in hand. "We've got to do something about this. As far as you know, Jesse, has he got any enemies in his job, his social life or . . . ?"

"None. He told me so. Nobody."

"Sounds almost like a hitman from the Mafia is out to get him," muttered Shadow.

Everybody turned to Luckstone's aide. This was the first observation he had uttered all evening, except for the business calls.

"He never had dealings with any criminals," Jesse dismissed Shadow's implication. "No drugs, nothing. He's a law-abiding citizen. He won't even smoke in elevators."

"But, honey, why would anybody want to harm your father?"

Jesse stared into Nicole's troubled face, then up at her grandfather's. "What do *you* think, LL?"

The billionaire stuffed both hands into the pockets of his pants.

"How the devil would I know? But that shouldn't prevent us from helping him. What we need is action!" LL thought very hard for a few moments, then turned to his aide. "John, get hold of half a dozen security men in London and tell them to guard Hammer, in shifts; have them move him to a place in the country. The Scottish Highlands, if necessary. Any place where it's deserted. And rent a house there so they can check on any strangers approaching and . . . Nicki, didn't you tell me he wanted to paint?"

"Yes."

"Well, he can paint there to his heart's content."

"But my father has a job, LL," Jesse protested. "In a couple of weeks he's supposed to get back to Elwin, Boyd & Cohn."

"Nonsense—of course he doesn't. I own the agency. I'll speak to

Gustafson to keep the job open for him till all this blows over. In the meantime, John, cable our London office to put fifty thousand pounds at Paul Hammer's disposal. I think he'll swallow his pride accepting the money in an emergency like this. In any case, that should take care of the incidentals, bodyguards, the cottage, painting paraphernalia, and whatnot."

"Aw sweetie!" Nicole leaped to her feet and rushed around the table, flinging her arms around Luckstone's neck. "You're the greatest—I love you."

"Hey, you're strangling me, Nicki!" LL roared with laughter, but did not fend her off as she hugged him and showered his face with kisses.

"Isn't he the most wonderful man in the world?" Nicole turned to Jesse as she slumped back on her seat, all flushed and happy.

A sharp stab of pain at this unconsciously honest remark nicked Jesse's heart. Not he, her fiancé, but her grandfather occupied the most important place in her heart.

"Come on, cheer up, Jesse," shouted the billionaire. "I promised to look after him, and I'm a man of my word. Am I not, Nicki?"

"You're everything you say, Gramps," she beamed at him.

"Well, go ahead, John!" Luckstone exhorted his chief lieutenant. "What are you waiting for? Send the telex so they have it first thing in the morning and can. . . ."

"I will, LL," Shadow interrupted, dabbing at his damp forehead with the napkin. "But I can't leave instructions with security overseas unless I know where they can reach Mr. Hammer."

"Absolutely right!" laughed the exuberant industrialist. "What would we do without the wisdom of John Shadow? Always asking the right questions. Don't you agree, Jesse?" But instead of a response from the young doctor, he heard the hiss of an exasperating sigh emerging from Shadow's lips. "Come on, John my boy," Luckstone seemed slightly disconcerted, "let's not start sulking again! I've given you credit where credit is due. What more do you want?"

LL turned with a mien of disdain, yet affected superhuman patience, to Jesse. "Tell him yourself how much you appreciate his help, Jesse. My good friend here thinks he's been slighted lately for all his good counsel, when I've told him a thousand times that he's my right-hand man in every conceivable way, ever since we first set out to base our companies on the German and Japanese concept of great economic benefits for their employees. Your father is one of them, Jesse, and you can thank John partly for this good fortune. He made sure that

Elwyn, Boyd & Cohn—the whole Eastern Seaboard conglomerate—is not like so many American companies—boilers of fear, greed, back-stabbings, excessive work loads, alienation. Go ahead, you thank him too for his invaluable contributions in this scheme of things."

"I never implied anything of the sort, LL, that I'd been slighted." Shadow regarded his employer reproachfully. Spots of embarrassment burned on his cheeks, much to the amusement of Louis Luckstone. "I don't need his endorsement."

"But I appreciate your help, Mr. Shadow," Jesse said, his voice noticeably lacking any enthusiasm. He was more concerned with his father's safety than Shadow's vanity, his petulance and obvious craving for recognition. "We all do, I assure you."

"Then we need your father's address," Shadow said gruffly. "Without it, we can't help him."

But Jesse had returned once more to his deeply troubled inner self, wondering whether he had acted wisely in revealing so much about his father' secret. He gazed blankly at the exquisitely arranged bouquet of violets that graced the dining table in a Baccarat bowl, forming its forlorn centerpiece.

"Jesse!"

The young doctor was startled back into the real world of finances and subterfuge. "Sorry, darling."

"John wants to know where your father is staying now."

Once again, Jesse faced the trio confronting him expectantly.

He shrugged, embarrassed to admit his ignorance. "Father didn't tell me. I think he's afraid to let anyone know where he can be found." He got up and strolled to an armchair near the unlit fireplace. "After those attacks on his life, I can't really blame him. Of course, he had no way of knowing about your offer of help, LL."

"Well, how about *you* sending him the money next time he calls, Jesse?" suggested the magnate. "That way he won't have to worry about being involved with anyone but you."

Jesse turned around to face Luckstone, more than a bit ashamed for having given in to suspicion, for ever having mistrusted LL in the first place, and even more for being so powerless to lessen his father's present danger when the means were at hand. "But what's Dad going to do in the meantime?" he asked. "I'm not even sure I'll hear from him soon. By now he may be anywhere—in Wales, or somewhere on the Continent. Christ!"

A philosophical shrug raised Luckstone's shoulders. "That's a risk he's got to take now. There's nothing anybody can do at this point to help him, not till you know where to reach him."

Looking at LL, Jesse's eyes became unexpectedly misty. "Thank you, sir, for offering to come to his aid. I always knew . . . I could depend on you."

19

The Audi 5000 which Paul Hammer had rented in Frankfurt, West Germany, was humming merrily down the E-4 straightaway of the Autobahn. Soon after he had left the airport, Hammer flicked on the wipers to clear away the droplets of rain which began running down the windshield. It was a desolate day, gray, blustery, the slick road almost devoid of traffic except for an occasional truck whooshing past him on the other side of the divider. Row upon row of tall fir trees stood beside the road like dripping wet sentries, alternating with miles of sodden farm land and fog-enshrouded woods.

Hammer had to travel south as far as Freiburg, then get off the E-4 and make his way east on Highway 278 to the village of Hinterzarten, about 25 kilometers away in the Black Forest. That was where he would meet his dear friend Karl Ludwig. He planned to stay with Karl for a day or two and go on from there, with him, to pick up the next witness to the Treblinka murder—a man named Kurt Frank.

Even now Hammer shook his head in disbelief, unable to accept the fact that both of these men, forty years ago, had worn the same uniform as SS guards, wielded the same power over life and death of millions in Treblinka and later in Auschwitz, and yet were as different as Jekyll and Hyde then, and probably now.

SS Sturmbannführer Karl Ludwig was a tall, blue-eyed, blond Aryan, in his youth the perfect example of the superior Nordic type portrayed in Nazi posters of the 1930's, the true Germanic *Übermensch*. At the age of 23 he had volunteered to become a guard at the most notorious of all Nazi extermination camps: Treblinka.

SS officer and camp guard Karl Ludwig was the most beloved man in Treblinka and Auschwitz, worshipped by every prisoner, by every Jew who ever came in contact with him.

Hammer glanced into his rearview mirror to make sure he was not being followed; there was only a milk truck. His thoughts quickly returned to remembrances of the heartwarming episodes he had witnessed involving Karl Ludwig in both concentration camps, Treblinka and Auschwitz-Birkenau.

All this came out in written depositions in the postwar trial in West Germany. In 1947, some of the Auschwitz guards had been hunted down, and their courtcase made headlines all over the world. Tears of gratitude glistened in the eyes of the dozens of former inmates called upon to testify on behalf of *Sturmbannführer* Karl Ludwig, and the stories they recited nearly canonized him as a saint in the Western press.

Strutting through Auschwitz in his gray-green uniform, Ludwig had always checked carefully to be sure no other guard was in sight before distributing slices of bread to the prisoners—edibles he frequently carried in every pocket of his fieldcoat.

Not only had he secretly brought them nourishment, he had entered their Birkenau barracks at night, sometimes hiding blankets under his coat, sometimes boots filched from the storage chambers, boots to wear or to use as pillows during the night.

As one of the highest ranking SS men in camp, he had ready access to the hospital, the experimental station, and here he absconded with medicine, drugs and pills and then dispensed them among the prisoners to ease their lot. Four prisoners, just out of their teens, bore witness that he had actually pulled them naked out of the lines, much to the consternation of the Lithuanian SS record keeper. While the female orchestra on its wooden platform played *Tales from the Vienna Woods*, Ludwig had ordered the Death Roll Call statistician to leave the four youngsters on the death list, since they were allegedly needed for medical experiments in the labs of Josef Mengele and Wolfram Sievers, in their dissecting rooms behind the wooden partition of Crematorium 5. Instead, he had taken the doomed prisoners to the Undressing-Delousing Station, ordered them to get dressed and led them to the garage in the German officers compound while the latter were having their dinner.

Then, risking his own life, he hid the four youths in the trunk of his military vehicle and smuggled them past the sentry box to safety, to a farm thirty kilometers away, where one of the few Poles willing to risk his life for the Jews provided refuge for the prisoners. False papers and, finally, freedom were arranged for them. Subsequent testimony revealed that Ludwig had undertaken this sort of daring rescue not once but four times in all.

On these occasions he reported to the Auschwitz *Schreibstube* that he had personally shot a number of prisoners to prevent their names from being added to the *Sonder-Behandlung* and *RSHA* lists of inmates earmarked for liquidation.

Karl Ludwig himself testified after the war that unfortunately he was not always that lucky. Many of those he tried to save were exterminated, anyway. Frequently bodies were in great demand, especially when requisitioned by SS doctors *Hauptsturmführer* Ritt and *Obersturmführer* Weber, who needed the human flesh for growing bacterial cultures. Ritt and Weber were loath to use horse flesh in their experiments—horses were too valuable in wartime.

Ludwig was also powerless to prevent the annihilation of small transports made up of less than 200 prisoners. These were always shot individually through the base of the skull with silenced small-bore rifles by *Unterscharführer* Stark who later was promoted to supervise the running of the crematoria.

Karl Ludwig was one of the first Nazi officers the prisoners faced when they reached the camp. Entering Auschwitz through the main gate with its steel-plated motto *ARBEIT MACHT FREI* (WORK LIBERATES) set above the portal, meant that one entered a death zone replete with electrified barbed wire and watch towers topped by machine guns. Frozen to the barbed wire were uncountable corpses of inmates who preferred electrocution to festering wounds, typhoid, cholera, tuberculosis, the constant beatings and whippings, the starvation rations and medical experiments to which they were subjected before being sent to The Showers.

Karl Ludwig testified that other prisoners were forced to remove the corpses from the barbed wire and that the euphemism—The Showers—was a term thought up by his colleagues SS *Hauptsturmführer* Hans Aumeier, the short stocky *Lagerführer*, and SS *Untersturmführer* Max Grabner, chief of the Gestapo's political department. Whenever the green-blueish crystals of the Zyklon B gas pellets had been poured through the vents in the roof into the gas chambers, the nearby truck engines were turned on full throttle by Aumeier's men to prevent the screams and poundings of the dying from being heard in the rest of the camp. The SS men Boger, Moll, Kurschuss, Schwarzhuber, Gorges, Buntrock and Quackernack usually cracked jokes at those times, laughingly remarking that the water of The Showers must be particularly hot today to make the bastards scream so loudly.

It was Karl Ludwig's duty to calm the new arrivals with a little speech. They were all going to be disinfected, he'd tell them, in The Baths, before they could retrieve their clothing in the Changing Rooms. They should always remember exactly where they left their garments. And that hot soup was waiting for them after the Disinfection.

Sometimes this speech of deception did not work, nor the signs "Cleanliness Brings Freedom," and "One Louse May Kill You" that had been nailed to the walls in the Changing Rooms. On such occasions all hell broke loose. Karl could do nothing but retreat and let the SS *Unterführer* take charge of the resulting massacre, with acts of brutality that beggared description. Without mercy, they beat and clubbed the old and the sick, as well as the children and their parents. Forced into the gas chambers, the Jews now became the targets of Alsatians. The dogs, at last maddened by the scent of blood, leaped like starved wolves at the naked prisoners and bit them savagely.

When even clubbing and whipping and crazed dogs didn't do the trick, *Oberscharführer* Voss regularly would try *his* version of speechmaking; he asked the uncontrollably bleeding death candidates what they thought they were trying to achieve by behaving with such obvious disregard for the welfare of their children. Didn't the elders realize that they were frightening the little ones with their mad tactics? Did they really want to make their last minutes alive needlessly distressing for their beloved little children, when all they had to do was to walk peacefully into the gas chambers and die heroically, as befitted the descendants of the Old Testament? Generally some of the prisoners would cry out that they were willing to work eighteen hours a day, seven days a week, even for the Nazis, at no pay, and it was at that point that the SS men finally saw it was no good arguing with the obstinate Jews.

As a last resort SS guards Voss, Hössler, Gorges, Kurschuss, Palitzsch, Dylewski and Quackernack always brought machine guns into the corridor that led from the Changing Rooms into some of the gas chambers and systematically mowed down the naked inmates by the hundreds. Some of them drowned in their own blood. At the conclusion of this massacre, those not fatally injured usually were finished off with 6-mm. small-bore guns held to their skulls.

Nearly all of the new transports arriving at the death camps firmly believed in Karl's soothing promise of hot soup waiting for them after The Showers and meekly entered the chambers, a thousand at a clip, naked and without a word of protest. Frequently *Lagerführer* Schwarzhuber and Dr. Josef Mengele would peer through a peep hole in the door to determine whether there were still any signs of life after ten minutes. Sometimes the camp doctors left the light on in the chambers throughout the gassing to watch the entire lethal process—the primary excruciating irritation in the victims' throats and eyes, then the explosive pressure in their heads before the final stage was reached and their lungs collapsed. At that point Mengele always ordered the *Kommandoführer* to switch on the fans to disperse the gas. The double doors would be bulging outward under the weight of bodies which had struggled on top of the weaker victims, hoping to snatch a breath of air through the cracks in the door. But to no avail. As soon as both wings of the double door were unbolted the corpses tumbled out, 20, 30 at a time, all of them covered with vomit, urine, menstrual blood, excrement. This stench, mingled with the sickly sweet smell of burning metaldehyde from the Zyklon B pellets, belched out of the gas chamber, and the *Totenträger* immediately had to hose down the corpses to neutralize the gas and cleanse the bodies.

This chore was always performed by prisoners. Next, Karl Ludwig had to supervise the stretcher-bearers, of whom Paul Hammer often was one, to pry apart and disentangle the warm bodies, with some of them lying in each others' arms while others were intertwined in the horrifying throes of a terminal death struggle. Most of the victims' faces had turned blue. Their fingers had been bitten through and many had torn fistfuls of hair from their own heads in their final agony. The pregnant women frequently aborted in their last distorted spasms of life. Paul Hammer, like other corpse bearers, had to wear gas masks during these assignments, since neither water nor fans could disperse the gas completely.

Karl Ludwig rarely watched these post-mortem operations, although he was supposed to. He was more concerned with helping those who could still be saved, who had not yet entered the chambers.

On many occasions Paul Hammer had seen Karl ease the final hours of the Mussulmans, the starved and exhausted wrecks who had lost the will to live. Their bodies had long burned up the fuel reserves stored in their livers and fatty tissues and were feeding on the breakdown of proteins in muscles and hearts. Their blood pressure, pulse rate and body temperature had dropped to frighteningly low levels; men became impotent, women stopped menstruating, edema set in, vital body processes were disrupted, intestinal walls were damaged; typhoid, diarrhea and pellagra deprived the bodies of the potassium and the fluids needed to control the rhythm of their heartbeats. At that stage, all Karl Ludwig could do was to cover the totally emaciated bodies, the skin and bones of the Mussulmans, with blankets stolen from the Felt Acquisition Storage Room, and perhaps save them the ignominy of being dragged off to be tossed, still alive, into the raging fires of the crematoria.

Off and on Karl was transferred from the old camp Auschwitz I to the highly efficient, modern mass murder factory Auschwitz II-Birkenau.

Here, on one occasion, he was to oversee the construction of a colossal water tank that was to help Dr. Rothe, the SS camp physician, in the drowning of babies and young children. Camp *Kommandant* Kramer and *Lagerführer* Hössler were to receive daily reports on the progress of the machine, which was designed to snuff out, hourly, the lives of about three hundred children aged ten and younger. The machine was to work around the clock, seven days a week.

Drowning children was already common practice. But the Supreme Commander of both camps, Rudolf Höss, felt that the process should be expedited. Thus, by placing a rod at the height of 1.20 meters, the SS weeded out the tiny tots who were useless to them alive but could not be accommodated in the overcrowded gas chambers. Children who passed under the rod without touching it with their heads were drowned immediately. In order to improve the efficiency of this mass drowning, Karl was to supervise the machine's swift construction. Whenever he was left alone, though, he managed to damage some part of the intricate machinery. After a few months of delay and failure, "Project Big Neptune" was abandoned, much to Höss's regret.

Where had it all started, this abominable madness, and why, this hell beyond logic, beyond comprehension, Paul Hammer wondered as his thoughts once more strayed from the acid-etched images of past beatings, gassings, tortures, to the present.

For a few seconds he took his eyes off the rain-spattered *Autobahn* to see if anybody was following him. Rivulets of water sluiced down the rear window. He knitted his brow. The milk truck was still behind him, a good hundred yards or so. Just as Hammer made up his mind to concentrate on the road ahead again, the truck glissaded into the upper corner of the window, then faded from sight altogether—it seemed to be literally whipped out of his field of vision. Too late Hammer realized that it was the back of his own Audi that was lurching in a drunken tailspin through the downpour. At once he gripped the steering wheel with both hands, tightly, trying to jiggle the car with extreme caution back into his lane. He took his right foot off the accelerator, ever so slowly, pumping the brakes, and brought the vehicle one more time under control. A close shave!

Hammer shivered faintly, then relaxed with a sigh of relief. Survived once again!

But then he always knew he *was* a survivor. He simply would not allow anything—natural disasters *or* concentration camps—*any*thing, *any*one, to kill him.

Only one thing seemed to go wrong in his life, it became abundantly clear to him: most of his fellow sufferers—his parents, friends, wife, Danny—did not fare as well as he did. Luck had escaped *them*. Death alone appeared to be *their* savior, Hammer brooded in a mood wavering increasingly between anger, frustration and bitterness. But was this all it amounted to, he asked himself. Death being a saving grace? Nothing else? Was that ignoble ending in the death camps, indeed, part of God's Mysterious, Undecipherable Design? The Creator's Design, in Whose Sacred (or Sadistic) Realm—called Life—the young, the innocent, the talcum-powdered, downy-cheeked warm babes were condemned to suffer untold agonies, drown in tanks of water, in their own blood, or get hurled alive, like Mussulmans, into roaring furnaces, and four-year-olds were used as guinea pigs for senseless medical experiments, their eyeballs punctured with malaria-infested needles, while just a couple of miles up north from this diabolical scene of screeching dementia, across the raw-earthed Vistulian plains, a Polish farmer's wife baked a dozen cabbage rolls of *golabki*, stuffed with pork, rice, eggs, onions and lots of spices. The iniquity, the vile unfairness of it all, boggled the mind. And what about the skin of young Jewish mothers, of old Serbian gypsies, turning blue, then the color of daffodils, as clouds of the searing poison gas shred their lungs to tatters, while in other parts of the globe, at precisely that moment, theaters crammed with thousands of merrymakers in Manhattan and on London's Leicester Square howled, whooped and shrieked with laughter at the antics of Abbott and Costello going through their "Who's on First?" routine?

What in the name of heaven did God, Yahweh, Allah or Whoever was in charge Up There, mean to prove by this monstrosity, this criminal injustice, Hammer pondered, banging his fists furiously on the wheel. Why would He create two universes on this, His Own, planet diametrically opposed to each other? One of death, of execrable torture, of screams for help unheard–a cauldron run by homicidally crazed henchmen–while three miles, three hundred miles, three thousand miles away, the sun shone on gurgling babies fattened on Nestlé's formula, and the moon on laughing theatergoers?

Two irreconcilable genetic systems, evolutionary spin-offs, on the same Mother Earth, peopled by the identical biologically developed species, *Homo sapiens*, yet creating worlds completely alien, totally apart, out of kilter, two human races at odds with one another, in a paradoxical clutch on the same piece of rock—again, one cosmos condemned unnecessarily to a living death under smokestacks belching forth flesh and bone; the other cosmos a life devoted to selecting fresh grapefruit at the supermarket, or fixing a flat at the local gas station, recuperating from the flu with a good read, packing for a two-week vacation to Hawaii, hoping for a simultaneous orgasm in bed, debating the existence of God. . . .

"God!" Hammer harrumphed the name out aloud in the car, almost with a sneer of disgust. Had *He* wreaked this calamity, this excremental lunacy? KL Auschwitz? KL Treblinka? KL Bergen-Belsen? Did He, in fact, sit up there on His Golden Throne, laughing His friggin' head off? And get a kick out of people dying forever of terminal cancer? And kids of Down's syndrome?

Or was this merely man's monumental copout, blaming everything on the invisible scapegoat, poor ol' God? On the other hand, perhaps this chaotic insanity against the Jews, the gypsies, the Slavs, the slaves, the innocent, originated in the perfervid mind of only one man. In Hitler. Or was this also too simple a solution to the unanswerable question: Why? Then again, had evolution planted the seed of destruction, of malignancy, in the German character—(which, incidentally, also produced a Bach, Goethe, Einstein)—by instilling in generation after generation the bacillus of unquestioning obedience, Prussian education, parental super-discipline, submissive fealty to the State?

But in that case, why did so many millions of Frenchmen, Poles, Ukrainians, Greeks, Belgians, Austrians, Italians, Latvians, Estonians, Lithuanians, Czechs, Hungarians, Rumanians, Bulgarians, so readily embrace the tyrannical pestilence of Fascism, of Nazism, too, and everything it involved? And why did they still volunteer to participate today in the slaughter of the innocent under different flags?

Hammer felt that it must have boiled down to two different time zones, as in a science fiction movie, two hemispheres, two globes inside man's mind. The evil globe and the good one, with each struggling to gain supremacy over the other. By a fluke of history in the 1940s, of nature maybe, or by Divine guidance, the evil hemisphere had managed to amass uncountable souls willing to do the bidding of just one man; they were eager to let their Cro-Magnon selves be seduced to do legally what each man in his heart knew to be illegal—or they would not have attempted to flee the hangman's noose at the end of their blood-soaked reign.

The hatred, then, was there all along, in the human heart, a pressure cooker flooded to the brim with loathing, and the lid had blown off when the heat was turned on, when the signal finally came. Not just the barbaric, single-minded anti-Semitic Jew-baiters were given free rein to act without restraint, but the millions of frustrated, the embittered, the sickeningly hopeless misfits, nature's punks, brutes and degenerates—all of them were unleashed. With not a word of reprimand!

Eichmann's and Heydrich's Wannsee conference on January 20, 1942 was not the beginning of the "Final Solution"—the birth of hatred lay deeply embedded in the human genes ever since the Pliocene epoch, from way back. Hitler had simply dropped the green flag. Bloated with his own glory, his spurious economic and military triumphs, he felt justified and reinforced by mass adulation, to play the role of God. And there was no reason for the grateful barbarians to question him, to doubt him ever again. Before God, Hammer knew, you did not ask why. You did your duty. You asphyxiated and incinerated people en masse. Period!

God's, the *Führer's*, words had vanquished the weak, the undesirables, for a dozen years, the minorities that could be bullied easily. The ultimate joy of all dictators! Amen and *Sieg Heil*! Blood flowed, wounds festered with pus, skeletons shuffled obediently to their deaths, because Adolf Hitler willed it so. To purify *Homo sapiens* and convert the human species into an Aryan *Homo neanderthal*. Hitler had thought it all out in detail; he tried to make all humans into instruments at his disposal alone, make them wholly responsive to his and nobody else's will. The answer: Hitler craved the *Ring des Niblungen*.

Hammer recalled reading about this manic, operatic scene. In the stenographed table conversations of April 1943 at the *Wolfsschanze*, Hitler had made it official. He tossed it out, offhand, to his SS automatons, his roboty underlings Himmler and Kaltenbrunner, between mouthfuls of chocolate éclair and slices of *Schwarzwälder Kirschtorte*, that henceforth the gas chambers of Auschwitz be used exclusively for the Jews . . . (then in an aside) and maybe for the Slavs and gypsies as well if there were sufficient facilities.

Heels were clicked. The stamp of approval was applied. The fate of six million sealed. Between chocolate éclairs and slices of Black Forest cherry cream pie. Genocide decisions to the strains of a Furtwängler recording. . . .

Even forty years later Hammer could not help marveling at the gargantuan enormity of man's gullibility, his foolishness, bestiality. Few stars shone, then, in the obliterating darkness blanketing Europe's continent—too precious few sparks.

Sturmbannführer Ludwig was one of those sparks, those miniscule pinholes of light in the night choked on its own stinking smoke of burned human flesh. In Treblinka first, more audaciously later in Auschwitz.

Paul Hammer could barely trust the veracity of his own memories. Although untarnished by anything even remotely akin to fantasy, they seemed to be propped up, for all their melodramatic underpinnings, on nothing but a base of absolute delirium. Yet each sliver of remembrance was true.

For instance, when *Kommandant* Rudolf Höss, who never saw anything sinister in the lunatic policies being piped down to him by the rampaging ideologists from the summit of Berchtesgaden, when this brute could not have it his own way in expeditiously dispatching the undersize children to their premature deaths via drowning, Karl Ludwig volunteered to pluck from the overcrowded Children's Camp those youngsters who could pass the physiognomic tests set up by four harebrained Nazi schemers. Rather than seeing some of these youths go to waste by following their elders to the grave, Karl selected dozens of "Nordic"-looking types—uncircumcised, blond, firm-bodied, blue-eyed, straight-nosed, physically perfect boys and girls—milling aimlessly amidst the pneumonia-riddled cadavers lying frozen in Auschwitz's wet mud, and he registered as many of them as he could—Danes, Ukrainians, Latvians, Estonians, Hungarians—for Himmler's idiotic *Lebensborn* operation. The sole purpose of this sordid SS department was to kidnap these young Nordic types from Hitler's occupied lands. In the end, tens of thousands of them were sent to childless German families—far fewer than the Nazis had hoped—so that one day they in turn could be part of Nazi stud farms and reproduce their own kind of *echt*-Siegfrieds and Brunhildes and, in doing so, eliminate all traces of dark-haired, Mediterranean characteristics from the future Germanic progeny.

Better by far to ship these orphaned children—their original names forever expunged—to the safe, healthy environment of country and suburban life in the German Reich, Karl Ludwig figured, than to have them end up, as most of them finally did, in Birkenau's satanic cul-de-sac, the super-efficient Teutonic gas ovens.

Dammit! Hammer knew that Ludwig was the bravest, the most decent man he ever met. Courage and decency were the only excuses for his extraordinary deeds.

During the trial, SS man Karl Ludwig was compared to the White Rose anti-Nazi group in Munich, of which Paul Hammer's parents were active members, to Witold Pilecki, the Gentile Pole who had himself arrested and sent to Auschwitz so he could organize a rebellion from within, and to Sweden's Protestant Raoul Wallenberg, who with utter disregard to his own safety managed to save more than 90,000 Jews in Hungary from deportation to the death camps. The White Rose members were executed by the German Nazis (Hammer's parents among them), Pilecki and Wallenberg by the Russian Communists. Only Karl Ludwig had survived. Feted by many of his fellow postwar Germans as a hero for risking his life against absolute evil, he was later shunned, ostracized, held in contempt by the surviving members of the *Waffen SS* who had been trained, with him, in a camp called Sachsenhausen to perfect the art of inflicting cruelties on defenseless prisoners. Being ignored by the SS did not disturb Karl Ludwig in the least. He grew older gracefully and retired in the mid-1980's to the small village of Hinterzarten, on the outskirts of the Black Forest—a tourist resort celebrated for its innumerable fine hotels.

It was one of the rare strokes of good fortune in his life that Paul Hammer had accidentally bumped into Karl Ludwig after the war. This unexpected encounter occurred at the Titisee, deep in the Black Forest, where Hammer was vacationing in the early 1980's with Jesse, and where Karl happened to be working at the time. In spite of the time span of almost forty years since they last met, Karl's features had hardly changed. Mostly, his hair had turned white, and Hammer recognized him immediately.

Now Paul Hammer was to meet with Karl once more. Stopping at a restaurant near Strasbourg for a lunch of the only meat he could stomach, beef tartar, Hammer reflected that, had it not been for Karl, he would surely have been gassed in Treblinka about an hour after Glückstein had dispatched his mother.

20

As Hammer climbed back into his Audi for the final leg of his trip to Karl Ludwig, he strained to recall the details surrounding his first encounter with the man in Treblinka, but somehow he couldn't focus his thoughts. That damned steak tartar he had eaten at the Strasbourg rest stop was the most vile tasting meal he had consumed since his days in the camps. As he steered his car along the slippery highway, he began to feel increasingly, painfully nauseous. Beads of perspiration soon dribbled down his face, even though it was dismally wet and chilly outside.

From Strasbourg it was still a few hours' drive to the village where Karl Ludwig lived. With each mile he drove, Hammer became more and more ill. He considered pulling over to the side of the road but felt that he would be better off reaching his friend's home and recuperating there, perhaps with the assistance of some herbal tonic Ludwig could concoct. He was well versed in the healing powers of plants and herbs and would surely have some suggestion for dealing with what now seemed a certain case of food poisoning.

For the past forty years Karl had dedicated his life to the propagation of nature. He had sought out the refuge of trees and become a forester. Until his compulsory retirement a year ago, at the age of 65, he had devoted himself exclusively to the well-being of flora and fauna. After observing with his own eyes the abysmal depths to which humans could sink, he was so revolted by working with people that he sought and found solace only among the towering trees of the *Schwarzwald*, the Black Forest.

The psychic defense system he had built up around himself in the nightmare of Treblinka, Sobibor and Auschwitz, the numbness with which he deliberately novocained his mind and spirit in those dark, blood-stained days, gradually fell away from him layer by layer as he reveled in the solitude of the woods. He declined offers of friendship from every quarter, fearing that among those he might befriend would lurk another monster in human guise. Early in the 1960's, though, he fell in love with a clerk at the forestry's administration building in Freiburg im Breisgau, a widow, Hilde, who was ten years his senior. Despite his initial resolve never to become involved with another human being, he could not fight the primary force of love, and they married.

Since Hilde was too old to bear children and the adoption services considered the couple not suited to raise a child because of their advanced years, they traveled to Greece to adopt a child there. They had no difficulty finding a baby boy to their liking and returned to the Black Forest, where they brought him up in a loving, happy household.

But early in his elementary school years the boy began to display uncontrollable temper tantrums. The doctors and psychiatric specialists were at a loss to explain the child's behavior, which became increasingly destructive. Finally he had to be removed from school. Hilde tried to raise him at home and educate him while Karl was out at work. One day, when the boy was fifteen, he locked Hilde into the bathroom and proceeded to destroy the Ludwigs' entire cottage, breaking everything his strong, young body could get his hands on.

The child was sent to an asylum, but this family tragedy was compounded by a new blow of fate. Because a few months later, the boy's adoptive mother, Karl's wife, drowned during a Sunday outing, in a nearby lake. Karl went into a state of shock for a full year, attempting to readjust to a life without the only person—apart from his parents—he had ever allowed himself to love. He never married again and, except for his job, had no interest in human contact of any sort.

When Hammer first recognized Karl two years ago at the Titisee, where the forester had been supervising the planting of pine saplings, both men embraced unashamedly and wept in each other's arms. Jesse was introduced to the man who had saved his father's life and the lives of countless others, and the two men reminisced about the years since their last meeting during the trial of the SS guards in 1947.

Ever since that fortuitous reunion at the Titisee, they had stayed in touch by dropping a few words to each other from time to time. From one of these communications, Hammer learned that Karl had finally retired to a house near the village of Hinterzarten, and it was at this address that Hammer reached him by phone prior to leaving Frankfurt, explaining that he must see him on urgent business.

And the way he felt at that moment, the urgency of being with his friend could not have been greater. The feeling of nausea had doubled, redoubled, and doubled again, until the spasms in his gut were nearly crippling. His heart started thumping wildly, its rhythm becoming increasingly erratic, and he sensed the colors of rainbows bulging around the edges of his eyeballs. Hammer could hardly concentrate on his driving down the wet highway. Every time another searing pain erupted in his bowels, he shut his eyes instinctively—a sourness sloshing inside his mouth—then forced them open again, swerving the car back between the lines. He had never had a reaction to food of any sort which could equal this agony.

Panic-stricken, Paul Hammer's icy hands clutched the steering wheel of his Audi. He centered all his hopes now on his friend's being able to come up with some quick medical assistance. It was only a few more minutes to Karl's village, but Hammer was not certain he could make it before the nausea got the better of him and he succumbed to the poison in his system. Still, the closer he drew to Hinterzarten, the more determined he became not to allow Luckstone his victory.

Hammer looked into the rearview mirror. For a number of miles he had been aware of the milk truck behind his Audi. In no time a nameless uneasiness clutched at his throat. Was the driver of the truck one of Luckstone's assassins? For more than an hour now, he had not let Hammer out of his sight, coming closer and closer. Hammer wondered whether he should take the risk and slow down to let the truck pass or try to race away from him and see if the truck likewise picked up speed to stay close to the Audi. He decided on the latter. His suspicion soon turned to icy fear. The milk truck also accelerated. Perhaps the agent in the truck had been following him ever since he left Frankfurt and even waited for him in a side street while he had his meal in Strasbourg.

Suddenly it occurred to Hammer that the meat he had eaten in the restaurant may have been deliberately poisoned. While he was waiting for his meal, LL's hitmen could very well have slipped past the chef and added some tasteless poison to the steak tartar.

With teeth gritted and stomach roiling, Hammer drove on in a stupor, plunging straight ahead. His entire being filled with the steady thrum of the rain, but mercifully at long last he came in sight of Karl Ludwig's country lane, then finally his home. As the Audi rolled to a halt, Hammer saw Ludwig open the door of his home and approach the car. The milk truck was nowhere in sight. Realizing he had made it, Paul Hammer's strength gave out. His head slumped on the steering wheel. Instinctively, he reached for the car keys and fainted.

At once the older man was at his friend's side, slapping his face to wake him and helping him the few feet into his ramshackle house. Hammer began to rumble in weak hysterics about poison in his food. Karl Ludwig nodded, made quieting, murmuring sounds, and got his woeful guest into bed.

He quickly prepared a mixture which he urged Hammer to down.

Too weak to resist, Hammer drank the potion, still pleading ineffectively for professional medical attention. As Ludwig's palliative took effect, with a heavy dose of Fernet Branca as one of its key ingredients, Hammer stopped even attempting to explain and fell irresistibly to sleep.

Karl forsook his carefully prepared evening meal and remained in an armchair beside his bed, dozing occasionally himself; he was happily awake two hours later when Hammer stirred once more.

The potion indeed had largely eliminated the nausea, much to Paul's amazement. For a moment he began to relay his suspicions about the poisoning, then realized that without the entire story as background, he would sound like a raving lunatic. Lying back into the plump goose-down pillows, and overriding Karl's request that he simply rest for now, Paul Hammer at long last unburdened himself, telling all that had transpired in the last few days to a soul he knew would not only listen with the greatest sympathy, but with strong personal interest as well.

It came as a shock to Karl Ludwig when Hammer voiced his suspicion that, far from having mellowed with old age, Glückstein could very well have been responsible for the renewed attempt on Hammer's life, this time in the Strasbourg restaurant. But lacking any conclusive evidence and seeing the immediate improvement his herbal tonic had produced, Karl was reluctant to point the finger of guilt at the billionaire for this deed.

Nevertheless, Karl himself had had his own run-in with Glückstein in Auschwitz, at least indirectly. There was a female prisoner named Irene Fischmann, a woman who played a large part in the lives of both Ludwig and Hammer during the Treblinka-Auschwitz days. More importantly, she figured prominently in the life of Kurt Frank, the sadistic SS officer.

Karl, however, hated the idea of ever getting in touch with Kurt Frank again, even if it was vital to Paul's interests. Evidently two years earlier, Kurt had been released from jail after serving almost thirty-eight years for the bestial crimes he had committed in several concentration camps; his immediate superior, Treblinka's ruthless Camp *Kommandant* Stangl—the other eyewitness and recipient of Paul Hammer's charcoal sketch back in 1943—had died in the 1970's in prison.

Although Karl Ludwig was opposed to contacting Kurt Frank again, he wondered out aloud about the concentration camp inmate Irene Fischmann, who had also witnessed Glückstein's murderous attack on Paul Hammer's mother.

"Perhaps you're right, Karl," Hammer pondered the suggestion, gently rubbing the sore region of his stomach. "After all, why should the media pay any attention to what an ex-Nazi like Kurt Frank testifies? At least with Irene they have a witness who not only was a prisoner, but a Jewish one at that."

"Exactly." Karl nodded. His sentences were short, his voice monotonous, lifeless, as if any communication with another human being was difficult, even painful for him. "They wouldn't believe me either. I was a member of the SS, remember?"

"Nonsense, Karl! You were a saint in the camps. All the prisoners loved you."

"Don't say that! I'm no saint. I detest the human race, Paul—that's not a prime qualification for sainthood. Besides, Irene will be more acceptable. A Jewish prisoner bearing witness against another Jewish prisoner isn't easy to dismiss."

"But you are coming too, Karl, aren't you?" Hammer turned his head on the pillow, dank from perspiration, his eyes anxiously following Karl as he shuffled to an old-fashioned roll top desk and sifted through some correspondence. Although Hammer had taken care not to reveal anything about Danielle's death and the shooting incident in the Cotswolds, fearing that such a violent report might scare his host and dissuade him from coming along to the States with him, he still could not predict Karl's decision.

"I don't relish the idea, but I suppose I will." He seemed to have found what he was looking for and returned with an envelope to his armchair. "I had a letter from Irene a month ago. Curious, isn't it?" He sank back into his seat. "I mean, a Jewish prisoner of a Nazi death camp actually corresponding with one of her captors."

"Stop saying that, Karl! Regardless of how you feel about the human race, except for the surviving Nazis, the whole world loves you."

"Rubbish! The world forgot long ago. I'm glad it did."

"Some of us remember! Karl . . . did you ever answer Irene Fischmann's letter?"

"Of course. Hers and those of all the other prisoners who wrote to me."

"Well, in your correspondence with Irene, did you ever mention that her old lover and persecutor was still alive?"

"You mean Kurt? Kurt Frank?" Hammer nodded. "Sure. I gave her his address after he got out of jail, but I'm glad she didn't want to have anything to do with him. Memories, you know."

"Can't really blame her, can we? Though I could never understand how she could stand being mistress to the sadistic swine."

"Fear, Paul. At first at least. If an SS man wanted sex with a Jewish girl, she gave it. Period. Or it meant instant execution. So she submitted. After all, she was an adult woman, a teacher of English. The odd thing is that rotten, evil, savage as he was, a strange deep relationship developed between them."

"I remember. Treblinka, Sobibor, Birkenau—he took her along wherever he was transferred."

"Yes. So long ago, and she's still obsessed with the past."

"Aren't we all?"

"But not enough for her to exchange letters with Kurt."

"To hell with him! As long as Irene is willing to come along with us to the States and expose Glück . . . or Luckstone as he calls himself today, we don't need Kurt. Are you sure she'll come, though?"

"If you offer her a free trip, like me, and pay her expenses. She still gives English lessons, but now only to a few private students; she can barely make ends meet."

"It goes without saying I'll pay her way as well."

"Then I'm sure you'll have your two witnesses, Paul." He got up and put Irene's letter on the table. "There are hardly any others left. As you know, many of the Treblinka survivors were gassed in Sobibor and Auschwitz; most of the rest and those who escaped have died since the war. Luckstone has good reason to feel safe." Once more he approached Hammer's bed and tucked him in warmly. "Get a good night's rest now. We'll make plans tomorrow to drive to Irene's place. Are you certain the medicine helped you a bit."

"Absolutely. Thanks again, Karl, for everything. I seem to spend my life thanking you."

"Nonsense." Karl stood up straight and stretched his arms. "Sleep well now. It may turn out to be quite an exciting day tomorrow with fiery Irene Fischmann," he chuckled.

21

During the night Karl's potion had lost its efficacy, because around two in the morning Paul

Hammer woke up, bathed in a cold sweat, lying with his throbbing head in his own vomit. Violent stomach cramps shot through his insides. Convulsions sent jolts of pain through his joints and muscles. He was in such agony that every time he tried to rise to go to the bathroom, stabbing pains seemed to harpoon his intestines and rip them open. He sank back into his pillow exhausted, demolished.

With all his remaining strength Hammer made an attempt to rouse Karl in the next room by shouting, and only after a considerable time did he succeed in waking his host. Karl was so shocked at the state of Hammer's progressive ailment that he immediately called up his longtime family physician, Dr. Maier, in nearby Freiburg im Breisgau, to summon him to his friend's bedside. The elderly doctor felt under the weather himself, though, and could not make the twenty kilometer trip to Hinterzarten. He asked Karl instead to bring his ailing guest at once to his Freiburg residence so he could tend to him personally.

Karl donned his street clothes quickly over his pajamas and rushed out into the frosty night to start up his car and warm it for his sick friend. For five minutes he struggled to get the engine revved up, but nothing seemed to work. It just stood there—a rock of Gibraltar on wheels. The battery probably was dead. He knew that every second counted. Paul Hammer was in agony, vomiting green slime. He obviously had a case of food poisoning, or worse, and the remaining contents of his stomach had to be pumped out in a hurry.

Karl rushed back into the house, immediately conscious of the sour stench of vomit, and attempted to rouse his friend. Hammer appeared to be unconscious, as though he had lapsed into a coma. But this was no time to be gentle. Karl shook him roughly by the shoulder, wet from the disgorged food, then slapped his face two, three times.

"Your keys, Paul," he shouted.

"What?" Hammer's speech was slurred; his eyes opened, glazed, vacuous.

"Your car keys. My car's on the fritz. The keys, *please*, Paul!"

Hammer turned to point in a daze at the dresser. The room swam, turned a somersault, and he blacked out again.

But in that split second Karl had seen them. The keys. On the dresser. Snatching them with his left hand, he buttoned up his coat to keep out the bone-chilling wet wind and made a dash out into the starless night to warm up Paul Hammer's Audi.

There were half a dozen keys on the steel ring, but fortunately the second key he tried opened the car door while the next key slipped easily into the ignition lock. Hands trembling with excitement, nervousness, the freezing weather, Karl Ludwig made the engine obey at once. His right foot stepped on the accelerator and pumped it gently. Paul Hammer's eyes unglued at that moment. His pain was excruciating; he glanced around the room, hoping to see his friend help him get up and into the car. With a feverish glimmer in his eyes, he focused hard on the closed door.

The next instant the door blew open. Like magic, an invisible hand lifted the door from its hinges, flung it across the guest room and sent it crashing squarely on top of Hammer's chest. Before his tiny blip of a scream could grow to full magnitude, the colossal explosion outside raged through the open door into the house, pressing him deeply into the mattress.

Everywhere window panes shattered. Vases leapt from tables, mirrors cracked and furniture toppled. A picture depicting Dürer's *Praying Hands* over the bed swung back and forth, then slid down the wall, crashing on top of the door. The detonation seemed to have sucked the air out of the room, depriving Hammer of breath. His body arched up against the weight of the door, then collapsed back into the bed with such force that the bedstand folded in two, pinning him within its broken frame. Fiery shafts of pain shot through him. The explosion's echo hung in the air, flapping back and forth in his ears, and he fell once more into a dead faint.

Thirty-six hours later, Paul Hammer had regained enough strength in the nearby hospital to speak to Dr. Ronze, the local physician. When neither Karl Ludwig nor his sick guest had showed up at Dr. Maier's residence by late morning and all phone calls to the Ludwig home proved futile, Maier had called a younger colleague, Dr. Ronze, in an adjacent village to go out to take a look at Ludwig's ailing friend. The pitiful sight that met Ronze at his arrival in Hinterzarten's outskirts that morning was enough to cause him to slump back into his car seat; he stared aghast at the smouldering ruin of the building in the narrow country lane, then gaped in bewilderment at the hordes of firemen and police swarming all over the place and interrogating Ludwig's neighbors.

Half the house was totally demolished. Soon after the explosion, the local constabulary had found Paul Hammer in the guest room in a deep coma, under the blown out door. They took him immediately to the nearest hospital.

Hammer's rented Audi was a total loss, a mass of twisted chrome and steel scattered over most of Hinterzarten. Karl Ludwig himself could not be found. His body had been completely obliterated by the monumental explosion. Later, parts of his limbs, head and torso were discovered, strewn on neighbors' roofs, as far as a quarter of a mile away.

For twenty-four hours the police interrogated a stunned, weakened Paul Hammer in his hospital room, asking over and over exactly what had preceded the detonation. What was his business in visiting the recluse Karl Ludwig? What was his relationship to him? In a daze, Hammer told the officials that he had come to visit the dearest friend he had in the world, one of the unsung heroes of World War II, and that he was heartbroken over the horrible death of his comrade in war and in peace.

Hammer knew that it would have been suicide to volunteer an explanation of the circumstances surrounding Danielle's similar ending to the German authorities. They might arrest him on suspicion of murder, since he seemed to be leaving a trail of corpses behind.

The fact remained, though, that Witness Number One had been conveniently eliminated by LL's henchmen. How they had tracked Hammer down again, he could not imagine. Only one thing was certain to him. The bomb, the plastic explosive placed in the car's undercarriage, again was meant for him alone. Or the killers would have attached such a device to Ludwig's car too. Yet even in bungling their assassination attempt, they had unwittingly deprived Hammer of someone who could bear witness on his behalf against Louis Luckstone: Karl Ludwig.

But Hammer had no intention of giving up now, least of all with still another death to avenge. There was one more witness, though, Irene Fischmann, who had observed Glückstein kill his mother.

Irene Fischmann. He did not recall her address on the envelope that Karl had left on the table. After the latter had retired for the night, Hammer had read the letter to acquaint himself with her life since their paths separated in 1947. Without this address, he would never have known where to find her nor, indirectly, her former lover, the infamous SS officer Kurt Frank.

It was only two days after being admitted to the hospital that Hammer learned from the local physician that medical tests had proved conclusively he was suffering from a simple, albeit severe case of ptomaine poisoning. There was no substance in his blood or stool to justify the conclusion that his sudden attack could be attributed to any other poisonous ingredient. Ironically, then, it was a sickening meal which had kept *him* out of harm's way.

Having sufficiently recovered from the toxic aftereffects of the steak tartar, Hammer asked the police if he could visit Karl Ludwig's destroyed home, ostensibly to remove his suitcase, but in truth to pick up Irene's letter to Karl.

As the officers and he were entering the guest room, still in a shambles, a fastidious detective inspector demanded to see Hammer's passport. While the latest entries in it were scrutinized, Hammer spotted Irene's envelope on the floor. It lay beside a broken table lamp, partly hidden under a stack of books—works by Elie Wiesel, Isaac Bashevis Singer and Simon Wiesenthal. Dropping a box of matches and scooping it off the floor, Hammer simultaneously managed to spirit away the letter, unnoticed, into his pocket.

The detective then asked Hammer not to leave Hinterzarten until the authorities had checked with the London Metropolitan Constabulary and New Scotland Yard.

Of course, Hammer could not afford to wait for the Yard to report to the Germans that a female friend of Hammer's had been blown up in similar circumstances just days earlier and that they had told him not to leave England. He nodded gravely, returning the passport to his jacket, and promised to wait patiently at the local Park Hotel Adler.

He got a room in the hotel, paid a week in advance, and took the first available bus out of the village. In the next town he changed into another bus and two hours later reached Donaueschingen, where he rented a new car, a Mercedes this time, and drove for a few hours up the highway to Schwenningen, always taking care that nobody was following him for any measurable length of time. Any driver he noticed lingering behind his automobile for more than five minutes he gave a chance to pass. He knew that since leaving Hinterzarten he had *two* hostile forces to contend with: Luckstone's goons, and the German police authorities, once they found out about the victim in London and that he had flown the coop in Karl Ludwig's village.

Just before supper time, Hammer stopped in the village of Aldingen, on the Neckar River, and took a room for the night at the local inn, using an assumed name. He had a very light meal, then placed a long-distance person-to-person call to his son in Sullivan County, New York.

22

In New York it was five hours earlier, around noon, and Nicole was just picking Jesse up in his office for a leisurely lunch together when the phone rang.

Shock and despair on Jesse's face became evident to Nicole as soon as the broken voice of his father thousands of miles away summarized the string of tragic events still hounding him. Jesse slumped into his chair and was hardly aware of Nicole's crestfallen features as she observed her fiancé stare blankly into space. After a minute or so she stepped over to his secretary's vacant desk, picked up the phone, and sat down to eavesdrop on the intimate transatlantic conversation between father and son.

In stunned silence, the young lovers listened to the tale of murder unfold in a voice that was by turns steadfast, then reduced to a quivering stammer of words. Finally, there was nothing, only a tear-filled hush. Paul Hammer was unable to continue after he gave his account of Karl Ludwig's body scattered over parts of Hinterzarten.

Nicole closed her eyes for a moment, allowed the stillness to persist briefly, then revealed that she was on the line. She said emphatically that she wished she could be with Paul to comfort him. She continued breathlessly that her grandfather would be shocked to hear of these tragic occurrences.

"In fact," she announced, "he has offered to provide you with around-the-clock protection, starting immediately. All you've got to do is to give me your address, and LL will see to it that bodyguards are dispatched to you at once."

There was a bitter chuckle at the other end. "I'm sure that he'd like to know my whereabouts, child. So he could take care of me for good."

"Exactly. That's what he said."

"Nicole, I think you misunderstand. *He*'s the one who's trying to get rid of me."

"Father, please!" Jesse shouted into the receiver, avoiding his financée's numbed expression across the room. "There's no need to drag Nicole into this."

"What *is* this?" Nicole telegraphed a puzzled, then infuriated look at her lover. "What are you saying, Paul Hammer? This is ridiculous!" she suddenly shouted into the phone, her temper coming to the fore. "I offered you money. You declined to accept it. My grandfather promises you protection twenty-four hours a day, all expenses paid, and you imply that he's out to kill you. I'm sorry you can't accept aid given to you in good faith and. . . ."

"Nicole, please let me handle this!" Jesse interrupted miserably, again seeing everything evaporate through his father's intemperate remarks.

"I didn't mean for you to hear any of this, Nicole." Hammer's voice came fadingly through the wires. "I know you're in no way to blame."

"But you blame *him*, don't you?" She stood up, her fingers curling tightly around the receiver so Jesse could not notice how hard she was trembling. "Blame him through some crazy paranoia of your own. God, I know LL has enemies, plenty of them. But what has he done to you except to offer to help you?"

"Listen to me, child. All I. . ."

"No—*you* listen to me! Let me tell you once and for all that LL has no intention of prying into your whereabouts. He said that Jesse could send the money to you himself, fifty thousand pounds, so that you'd be able to hire the guards yourself. Now, if you want me to hang up, say so and you can tell Jesse yourself where you are."

"He'd always find me, Nicole, as he's done the last few days." Hammer's reply was tired, bone-weary. "I'm sorry if I. . . ."

"He?" she shouted, eyes flashing. "Did you say *he* and mean gramps? . . . I say, *did* you?" She stared at the mouthpiece of the telephone, and when no answer was forthcoming slammed the receiver down on the hook. "Hasn't he grasped yet," she trembled with outrage, "that my grandfather is the epitome of goodness, that he's *incapable* of harming a soul?"

Jesse lowered his eyes.

"She hung up, Dad," he said feebly. "I won't reveal your address to a soul, I promise. . . . Dad?. . . . You know you can trust me."

He waited helplessly, but there was no response, only the crackling of static. Then there was a click. Paul Hammer had hung up.

Stupefied beyond words, Jesse replaced his receiver and glanced up. At the secretary's desk his fiancée confronted him with an air of utter and uncompromising defiance, and he knew that the time was at hand for a showdown.

"Well?" she demanded.

"I've never seen you like this, Nicki. Not since you left. . . ."

"Cut it out, Jess! You're not leveling with me. What's your father talking about? That gramps is out to kill him?"

"I don't know. You heard exactly what I heard. No more, no less."

"You're holding out on me, Jesse, and I don't like it."

"What's gotten into you suddenly?" Jesse rose from his chair and walked over to her. "How can you accuse me of trying to keep you in the dark?"

"Because you didn't challenge him about this ridiculous accusation, that's why." She did not budge, simply folded her arms as he took her by the elbows and planted a kiss on her forehead. "For the last time now, Jesse, I want the truth. I mean it."

Jesse heaved a deep sigh and gazed deeply into her eyes. "All right," he said finally, "if you insist. I had hoped to evade the issue, but I see now you won't let me." He moistened his lips. "Okay, Nicki, the sad truth is that sometimes my father is mentally disoriented. By. . . ."

"What?" she exclaimed.

"Let me finish, please! By disoriented I mean that he suffers from delusions, a persecution complex, all as a result of his terrible wartime experiences. What happens is that he actually relives some of these traumatic events, just as you went through your phase reliving the dreadful experiences of *your* youth. Only with you the resulting symptoms were complete withdrawal at first, then extreme anger. With my father, tragically, it evolves in delusions of death and murder. We all have our different avenues in resolving the problems that seem to be beyond help from the outside, and unfortunately dad is no exception."

"I see." Nicole met his eyes coolly, unwavering, but her voice betrayed no hint of compassion. "And why does he focus this. . . ." She groped for the right word, ". . . this hatred on my grandfather of all people?"

Jesse pursed his lips briefly. "Probably because LL is a person of power, absolute power . . . much like the guards who wielded absolute power over dad's life in the concentration camps. That's what I mean by his reliving these wartime experiences?"

But instead of answering, Nicole turned from her lover and picked up her pocketbook from the secretary's desk, then moved pensively toward the door.

"One question," she said, training her eyes once more on Jesse. "Why hadn't you told me about any of this before?"

"There was no need to. Dad hadn't shown any symptoms of this persecution mania in years. The Treblinka memories probably triggered it again."

"How interesting." Suspicion and mistrust pervaded the young woman's eyes. "I no longer know what to believe, I'm sorry. All this psychological gobbledegook. Look, Jesse. . . ." She shrugged. "I've lost my appetite. Besides, I'd rather be with gramps now . . . if you don't mind."

"Of course!" He crossed his study apprehensively. "Nick, I'm sorry too, if you still think I'm holding anything back from you after explaining all this."

Nicole's hand reached for the doorknob. A look of deep hurt, reproach, doubt, darkened her eyes. "Tonight then." Her voice was husky.

"Nick."

"What?" She had already opened the door.

"Aren't you going to kiss me good-bye?"

A tremulous breath escaped her. "I think I'm coming down with a cold."

Jesse stopped short, awkwardly, in the middle of the office, and thrust both hands into his pockets. "Well . . . don't mention anything to LL about this . . . about dad's call."

Nicole raised a surprised eyebrow. "Oh? Why not?"

"No need to make things worse by scaring him with any of this."

A stiffness shot through her slender body and she squared her shoulders. "I think you don't know my grandfather. He doesn't scare easily. . . . See you."

The door shut behind her. Once she reached the hallway, Jesse heard her footfalls on the marble floor fade away in the distance.

Alone now, Jesse's shoulders slumped. Suddenly he was terribly tired. A sense of despair, of a future blackened beyond his wildest imagination, filled him to the marrow of his bones. He dragged himself back to his swivel chair and, collapsing into it, realized that he, too, had lost his appetite, for lunch, for work, for . . . everything.

23

Paul Hammer had never heard of Frommern, a village so small it was rarely shown on maps. It was situated about forty miles north of Lake Constance and ten miles south of the Hohenzollern Castle. The envelope he had managed to filch, unobserved, out of Karl Ludwig's damaged house gave Irene Fischmann's address in Frommern, on the second floor of a two-family home.

One of the handful of survivors of Treblinka, she was about ten years Paul's senior, a senuously attractive Jewish woman forty years ago. In order to survive the death camps, she soon learned that everything she remembered of humanity, morality and principles had to be abandoned, sacrificed, for the most part. Whatever animalistic instincts remained had to serve the prisoners in enduring the elements and scraping and bowing before those who wielded absolute power over their lives. In the name of self-preservation, and spurred on by marrow-chilling terror, Irene had thrown herself—heart, body and soul—into the desperate struggle to survive, and by a quirk of nature her life was spared. She had served her master obediently, compliantly yielding to the unnatural whims of the monster who ran Treblinka in the *Kommandant's* absence.

That was more than four decades ago. Today Paul Hammer looked at her, aghast. Gone was the flirtatiousness, the feminine seductiveness that once surrounded her like the faint fragrance of fine perfume. The sensual allure had yielded to the pains and pressures of the decades. A prematurely old, stooping woman faced him now; her left arm, withered like a birch branch in winter, clung palm up to her midriff as if waiting for a handout. Only the deep brown, bright eyes still carried some hint of the devil-may-care hussy who had brazened her way through the macabre hell of the Nazi camps.

Yet today those eyes lay darkly embedded in a wrinkled, shriveled face, and for a few seconds Hammer could not tell for sure if he was in the presence of the woman who, long ago, tried to initiate him in the art of love-making. The eyes alone and her long untidy black hair gave her away.

She had been dusting the cluttered Victorian bed-sitter when he rang her doorbell—the dustcloth was still in her hand when she opened. Paul Hammer asked her if she didn't recognize him. When she shook her head, he gave her the one code word, "Michelangelo," the name by which he was known for almost two years in Treblinka, Sobibor and Auschwitz. After an incredible, aching moment tears filled her eyes and she reached for his hand. His arms encircled her frail, wasted body and they hugged unashamedly in the open doorway.

For hours life outside the tiny quarters ceased to exist and only the intervening period of forty long torturous years since they were liberated crowded the gabled attic with old ghosts and cobwebby events, adorned with the beads of tears of joy and remembrance.

Hammer spoke of his job and the early death of his wife, Linda, following a heart attack, of his obsession with work to the exclusion of everything else to bridge the jolting experience of her absence and of his efforts to put his son through college, and he told her of Jesse and his success, his impending marriage. But finally he brought up the real purpose of his visit, and he opened his heart to her, fully, about the events that led him to this fateful point, this quandary, about his scheme of retribution that seemed to be leading nowhere in the face of one of the most powerful, popular men on earth today. The enemy was Ludwig Glückstein, the very man who Irene had seen kill Hammer's mother. The man who himself, more than a year later, had maimed and crippled Irene Fischmann for life, and would have killed her if it had not been for SS *Sturmbannführer* Karl Ludwig and, ironically, the bestial Kurt Frank.

They shared recollections as Paul Hammer helped himself to some petits fours and a slice of the freshly baked *Napfkuchen* which Irene served under a window bordered by a box of dark red geraniums.

"Oh Paul . . . Paul." Irene set down her cup of coffee and started massaging her crippled left hand, its paralyzed fingers frozen bone-white and curled upwards like the open petals of a petrified flower. "The thought that Karl had to go like this, a man who saved so many, so nobly . . . I just can't grasp it yet. . . . And his beautiful letters to me."

"And what about me lying in hospital and hearing the news! Another wretched victim of Glückstein's henchmen."

"It's horrible! He never seemed to fear for his life—not even in Treblinka and Auschwitz. We were in fear of dying every minute, day or night, wondering whether it would be our turn next to be selected for The Showers. Only Glückstein—Baldwin—stalked the grounds, smug and superior, as if he were in charge everywhere."

"And using that Baldwin leg as a club, he *was* in charge. He still seems to be."

"Even when he was selected by Kiwe to go up the Road to Heaven, it was Kurt Frank himself who yanked him out of the line of prisoners. Kurt Frank personally saved his life. A beast saving a beast."

"I never knew that, Irene," Hammer exclaimed, placing his cup noisily in the saucer. "Kurt actually went out of his way to save Baldwin's life?"

"I should know, Paul." Irene nodded, flexing her pale stiff fingers back and forth. "Remember that Kurt told me he needed not only me but Baldwin too. To take the valuables, the jewelry from the new arrivals, so that Camp *Kommandant* Stangl could secretly slip them to SS *Brigadier General* Globocnik from Berlin; it helped to save his cushy Commandant's position at Treblinka. But Kurt needed my services too, to supply his own little treasure chest with the rings and the gold teeth I had to pull from the gassed inmates. And at night, of course, as his mistress."

"But he was so ugly, Irene, and you so beautiful. How *could* you do it?"

"Not much left of that beauty, is there?"

"Don't be silly!"

"No use pretending, Paul. I'm almost seventy, crippled, in constant pain, but I knew that if my beauty'd help me survive there, I'd use it. Pride and principles were a sure passport to The Showers. And thank God, monster that he was, Kurt wouldn't touch any woman but me."

"In camp they said. . ."

"I know what they said. That I was a whore. That I went to bed with the devil to save my life. And they were right. But I wanted to live, Paul. Although I've often wondered since, if I had known what was in store for me—the agony, my smashed shoulder, the years of loneliness, living on a monthly pittance, deserted and forgotten in this attic—if I had known all this, wouldn't it have been better if they'd also gassed me in Birkenau?"

"Stop it, Irene!" Hammer said sternly. "I don't want to hear this from you! Ever! You're alive. And I need you."

"Yes, I know, I know." She sighed. "Free trip, all expenses paid, and fifteen thousand dollars in the bargain if I tell the press what sort of a man Baldwin really was."

Hammer wiped his mouth on the napkin and regarded her anxiously. "You *are* coming along, aren't you? You're not letting me down? Not after what he did to ruin *your* life!"

"I'd like to, Paul. But the odd thing is that even if I do, it's more to do *you* a favor than to avenge myself for . . . well, this hand."

"You mean you feel no hatred for him at all, no sense of satisfaction in bringing him to justice?"

"What good would it do, Paul? My arm is gone. So is my life, in a way. Exposing him won't give me back one minute of the carefree life I could have lived. And bringing him to justice?" She shrugged. "He's too powerful. People read horror stories in the papers; for a few days they cluck their tongues over them, and then it's forgotten, dismissed from their minds. You know yourself how callous people have become, average, law-abiding people. Their attention span per scandal doesn't amount to more than a few days, at best. Next thing you know, they move on to the next crisis. There are too many human tragedies to choose from every day on TV . . . And Luckstone? My God, I'd rate him for a week perhaps, no longer than that. People just don't care."

"Meaning you won't stand by my side. He can send out his executioners and you would let him get away with it. Just forget about Karl!"

Irene's sad brown eyes pleaded with the man from her past.

"Don't corner me like this, Paul. It isn't fair. Having to make a choice is something I left behind in the camps. I'm an old woman now. Tired, beaten. I'm not out for blood—I never was."

"Yeah—I'm only too aware of that, Irene."

"Now don't give me this reproachful look! Paul, all I . . ."

"How d'you expect me to look? You'd have been my star witness!"

"But why me, Paul? Don't you think that Kurt Frank would be a much more reliable witness than me?"

"I don't know where he lives. Karl and I were going to visit him together too, but. . . ." Hammer tossed his head, as if to shake off the recent calamity. "Luckstone took care of Karl, and Karl took Kurt's address with him to the grave. Besides, I'd think it would be self-defeating to face the press with a witness who was one of the most ruthless SS men, who seemed to be fascinated by inflicting pain and death. Surely you recall his ideas of fun, or Sports Events as he called them, on the *Appellplatz*."

"Of course. How can you ever forget those races in summer, till one of the runners dropped dead and the others were dying of exhaustion? The thirst-crazed runners were forced to drink gasoline—remember? —and then the SS put a match to them and watched the wretched prisoners cough and spit long jets of fire and literally turn into living flamethrowers. They have a lot to answer for, Paul. Especially Kurt and that horror of horrors Kiwe."

"The Polish prisoners had a nickname for Kurt too. What was it still?"

"Lalka. But Kiwe had the more diabolical imagination. I remember him scattering rat poison and broken glass on the floor of your barracks one day. Then he forced some inmates to go down on their fours and lick the floor clean."

"All I can say is, Bless the Jewish prisoner who killed the bastard. Even on his last day alive, he still had his fun. With a young Jewish mother. She was forced to pour prussic acid into the eye sockets of her eight-year-old daughter and then had to watch the eyeballs melt and sizzle. And when the mother screamed she wanted to die, Kiwe barked at her that she couldn't die when *she* chose to but only when *he* wanted her to. All of this, amusements to while away the time till the next convoy of prisoners arrived. Stangl and Höss said it kept up the morale of their men and gave them a change from the tedium of mass murder."

"Nice bunch of people we lived with, Paul, weren't they?" Her voice brimmed with sarcasm.

"And can you imagine how much attention the press would pay to an animal like Kurt testifying against a Jewish inmate, a man who's a favorite everywhere now for his generous gifts to charity? But with *you* coming along, Irene, a Jewish death camp inmate who has seen him kill my mother with the Baldwin-leg and who has nothing to gain from bearing false witness against a fellow priso. . . ."

Hammer stopped in the middle of the word, gazing beyond the window box of geraniums and focusing on the quiet cobblestoned street below. He peered attentively at the corner grocery store, where fruits and vegetables were displayed in crates and boxes outdoors.

Irene frowned and painfully rose to her feet to follow his intense stare down to the tranquil village street.

"Anything the matter?" But Hammer did not seem to have heard—he just kept glaring into space. "Paul!"

Irene cast a worried eye on her old friend and sat down again.

"Now don't tell me you're seeing more of Glückstein's executioners."

The last few words had an electrifying effect on Hammer. He turned quickly to his hostess.

"You may be closer to the truth than you think, Irene," he said tensely. "That guy downstairs, in the red stocking cap, the one fingering the tomatoes—he's been in front of that grocery almost since you started serving the coffee. Have you ever seen him before?"

Irene's jaws fell open as she stared at her friend. Again, she got up, wordlessly, and glanced across the street, at Bruhn's grocery, then settled down once more.

"No, I haven't. Why?"

"Not only has he been hanging around that store for over an hour, but he's been looking up here, or over at my car, and then pretending to be interested in the vegetables again."

"Paul, I think you're seeing threats where there are none. There may be a perfectly harmless explanation. Perhaps he's waiting for somebody."

"Yeah. For me. Or one of his partners, possibly."

"Paul, please!"

"Irene, about five minutes ago he put on this red woolen cap and. . . ."

"So what! It's cool outside."

"My building's caretaker told me that one of the supposed repairmen from the London gas company who planted the bomb that killed Danny wore a red stocking cap."

This time Irene did not try to scrutinize the man in front of the corner store. Instead, her eyes swept blankly across the gables of the old houses opposite her, at their herringbone TV antennas, as if trying to block out the sight of imminent danger.

"You have no evidence, Paul, that he is the killer," she said softly.

"True. But I don't want to put it to a test."

Irene got up and again looked out the window. The man wearing the red cap was too far away for Irene to distinguish his features, but she could see that he was staring at her house.

"I wonder if he was also the one who planted the bomb in the car that killed Karl."

"He may very well be. Irene, look at me!" She turned from the window to confront a deadly serious Paul Hammer. "Once I leave here, do you really want to stay behind alone, facing that man out there, who may be out to get you?"

"Me? What have *I* done to him?"

"As little as Danielle and Karl. Who knows? The killer may have instructions from LL to do away with anyone who could be dangerous to him. It's becoming increasingly clear to me, Irene, that Luckstone must know that in Karl and in you he faces two very threatening witnesses. And he already terminated Karl."

Irene fell back into her armchair and clutched her crippled hand. Pain and fear brooded in her eyes. "You should not have come here, Paul, putting my life in danger this way. I'm an old woman trying to forget the past and deal with the present, however difficult my circumstances are. And now you come out of the blue and. . . ."

Hammer suddenly reached forward across the coffee table and grabbed her gnarled right hand.

"Irene, there's nothing I want less than to see any harm come to you. I tried my damndest to make sure I wasn't followed here; but then I never dreamed Luckstone would send men after me when I was with Danny or Karl. He is afraid, Irene, of what we might reveal about his past, and until we have spoken to the press in the U.S., he'll keep hunting us down; at least till we no longer pose a threat. It's no good shirking our responsibility now."

Irene shook her head, deeply troubled. "Here I thought I could live out my life peacefully in this tiny town, and then you come swooping out of the past, rip me out of my secure hiding place, and carry me back forty years to those days and nights of endless horror."

"I don't want to revive the past, Irene, believe me, but to kill it. Ask my son. I was perfectly willing to return to England and forget about Glückstein. I wanted to get married again, but he declared war on me and destroyed my dreams. For the second time in my life."

They sat uneasily in two dusty armchairs, silently gazing into each other's eyes.

"It would mean," she said in a tortured voice, "that everything depended on your other witness, wouldn't it, if I didn't come along?"

"What do you mean? What other witness?"

"That brute."

"Kurt Frank?"

"Yes."

"He is the only one alive who could explain to the world why he used his position as adjutant to the *Kommandant* of Treblinka to save Baldwin from death."

"Paul, meeting this beast again after all these years would be quite a shock for an old woman like me. Karl sent me his address."

"I don't relish that meeting either; you understand, don't you? Especially after what he did to me on that first day in Treblinka, shortly after my mother was killed. I'll never forgive Kurt Frank for that."

A sad little smile added more wrinkles to the woman's face, transfigured with pain. "As long as I live I won't forget your terrified look when Kurt ordered you to rape me. Dear Paul, if we only knew then what we know now, it would have been so much simpler."

"I guess so." Hammer dreamily gazed at her cold hand in his. "I wonder if he still remembers."

"We'll have to ask him when we see him, won't we?" She smiled.

A look of astonishment displaced Hammer's faraway gaze. "Then you *are* coming with me?"

"What choice do I have? I'll feel safer with you now, I guess, than staying behind all by myself. Nothing ties me down here. I've only one English student left."

"Oh Irene!" Hammer leaned forward and planted a dry kiss on her brow, then watched her guardedly. "You do have a passport, I hope."

"Goodness, Kurt lives only two hundred kilometers from here, outside Munich. For that I don't. . . ."

"Not for Kurt. For afterwards. Once we've persuaded him to come along, we'll leave for the States. To face the press."

"Yes, of course. I'm sure Kurt would like that idea. Karl wrote me that Kurt would do anything to get his hands around Glückstein's neck. Kurt claims he was betrayed by him."

"That's a strange idea—the mighty SS officer betrayed by one of his own prisoners. Should be an interesting meeting. Come on, get everything ready. Just a small suitcase and your passport. If you forget any clothing, I'll buy it for you on the way. And I'll make out the check for fifteen thousand dollars for you, to compensate you for all this trouble, after we've seen Kurt."

"I don't want any money, Paul, I told you."

"You'll take it and find a decent place to live. An attic doesn't become a woman who has suffered so much," and as an afterthought, "and taught me about love."

Irene smiled playfully and rose to her feet. "My God, if Kurt had ever found out, he'd have sent both of us to The Showers."

"Well, we'll tell him now about our affair. And if he doesn't like it, so much the better."

She started to busy herself with removing clothing from her dresser. "Mustn't forget my medicine, and tell Anna, my neighbor, to look after the mail, pay my bills, and water the geraniums," she muttered, and suddenly looked up alarmed. "Do you think the American immigration authorities will let Kurt into their country if they know he was a member of the *Waffen SS*?"

"They won't ask him if he just comes as a tourist. I only hope he has a passport."

"He does. Karl wrote me last year that Kurt tried to emigrate to Latin America after being released from jail but then soured on the idea when some of the Nazi leaders over there didn't want him around."

"I wonder why. But *you* do have one, don't you?"

"Yes—right here." Irene removed her passport from the bottom drawer of a marble-topped chiffonier. "I needed it a couple of years ago for a trip to Rome, to one of the women who nursed me with my shoulder . . . Paul, is that man still outside?"

Hammer craned his neck over the window box of flowers. "Staring at my car now. Probably hoping to plant a bomb in it once it turns dark."

24

Paul Hammer wanted to reach Munich before supper and show Irene Fischmann around the place where he had spent his youth, but the excitement of the trip began to tell on her, and he decided to call it a day when they made it as far as Fürstenfeldbruck, about 25 kilometers outside the city.

After booking two rooms in a small inn and unloading their luggage, Hammer explained to Irene that he planned to return his rented car before supper and check out a new one early the next morning for the last leg of their journey to Kurt. That would prevent the pursuing assassin from planting a bomb in the automobile while they were asleep.

Irene readily agreed to Paul's cautious plan. She had now had a run-in with the man in the red woolen stocking cap. At first she had dismissed Hammer's suspicions of him as a sign of understandable but unjustified fear. But her skepticism quickly dissipated after they had loaded the trunk of the Mercedes with Irene's suitcase and started out shortly before dusk.

The man in the red cap did not, as Paul had expected, turn to watch them as they departed. In fact, he had his back turned to them. However, he was able to watch the proceedings without any difficulty by using the grocery store's open glass door as a mirror, which was reflecting the scene of Hammer and Irene preparing for the journey.

Once they had settled in the car, Hammer stepped immediately on the accelerator and raced down the deserted cobblestoned street. Keeping their eyes glued to the rearview mirror, both passengers observed the man making a dash for his sky-blue Opel. Hammer's worst fears had been vindicated. He gunned the Mercedes at once into a side street, roared in a full circle around the block and sped off through a labyrinth of Frommern's alleys, a maze of its byways. In no time it appeared they had lost the mystery man, but they were convinced that he was perfectly capable of catching up with them any time later.

There was no other automobile visible in the immediate vicinity of the inn in which they spent the night. As they stepped into their newly rented car early next morning Irene expressed her hope that they had finally gotten rid of their pursuer. Nevertheless, they made doubly sure on the final stretch of their trip down Highway E-61 that no one resembling the red-capped killer was following them. In fact, Paul made it his business to travel through Munich, hoping that if the murderer had succeeded in trailing them on the Freeway, they would now lose him in the heavy metropolitan traffic. About three quarters of an hour later, they emerged from the Bavarian capital, absolutely convinced that this time they were in the clear.

It was a foggy, raw day and, besides, the thick haze shrouding the countryside served for additional cover as the two old friends rode down the expressway away from Munich. Soon they were zeroing in on Kaisersdorf, a new suburb of Hohenbrunn where Kurt Frank had made his home after almost thirty-eight years of incarceration.

Nestled snugly in a valley among peaceful, wooded hills, the town was not far from walled cities, medieval courts and restored castles, yet seemed light-years away from the carnage and crematoria of the concentration camps. Frank's address turned out to be an ultra-modern housing project made up of three-story apartment buildings replete with pastel balconies, fistfuls of flowers in every window, and beds of exquisitely manicured shrubbery near the entrance doors. Across the street was a tidy park with swings, seesaws and slides, where children frolicked and played ball. A shopping center down the road was a perfect replica of its American counterpart.

Earlier in the day, Hammer and Irene had agreed not to reveal anything about the murders of Danielle and Karl Ludwig to Kurt, fearing that the disclosure might frighten him away from joining them on their trip to the States. At least so far, Hammer had seen no mention of Karl's death in the papers. At the same time they would have to concede that he had been killed in an automobile accident, just in case Kurt decided to get in touch with him.

In the midst of such glamorous new surroundings, it came as a surprise to the two visitors to discover that Kurt Frank occupied a one-room studio in the cellar, next to the garbage cans. The foul vegetable stench of the overflowing receptacles festered in the visitors' nostrils. The cans had been assembled in long rows on both sides of Kurt's front door, like a phalanx of silent, steel-helmeted sentries standing guard. A lone naked light bulb was the sole source of illumination in the basement.

Rapping his knuckles against the door, Hammer grabbed Irene's hand and with a barely suppressed tremor both stood facing the door, behind which lived one of the most diabolically brutal, inhuman monsters ever to walk the Earth.

A chain scraped on the other side of the door, the safety latch was lifting noisily, and the door opened a crack.

"Who is it?"

The voice was older, scratchier perhaps, but unmistakably that of the sadistic SS officer who had brought death and untold suffering to hundreds of thousands.

Paul Hammer stepped closer to the door. "Karl Ludwig gave us your address. We're friends of his."

Another chain was removed and the door opened. Electric light burned in the dingy basement room, although it was not noon yet. The two unnamed intruders held their breath. There he stood, towering over them, his bony death's head hunched on a pair of slightly humped shoulders. Time, a wasted life, bottomless cruelty and bestial memories had conspired to ravage his face, framed in grey muttonchop sideburns. Not the same man, surely, yet buried behind the aging flesh lay the core that drove him relentlessly, unquestioningly, ruthlessly, to obey the orders of his *Führer*.

Evil incarnate. Eyes, dimly grey, dead to suffering and love, eyes that had seen the most unspeakable human crimes, glowered back at the two. In Hammer's mind a frightening flash from the long-forgotten past thrust out the picture of the awkwardly huge frame of Kurt Frank in his field-grey SS camp uniform leading a band of pitiful boys and girls in rags and tatters to the open fire in the mammoth pit. This sulfur-fed pyre burned day and night in Treblinka, and was hidden from view by an eight-meter-high screen of beech trunks. A red cross set in a white circle had been painted on its front.

The children's tiny hands clung to a rope, and their spindle-thin matchstick legs stumbled and tripped and fell over the numerous branches and rocks strewn across the road. Not a single sound emanated from the long trail of children, about two hundred of them, for all of them were either mute, deaf or blind. They could sense the heat of the fire as they approached the pit; only a multilingual murmur occasionally enlivened the dirty, pinched faces of the blind youngsters as they began to slow down, suspicious, dragging their feet. When the two children in the front were less than half a dozen meters from the fire, SS *Sturmbannführer* Kurt Frank gave the back-end of the rope a sharp tug and the entire procession came to a halt.

The band of ragged toddlers stopped in the chill wind, sniffing the air like puppies sensing danger, waiting, dead eyes turning up to a dark, unforgiving sky. Frank removed a greasy package from his field-grey tunic pocket and unwrapped a thick liverwurst sandwich. He bit greedily into it and munched the food, savoring the freshly baked bread. Still chomping furiously, he stuck the sandwich into his mouth, leaving his hands free to pry the icy fingers of the mute child in front from the rope. Next, he lifted the barefoot little girl in both arms, stepped behind the screen of tree logs to the edge of the burning pit and with a mighty heave hurled her into the fire. No sound, no scream of terror, no motion of protestation other than the flutter of her torn thin dress issued from the rag of a human bundle as it flew through the air and landed in the roaring sea of flames.

Kurt Frank bit another piece out of his soggy liverwurst sandwich, watched the greedy fire engulf the small body as it arched up in silent agony and the mouth and eyes in the blood-red face opened up insanely. Then he moved back to the other side of the beech wall where the girl's companion in the front row, a boy of six, waited shivering in the cold, dull eyes turned heavenward. Again he disentangled the child's frozen fingers from the rope, lifted him with ease under his arm and flung him after the girl into the flames. No sound came from the child's gaping mouth. His vocal cords were scorched instantly, seared by the flames he sucked in with a wild frenzy. The dead pupils of his eyes split, like cracked eggshells, releasing a river of blood. His mop of flaxen hair hissed in a brief gust of flame.

Neither joy nor pity, neither revulsion nor indifference registered on Kurt Frank's face. His jaws disposed of the food methodically, and in-between bites he tossed live bodies through the air as if they were bags of garbage. If he appeared absent-minded to the outsider, this preoccupation stemmed from the fact that another group of prisoners was expected to arrive within the hour, demanding that the tiny tots be gotten out of the way expeditiously for the arrival of the new transport of human "refuse."

Paul Hammer had been a silent, though helpless witness. That morning, as on countless other occasions, it was his duty to camouflage "The Road to Heaven," the *Himmelfahrts Strasse*, near the gargantuan pit of flames, with fully leafed branches. This was the path, about a dozen feet wide with ten-foot high barbed wire fences on each side, through which the naked prisoners, in rows of five, had to run the ninety meters from the women's and children's undressing barracks down the hill to their death—The Showers. And the camp's "Beautification Program" demanded that the green branches from the nearby forest stay in place.

But that particular morning was more than four decades ago. Since then the world had undergone many cataclysms and catastrophes, and

Kurt Frank was no more than a purportedly chastened statistic.

The rawboned giant, stooped by height and age, now stared at the two disturbers of his privacy. He rolled up the sleeves of his white shirt.

"Karl sent you?"

"Yes," said Hammer. "You don't recognize us?"

Frank frowned suspiciously. "Should I?"

"Not even me?" Irene spoke up. "You don't even recognize me, Kurt?"

The former SS guard bunched up his furry brow at the sound of Irene's voice, trying to place it, wondering at the familiar way she used his first name.

"It's dark out there," he growled. "My eyes aren't that good any more."

"You don't remember your *Zigeuner*—your Gypsy?" It was the nickname he had given her in camp because of her black, unkempt hair. She watched anxiously to see how he would react to this prodding.

He peered out of his room at the ghosts from the long-ago past and said nothing, just gaped, slack-jawed. Then his gigantic hands reached forward to the woman's right hand. Gently, delicately, he pulled it up to his lips and kissed it. Without releasing her hand, his eyes fixed intently on Hammer, but after a while he shook his head.

"We met too?"

Hammer nodded. "When I was fourteen. Still don't recognize me? . . . Stangl used to call me Michelangelo, and you. . . ."

"Yes . . . yes. The painter!" His voice betrayed no emotion, only recollection. "You did that sketch of me shaking Himmler's hand. The Yanks took it from me and beat me up. Paid no attention to the Geneva Convention on how to treat prisoners."

"Do you still have that other sketch, Kurt?"

"What other sketch? . . . What was your real name again?"

"Hammer."

"Yes, Hammer. Paul Hammer. I remember now. What other sketch?"

"The one you ordered me to draw of me having sex with Irene. When I couldn't do it you threatened to shoot me unless I raped her in front of you and the others. You remember none of that?"

Kurt Frank released Irene's hand but would not take his eyes off Hammer's bitter, hard face. Finally he shrugged.

"That was then. Today is today. Many things happen in a lifetime. All right, come in. Place looks a mess, but I'm seventy and can't find anybody to help me. My pension isn't big enough to pay for a maid."

"Okay, okay," Hammer said impatiently and scanned the room as he entered.

While Irene's bed-sitter was nothing to rave about, Kurt Frank's abode was downright dismal, a picture of desolation, untidiness and discomfort, locked in perpetual cave-like darkness. Only a smidgen of daylight filtered through the street-level iron grill set back in the ceiling over an alcove. However a dangling unfrosted light bulb burned permanently to lend a livable brightness to the underground lodgings. Gogol's cavern for a twentieth century Dead Soul.

Two shaky, cane-covered straightback chairs were immediately cleared of dirty laundry so that Irene and Hammer could sit beside a table that was jam-packed with German and Allied tin soldiers of the First World War in battle formation.

Kurt tossed the clothing on a bed whose sagging mattress was heaped with piles of postcards. Irene cast a glance at a few of them, all sepia-toned pictures, and realized that they depicted German urban scenes taken at the turn of the century, or at least prior to the days of the Weimar Republic.

Hammer nodded at the armies of tin soldiers marching in static silence to their next battle stations.

"Couldn't get any Nazi soldiers?"

"What?" Kurt comprehended the question slowly. He squatted on the threadbare sofa and faced his two guests. Finally he responded, impassively. "It's difficult to obtain figures with Third Reich uniforms. But I could have if I had tried hard enough."

"Didn't you?"

A bitter grimace soured Kurt's harsh features still further. "Why should I? They let me down. Thirty-eight years in the slammer, and as gratitude I get not a single word of thanks from them. For doing my duty. No recognition. Bastards!"

"You mean your *Kameraden* don't want to help you? Not even to leave the country and settle down in South America? With them?"

"*Schweinehunde*! Even *they* turned their backs on me."

"They did?" Hammer sounded dubious. "You mean they don't recognize what you've done for the Third Reich?"

"They say I embarrass them. They've spent millions lately persuading the world that no Jew was killed, that it's all Zionist propaganda. And then I appear, a free man, after wasting almost thirty-eight years in jail, for running a German concentration camp. Too many witnesses testified that I had participated in the executions, running the gas chambers. They don't like having a newly certified Nazi war criminal smearing their propaganda image."

"And now? Would you join up again, knowing in advance that the same treatment was in store for you?" Hammer couldn't restrain his gloating as he stood there, relatively well off, in good health, fortunate even in his peril by comparison with this decrepit executioner.

"I told you I'm seventy. Why bring up that shit now? I don't want to get involved with anybody. You like some coffee?"

"No, thanks. We had a big breakfast."

"With Karl? Karl Ludwig?"

"With Karl! You mean you don't know?"

"Know what?"

"That Karl died a few days ago."

Kurt's cheeks worked hard, bunching up. His eyes remained dull, lifeless. "How?"

"Why should you care?" Hammer said brusquely. "Your whole life has been devoted to killing. Why bother about one more life?"

"He was nice; a coward, though."

"No, he wasn't a coward, Kurt. He was the bravest man I ever met. He wore the SS uniform but risked his life to help those who were powerless against bullies like you. And he was no *Kamerad* of yours, Kurt. Remember, he testified against you."

"I don't care. That's all over. At least he corresponded with me. The others remain silent—the swine! How did he die?"

"In an automobile accident."

"Well, we've all got to go some time." He glanced helplessly around the room, at the picture of Frederick the Great hanging on the grey, grease-spattered wallpaper. "All right then—why did you come to visit me all of a sudden?"

"We need your help, Kurt," Hammer blurted out, no longer beating around the bush. "It's about a mutual friend of ours. And yours. Do you remember a prisoner named Ludwig Glückstein?"

Spasms ran down Kurt Frank's lean bony cheeks at the sound of this name, and his nostrils flared. For the first time a strange light entered his dull eyes, causing them to burn like dark lumps of coal. He rose from the sofa and shuffled to the iron grating at the other end of the room, looking away from his guests, and taking note of the dreary, grey light trickling stingily between the dozen rusty bars.

"I had more light in prison," he reminisced grimly, turning back to his visitors. His head almost reached the ceiling. Paul noted a blue vein throbbing in his temple. "Glückstein, it's all his fault. He betrayed me, he gave me away to the police." Bitterness crept into his voice. "I saved his life, rescued his little girl Inge and kept her hidden in my house at the risk of my own life, and then he repaid me by handing me over to the military authorities. Forty years of my life down the drain, and now only a few pennies pension in this dungeon to keep my body together. All because of Ludwig Glückstein. I should have shot him the day he arrived."

"Why didn't you?"

"That's my business," he snapped testily.

"So, all you have left is playing with World War One toy soldiers and staring at Frederick the Great."

"He was the *Führer's* idol. Only the dead should be honored. I hate people—all people. Even to the *Waffen SS* groups here I'm poison, a constant reminder of the camps they deny ever existed. So they avoid me too. Everybody does. Damn them all to hell!"

"You moan about the present, Kurt," Irene said at last. "Do you feel any remorse about the past?"

"Remorse? You'll never hear *me* echo that old routine that all I did was my duty, that I only obeyed orders. That's too easy. No, Gypsy, I killed because I hated the human race. Jews, gypsies, anti-Nazis, priests, that was only an excuse for most of us. We were not selective killers. We were killers. Period. We killed thousands of Catholics, monks, nuns. You, Paul, you aren't Jewish. You wore a red triangle on your Auschwitz uniform, and we got rid of your family."

"But you tried to join *your* family after being released from jail. The Nazi family. Still have that hankering for the old tribe, haven't you?"

"At first, but no longer. For Hitler, yes. If he were alive today, even in the deepest, most malaria-infested jungle, I'd follow him, serve him, as bodyguard, bootblack, cook, anything, just to be close to the man."

"I know, Kurt," Irene said softly. "You never had a father, so you're still feeling the loss of that one man who commanded your loyalty, your respect."

Kurt stared down hard at the crippled woman for a long time. "Perhaps. You always knew me better than anyone, better than Stangl in Treblinka, Höss in Auschwitz. See that, Paul Hammer? Irene is Jewish. I was cruel to her, often, I don't deny it—I don't have to any more. But she's the only person who's ever been close to me. She and Inge."

Hammer looked perplexed. "Inge?"

"Glückstein's daughter. I would not let her go the The Showers. She stayed hidden in my house. If Stangl or Höss had known who she was

I'd have been court-martialed. The firing squad. But I saved her."

"Why?"

"None of your damn business! Even Irene doesn't know the whole truth."

Hammer got up and faced the second-in-command of the Treblinka death factory. Usually he felt inadequate and insignificant when in the presence of taller people. But this time he knew he must take command of the situation, appear sure of his stature and his stance in order to win over this loathsome figure of faded Nazi glory who was so crucial to his plan.

"Kurt, before this day is out you *will* reveal that secret to us, because if you don't Glückstein will."

Frank glared down at Hammer, then retreated to a timeworn, ragged armchair close-by and collapsed into it.

"You're crazy, Paul. How do you know he's even alive?"

A reluctant smile of triumph insinuated itself into Hammer's handsome features.

"How could *you* know he's alive when you're always living in the past?"

Hammer nodded contemptuously in the direction of the tableau of World War One miniature toy soldiers on the kitchen table and the postcards on his bed.

"Well, Kurt, prepare yourself for a shock!" And Hammer proceeded to summarize his new relationship to LL and the latter's status in world politics, commerce and philanthropy. Throughout the long recounting the former SS officer stared venomously at the face of his ex-prisoner but did not interrupt him. When Hammer had finished the tale, Kurt rubbed his eyes with his enormous hands and sank back into the chair.

"Four long decades I've waited for this moment," he said hoarsely. "I've dreamt of revenge all those years I was wasting away in jail, and here you come and offer it to me on a silver platter."

"Now wait, Kurt, let's get one thing straight," Hammer said firmly. "You may have waited forty years to get even with Luckstone—that's his new name—but remember that I have another debt to settle with him. He killed my mother. The day I arrived in. . . ."

"I remember," Kurt interrupted icily. "With the piano leg. I saw it with my own eyes."

"You do? Really?" exclaimed Hammer. He took a couple of brisk steps forward and, much to Kurt Frank's amazement, vigorously pumped his huge hands. "Thank you, Kurt, thanks. That's all I wanted to know, to make sure you were a witness of the crime."

"I don't understand," Kurt peered from Hammer to Irene and back to Hammer again. "So I'm a witness. Glückstein interrupted my looking at your drawing of Himmler shaking my hand—who cares?"

"The world will, especially the reporters in the U.S. who're opposed to the present administration in Washington. They care. And the public will. That's why we want you to help us."

"You mean help you destroy him by giving him a bad name? Nonsense! I'll wring his neck!"

"You'll do nothing of the kind," Hammer said commandingly. "We'll break no laws. Everything is going to be aboveboard. We're going to destroy him subtly. Legally. Me with my mother. You with your story. Irene with being crippled by him."

"But how? By speaking to the press?"

"Right. At a news conference. Let the world know everything *we* know about him."

"Fair enough. But I think it would be better still if we first faced Glückstein in person and. . . ."

"No!" Hammer cut in fiercely. "That'd be too dangerous."

Frank's face immediately clouded over. "Why?" he demanded tightly.

Hammer's brief glance to Irene told her that he had almost slipped and revealed the attempts made on his life.

"I mean it's dangerous confronting Luckstone himself because he could have us knocked off on his estate as intruders and no one would be the wiser for it. Much better to tell everything to the media directly."

"No! Then I won't go along," Kurt raised his voice and clenched his hands. "You want me to go along, you let me see Ludi first."

"See who?" Paul shot back, already sensing trouble.

"Glückstein!" Kurt shouted. "I always called him Ludi."

"But why in heaven's name?" Irene said, exasperated. "What purpose would that serve, confronting him?"

"Can't you see, you two?" A strange, almost malevolent light entered Kurt's glacial, grey eyes. "It would give me . . . give us a chance, first of all, to settle a personal debt with him. We can destroy him twice, Irene. Twice. First when coming face-to-face with him, then again when the press hears our side of the story right in front of the Big Man himself. On his own home ground."

"I don't like it," said Hammer, fully conscious of the sharpshooters who might lurk at Rosedale. "It's still too risky, Kurt."

"You want me to come along, don't you?"

"Of course."

"Then you play it my way," Kurt said with an air of finality. "Why are you so dumb, you two? Can't you just picture it? We face him first and watch him squirm. Let him know that there are at least three people who've penetrated the most closely guarded secret of his life. The truth is out at last. Three witnesses—and he can't do a damn thing about it. We're going to break his balls in private first, Paul, and then announce that the news media are going to finish him off in public that same evening. We'll see him sweat, Irene, sweat blood. And even *that's* too good for the bastard after what he's done to us. But at least now we'll enjoy the supreme moments of *our* lives. We'll see him die before our eyes, *twice*. Do you understand now?"

Hammer stared at his former captor, then regarded Irene pensively, but she only nodded.

Kurt waited a few anxious seconds. At last he rattled on, "If you're so scared of what the old bastard might do to us on his estate, then why bother to go through with it at all? He could have us tailed, even if we only see the press, till he got us in his gun sight."

The three glowered at each other in tense silence, things more unresolved than ever, when Kurt suddenly asked, "Have you got a lawyer in the States, Paul?"

For a moment Hammer was confused by Kurt's strange question. "Yes, an attorney. Why?"

"Drop him a note. When I was in jail and had a particularly nasty and rough guard in charge of me, my defense lawyer told me to send him the name of that guard and describe the harassment by registered mail, just in case I was found dead one day. And that's what we're going to do. Prepare a signed statement including what we know about Luckstone and the fact that we're going to see him about this. Then we send it off by registered mail to your attorney, with instructions to make the contents public seventy-two hours after receipt of the letter, if we haven't contacted him first. That way we're covered, and we can let Luckstone know about it in case he tries anything funny with us. But we must see him first, I insist on that. Or you can count me out."

Hammer mulled all this over, briefly, and for confirmation glanced at Irene.

"Sounds reasonable enough to me," she said simply and cast her eyes down, massaging her atrophied hand.

"Okay," Hammer nodded in agreement, accepting the fact that he was clearly outvoted. "Maybe you're right."

"Good!" Kurt slapped his thighs as if rubber-stamping somebody's execution order. "That's settled then. We're going to see Ludi first and. . . ." His enthusiastic suggestion broke off in midstream, and he glared at Paul Hammer. "But how're we going to get over there? I have no savings with my miserable pension."

"Don't worry about that," Hammer said quickly. "I wouldn't expect you to pay for the trip. I'll take care of all the expenses and . . . you do have a passport, don't you?"

"I got one when I first considered emigrating to Argentina."

"Good. Now listen to me—if you play ball with us and reveal your relationship with Glückstein to us—now!—then when this is all over, I will pay you fifteen thousand dollars as a bonus."

As the sound of the sum of money rang in his ears, echoed in the cramped, garbage-reeking quarters he called an apartment, Kurt's eyes began to glaze over, his hands to tremble so violently that he had to join them in a tight, strangulating clasp. A moment later he chuckled, and he let the chuckle surge into a full-throated laugh, a laugh which grew increasingly thunderous until it reverberated through the room with a roar and a shriek so diabolically unbridled it seemed to want to burst through the walls. Tears trickled down his hollow cheeks and ran into his muttonchop whiskers. But then, just as abruptly, he sliced off his laughter and banged his fists on the arms of the easy chair.

"You're . . . you're not just leading me on, Paul, are you?" he bellowed.

"Absolutely not, Kurt," Hammer said, straining to appear irreproachably sincere. "I've never been more serious in my life. Okay now, I've been honest with you, but now you must level with us."

Kurt calmed down with some difficulty. A frown settled on his brow. "Level with you?"

"Tell us the truth, everything about you, your youth, why you saved Glückstein and his daugher Inge, everything. If Luckstone knows something you withheld from us, he might be able to use it in his defense against us. Our own case must be ironclad. You understand?"

"I can tell the Yanks things that'll flabbergast them."

"You do that, and I'll translate it for you."

"What for? I've spoken English longer than German. Don't forget I've been in an American jail for almost forty years. Sit down, Paul! You make me nervous standing there. You want some coffee, some dry bread?"

"I told you we're not hungry," Hammer said, again settling down on his caned chair. "Sounds strange coming from you—offering me coffee and a chair when I remember you pulling exhausted women from the ground where they had collapsed on the *Appellplatz* during roll call and then having them tied to the whipping block so one of your guards could lash them till the skin hung from their bones in tatters."

"Right. You've got a good memory. Remember what I called those events? Concerts. Sports Events. Not that I'm strong enough for that circus today. But don't expect me to say I'm sorry, Paul, because I'm not. I've never once felt remorse about my past. I told you—I'd be happy to do it all over again, given the chance, Jews or no Jews."

"You're nuts, Kurt, sick." Hammer's eyes blazed with anger as they swept across the table of World War One battle scenes and settled on Irene; she was sitting quietly on her chair in her long black dress, eyes downcast, and flexing her rigid, pale fingers. "Still dreaming of extermination camps!"

"Camps are of no use," Kurt said contemptuously, eyes not wavering from Hammer's enraged face. "The only way of solving the world's problem of hunger today, of overpopulation, *Lebensraum* and unemployment caused by computers and robots, is by mass starvation, or better still nuclear annihilation. Viet Nam, the Middle East, Ireland, they're chicken shit conflicts. Most effective would be to sterilize everybody, *all* adult men and women. Even solves that idiotic abortion issue. So you see, I was just one of the advance troops and should never have been convicted."

"All right, I don't want to hear any more about it! Just as long as you don't bring any of this up when talking to the media. Or you'll ruin *everything*. For us, for yourself. And not a word about how you enjoyed killing Jews and. . . ."

"It *wasn't* Jews. You're an imbecile if you still think that. It was a matter of killing people. Period."

"Okay, people then. But be prepared, Kurt. The press will want to know about your personal life, especially how you became one of history's most famous mass murderers. Things like that don't just happen overnight. After all, your parents didn't raise you to become a killer."

"My parents! That's a joke!" Kurt Frank gave a hiccup of a bitter laugh and slouched back in the frayed chair, which had a rusty spring protruding from one of its arm supports. "Ask Irene here, my little Jewish girl. *She* knew how to mother me. Didn't you, Gypsy?"

With that he reached forward and clasped Irene's uninjured hand in both of his. Two hairy claws encapsulating a wan, broken spirit. Irene sat up, stiffly erect, her face hardening into a graven, marmoreal mask, eyes focusing on him in a frozen fish-stare.

"Kurt," she whispered. Splashes of red blotched her neck.

"Why don't you leave her alone?" Hammer blew up. "Goddamnit! Can't you see how she's suffering?"

Kurt jerked his hands back as though he had touched a live wire; his pupils dilated with barely constrained resentment. "Don't you tell me what I can or can't do in my own house!" he snarled. "And sit down! You're making me nervous. Why the hell are you so jittery?"

Paul Hammer had risen and, like a machine driven by the uncontrollable energy of old hatreds, old memories, started prowling around the subterranean pigsty Kurt referred to as his 'own house.' "I asked you what makes you so jittery," Kurt demanded gratuitously.

"Everything. You. This place." Hammer came to a halt in front of Kurt's bed. "What in God's name is *this*?" he growled, pulling a scratched, old 78-r.p.m. record from under the pile of antique postcards. "Beniamino Gigli sings Verdi and Puccini," he read from the label. "Since when are *you* interested in music?"

"Just put it back on the bed!" Kurt made no bones about being irritated by Hammer's probing into his private feelings. "It's the only record I have. . . . Nothing wrong with being moved by good music, is there?"

"Moved! *You* being moved?" Hammer uttered a sarcastic laugh, tossed the record back on the bed and glanced around. "Where've you got the phonograph?"

"In school, a few blocks away. I can't afford to buy one, but I got permission to play the record at night when the school is deserted." He shrugged somewhat sheepishly. "So happens operas bring tears to my eyes."

"Christ!" Hammer dropped back in his chair. "Now I've heard everything! Shedding tears over an aria, but dry-eyed when it comes to killing ten thousand children!" He shook his head in disbelief, baffled by his own morose thoughts. "It's so senseless. Art touches your heart, but life doesn't. God!" He stared grimly at his host. "What sort of a crazy nation *did* I come from!"

"Now cut that out!" Kurt exploded. His fist crushed the armchair's corroded spiral. "We're no better, no worse than the rest of the world. Governments *still* practice mass murder. Like they did in Greece, Iran, Russia, Cambodia, China, not even that long ago. And soon tourists from all over came to visit these places in droves, anyway. So just stop your belly-aching! Because the world *never* gave much of a damn, Paul; it always *was* rotten, and always *will* be."

Irene raised her tormented eyes to her former jailer. "Maybe you only see everything as rotten, Kurt," she said quietly, "because you yourself are so. . . ." She stopped herself, just in time, the old fear of 1943 creeping back into her eyes.

25

"Say it, Irene! Out loud!" Kurt prodded her. "So rotten; that's what you wanted to say, right? Well, I was. Morally degraded. Befouled. My whole life. Even in the years of glory. My Thousand-Year Reich. Ha!" His angry eyes swept back to Hammer. "What do *you* think, Paul? About my being forged by events. Do people shape history, or does history shape *us*? Even in jail I couldn't figure that one. But perhaps *you* can, especially since you want to hear my story. . . . Like, for instance, how history entered *my* life already when I wasn't even two. First, there was my father . . . killed in World War One. I never knew him. And then, eighteen months later, that bitch of a mother of mine . . . yes, I said bitch—I should have shoved her into a gas chamber—she abandoned me when I was three."

"Why?"

"How do I know? I suppose she was young, a woman with no husband and better things to do than spend her time raising a little boy. It was the end of World War One. There were people starving in Germany, children and adults alike. Terrible poverty everywhere. Indescribable inflation. Soon a loaf of bread cost a hundred billion Marks. Nobody liked the responsibility of an extra mouth to feed. Besides, I was not a prime candidate for a family and love and attention. I was ugly, Paul, frighteningly ugly, even as a child. No relatives wanted to take care of me, so off I went to an orphanage. The staff kicked me around, shunting me from family to family. I tried to make friends with each of them—God knows I tried—but hard as I did, to please them, to ingratiate myself with them, nothing seemed to work. By the time I was eight, I'd been farmed out to fourteen different foster homes. I wanted to love them and be loved by them in return, but nobody ever gave me a chance to. They strangled love inside me. I couldn't stand it any more, feeling unwanted, unloved, and one day ran away from the orphanage. I slept in doorways, gutters, coal bins, and one winter morning was so starved I stole an apple from a grocery store. They caught me, threw me into jail, with thieves, rapists, murderers. Moabit Prison, in Berlin . . . Eight years old! But even that was nothing compared to my ninth birthday in the pen."

"What do you mean?"

"Early in the morning a group of prisoners came to my cell and presented me with a birthday gift. A little kitten. God knows how they got hold of it, but they told me it was mine and to take good care of it. I could have hugged each of them. I wept with joy, Paul. Nobody had ever given me a present in eight years. It was the most beautiful cat I had ever seen, and even though I was hungry most of the time I saved some of the dry bread we got and gave it to Marmalade—that's what I called the kitten. I sat on my bunk all day long cuddling it, holding its warm furry body to my cheeks and kissing it.

"Up to that moment in my life, it was the only thing I had ever loved and that seemed to love me back. That morning and afternoon must have been the happiest hours in my life. Because then they came back in the evening, the same jailbirds who had given me the animal in the morning. All twelve of them, Paul, while I was taking my weekly shower. And the biggest among them, Bruno, he had taken the kitten from my bunk to the shower stall, and there they stood now, the twelve men, naked like me, and they kept staring at me.

"I asked Bruno why he had taken Marmalade out of my cell, and he only peered down at me. Then he opened his mouth, wide, shoved half of the kitten into his mouth and bit Marmalade's head off. He spat it out and threw its wriggling, bloody body into my face. I screamed, and he grabbed me by the throat that I almost choked.

"The same thing will happen to me, he shouted, if I didn't give. Now! I didn't understand at first what he meant. I was too frightened. But then one of the brutes held my arms, another grasped me by the legs; they bent me over, and each of them fucked me in the ass, fucked me so hard with their big pricks that the blood poured down my spindly legs. . . . Happy birthday, Paul! Happy ninth birthday!"

"Holy shit!" Hammer got out of his chair, but the next second sat down again as though realizing that there really was no escape from this gloomy mousetrap. He glanced around, confused and agitated, and inexplicably thought that only the warmth of a hearth, of a fireplace and a dark ruby claret glowing in a goblet could cheer up this

155

drab cellar.

"People make me sick, unmitigated bastards, all of them!" Hammer said huskily, as cold rage invaded his brooding features. "You know, I remember reading a passage in a book by Mark Twain, years ago, something I've never forgotten: 'Of all the creatures that were made,' he wrote, 'man is the most detestable. Of the entire brood he is the only one, the solitary one, that possesses malice. That is the basest of all instincts, passions, vices—the most hateful. He is the only creature that inflicts pain for sport, knowing it to *be* pain.'"

"True, I can attest to that." Kurt nodded grimly. "That's when I started hating men, all men. On my ninth birthday. And all women, for not wanting to be a mother to me and saving me from this nightmare of a childhood. Every night I prayed that they should die, all of them. I would have been a fool not to. When I. . . ."

"How long did you stay in prison?" Hammer asked shakily.

"Six months. When I was released they sent me to a new orphanage, and to a *Volksschule*, in Munich this time. That was in 1924. I was still nine years old. But here the children made fun of me, beat me up because they thought I was a monster. I looked like one all right, had been in jail and wasn't very bright—which isn't too surprising if you consider that I was pulled out of school every time I was sent to another family and summers had to work on the land until midnight. So this time children ganged up on me. They tore up my homework, poured ink over my hair, down the only suit I owned and . . . God, how I hated them, Paul! How I wanted to kill them . . . children . . . and still do!"

All of a sudden Kurt Frank's hands joined and the ten fingers locked into each other, like giant pincers, as though they were trying to press, to squeeze the last ounce of breath out of the human race. "Anyway," he paused with a sigh as his hands relaxed and plowed through his unkempt grey hair, "there was nothing I could do but stick it out. Then came 1925, and I knew there were no takers, not at my age. I felt rejected by everybody.

"That is, until the day a new student was inducted into my class. He was a Jewish boy, and he asked me a few weeks later if I wanted to visit him at his home some weekend. I was ten years old and nobody had ever invited me to their home or even spoken a kind word to me. All I could do was blurt out 'yes' and run away into the toilet. And you know what? I burst into tears. I figured the boy must have been insulted that I left in such a hurry without even thanking him because he didn't repeat his offer. I was sure he had forgotten all about it. And then we broke for our summer vacation. He approached me in the school yard and I figured he came to say good-bye, but instead he asked me if I could arrange to spend the eight weeks with him and his family in Berg on the Starnberger Lake. You can imagine how glad the orphanage was to be rid of me for the summer. It agreed to release me on the spot."

"Kurt," Irene broke in gently. "You didn't tell Paul who the boy was."

"Let him guess."

"Come on, Kurt, how do I know who your friends were in 1925? I wasn't even born yet."

"Well, the boy's name was Ludwig Glückstein."

"Good Lord! You mean you knew. . . ."

"Yes, I've known that son of a bitch since 1925. Sixty years."

"But how on earth. . . . Why would he want to invite you?"

"Paul, he was the greatest—the only—friend I ever had. Gentle, compassionate, understanding. I'll never forget that Friday in early July '25, when his father's four-door Packard sedan picked me up at the Munich orphanage and we rode to his family's beautiful mansion on the lake. I had never seen anything like it or experienced anything like the kindness of his parents. It was indescribable. Ludi—that's what I called him after the first week in Berg—saw an underdog in me. Before we ever met in Munich he had been taken out of a school in Unterhaching because he was the only Jew in the school there and the Catholics would pull down his pants to look at his circumcision, then grab him by the arms and legs and whip his penis with birch rods. Almost everybody in the south of Germany was a rabid anti-Semite, young and old, years before Hitler—all of them perfect, ready-made material to manipulate for his own use later.

"So, we were two underdogs—we had that much in common. He taught me math and geography, and I showed him how to change washers, fix furniture, gutters, electrical appliances and drains and toilets, which I had learned when I was staying with different families. And then came the happiest day of my life, when *Herr Direktor*, Ludi's father, asked me if I didn't want to stay on with the Glücksteins. Ludi had no brothers or sisters, *Frau* Glückstein couldn't have any more children, and he was glad to see what a calming influence I was on his nervous son, how well we hit it off together, and how we helped each other out."

"But you're Catholic, Kurt," Hammer interrupted. "Didn't it disturb you to stay with a Jewish family in the most conservative, religious part of Germany?"

"Why should it? I never got anything out of religion except getting kicked in the ass, and the fact that Ludi was Jewish didn't mean a damn thing to me. If they had asked me to convert to Judaism as a precondition for adopting me I would have done it without giving it a second thought. But they never asked me, because they themselves never practiced their religion. They said they were German first, and everything else took last place. Besides, *Herr Direktor* was too busy traveling to his factories all over the world, and *Frau Direktor* was always ailing—I think she had gallstones. Ludi and I spent every minute of the day and night together, going to school, doing homework, on vacations, playing sports. I no longer cared if the other kids teased me. At last I had found a family that loved me, that's all that mattered. I had the best brother in the world—Ludi *was* like a brother to me—my grades improved, my whole life centered more and more on the Glücksteins. I lived for them, and while working on the masses of flowers on their large estate in Berg I made up my mind to become a landscape gardener.

"Although I was legally adopted, the Glücksteins arranged that I keep my original name. My real mother had remarried and found out where I was through the orphanage. She visited me once in the house on the Starnberger Lake and asked me if I wanted to return and live with her again. The bitch had her nerve! I turned her down flat. Obviously she realized that I was quite talented with mechanical contraptions and in the garden. It probably occurred to her that with my know-how I could bring quite a few Reichsmarks into her new family. I really got a kick out of seeing the hurt in her face when I told her to go piss off. That whore abandoned me when I was three; she had it coming to her. But you've got to remember the year I told her to go to hell—1934. I was nineteen at the time and Hitler had already been in power for a year.

"And then it happened, on a rainy day, in March 1934. I recall it all, like it was today. Ludi and his father were going on a business trip to Zurich, where Ludi's Uncle Harry was the director of a bank. You see, the Glücksteins were extremely rich, with property, factories, banks all over the globe, so that the inflation of the Weimar Republic didn't affect them very much. I was sitting pretty, running not only the huge garden at Berg but the twenty-four-room mansion as well. It was in quite a state of disrepair and needed a full-time employee to fix things. So my hands were full. But I loved it; I felt needed. Financially, I had nothing to worry about, and I didn't give a fig about politics. Hitler was just another politician to me, nothing more. Since leaving school I was kept busy with the estate; I stayed behind its walls and nobody made fun of me. In fact, that March I had the run of the house to myself, except for a couple of maids, because *Frau Direktor* was in the hospital for an operation.

"About three hours after Ludi and his father departed on the train—I had chauffeured them myself to the station in their new Horch—I had a few visitors, members of Hitler's S.A. They informed me that Glückstein's trip to Zurich was only a ruse to be away from their property, since they apparently lacked the heart to tell me to my face that in view of the new Nazi policies they no longer wanted a non-Jew in their midst. The Glückstein's wanted me off their land. These men actually produced papers—years later I discovered they were forgeries—that they had invalidated the adoption records and really were serious about the break.

"At first I laughed it all off in disbelief. Then I was stunned, the more documents they came up with. Finally, when more and more evidence was produced, including a maid—the cook—who was bribed by the S.A. to corroborate their statements, I was so upset I went berserk. I sobbed. I had been betrayed by the family I loved more than anybody. I would have laid down my life for them.

"The next few months I lived in a trance. The storm-troopers ordered me to pack a small valise with my belongings and that very day in March of '34 shipped me off to Berlin, keeping me under constant guard. I might as well tell you what I learned after the war, when my real mother visited me one day in the American jail—that it was she who had first alerted the S.A. to get me out of the Jewish home. My turning her down had stung her so deeply—and never mind how she had hurt me as a child—that she tried to turn the tables on me by paying back in kind for my so-called ingratitude and making me sever all ties with the people who had been a true, loving family to me for almost ten years."

"And naturally you were taught to hate your benefactors," Hammer commented sarcastically.

26

"The Glücksteins—all Jews! As an Aryan I was more than welcome to the Nazi ranks, and they were glad to see me divorced from the Jewish family that had adopted me. I was sent to an SS training school for a starter, to Sachsenhausen, near Berlin. I hated it, all the military drills after that wonderful decade in the luxurious surroundings of the Glücksteins. But at least the taunting was gone—nobody teased me as they did in school about my appearance. Even so, I was still the outsider. Nobody really wanted to be close to me either. In the five years, right up to 1939, no one ever asked me out once to join them for a drink." Kurt's fists bunched into veritable sledge hammers.

"I became morose again, disillusioned, and felt that I had been rejected once more, this time by the adult world. I started hating everyone again. Then came years of indoctrination, and gradually I began to believe what the Nazis said, because miserable as I was I *had* to believe in something. But I didn't just hate the Jews. I saw a Jew in almost every human being. The Jews, the human race, had stabbed me in the back over and over, and I swore that one day they'd pay for it. The only one I fully respected by 1938 was Hitler. I suppose he *was* a surrogate father for me, *Herr Direktor's* successor, and I loved him with a passion. I was ready to get even with the human race for treating me so shabbily. The world was a ghetto to be eradicated, and Hitler gave me an excuse, a way to give vent legally to my murderous feelings.

"Later my American prison psychiatrist made all this clear to me, how it helped to dull my inner pain, embracing Hitler's powerful theories and enjoining upon me eternal loyalty and submission to his government; especially how I enjoyed the respect given me, my new stature. You see, meanwhile I had been promoted to *SS Rottenführer* and transferred to the *T4* Division and. . . ."

"*T4?*" Hammer sounded puzzled. "What does that mean?"

"*T4* stands for *Tiergartenstrasse 4*, in Berlin-Charlottenburg. Headquarters for the *Central Foundation for Institutional Care*. Sounds positively benevolent, doesn't it? But in truth it was the Office for Euthanasia of the Physically and Mentally Handicapped. The planning for the organization came directly from the *Führer's* Chancellory, a special department Hitler created to administer private affairs and to consider petitions addressed to him personally. *Reichsleiter* Philipp Bouhler headed it, and he ordered me to assist *SS Oberführer* Back, *S. A. Oberführer* Blankenburg and Professors Nitsche, Heyde and Dr. Mennecke, in running the place."

"And you did?"

"You know very well, Paul, I had no great love for humanity, least of all the dregs of the earth. Sitting at a desk and arranging for the elimination of the incurably sick, the hopelessly malformed, didn't faze me at all under the circumstances."

"The first step to Treblinka," Hammer observed darkly. "In other words, you started out as a desk murderer."

"Don't be so damn patronizing! All this wailing—damn you! Much ado about nothing! I certainly didn't play noble like the Bishop of Münster, Count von Gahlen, who attacked the Euthanasia program at once. In any case, some of the elimination processes were perfected on the retarded people in the 1930s already, and on occasion I had to visit some of these places and write a report for Bouhler. You can imagine how thrilled I was to learn that Hitler himself saw copies of my reports."

"And you felt nothing, no pity, no revulsion at that time, that a government should actually order the mass murder of thousands of innocent, defenseless men, women and children?"

"A thought like that would never even occur to me, Paul. Yes, at first I didn't like to peer through the peepholes when the incurably sick were gassed, but when I was ordered to describe their death in a report to Bouhler I was forced to observe it. Yes, again I admit, in the beginning I felt sort of queasy seeing the patients gasp for air, but the whole thing lasted less than a minute, all that jumping and leaping about, the scratching of their faces, the clawing of the walls as they tried to snatch some air from God-knows-where, and then I told myself that I had been treated brutally, almost like they were, ever since I was born and nobody ever gave a damn about me."

"Nice way of rationalizing it."

"*I* didn't instigate the program," Frank snapped irritably. "Besides, how many people could claim that their reports were actually read by the *Führer*? It made me feel important. If I had objected, I'd have joined those naked, dancing bodies struggling for breath in the gas chamber, and someone more accommodating would have taken my place."

"How long did you stay with *T4*?"

"Till August '41. Bouhler came to see us that summer and told us that Hitler's private train had been held up outside Hof, near Nuremberg, when mental patients were loaded from cattle cars into trucks. When that happened, a crowd of spectators jeered the *Führer*—the only time he was booed while in power, I'm told—and he ordered Dr. Karl Brandt, his personal physician, to call Bouhler and stop the Euthanasia program immediately."

"What then?"

"Globocnik called me to. . . ."

"Who?" asked Hammer, absently toying with one of the tin soldiers.

"Irene surely remembers. *SS Obergruppenführer* Odilo Globocnik, Brigadier General Globocnik. He summoned me to his office to help him set up the extermination camp near Treblinka. He was in charge of exterminating Europe's Jews in Poland. No, my mistake—first I had to help construct the camp at Sobibor where Wirth was the *Kommandant* and Oberhauser his aide. The real joke is that Oberhauser runs a wine cellar here in Munich today, and I asked him last month if I could have a job with him—anything, cashier, dishwasher—but the bum turned me down flat; he didn't want to be reminded of the past all his life, he said.

"I remember June of '42, though, when that bastard introduced me to the twenty-five *Arbeiterjuden*, who had been forced to build the gas chamber in Sobibor. To try out how successful their job was, he lured those Jews inside, on the pretext that they were to paint the walls, and when they had finished, the Polish guards slammed the doors shut and gassed all twenty-five of them. The Showers were in perfect working condition."

"Christ!" The miniature soldier dropped out of Hammer's hand on a toy cannon.

"The ironic part is that the twenty-five Jews were among the thousands that had escaped to Russia before July 1941, and because of the Hitler-Stalin Peace Pact, Stalin shipped them all back to the German Nazis in Poland as a gesture of gratitude for the pact."

Hammer could only hold his head in wonder at the horrors unfolding before him.

"You want to know something else that will strike you as funny? I actually *liked* the mentally retarded and all those incurably crippled prisoners. They were worthless, yes, but at least they didn't hurt anyone. And not one of them ever laughed at me."

"My heart bleeds for you," Hammer said bitterly.

"Yeah. A few happy years in my youth, then killing mankind

because mankind always hurt me. And now. . . ." He shrugged. "A tiny pension to keep me and my bowstring hemp alive." And he gazed at his plant.

"I can't feel sorry for you any more, Kurt," Irene said quietly. "My whole life has been pain—and submission. My family wiped out only minutes after our arrival in Treblinka; then my shoulder smashed to pieces in Auschwitz, and after the liberation trying to eke out a living with one hand, giving English lessons to a few private students, but never enough to save anything for the future. All I know is agony, day and night, even now. Life has deprived you of power, Kurt. It has deprived me of everything of value in life, even of laughter. I haven't laughed since 1941. And now, like you, I subsist on a miserable pension. The irony is that you get your pension for being my captor, I for being your prisoner. Makes no sense."

"Exactly what I say—life makes no sense. You just live. Period." Kurt's laughter boomed in the low-ceilinged, cramped basement room.

The herculean, broad-waisted man got up and shambled to the two-burner stove next to the battered kitchen table, where a couple of open cans of tuna fish and sardines sat half empty. He picked up both cans and one after another tilted their contents into his mouth.

"See? That's my lunch. Ludi probably eats from sterling silver plates and drinks fine champagne. Makes no sense either. But fate wants it that way."

There was a scraping sound above them on the street. Kurt waved an arm with an air of disgust towards the source of daylight in his dingy cellar abode.

"See what they're doing to an old man like me?" he shouted over the din, striking his head on the bug-laden flycatcher hanging from the ceiling.

Paul Hammer and Irene looked up and to their amazement saw a steel plate being shoved over the bars that let the daylight through. It blocked the opening completely. Only the feeble ceiling light illuminated the room now.

"They're hosing down the street again," Kurt explained. "The maintenance men always push that thing over the grate so the water won't pour in. You know, once they forgot to put it back in the hallway after they finished," he groused. "There's no way to lift if from here. I had to dress, go outside and move it myself. Must have weighed two hundred pounds, the damn plate. These young workers have no respect for their elders."

"For crying out loud," Hammer mumbled. "*You're* the right one to talk about respect for one's elders."

"What?" Kurt dropped back into the beat-up armchair and glanced up at the grill that was now completely barricaded. "Well." He shrugged. "I suppose you can get used to anything, considering the alternative. Light, darkness—life, death—they're all the same—interchangeable. Nothing really matters."

"It depends on which side of the crematorium wall you're on, Kurt," Irene said. She wrinkled her nose in obvious distaste as she looked around the untidy room, now darkened and more forbidding than ever. As if she were about to have a fainting spell, she placed her good hand delicately on her forehead. "This room is awful," she muttered. "And that smell of gasoline gives me a headache."

"Somebody must be fixing his car on the street," Kurt suggested, smiling at his mistress of forty years ago. "Dear Irene, we have one thing in common now. With old age you have also become ugly, like me."

Exploding with anger, Hammer banged a fist on his kneecap. "How the devil could you ever love a man like him?" he burst out, disgusted.

"In hell vice becomes virtue, Paul," Kurt answered for Irene, his guarded smile broadening into a grin. "Why *not* love someone who saves your life?" The grin vanished from his Mongol-boned face. "You're right, though, this gasoline leak does stink the place up."

"Never mind the stench!" Paul Hammer cut in impatiently. "What I want to know is how you met up with Glückstein again after you got to Treblinka, and why you'd want to save his life if you felt he betrayed you."

27

"Yeah, I did feel betrayed." Hammer's testy reminder jogged Kurt Frank's memory. "Before he made his appearance there, though, Stangl and I were transferred to Treblinka, leaving Reichleitner in charge of Sobibor. And in Treblinka, one of my many duties was to scan the lists of new arrivals and select the tradespeople we needed for the construction and maintenance of the camp—the able-bodied inmates like carpenters, goldsmiths, dentists, painters, cooks, seamstresses, doctors. Less than a thousand for the entire complex, just a basic crew, the best . . . the youngest and strongest. We had the pick of the crop of the million who ended up in Treblinka. *Hofjuden, Goldjuden, Platzjuden* we called them. Remember?

"The first *Kommandant*, Dr. Eberl, had made a mess of things. He wasn't so much interested in the efficiency of the gassing process as in the fun he could have with the new inmates. He'd have Jewish girls as young as eight dance naked on tables while the guards were having their meals, and then for after-dinner entertainment use the girls they didn't want to sleep with for live target practice.

"So Globocnik got rid of Eberl and we took over. After three weeks we could already report good progress to Globocnik. Usually by eight A.M. a transport of two thousand new prisoners would arrive. By ten A.M. they all had been gassed, and after they had been stripped of their valuables they were buried, later dug up and cremated."

"And efficiency is the word you like to attribute to this system?" Hammer asked caustically.

"Don't be a sap, Paul!" Kurt flared. "You lived through it all as a *Goldjude*, even though you're Aryan. So don't play the innocent with me again."

"Please! Please, Kurt, Paul!" Irene interceded with uncommon vehemence. "Let's not argue about things that can't be changed. Besides, you did bring something up, Kurt, that involves me personally. At least later, after Glückstein finished with that job."

"What's that?"

"Stripping the corpses of their valuables."

"Yes. Helped save your life, didn't it? And it's all due to the arrival of Ludi in Treblinka."

"I don't understand," Hammer said, frowning. "What has Irene got to do with Glückstein and the jewelry on those corpses?"

"Well, it all started in the autumn of 1942," Kurt explained, "when I came across the Glückstein family on the list of new arrivals. It was just a fluke that I picked up their names among the thousands on that list, but there it was. I asked Stangl if I could speak to Ludi in private for a few moments since I had known him in school, and he agreed."

"I remember it being a reasonably warm day for October—blue skies, a brisk wind, bronze beech leaves from the nearby forest flying everywhere, but not too cold, with the sun shining brightly as the train rolled into the station. At that time, of course, in '42, you hadn't painted the hands of the clock on the station building yet, Paul, and the flowers hadn't been planted either. Remember? So everything looked kind of primitive. But God knows, we tried our best to make the place look more civilized and. . . ."

"Stop that bullshit, Kurt!" Hammer sliced in angrily. "You're making me sick. Civilization is the last thing anyone would associate with these camps!"

"Will you control your hysteria, Hammer!" Kurt snapped, his beetle-browed glare trying to stare down his guest. "You may be paying for my cooperation, but I don't have to put up with all your sanctimonious crap! Okay? . . . Anyway, I saw from the roster of prisoners that Ludi was due with his family in the morning and that he had a daughter named Inge who was seven or eight years old. Ludi had married a girl he met in Switzerland shortly after I left the Glücksteins, I learned later. So, when they got to Treblinka, I drew him and Inge aside and left his parents and his wife on the *Appellplatz*."

"Damn fool!" observed Hammer under his breath. "All that money and they never emigrated."

"Puzzled me, too. After he had gotten over his first shock of seeing me so unexpectedly, and in the uniform of an SS officer moreover, I posed the same question to him."

28

"We never thought it would come to this," Glückstein said, shivering in the brisk cool wind as the three stood behind the SS mess hall on Treblinka's Kurt Seidel Strasse. "But what are you *doing here*, Kurt? In that uniform! And why did you run away in '34?"

"Papa, where is Mommy?" Inge was clinging desperately with both arms around her father's leg. Her black eyes pleaded with him, round and large, and as she swept her long untidy chestnut hair out of her face, the tear-streaked, pale cheeks bore silent witness to the hunger and the filth to which she had been subjected on the freight train.

"We'll see her in a few minutes, Inge."

"I'm hungry, Papa," the little girl whimpered.

SS Sturmbannführer *Kurt Frank quickly reached into his pocket and produced two Sarotti chocolate bars. He squatted down on his haunches and peered into a pair of very black, very grave eyes.*

"Do you like milk chocolate, Inge?"

"Thank you. Can I take one to Klaus?"

"And who is Klaus, Inge?"

"*Not right now*, Liebling. *Just hold on to Papa's leg and save one bar for Klaus.*" Glückstein *turned back to his captor when Kurt stood up again.* "Klaus is my son. He's three and a half and waiting on the square with Hanna, my wife. Now look, Kurt, why did you leave us? And what are you doing here?"

"Just relax now, Ludi! Remember we don't have much time."

"I'm dirty, Papa!"

Again Kurt bent down and brushed the hair from Inge's brow. "In a few minutes I'll get you some pretty, new clothes," *he said to the frightened girl clutching her chocolate.* "Then I'll get you some hot soup and put you to bed, all right? But let me talk to your Papa first."

"All right," *she whispered, half-hiding in girlish embarrassment behind her father.* "What is your name?"

"Kurt. I'm your Onkel *Kurt.*"

Part embarrassed, part flirtatious, she planted a hurried little kiss on Kurt's big hairy hand, then buried her face in her father's leg.

"She has your eyes," *Kurt said, rising to his full height.* "Now then, that letter the Nazis showed me, Ludi, it told me everything."

"Which letter?"

"The one invalidating the adoption."

"What are you talking about?"

"Your family's decision to get rid of me because I wasn't Jewish."

"Kurt, we never invalidated a thing. There was no reason to. After all, my parents adopted you, knowing full well you weren't Jewish. We loved you. You were like a brother to me."

"But they. . . ."

"It was a forgery, Kurt. How do you think we felt coming home from Zurich a couple of days later, the maids gone and the house, the furniture, smashed to pieces?"

"The furniture! . . . I had no idea. Who'd want to do a thing like that?"

"Maria came to visit us a year later, with her swastika badge, and told. . . ."

"Maria? The cook?"

"Yes. She had also disappeared when we got back. But when she visited us she said it was you, that you couldn't stand seeing Jews like us exploiting the German nation."

"That's a lie. A put-up job. In fact, it was Maria who corroborated the S.A.'s statements that you wanted to get rid of me."

"Look, we were both tricked, Kurt, but what could we do? I left Germany soon after, joined Uncle Harry in Zurich, became a partner in his bank, then married a Jewish immigrant there, also from Munich, and had Inge and Klaus."

"And you returned to Germany?"

"I had to. In the summer of 1939. I tried everything I could to persuade my parents to leave Germany before it was too late, but Father didn't think it would come to war—certainly not to deportations. And with Mother always ill, it was impossible to find a country willing to accept her as an immigrant. And then the Swiss wouldn't take us back into their country, and I was trapped in Berg with my children and Hanna. We couldn't get out any more. All the foreign quotas for German emigrants were oversubscribed. War broke out and we were sitting ducks. That is until now. So, what's going to happen, Kurt? What are you going to do with us?"

Kurt grabbed his friend by his arms, glancing around first to make sure there was no one around. But the rest of the camp guards and kapos were about half a mile away, out of sight, supervising the transport's annihilation.

"Listen, Ludi, you've got to pull yourself together now. When I saw your name on the arrivals list last night I came up with a plan to save you. If you play along with me. . . ."

"What do you mean, 'save me'?" Alarm showed clearly in Glückstein's unshaven face. Behind him the green Bavarian-style windowshutters flapped in the breeze against the mess hall building with a loud clap. He whisked around, startled. "What was that? Gunfire?"

Kurt slammed the two shutters closed and swung Glückstein around forcefully to face him. "Look, Ludi, we can't stand here forever. I can save you. As long as I'm around you're safe. But. . . ."

"What's all this about being 'safe'? I'm willing to work, Kurt. You know that. But what about Inge here? And my family?"

"I'll take care of Inge. A number of unmarried SS men have taken on kids, even Jewish ones, or women to serve them as concubines."

"Hanna! What are they going to do to her? She's strong, Kurt; she's lived in Switzerland since 1933 and was going to be naturalized after we returned to Zurich. She can work in the fields. Father can do the *bookkeeping and I. . . ."*

"No! Listen, damn you!" Kurt shouted, and for an instant clamped a hand over Glückstein's mouth.

Inge started to cry softly, burying her face again in her father's trouser leg, unwilling to be witness to the ugly scene evolving above her.

"You're frightening Inge!" Glückstein said angrily.

"For the last time, Ludi!" Kurt pressed the words through his clenched jaws, eyes shifting nervously about to make certain that they remained unobserved. "Nobody is going to work in an office, or in the fields. You will become a kapo, the. . . ."

"A what?"

"A kapo. Camp police. Seeing to it that the operation runs smoothly."

"What operation?"

"That's what I'm trying to tell you. Hell, why do you make it so damn hard? Have you no idea what's going on here? What Hitler has planned for you Jews?"

The color in Glückstein's face drained away. He stared, unblinking, at his old friend.

"Ludi," the SS officer's voice was a mixture of soft-spoken pleading, an appeal to reason, and an inherent threat. "It's up to you now. If you want to live, do as I tell you. If not, you and Inge will follow the rest of the convoy."

Glückstein swallowed hard. "Follow?"

"To The Showers."

Incredulity, puzzlement and confusion mingled in the prisoner's eyes. "The Showers?"

"That's what they're called for the prisoners' benefit." Kurt glanced at his watch. "This new transport has been here about fifty minutes. Of the two or three thousand people that arrived with you less than an hour ago, half of them are dead already."

"Oh my God!" Glückstein's hand flew to his mouth. Tears sprang to his eyes, squeezed out of them and rolled down his stubby cheeks. The cold wind blew a lock of hair into his face. "No, Kurt, you're lying. They told us in Munich. . . ."

"I don't care what *they* told *you*," Kurt broke in brusquely. "Hitler's policy is to annihilate Europe's Jews—damn it, he said so himself in a 1939 speech—and this is one of his extermination camps. You can't escape from here. Nobody can. Except for a handful of the arrivals, everybody is gassed; sometimes ten thousand a day, men, women, children, and if you won't let me help you, then you too. . . ."

Glückstein whirled away from his friend and doubled up. A stream of *yellow-greenish vomit spewed out of his mouth, forming a slimy thick puddle on the frozen ground. Amazed by the unexpected spectacle, Inge released her father and forgot about her tears and her shyness. For a brief moment she was fascinated by the strange discharge. A second later, repelled by the sour stench, she spun away in disgust and ran to the SS man to hide her face in his trousers.*

At once Kurt lowered himself to her level and opened one of the softened chocolate bars, stuffing half of it into the girl's mouth. Inge at once began to chew it vigorously and broke off another piece.

Kurt stood up again when Glückstein had calmed down a bit. The striken Jew approached Kurt, the tears still flowing down his cheeks.

"My family?" The words spurted out tremulously. "They. . . ."

"Ludi," Kurt said quietly, "your family is eating milk chocolate. This is your family."

"But . . . I spoke to Hanna less than half an hour ago and asked her if she had packed my camera."

"Your luggage is already being sorted by the Arbeitsjuden *and will be shipped back to bombed out German civilians."*

"Oh God! . . . and . . . Klaus, Mutti, Papa?"

"In about half an hour you will see smoke coming out of Camp Two's crematoria—cement pillars really. Watch that smoke, Ludi! Because in those black clouds you'll see the spirits of Hanna and Klaus, and I'll see Herr *and* Frau Direktor."

Glückstein had finally heard the death sentence pronounced on his innocent family. He could no longer control himself. Sobbing, he fell against his friend's grey SS uniform, crying out aloud the names of his closest kin and banging his fists against the Sturmbannführer's *chest bearing the white eagle with the wreathed swastika in its talons. Kurt did not move. He remained stock-still as an unbending oak, just stared at the lovely little girl solemnly chewing the second candy bar she had planned to save for her brother Klaus and getting the brown sticky sweetness smudged all over her cheeks. Above them now was an overcast of grey fleecy clouds through which the sun peered dimly, like a pale, demented ghost.*

'Ludi."

Glückstein's body was racked by sobs; he simply could not stop.

"Ludi. . . . We've only got a few more minutes. You must tell me now whether you've got enough courage to go on living or want to follow your family. . . . Listen, for Chrissakes! Ludi!"

Kurt shoved Glückstein brutally from his body, wrenching the distraught man's arms from his neck.

"Answer me! Do you want to live or die? . . . Speak, goddamnit!"
Glückstein shook his head, his jaw slack and dribbling. He was sobbing uncontrollably now, blubbering great, wracking gasps that made it impossible to distinguish one word from another.
"For the last time, speak!" Kurt Frank barked at him. "What is it to be? Life or death?"
Glückstein lifted his face. "Death . . . I want to die." Tears streamed down his soiled face. His eyes were red from crying. "I don't want to live without Hanna, without Klaus and. . . ."
"All right. I tried. At least I tried. Take Inge's hand and I'll show you the way to Camp Two."
"Camp Two?" he sniffled.
"The Death Camp. The gas chambers. Our new incinerators. Come on, let's not waste any more time. Take her by the hand."
Both men stared at the little girl in the fire-red fall coat as she licked chocolate from her fingers and gazed up at the two tall men with her grave, trusting eyes.
"Hurry up, Ludi. Take her along. To be gassed."
Glückstein dried his tears with his hands and blew his nose in a dirty handkerchief.
"If I . . . Kurt, what would I have to do to keep her alive?"
"Become a kapo. In Camp Two. Pull the rings from the fingers of the prisoners after they're gassed."
"No! Not that, Kurt! Never! It's as though I was killing them."
"All right, let's go! Somebody will be only too grateful to do it, if it means life to him."
"Wait! What then? What happens to the jewelry?"
"You put it into buckets. Where you have difficulties you clip off their fingers at the base with special shears. The valuables are forwarded to the Reichsbank *in* Dresden and Berlin. Then you and the other Arbeits-juden *hand the corpses over to* SS Scharführer Horn *who's in charge of burning them."*
"God!"
"Stop calling on God, Ludi! He won't help you or the millions of corpses. Just as He didn't give a shit when He gave me my ugly face. He doesn't give a damn. So why should you? Now listen and listen carefully to what I'm going to tell you. I want both of us to come out of this camp alive when the war is over. We can do it. I don't know if the Führer will pull it off—win the war for Germany. It's almost November 1942 and, truthfully, the war doesn't look too rosy for us. Montgomery is beating us in Africa; U.S. troops have landed there too. We're already retreating

in Russia; the second winter there is going to beat the hell out of our troops—I'm certain of it. There's a good chance Hitler will lose this war. I tell you this because you are my brother, the only person I've ever loved. If anybody else heard this defeatist talk I'd be shot on the spot. So we've got to prepare for all eventualities. Do you follow me?"

"I don't understand. Prepare for what?"

"Prepare for our lives after the war. It may not come for three or four more years, but that gives us enough chance to have something to fall back on when we get out."

"Kurt, I don't know what you're talking about."

"I figured it out last night when I saw your name on the list. When you pull the valuables from the corpses, you'll be all alone. You'll place the best pieces on top of the buckets and bring them down into the Valuables Office to which only Stangl, the Kommandant, and I have the keys. I'll be there, alone, waiting for you, to skim off the biggest diamonds and rubies and whatnot, and hide them."

"But why? If you show them off in Germany when you're on leave, or sell them, won't the Nazis shoot you?"

"Sure, they would. For absconding with Reichsproperty. . . . Psss! Quiet!"

The two men froze, rigid, and strained their ears. In the distance, a piercing scream cut through the increasingly chill autumn air; then absolute silence, except for the swish of the wind.

"What was that?"

"Maybe somebody got his throat cut. Or a girl raped. It happens every day. We call this Concerts. Sports Events. You've got to get used to the dark side of life, Ludi, or you'll go under, die. I had to do it. It took me a little while to accept it completely. But you've got to take a crash course. To survive. And if Stangl sees you're not giving it your all, killing a few of the prisoners. . . ."

"What're you saying? Kill? Me kill? Are you out of your mind? I can't. . . ."

"Yes, you can! And you will! The other kapos also said they couldn't. But if it means surviving in hell, you'll learn. . . . All right, forget that for now. About the jewelry: that's where we've got to work hand in glove."

"But I only pull them off the corpses, you said."

"And bring them to me. Now, each time I go on leave with the valuables, you, Ludi, will drop a note to your uncle in Zurich, Uncle Harry—I met him many times myself in Berg—that the jewelry is to be put into a safe in our names. . . ."

"Wait! Wait! You say you're going to deposit the jewelry in Uncle Harry's bank in Zurich? In our names?"

"Right. Nobody will be able to touch the safe-deposit boxes but us."

"If I live that long."

"You will. I'll see to that."

"But that's blood money, Kurt. Valuables of my Jewish brothers and sisters."

"Would you rather see it all go to Schacht and the Reichsbank?"

"But he wouldn't do it, Kurt."

"Who wouldn't do what?"

"Uncle Harry. If you told him the truth about the jewels—and you'd have to—and that you're an SS guard here. . . ."

"Not a guard, Ludi. I'm the aide to the Kommandant."

"You . . . oh God no! In charge of gassing the Jews! . . . You. . . ."

"Münzberger handles the gassing. Also the Ukrainian Ivan the Terrible, and others."

"But you virtually run the extermination of millions . . . of my mother, my father, wife, son. . . ." Tears again ran down his cheeks.

"Will you stop it and pull yourself together now!" Kurt shouted. "I did not volunteer for this job either."

"But you could get out of it."

"And have someone else take over while I end up at the Russian front? Ludi, you can't escape this madhouse and neither can I. We've got to make the best of this rotten world. . . . Now, why do you think Uncle Harry won't go along with our scheme?"

"He's Jewish, Kurt, like Dad, like me, but he's a devout Jew. You don't imagine he'd keep this jewelry in storage for an SS man?"

"All right, not in our names then, but in yours alone, for after the war. Tell him that only you can withdraw the valuables, so you can return them to the survivors of the camp later. That's what you'll write to him. Of course, he doesn't know that there won't be any survivors. And whenever I go on leave with a new supply, you give me a letter proving to him that you're still alive, mentioning some current news item. But only you and I know that when this is all over we'll split the proceeds fifty-fifty. What do you say, Ludi? Just keep in mind that I'm laying my life on the line by doing this—risking everything by taking the jewelry out of the camp."

"What about me? The risks I take as a Jew in a death camp?"

"Not as long as I'm around, Ludi, I swear. And while I'm away in Zurich, a man named Karl Ludwig will look after you. Best of all, though, with the valuables in your name only I have a special incentive *in keeping you alive. But remember, if you go against me, doublecross me in any way, I'll have Inge in my house. And I certainly don't want to send her to The Showers. In your presence."*

"Oh God, God, what are you saying?" The tears were blinding him. "Worked it all out, haven't you? Every ghastly detail."

"Can you think of a saner solution in this boneyard? Even if it all seems hopeless now, for you, isn't it at least something to look forward to? You and Inge coming out alive?"

Glückstein seemed to deflate with a deep fatalistic sigh. "I'm in your hands, Kurt. What other choice do I have?"

"Good. That's settled then. I'll get you your kapo uniform and show you to the living quarters of the work-Jews. Inge will stay with me. I've got a Polish maid who'll look after her."

But Kurt Frank did not take his eyes off his friend, off Ludwig Glückstein's scraggly beard. He was fearful that his captive would start crying again any moment and possibly even change his mind, torpedoing all those carefully laid plans Kurt had propounded with such pressing conviction, such persuasiveness.

"For God's sake, get a hold of yourself now!" The SS man's plea was a desperate blend of anguish and menace. "And stop bawling like a goddamn child! It's too late for tears, Ludi. You're in hell now, realize that! And hell knows no pity, no tears—only hatred . . . And death!"

29

"So that's how it started." Paul Hammer nodded grimly. "It took him just a few months to turn into a brute."

"Most kapos, in the various death camps, learned the lesson of survival sooner or later. By the time you arrived in Treblinka he had already been steeped in death and sadism for four or five months, day and night. What *could* he do? He knew there was no outside help for him, or anybody. No pope, no priest, no nun praying outside the barbed wire fence then, even though Pope Pius XII had been informed in writing of the various extermination camps. No, all you saw outside those electric barbed wires and watch towers with machine guns in the early Forties were hordes of Polish women and men from neighboring villages bartering with Lithuanian and Ukrainian guards, haggling over the prices the camp guards demanded for the looted possessions of the new arrivals. But, of course, that was chicken feed compared with *our* gold. Only the bastard betrayed me after. . . ."

"Oh my God—look!"

Irene had jumped up and was pointing with her good hand in the direction of the door. The two men turned and saw a flame burning fiercely on the cheap runner protruding from the entrance of the tenement.

Hammer shot out of his chair, blanching. "Jesus—how did that get started?"

"What the hell *is* this?" The hulking figure of Kurt Frank strode toward the rug and stepped on it furiously with both heavy boots as the flame suddenly spread across the entire rug.

"Throw it out, Kurt," Irene shouted. "Out into the hall!"

Kurt picked up the burning runner with one hand and headed for the door.

"Goddamn! It's soaking wet," he exclaimed. "With gasoline."

His hand fastened around the doorknob and pulled the door toward him. It did not open.

"What *is* this?"

He pulled again, with all his strength, straining hard. It would not budge. He had already turned the locks and shifted the bolt, but still the door did not yield.

He spun around to his two guests, his face grey as slate, eyes bulging with horror.

"We're locked in. Trapped. Somebody. . . . Damn it!"

The runner suddenly burst into a sheet of flames in his hand and he tossed it away in shock, whipping his scorched hand back and forth through the air.

"Look!"

Hammer pointed to the large moth-eaten carpet covering the entire floor of the room. Here, too, the material began to smoulder, sprouting little flames in various spots, and suddenly bursting into flames, everywhere.

"Jump on it, smother those flames!" Kurt shrieked, trying to stamp them out himself.

The runner he had tossed away had landed on a carton containing old photos and celluloid reels of World War One battlescenes. Before anybody had a chance to move, the whole carton blew up in a puff of smoke, a sudden hiss of flames.

"No!" he screamed. "Not my pictures! All my savings went. . . ."

He dashed around the table as Hammer ran for the door and tried to pull it open himself, but without any success. Smoke began to smart their eyes, to fill the room. Irene was coughing and holding on to the center table with the tin soldier tableau arranged in World War One battle formation. But the smoke became thicker, blacker, increasingly acrid.

"We're trapped," Hammer cried out and turned toward Kurt, who was attempting to push away the heavy steel plate through the bars of the street grille with a broom stick. It was no use. The plate would not be dislodged. Disgusted, he hurled the broom into the corner.

"My God!" Irene turned to the two men. "Somebody is trying to kill us."

"The phone, Kurt. Call the police! The fire unit!"

Kurt sped across the room, coughing, spitting the sulphurous, burning taste out of his mouth; he dialed the operator and barked into the receiver that three people were trapped by fire in the basement of Bundesgasse 5 and choking to death. He listened for a second, said yes and slammed the receiver down.

"Into the wall closet!" he shouted.

"What about the toilet?"

"It's outside, in the hall. Hurry! Into the closet!"

Kurt Frank yanked the closet's sliding door open. In a flash, Hammer had grabbed bundles of clothing hanging inside and thrown them out into the burning room.

"What the hell do you think you're doing?" Frank screamed, outraged.

"We'll need some air till the fire engine gets here," Hammer snapped back, unfazed by Kurt's manic eyes.

"They're mine, you idiot," Kurt yelled, watching helplessly as his suits landed in the fire. "It took me a year to save the money for them. They're all I have, you bastard."

Irene buried her face in the crook of her good arm. "I can't breathe. The heat! God, I think I'm going to faint."

"Hold her, Kurt," Hammer shouted. "Hold her while I empty the closet."

A few more jackets and pants flew through the air into the raging inferno. The smoke became denser by the second, more impenetrable, the tin soldiers battled in clouds of poisonous vapors as Kurt pushed the invalid woman into the closet.

"Do you know the phone numbers of your neighbors upstairs?" Hammer shouted.

"Not by heart. They're in the book over there in the. . . . Hell, it's burning. . . . Hurry up! Get in!"

The three huddled in the small closet and slid the door shut. So far, little of the smoke had penetrated into its interior. The pitch-black darkness smelled of damp clothing and mothballs, but already the scent of burning fabric had tinged the air.

For a few minutes the three did not utter a word, their silence broken only by an occasional cough until their lungs had been cleared of the smoky fumes they had inhaled earlier. They could hear the snap and crackle of the fire outside the closet, systematically laying waste to Kurt's furnishing.

"Somebody is trying to kill us, Kurt," Irene gasped, and desperately gulped in a swallow of air. Even here she felt like gagging.

"Not you, me!" Frank said bitterly. "If only those goddamn fire trucks would come. He's trying to kill me, I know it."

"Who?" Hammer was confused, bewildered.

"Cohn. David Cohn. He lives on the second floor and knows who I am. He's a Jew, and I've been told he hates me. Wait till I get my hands around *his* neck."

"Kurt, stop it!" Hammer shouted. "It isn't David Cohn—it's Glückstein. He's the one after us."

"You're getting paranoid, Paul. He doesn't even know where I live."

"Don't you tell me I'm paranoid! You begin to sound like my son. He also. . . ."

"For God's sake, stop fighting, you two!" Irene's frightened plea cut into their squabble. "Be quiet and conserve the oxygen in here, or we'll all suffocate."

They knew that Irene was right. They *had* to save their strength. Nobody uttered a sound. They stood rigid, motionless.

But their anguish proved too strong. The resolve that they stop squabbling grew on them like a scab to be pried off at all costs.

"Shit! Why isn't the fire engine here yet?" Frank shouted, completely unnerved now, as if Irene's appeal had never been voiced.

"What're you getting so excited about?" Hammer couldn't help taunting his former sadistic jailer. "You afraid to die? I thought life and death are the same, interchangeable, and neither matters too much."

A new stillness descended on them in the darkness, like a fourth companion. Three hearts pounded painfully behind constricted rib cages, and the beat of their pulses drummed in their ears.

Then, the anxious whisper: "What d'you mean Ludi is trying to kill us?"

"His men no doubt followed us," explained Hammer. "They must have squirted the flammable liquid under the door. I thought I had shaken them, but they're expert at that sort of game. A few days ago they tried to kill me, but instead they blew up my fiancée."

"What? Why didn't you tell me? Why would he. . . ?"

"Because he knows I'm ready to reveal the truth about him. I'm the only surviving prisoner from Treblinka he knows of that could spill the beans about his past. It would ruin him, not financially, maybe, but make him a public outcast."

"There are SS men left who could. . . ."

"No one would give a damn about the testimony of an SS guard testifying against a Jewish prisoner, normally. But with me and Irene to back up your story, we can be very convincing."

"They would have believed Karl Ludwig."

"Kurt, Karl Ludwig was killed a few days ago, also by Glückstein's men."

"By Glückstein's. . . . But you said Karl died in an automobile accident."

"In a car, yes. In *my* car. Blown up by dynamite meant for me."

"Holy shit! Did you know about this, Irene?"

"Yes, but we didn't think he'd get us here, and there was no reason to scare you with all this information."

"Scare me!" Kurt shouted. "He doesn't. . . . Yes, he does. He's too damn powerful. And I let him survive. He got the money through me, the rings, watches, buckets of them. They're part mine!"

"Now don't start that again," Hammer overshouted the former SS man in the dark. "Or you'll ruin it all. If we get out of this alive, it's to tell the truth about Glückstein, not to claim some personal fortune for yourself."

"What the hell do you. . . ." Kurt silenced his own outburst abruptly and sighed audibly. "I guess you're right."

"He knows where you live, Kurt, and none of us can afford to rest now till we have it out with him. As a witness, he'll try to get rid of you too . . . if we don't act first."

"I suppose so," Kurt muttered grudgingly.

"But I warn you: one of your outbursts and I'll. . . ."

"Quiet! Listen!"

The three pinched their eyes tight-shut in the pitch-blackness and strained their ears. Pearls of sweat rolled down their faces, blinding them as the smoke began to seep through the tiny rail-track under the door. Outside, the clanking of bells, the sirens of fire trucks now could be heard distinctly, racing, coming closer. Voices. Shouting. Footsteps, and the scraping of the steel plate being removed from the street grille.

A minute later, the first ax blows. Heavy objects, garbage cans falling about noisily. More shouting in the basement hallway echoing back and forth. Ax blows again, the shattering of windows sounding miles away. The three captives in the closet were coughing more strenuously, gagging, as the inside of their sanctuary turned thick with smoke, and became a living furnace.

"Bury your faces in your jackets," Hammer croaked out, barely able to constrain himself from retching.

"I have no jacket," Irene whispered.

"Here . . . against me. . . . Hold your face against my shirt." It was Kurt's voice. Then: "She's fainted . . . Paul, she collapsed. . . . Gypsy!"

A thunder of footfalls outside, something being dragged across the floor . . . and the rush of high-powered jets of water. Sulphurous, hissing steam snaking venomously beneath the sliding door. Hammer was close to blacking out, but he knew that the sound of water rushing in meant that, once more, LL's men would not succeed in extinguishing his life, nor that of his two witnesses.

Another fraction of a second and, as if by God's own hand, the sliding door was drawn open. Respirators were clasped on the three faces struggling for breath, and smoke and flames belched through the blistering heat into the closet. One last picture registered in Hammer's oxygen-starved mind before he fainted: the sight of masked beings, looking like extraterrestrial creatures from a science-fiction movie, coming out of clouds of black and orange smoke and dragging their three helpless victims through the roaring blaze of Kurt's past, out onto the cool Bavarian street.

30

An hour before dusk, kicking and cursing his way through the sodden, charred rubble of his worldly goods, Kurt Frank pulled his passport, moist but undamaged, from the blackened hulk of a chest of drawers. His resolve to go along on Hammer's journey of retribution had grown irrevocable as he surveyed the ruins of the little life he had tried to eke out for himself since leaving prison.

Hammer had the money to get him on his feet again; he had already promised to buy Kurt some new clothing to replace his scorched wardrobe, and to take Irene and himself away for a couple of days rest, of recuperation, at Lake Geneva after their fiery ordeal. Yes, he would cooperate—who could resist the opportunity to earn $15,000 by taking revenge on the swine that had condemned him to a life of unending suffering?

After returning from Switzerland, Kurt Frank and Irene Fischmann picked up their visitors' visas at the U.S. Consulate in Munich, and the next afternoon already—following a furtive, clandestine trip to Frankfurt during the night—Paul Hammer and his two prize specimens boarded a gleaming Lufthansa jet for the flight to the States.

Tempers between the two men had simmered down in the meantime, but a new, rather childish sort of competition was breaking out now.

Like two teenage boys courting a young lady, Kurt and Paul were falling all over themselves in catering to Irene's every need. Each time they reached a doorway, the two men vied for position to hold the door open for her. When they ate their meals, they each offered to pass her the tastiest morsels on the table, or to refill her glass with wine, and argued openly about who should have the privilege of ordering the lady's meal. At first, Irene found all this consideration and courtesy most flattering, then amusing, but by the time she was on the plane and in the air, her patience had worn thin.

Irene finally had enough of their attention-getting stratagems, and she began to recite point by point the indignities she had suffered in the last few days due to their overzealous behavior, as if each of them tried to outdo the other by proving that he alone was the man with the greatest, the most enduring influence in her life. All she wanted was to get this business over with. Meanwhile they should treat her simply with kindness and respect.

Kurt immediately reacted by showing that she had deeply offended him. He sulked and shut his eyes. Hammer sank back in his seat after her mild tongue-lashing, listened to some classical music on his headset, and—for his turn—tried to disregard Irene's snub by reflecting on the safety measures he had taken. Once more, he went in his mind over the passengers who had boarded the plane with his two companions. Since he had seen to it that they would be the last three passengers to get on the airliner, there was no chance that anybody could possibly have followed them on to the plane.

Hammer was also grateful to learn the day before that the municipal authorities of Kurt Frank's home town had concluded after a brief investigation that a former disgruntled wartime captive of Frank's probably set the fire to the basement, and forthwith they absolved him of all responsibility in the destruction of the property.

The Jewish tenant, first suspected by Frank, David Cohn, was exonerated likewise; he had been away with his family all month in Paris.

Irene, too, was calmer now. Her eyes were closed as the jet headed out over the Atlantic. Perhaps she was right in dressing down her two male acquaintances, Hammer deliberated. Possibly their overzealousness *had* been laced with a touch of jealousy. A conclusion not to be dismissed out of hand, he felt, when considering the nature of his own relationship with Irene, beginning so painfully, so publicly, in the cold Treblinka afternoon four decades ago and growing into a true bond in the ensuing months.

As a Brahms symphony at last lulled Hammer into a state hovering between dozing and memory, he envisioned his first meeting with Irene, and the circumstances which led up to it as they had been revealed to him by Kurt Frank.

31

SS Scharführer *Küttner, forever known as Kiwe by the concentration camp prisoners, was engaged in a running battle with* SS Sturmbannführer *Kurt Frank. On the day of*

Paul Hammer's arrival in Treblinka, in February 1943, the two men had already butted heads over a little Jewish tailor named Aronson. In the late morning, as Aronson was picking up a pile of clothing the women had left behind in the Undressing Barracks before being gassed, he came across the coat of his own daughter. He became hysterical, incoherent, rushed back to Camp One and pleaded with Stangl himself for his daughter's life.

He needed an assistant, he cried—for a seamstress—and his daughter, who was the best seamstress in the world, was now being led to the gas chamber. Camp Commandant Stangl, dressed in the white coat the inmates had made for him and scratching himself all over because of the sandflies, reached into his pocket and signed a chit, stating that the tailor's daughter could be spared. He handed the paper to Kurt Frank, who rushed up to Camp Two. There, Kiwe was ordering Münzberger and two drunken Ukrainians to start the gassing operation. Frank yelled at him to delay the action by a minute, but Kiwe ignored the annoying interception and screamed at the three men to hurry up with the execution of his order.

Kurt Frank pointed to Stangl's chit. Kiwe simply ripped it out of his hand and tore it up, ranting that the Führer's orders superseded Stangl's. Frank raced back to Stangl's side, with Kiwe limping only a few steps behind, to report the act of defiance to him. But Stangl just waved all this aside; it was only a Jew's life that had been snuffed out, he said, it wasn't worth an argument. Frank was livid with rage—Stangl had not supported him, his own aide, when he had been challenged publicly by an underling like Küttner. The other guards just stood there, watching and chortling. Frank realized that Stangl was deliberately undermining his authority.

It was later that same day that Kiwe spotted Paul Hammer standing nearly alone on the Appellplatz. Kiwe was not aware that Stangl himself had spared Paul's life—he had been up in Camp Two when the trainload of prisoners arrived.

The fact that Kurt Frank was also present on the Appellplatz and not taking any action toward the lone boy should have alerted Kiwe that there was some special circumstance in keeping Paul Hammer alive. But instead, Frank's presence only goaded Kiwe into immediate action, offering an opportunity to display his superior savagery right under his rival's nose. He came storming down the Reception Square with his familiar limp, screaming at the top of his lungs.

"Why isn't this Jew-pig in The Showers? Nearly the whole transport has already been taken care of."

Paul Hammer looked up from the shoe he was tying. "Because I'm not a Jew," he yelled back, rising.

The beetle-red Kiwe tore past Kurt Frank and, without warning, slammed his fist into young Hammer's face. The 14-year-old's head snapped back. Blood spurted from his nose, and his upper lip split open.

"You don't address a member of the Third Reich until spoken to, and you never *raise your voice, pig!* Is that understood?" His face was inches from the bleeding boy's, his breath reeking of salami. "I asked if this is clear!"

Paul was doubled up, spitting blood on the cobblestones.

"The Kommandant *has given him a dispensation*," Kurt Frank cut in roughly. "Nobody's to interfere with him. And that includes you!"

"Is he telling the truth that he's not Jewish?" Kiwe was far from being appeased.

"Yes."

"Then why is he here?"

"Parents were arrested for distributing anti-Nazi leaflets."

"What!" Kiwe wheeled around, his peasant face livid with rage.

He yanked Paul up by his hair and dealt him a kick with the point of his jackboot so ferocious that the boy catapulted forward and struck the ground with his head, in the puddle of his own blood.

"A traitor's son! This son of a whore should have been shot on the spot." The SS man leapt forward and pulled Paul up by the nape of his neck, as if he were a rabbit. "Shooting is too good for you, you scum! Now stand up! Stand up when a member of the Waffen SS *addresses you.*" Still fuming, Kiwe turned toward Kurt Frank. "What's the matter with Stangl? First Aronson's daughter in Camp Two, and now this vermin."

"Let him go, Küttner! You sent that Jewish girl up the chimney already, despite Stangl's orders. Will you be guilty of insubordination twice in one day?"

"I obey the orders of the Third Reich," Kiwe screamed back.

Kurt stood his ground and barked his commands with total assurance. "I order you to take your hands off this boy, Scharführer. He's protected under the orders of the Kommandant."

Kiwe glared at the trembling, weeping boy and released him, but the next second he unbottoned the flap of his holster, withdrew his pistol and without explanation ordered Paul to come along with him.

Kurt Frank and a few of the SS men in the vicinity followed quickly as the two headed for the enormous woodshed at the far end of the

Appellplatz. *The door opened at that very moment and the huge kapo who had killed Paul's mother emerged but quickly retraced his steps into the woodshed when he noticed the others entering; they paid no attention to him.*

There were long logs of pine, beech and birch on the ground, stacked in neat man-high piles, all the wood that was needed for the construction of the new living quarters of the SS. Once under the corrugated tin roof, Kiwe whipped the terrified boy around to face him.

"I don't believe you are Aryan," he challenged the teenager, pointing his Luger between Paul's eyes. Meanwhile Kiwe had reverted to his normal color, with skin as pale as an albino's, contrasting with piercing blue eyes and a shock of bright red hair topping his bare head. "You lie to us," he said through clenched teeth, "and I'll finish you off, here and now, and never mind what the **Kommandant** *said."*

The door of the woodshed slammed shut and everybody turned around. SS Sturmbannführer *Karl Ludwig had planted himself by the door, next to Kapo Glückstein, legs spread and arms held akimbo.*

"But I am Aryan," the boy insisted, his eyes shifting in terror from one SS man to the next.

"Prove it."

"How?"

"Pull down your pants!"

"My pants! No! I won't!"

Kiwe lifted his 7.65 mm. pistol a bit higher and stuck the barrel into Paul's left ear. With his thumb he snapped back the safety lever.

The boy glanced around helplessly, seeing only the stony faces of the SS officers enjoying this unexpected bit of fun.

"Take your suit off!" Kiwe commanded once more.

Slowly, reluctantly, Paul began to untie his shoe laces, then unbutton his jacket and pants. He stood shivering in his soiled underwear. Tears shimmered in his eyes.

"Everything!" roared Miete, another SS man, watching beady-eyed as the boy, weeping softly, put down his artist's materials and pulled his undershirt over his head, then dropped his shorts on the ground. His penis had shriveled in the cold, and fright made him break out in goose flesh all over. Everybody stared at his genitalia. He was not circumcised.

There was a hiccup of a snicker, then a burst of giggles from one or two of the onlookers, and at last the shed rocked with laughter as the scared youngster stood naked among the wood piles, modestly covering his genitals with his hands.

"What sort of man are you?" Miete cried out between shrieks and loud guffaws. "You have a prick like a two-year-old."

Paul bowed his head, and even though ravenously hungry, frozen, grief-stricken, felt his face burn with mortification.

"Enough! I said enough!" shouted Kurt Frank, and the laughter immediately died down. "All right, what I want you to do now is draw," Kurt addressed Paul. But the youngster did not move. He was petrified. "Did you hear what I said?"

Paul lifted his head, fear of the new unknown gripping his innards.

"Draw?"

"Yes."

"I'm cold. Can I dress first?"

"No. Draw first, then dress."

"My mother is dead." The boy shivered. "I'm so . . . ."

"I said draw!" Kurt bellowed and also removed his gun from its holster. "You don't need your mother for that."

Paul became increasingly terrified. His whole being, chilled and bony, was rent by quiet little sobs.

"Do you hear what the Sturmbannführer said?" screamed Kiwe. "The son of a sow that dared to challenge the Führer now has the nerve to shed tears over her! Draw!"

Paul wiped his blood-streaked face with the back of his hands and picked up the sketch pad and charcoals.

"Come on, quickly, or you'll follow the rest of your family. There are plenty more engine-exhaust fumes left to gas you."

Paul rubbed his arms briskly; they were blue from the cold.

"What . . . what do you want me to draw?" he asked Kurt Frank.

All eyes turned to the second-in-command of the extermination camp.

"I want you to draw Hitler and . . . No, you already did that. I know—make a sketch of two people fucking."

Gales of renewed laughter echoed from wall to wall, but none louder than that of Glückstein, as Paul felt himself go weak in the knees.

"Fucking?"

"You heard me! Quickly now!"

"But how . . . I don't know how . . . I've never seen it."

New screeches of laughter erupted under the tin roof.

"What d'you mean you don't know?" Kurt Frank accosted him, becoming increasingly ill-humored.

"I . . . I've never seen . . . never done it."

Loud gleeful "Oooohs" and "Aaaahs" accompanied this bit of news.

"You haven't? Ever?"

"*Never.*"

"*Just figure it out for yourself.*"

"*I don't know how. Can I have a slice of bread now. I haven't eaten in two days.*"

"*No, you can't! Not till you've drawn a man and a woman screwing.*"

"*But I . . .*"

"*Are you deaf or something? I'm losing my patience with you.*" Kurt's voice became menacing. "*You* can *do it—and you will—now!*"

"*Herr Sturmbannführer!*" Kiwe's heels clicked together like the fusillade of guns in a firing squad. The pale-skinned SS man now feigned fawning subservience to Kurt Frank, seeing that the fun was going his way. Brute sex had become an artistic sideline of his ideology.

"*What?*"

"*With your permission, I'd like to bring a girl down here so she can teach him how it's done. Then he can make a drawing of his fucking lesson.*"

Paul's chin dropped on his chest as the tears continued dribbling down the ridge of his nose.

"*Mutti . . . Vati,*" he whimpered, envisioning his parents in his mind, only dimly aware that Kiwe had left the woodshed.

The booming slam of the metal door a few minutes later started Paul out of his misery. He hardly dared to look up. When he finally did, his eyes came to rest on a completely naked female who, like him, was trembling with cold. She padded, barefoot, across the icy, concrete floor and had one arm folded horizontally over her breasts, the other hand covering her pubic area. Her skin had taken on a translucent, milky-white hue. Frightened out of her wits, she stared at the young male prisoner across the pile of beech logs from her.

A sharp command from Kurt brought the young woman to a halt. She appeared to be past her mid-twenties, with raven-black hair, long and unkempt, and was a trifle plump. The two naked prisoners faced each other silently, immobile, less than ten yards apart.

Kiwe whispered something into Kurt Frank's ear and the two parted, saluting each other with a backward flip of the hand.

"*Her name is Irene,*" announced Kurt Frank. "*You have exactly three minutes, starting now, or you'll both go to the gas chamber.*"

Like a bucket of ice-cold water, the words sent the goose bumps in prickly showers down Paul's entire body now.

"*Come on,*" Kiwe shouted. He had returned from one of the woodpiles with a thick branch, wielding it menacingly in his hand. "*You've got enough brains to know what to do. Get started!*"

The frightened young couple looked from one SS guard to the other, finding only poorly suppressed smirks on their faces, but finally the prisoners' eyes crawled guiltily down one another's bodies. Both were aflame with humiliation, guilt, embarrassment, as their gaze wandered from their chests to their pelvic areas, then focalized unwillingly on their genitalia while, around them, the guards leered lasciviously at the two and waited for the performance to start.

"Hurry now—on the double!" Kurt yelled. "Thirty more seconds standing there like dumb idiots, and both of you will be hacked to pieces . . . You there, the woman . . . Irene, du Sau-Jüdin, you're old enough to know. Show him how it's done. Quickly—we haven't got all day."

Moving slowly, unsteadily, as if she were in a torpor, the nude woman advanced on the trembling boy who was holding on to a protruding log of beechwood for support.

She sensed that her whole life, for whatever it was worth, depended upon her ability to get herself sexually entangled with this shy boy, to arouse him successfully in front of these brutes for their bestial entertainment.

"I told you to move, you slut!" Kiwe raved, whipping the fat branch with a swishing noise through the air and smacking it sharply across her buttocks.

Irene was jolted forward by the stinging blow. She uttered a little cry, grimacing with pain, and rubbed her backside rapidly.

"Fuck that son of a bitch!" screamed Kurt Frank, himself aroused now by her tardiness, the remote foreplay of the naked captives. "I want to see his cock inside you now! Verstanden?"

Irene's hand reached out timidly for the shaking youth, and at last the flat of her palm came to rest on his chest. Imperceptibly, almost dawdling, her hand made its way down in little circular motions.

"Faster!" Kiwe yelled, wiping his brow with a red handkerchief. "Feel him! I want some action, some passion!" He sounded like a movie director in some demented pornographic production.

"Put your hands on her tits!" ordered Unterscharführer Miete.

Except for Glückstein by the door with his piano leg, only German SS officers were present at this perverse performance—none of the Poles, Ukrainians, Lithuanians, no other kapos. This "concert," this "sports event" was reserved for the benefit of the Herrenvolk only.

"Come on, Michelangelo, her tits—suck 'em!" bellowed Kurt Frank.

With growing panic, Paul's eyes swept around the shed, not knowing how he was supposed to behave in spite of all the graphic instructions shouted at him from all corners of the shack.

"Suck her tits, I said!" screamed Frank, hardly able to restrain his own lust, then saw the boy drop the sketching paraphernalia.

Irene's left arm came around the boy's neck and she pressed his head down toward her, gently, until his lips touched the softness of her breasts, prickly with the bitter cold.

His mouth was on her nipples now and the tears came streaming down his cheeks. His stomach churned, felt hollow. He could not concentrate on anything but the thought of eating something, some dry crust of bread, ham, eggs, anything; he was starving. He was not interested in the woman's breasts; they smelled of sweat, unwashed. And tasted salty from his tears. Yet even they failed to rinse the odor from the roseate circles of her bosom.

"Lick them, goddamn you!" Rottenführer *Münzberger* shouted. He had come down from the gas chambers especially to join in the fun after Kiwe had picked Irene from the line of death candidates. Without such "recreation," the extermination operation would be unbearably boring. Paul's tongue flicked out obediently and licked his tears from her pinkish areolas, the jutting nipples.

The woman's hands hovered on his belly, over his pubic hair, and seemed to freeze there. Her eyes were closed now, shutting out the brutal nightmare around her.

Paul thought to himself, why did they have to select such an old woman for him? She must have been almost twice his age, he supposed. Far too old. He had always fantasized in bed about the fifteen- and sixteen-year-old schoolgirls from his Munich community. God, he prayed speechlessly, please don't let my sweet angel of a mother see me now, like this, from her seat in heaven!

"Jew-cunt!" Kurt yelled and waved his Luger impatiently in his hand. "I want you go give him a hard-on, now! You hear? Now!"

Paul began to shake violently as he felt her hands descending the last few inches to fondle his penis. Nobody, but nobody except for himself, had ever touched him there. It was still small, shriveled from fear, cold, hunger, humiliation—a stunted phallic instrument. His stomach growled noisily, and two of the SS men roared with renewed laughter while the others unconsciously followed Frank's example, toying with their pistols.

Irene's manipulation of Paul's penis became more frantic, more panicky. She pulled his foreskin back and forth while his mouth remained frozen to her right nipple. With the other hand she cupped his scrotum. Her frenzy increased and she began to hurt him. Nothing seemed to work. The blood which was supposed to rush to his phallus, to swell it to long rounded hardness, stayed put, stubbornly, like stagnant water, behind the dam of grief and hunger.

"Hey, Jew-bitch!" Kiwe bellowed at her. "I want you to screw him. Now! Do you hear?" He aimed his Luger at Irene's head. "Give him a hard-on in sixty seconds, or it's into the fire with you—with both of you. Sixty seconds!"

And for emphasis he dealt her buttocks a vicious blow with the thick branch.

Stricken with panic, Paul suddenly wanted to live, not to die in a gas chamber. He took hold of his thoughts, summoned up all the lewd pictures his young mind had imagined in bed alone when still in Munich, in the safe warm confines of his parents' home. Movie stars from Hollywood's Broadway Melody *films,* UFA's Der Ammenkönig, *and especially the young naked women leaping in slow motion during the opening scenes of Leni Riefenstahl's* Olympia *reeled with him now in an imaginary bed, spreading their legs for him, girls on Munich streets he had secretly admired from afar—all to no avail. It simply did not work. His penis remained limp, shrunken to an abnormal size, as if hiding away in shame.*

"A young girl," he whimpered. "If she were only younger."

Irene uttered a curse, roughly pulled the boy's face back up from her breasts and kissed him hard on his mouth. But his lips were shut tightly. She drew back, eyes flashing angrily. Her life was at stake too. The killers were getting impatient with her. She sank down on her knees and stopped with her face in front of his flaccid sex organ.

The SS men started to applaud wildly—to spur her on.

Paul shut his eyes, mortified. He froze, standing upright, stiff as a pillar, feeling the hot tears stinging his face, squeezing out from under his lids. Slowly, he became aware of her mouth closing warmly around his penis, moving back and forth, rapidly, the wet sucking sounds interrupted only by his heart pounding achingly inside his chest and his ears and the loud cheers of the SS officers urging her on with her fellatio.

He did not know why, but suddenly he cried out how hungry he was. And the SS men only laughed that much harder, some of them shouting back that he should eat her *in that case.* Even they were no longer conscious of the passage of time. Irene kept on sucking him, frenziedly, as she had been doing far beyond the allotted sixty seconds limit. With a sinking heart she realized nonetheless that it was no use. He still had no erection.

Suddenly the laughter of the camp officers died down. Horrified that the moment of truth was at hand, the bewildered boy opened his eyes and to his astonishment saw one of the men, the SS officer who had posted himself with arms planted akimbo by the door, go from one guard to the other and whisper into their ears.

Only Irene did not seem to notice what was happening around her. In a new act of desperation she grabbed the boy's buttocks, governed by the instinct of self-preservation only and, infuriated, continued to fellate him with an animalistic fierceness, until the very moment that the door of the woodshed creaked open noisily and Glückstein and the SS men filed out, one by one, snickering.

Irene drew back, staring incomprehensively at the small penis. It had barely grown, still hung wet, limp, from the youthful underbrush of pubic hair. But then she noticed that a sudden stillness had fallen around her. With a gasp of shock, she realized that she and Paul were alone in the huge shed except for the officer who had stood near the door.

The SS man shut the door now, peered through a couple of windows and hurried to the pyramid of long-stemmed pine logs against which the unsuccessful obscenity had taken place.

"Get up!" he ordered brusquely, and Irene rose stiffly from the frozen ground, rubbing the dirt from her kneecaps. "Here, eat this, both of you. Quickly!"

And with this, Sturmbannführer Karl Ludwig entered Paul Hammer's and Irene Fischmann's life. He had removed two rolls of bread from each pocket of his field-grey tunic. The two nude prisoners stared dumbfounded at their captor.

"Come on!" he whispered urgently, darting a furtive glance through one of the windows. "Eat it! For God's sake now! You have exactly five minutes. I'll be back in a couple of minutes. When you finish the rolls, huddle up together to keep warm, and don't move from this spot!"

Having said this, he rushed past them, around the hoards of lumber and out through the other door at the far end of the shed. No sooner was he gone when the two captives sank their teeth into the fresh rolls and wolfed them down. At first their stomachs rebelled against this sudden onslaught of dough, but seconds later their innards became increasingly tolerant of the sudden intake of food and accepted the morsels of bread gratefully.

It was Paul who, having finished his roll first, threw his arms around the woman's waist and hugged her tightly to generate some measure of warmth. Oddly, he felt an unexpected stirring now in his groin. He no longer understood what was happening to him, his mind, his body. Inexplicably, he started weeping again, softly, in the crook of her neck, and Irene hugged him gently, still chomping the last mouthful of bread, brushing her lips over his boyishly downy shoulders and stroking his cold, goose-pimply backside.

Suddenly the door through which Karl Ludwig had made his exit was flung open, and the two naked prisoners flew apart, their hearts pounding mercilessly. They could not imagine what new terrible acts of sadism waited for them.

To their utter surprise they saw **Sturmbannführer** Ludwig shut the door softly, a nude young girl now by his side. She could not have been more than fifteen years old, Paul reckoned, with long flowing golden tresses draping her bony shoulders and a skin as translucent as the finest porcelain. Her breasts were the size of small apples, and the fluffy bit of blond pubic hair left the split of her vagina barely protected and vulnerable. Tears coursed down her face as Karl Ludwig pulled her behind him by the wrist and hastened to the two waiting inmates.

"Her name is Luzie," he started speaking even before he had reached the two; the breathless urgency in his voice did not escape them. "She kept screaming that she did not want to die. So I pulled her out of the line of people queuing up to be gassed and . . ."

Luzie hid her face behind her free hand and started to sob.

"Her parents were already in The Showers, and she knows that by now they're dead." He wheeled around to her. "Come on, pull yourself together now!" he barked. "Stop whining if you want to live."

He pressed the girl's hand down and grabbed her by the shoulders, gazing into her tear-filled young eyes. "You want to stay alive, don't you?"

She opened her mouth, but the words wouldn't come out—only a tremulous gasp. She nodded.

"All right then. You can stay alive. You only have a few seconds to make up your mind. If you will make love to this boy, now, you . . ."

"No . . . no!" Luzie stepped back, aghast, her hazel eyes wide with fear. "Anything . . . anything but . . ."

"Listen, girl! You have a few seconds to decide whether to live or die," Karl Ludwig bellowed as Luzie stared in mute horror at the blood-caked face of young Hammer. "There's a pack of animals outside that wants to watch the boy here fuck this woman, but only a young girl like you can arouse him. If you say No, all three of you will march straight from here up the Road to Heaven; you'll be gassed in ten minutes, then cremated. Now then, do you want to go up in smoke, Luzie—look at me, damn you! Do you want to have this lovely blond hair, your face, your skin burned to ashes in a few minutes, or do you. . ."

The girl spun around, but instead of running away, out of the shed, she flung her arms around the waist of the SS man and sobbed, sobbed so hard that her body and her legs shook uncontrollably.

The SS officer slipped one arm protectively, soothingly, around her back and with the other beckoned to Paul to approach the girl. Luzie raised her tear-stained face to Karl's.

"I . . . I have never . . ."

"Neither has the boy; he's just as frightened as you," Karl whispered into her ear. He glanced at his watch just as Paul pressed his body against Luzie's backside. The touch of his skin against hers seemed to send a jolt through her. She uttered a little, bird-like cry and fastened her grip more tightly around Karl. He in turn quickly pried her arms from his midriff and twisted her around to face Paul. Disgust, guilt, a flood of emotions overwhelmed her then. She shut her eyes and braced herself to wrap her arms around the boy's nakedness. And still, her torso, its lower half, frantically tried to isolate itself from any genital contact with the teenaged lad. But only for as long as she could.

Paul suddenly felt highly conscious of her breasts, of her nipples rubbing softly against his chest; and the touch of her satiny skin, the warmth of her body began to stir eddies of passion in his mind, his mouth, his groin, as almost against his will, and still filled with shame, he sensed his small member swelling, gorging on a rush of blood. Both of his arms forced Luzie's delicate body against the full length of his own. Crying with embarrassment, he felt the enormity of his erection now against the fluffy growth of her pubic hair; and his lips, his tongue, thirsting for more, much more, sought out and wetted the back of her neck.

"Quickly! Irene, lie down! Here!"

Karl Ludwig had ripped an oil-stained sheet of tarpaulin from a pile of carefully stacked timber and spread it on the concrete floor.

Paul heard the commotion on the floor behind him, and the next instant felt himself torn out of the soft, trembling embrace of the young girl and flung on top of Irene, who was already lying on her back, legs spread wide apart.

"Stick it in her, damn you!" shouted the SS man, and in the resulting confusion he literally had to guide the befuddled boy's erection into the woman's dry and tight vagina. Paul's initiation into sex had been completed. The rape as a political statement finally became reality.

Luzie immediately shrunk back, watching in tear-streaked horror, yet fascinated by the prefabricated dipping of one genital into another, as the youngster began to pump deliriously into the vitals of the prostrate woman, his face buried in her gypsy-black hair only inches from the oily canvas.

Karl Ludwig had achieved what he set out to do. He swung around, rushed past the stacks of cut wood and stormed out of the shed, shouting, "Kurt, they're doing it. Quickly, men—everybody!"

Like a gaggle of geese in field-gray uniforms, half a dozen men flocked back into the ill-lit shed and marched past the masses of timber and lumber to see the sexual spectacle.

Now more reminiscent of a procession of defrocked priests, they gathered quietly around the two prisoners unlovingly going through the mechanical motions of intercourse.

Tongues moistened dry lips. Kiwe ran his hands through his thick shock of red hair. He was aroused, not because of the up and down physics of the sexual rites being acted out in the dirt for his benefit, but because he had caught sight of the graceful figure of Luzie, who on seeing the six giant SS guards had retreated in terror behind a splintery stack of wood.

"Get finished with it, Michelangelo; then six sketches for my men!" Kurt's order boomed through the tin hut and interrupted Kiwe's salacious reverie about the pale girl.

The tossing and writhing of the naked flesh on the tarpaulin no longer held their interest as five of the SS officers began to file out through the front entrance. Just as Kurt was going to shut the door, he turned around and saw Kiwe grab the young girl's hand and yank her in the opposite direction, toward the door through which she had originally entered with Karl Ludwig.

"Küttner!" The name reverberated through the woodshed.

Kiwe and the girl abruptly rooted to the ground. "Where the hell do you think you are going?"

Kiwe turned to his superior, spinning Luzie around with him. He stared at his nemesis, remaining tight-lipped.

At the other end of the building, the five SS men stopped to watch the scene of rivalry that threatened to develop now. Unaware of this new, ominous battlefield, Paul's mouth hungered for Irene's, and greedily nibbled her lips as she played her part in the grim drama, pretending to be rocked by a paroxysm of orgasm. A few seconds later the boy dropped off her body, sated, like a wooden log rolling from the top of its pile of timber.

Irene held the spent boy's hand in her own and stroked it tenderly. Sunlight filtered through the grimy window under which they lay and enshrouded her flushed face in a dusky halo—an imprisoned madonna.

Sturmbannführer *Kurt Frank could never fully explain his next move. Perhaps it was a moment of weakness, perhaps an act of bragadoccio to show Kiwe that he could conquer a lovely female without the aid of force. He strode back briskly to where the two spent lovers rested on the tarpaulin, snatched Irene's hand away from her exhausted partner and scooped her off the floor. Next, he dusted off her caked backside with his huge hands, then removed his jacket and draped it gentlemanly around her shoulders.*

"Can you cook?" he asked in a low voice.

Irene stared up at him with large fearful eyes and found scarcely the strength to nod at the ugly giant looming like a Cyclops above her.

"Come along then," he said softly. The next moment his head snapped up, and he barked at Kiwe. "Follow me!"

The two SS men and the nude females made their way to the back door where Kurt turned once more to the shed's interior.

"Hammer!" he shouted. The boy rose shakily to his feet and wiped the sticky inside of his thighs with his hands. "Unterscharführer *Miete will take you to your quarters and issue another suit to you—one with a red triangle to show you're a political prisoner—and something to eat. Then you do the six sketches."*

Miete clicked his heels and advanced on the youngster as the others left the glacier-cold tin hut.

Men with blue armbands and whips in their hands suddenly came toward Kurt. One of them reported that another transport was due within the hour. Kapo Glückstein, clutching his ever-present piano leg, was among them, as well as Oberkapo *Blau, a former school friend of Camp Commandant Stangl and more feared than some of the SS men. They were heading for the station ramps.*

"Glückstein!" Kurt called out, and Glückstein immediately dropped out of the column of kapos to approach the odd quartet of SS officers and naked women. He came to a halt a few steps from them and stood at attention.

"At your service, Herr Sturmbannführer.*"*

"Take Küttner's girl and give her the special treatment at the Lazarett.*"*

"Hey, wait a minute!" Kiwe protested at once. "What is this?"

"Kapo Glückstein," Kurt Frank overshouted Kiwe. "You heard my order. Take the girl to the Lazarett!*"*

"The Jew will not touch my girl!" screamed Kiwe. "I can have any woman I damn well please. You're having your woman, and I'm having mine."

Glückstein stepped forward and grabbed Luzie's free hand.

"Take your hands off her, you Jew-prick!" Kiwe shrieked. His hand was already unclasping his holster and reaching for his Luger.

"Are you defying my order, Scharführer?" Kurt Frank yelled, beside himself with rage. "Have you decided to make your insubordination permanent? In case you forgot, I'm a few ranks above you. You will release the girl at once to Kapo Glückstein."

"I don't want the Jew to touch the girl," Kiwe shouted back, undeterred.

"Then don't touch her yourself! She's Jewish too."

"If she goes to the Lazarett, then your woman also goes!" Kiwe's rage found no bounds; his entire body was trembling. "She performed the sex act with a member of the Aryan race—a crime punishable by death. She defiled his Christian blood. I've got the right, the duty, to kill her." And his hand tightened around his pistol.

Irene shrank back in horror, away from the feuding SS officers; she began to weep uncontrollably. Kurt Frank's eyes swept briefly in her direction.

"You so much as harm one hair on this woman's body, and I'll have you court-martialed, Scharführer!" Frank's titanic voice echoed from the buildings of the town square. "One more word of contradiction out of you, and I'll bust you down to nothing! I'll have you demoted to SS Anwärter, and if that doesn't help, I'll see to it that you're sent to the Eastern front. Verstanden? Dismissed!"

Kiwe stood stock-still; only the vein in his temple under his red hair pumped away madly. His crazed, icy blue eyes burned with venomous loathing.

"I said Dismissed, Küttner!"

Hesitantly, with a readily visible effort at restraint, Kiwe dropped Luzie's hand, and glared wordlessly at Kurt Frank.

The tears had long since dried on the girl's face. Not even the feeling of shame at being nude in the presence of these roughnecks, nor the bitter cold, bothered her as she followed the heated exchange of words of the SS men.

Kapo Glückstein took her hand and squeezed it. He even smiled at her as they walked in the direction of the "hospital." Kapo Glückstein explained to her that she was lucky that two SS men had openly expressed a liking for her. But first she must go to the Lazarett where they would see if she was healthy or suffered from malnutrition. She would be seeing the doctors soon, but to start with she should warm herself. She could stand at the edge of the burning pit and thaw out her hands over the flames.

Less terrified now, even trusting and thankful to be spared, she did as told by the kind kapo and held her arms out over the furiously burning pit after they had entered the **Lazarett**.

"You stay here," Glückstein said, caressing her pale cheeks gently, "while I get you something to wear and a bun that Kapo Siegfried baked this morning. He's a nice man, Reinhold Siegfried, and like you and me he's also a prisoner. Now just warm yourself, child."

The heat of the fire was already making her feel drowsy, a bit giddy—she hadn't had anything to eat for three days. For the first time since arriving at the camp, she bestowed a thankful little smile on a man.

He winked at her. Tears swam in his eyes. The sharp east wind must have affected them, she reckoned and turned back to the roaring fire. She stretched out both arms over it and aimed her eyes up through the open roof at the heavens to offer a soundless prayer that at least she would be allowed to live.

Glückstein swiftly stepped back behind her, raised the heavy bulk of the piano leg in a mighty swing over his head and with all his strength stuck the unsuspecting girl in the back of her skull.

Something cracked. The spinal cord. Her neck. Hair, arms, legs flying in a wide arc through the air, Luzie catapulted from the rim of the pit and without so much as a flutter of a cry dived into the sulphurous sea of flames. She was dead well before hitting the fire that would cremate her in a few minutes. Nobody at the camp knew her last name.

PART THREE: SURVIVORS

32

After arriving at JFK Airport, the three visitors spent one day in New York City's Hotel Tudor to recuperate from their jet lag. At night, they went to see the Broadway musical *Cats*, and the following morning they discussed plans for the confrontation with Luckstone at Rosedale.

Paul Hammer took the opportunity to write a letter, as planned, to his attorney, but thought it wiser to mail it inside another letter addressed to Jesse. He, in turn, was to forward it two days after its receipt to Hammer's lawyer. However, Jesse was to do so only unless instructed otherwise in the interim. If there was no news from the trio within seventy-two hours of the receipt of the letter, the lawyer was to make its contents public.

In the letter, Hammer outlined the situation, the murders which had already taken place, their immediate intention to meet with the billionaire at his home in Sullivan County, and the case against Glückstein, alias Luckstone. Kurt, Irene and Paul all signed the document, and it went off by registered mail to Jesse the following morning, just before the three began their two-and-a-half hour drive by rented car to Louis Luckstone's palatial estate.

Paul knew that Luckstone would be on the grounds when they arrived at Rosedale—for during Hammer's unexpectedly brief visit to the States, Jesse had mentioned that LL would be engaged in three weeks of continuing business consultations at his home before embarking on an extended trip abroad. And that visit, despite the eternity that had elapsed between then and now, had ended just about two weeks ago.

Originally their plan had been to get in touch with the press immediately after arriving in the States and to ask the reporters to be at Rosedale the following evening for an important news conference. But on second thought they decided against this arrangement since the press most likely was cautious enough to check back with the Luckstone headquarters and discover that the call was a hoax. Better to wait and, after confronting LL, make the date with the media directly from his own home. They would simply stay there for the reporters to arrive.

The gatekeeper at the entrance to Rosedale was understandably skeptical when presented with Paul Hammer's demand for admission to the estate, but he was willing to phone "Miss Nicole" and verify the story that the self-invited guest needed no prior appointment to gain entry to LL's home.

While remaining in their car and awaiting her reply, Paul Hammer gazed across the rarely traveled New Cochecton Turn Pike Road leading to the Luckstone property and for the first time noted the large bull chained to an iron rod in the middle of an untended pasture, huge patches of Queen Anne's lace making it look sprinkled with powdered sugar.

After a few minutes, the guard returned from his conversation over the intercom and, with an exaggerated show of civility to make up for his earlier brusqueness, let Hammer's car onto the grounds. He directed them to the Tudor house where Miss Nicole was practicing piano, some distance from the Executive Mansion, and instructed them under no circumstances to proceed to Mr. Luckstone's headquarters.

On the drive to the baronial residences beneath the majestic maples and elms, which were beginning to turn coppery gold, the three avengers met a column of Mercedes, Rolls Royces and Cadillacs coming toward them—plainly some of the corporate big shots who had completed their business conferences with LL for the day.

Irene and Kurt sat in the rear of their modest, rented Dodge, awestruck into silence and overwhelmed by the immense compound of luxurious villas, the expertly tended, seemingly endless beds of flowers, the tennis courts, swimming pools and, beyond them, the heliport from which several noisy departures were proceeding.

Kurt Frank leaned forward and mumbled something about investing the jewelry of the gassed prisoners in such peaceful surroundings. He remarked bitterly that the beautiful scenery reminded him of the woods north of Treblinka. Hammer braked the car to a halt abruptly in front of the Tudor-style manor and turned to his companions.

"Let me do the talking," he said quickly in English. "And don't confuse the girl by butting in with your share of the loot, Kurt! Understand?"

They heard the sound of piano music through the open windows on the ground floor—the deep, mournful sounds of Beethoven's *Moonlight Sonata*.

Paul recalled the first time he had met Nicole, when she had confided in him that she played the *Moonlight Sonata* only when she was in "a deep funk." He was sorry to think that this lovely young woman was so upset that she had to forego her minuets. He also wondered fleetingly whether this depressive mood could bring out her violent streak, particularly when she met the man who was upsetting her perfect world.

Hammer slammed his car door shut, as did Kurt and Irene on their side, and the music stopped in mid-phrase. Moments later, the door of the mansion opened. Nicole stepped out into the autumnal sunlight.

The clinging turquoise silk dress she wore had a slit up the side seductively drawing attention from the fabric's lustrous sheen to her shapely, tanned legs. Hammer's glance passed quickly from her svelte figure, though, to her face, which told a far less cheerful tale. It had greatly changed since their last meeting. The joy had drained out of it, and a bitterness had sculpted the flesh into a mask of bloodless, stony hardness.

A few pleasantries passed between them, Hammer introduced his friends, and the four settled down in the elegant Music Salon where Hammer and Nicole had their first heart-to-heart talk.

"Can I offer you anything?" she asked with strained politeness.

"No, thanks; we had something to eat near White Lake. We just dropped in to see you—and LL, of course."

"I don't think gramps has much time to see you today, Paul. He's tied up with his business meetings all week long." An uncomfortable silence descended for a painful, drawn out minute. Nicole broke the spell abruptly. "Paul, what did you mean a week ago on the phone when you said my grandfather was responsible for all those deaths?"

Hammer winced and shot a brief glance at his two friends.

"Look, Nicole, it's too long a story. I really don't want to start explaining things now. Let Jesse tell you. You're a nice kid and. . . ."

"Please don't be so damn patronizing!" Nicole sat up stiffly on the ottoman and a new arrogance appeared in her voice. "I'm a woman, not a kid! And what concerns your son, he will *not* tell me. Besides, we don't see each other as frequently as we used to."

"You don't?" Hammer had expected the rift, but pretended to be quite shocked nonetheless. "You don't mean the wedding is off?"

"I didn't say that. It's just. . . ." She shrugged. "He's very busy."

"He always was, and you two still managed to meet almost daily."

"Well, things change," she said icily. "And I don't like being taken for granted, not being taken into his confidence. He's as secretive about my grandfather as you are, and I resent it."

"I understand. Of course, I'm sorry to hear about this, Nicole." Hammer rose to his feet and his two travelmates followed suit. "Maybe after we've seen LL, I can explain what I was talking about on the phone."

Nicole also got up. "I'm afraid he won't be able to see you today, I already told you. He isn't in."

"He isn't? A moment ago you said he was tied up in meetings. And we just saw a parade of limos leaving as we drove up. Look, Nicole, I know he's in the executive wing. And he did tell me that I could see him any time I wanted."

"No!" The word leaped from her lips, an unquestionable command. "You won't! I don't mean to be rude, but I won't have you upset him with your outrageous charges. And if you persist, I'll be forced to call his bodyguard."

"His bodyguard! Nicole, I'm surprised at you. Please don't take this attitude. We didn't come all the way from Germany to be put off like this."

"From Germany! You mean your friends came to see him too? They know him?"

"That's right. And we're going now. Please don't put any obstacles in our way, child!"

Nicole did not budge. She faced the trio, not so much attempting to block their exit physically as presenting a pale apparition condemning Hammer's announced intention. When no further words were spoken, she stepped aside for them to pass. "I can't hold you back, Paul, but don't blame me for the consequences."

Hammer waited a moment longer, expecting her to elaborate on her implicit threat, but then led the other two out of the room and into the garden.

Nicole looked after the trio as they marched purposefully toward the Executive Mansion. She turned decisively and headed for the house phone, dialing two numbers.

"Grasser?" Her voice could not conceal her inner tension. "There are three people on the grounds. Two men and an elderly woman with a paralyzed arm. The smaller of the two men is Jesse Hammer's father. Please treat them with courtesy, but under no circumstances let them see LL till I've gotten in touch with you again. . . . Fine. . . . Thanks."

She hung up and momentarily froze, staring hard at the telephone, deciding on her next move, then made up her mind and dialed Jesse Hammer's office. She was determined to sound cheerful.

"Hi, Joannie. Nicole. Is the doctor available?"

Jesse's secretary spoke in a low voice. "Not really. He's finishing up a report for next week's Conference of the Neurological Society. But I don't think he'll mind a few minutes distraction. Hold on!"

There was a click in the line and Nicole's body stiffened.

"Darling?" It was her lover.

"Hi Jess. Good to hear your voice again."

"How've you been, Nick? I'm sorry I couldn't make it over to see you for the last few days."

"So am I. Jess, I must talk to you. I. . . ."

"Great. I'll be over tonight, I promise."

"No, I mean now. On the phone. Your father is here."

"What! What do you mean 'here'? In the States?"

"He's *here*, I'm telling you. I just spoke to him in the Music Salon. He's with two friends, a man and a woman."

"What's the matter with him? Without letting me know! What's the point of coming here for his vacation, then leaving two days later, and returning less than a week before it's up?"

"I don't get it either. That's why. . . ."

"Didn't you ask him what he wanted, why he came back?"

"All he said was that he had to see LL."

"Oh no, he doesn't!" The alarm in Jesse's voice rang loud and clear through the wire, instantly redoubling Nicole's anxiety. "Don't let him, under any circumstances!"

"I already told Grasser not to let them see gramps."

"Them? You mean his friends want to see LL too?"

"Yes. He claims they know him. They all came from Germany."

"For God's sake, don't let them get close to LL! Block them, anything! I can't get away from here now. Just keep 'em away from him till I arrive!"

"Do you think they may be dangerous? Armed?"

"I don't know. I can only guess at who they are."

"Well, tell me! Who?"

"Look, Nick, no more questions, please! We don't want to go through the same scene we had last week, so. . . ."

"For crying out loud, how do you *expect* me to feel?" she shouted into the phone. "First your father being so secretive—and now *you* lying to me."

"What d'you mean *lying* to you?" he cried out.

"Just like you lied to me last week when you said your father was suffering from a persecution complex."

"But it's true, Nicki. How can you say I was lying about that?"

"Because the two people with your father are no phantoms, no figment of his imagination, but real-life flesh and blood people out to get my grandfather. And you're *still* holding out on me! For the last time now, Jesse: are you going to own up? What are these three people after?"

"Now you stop it immediately!" Jesse raised his voice, turning away from his secretary in his swivel chair and staring out into the garden. "This is no time for ultimatums. You're behaving like a child, Nick, and right now we have real problems to worry about."

"Exactly! That's why I'm going to prove to you that I'm mature enough to deal with your father, whatever problems *he's* bringing with him. And you know what you can do with your secrets!"

She slammed the receiver on the phone. A chill ran down her arms as she clutched both elbows and stared hard into space.

The sound of glass shattering, like a window pane breaking in the distance, drove her to the open French window. Her eyes probed the sunny garden intently. Perhaps Grasser had captured the three intruders. Even her fiancé didn't know if these unwelcome visitors were armed. The very possibility of this threat sent her charging out onto the grounds.

There was no sign of anyone, not even of Grasser.

However, a few minutes earlier, before Nicole emerged from the Music Salon, the trio was scanning the premises also, from the safe vantage point of the wooded area near two of the greenhouses. In the distance they spotted one more limousine noiselessly gliding past the complex of buildings and up the driveway through the forest.

There was little doubt in their minds that Nicole would alert the bodyguard after they had challenged her wishes not to see her grandfather. At the same time they knew that they had to use a diversionary tactic in order to reach LL's Executive Mansion without being observed. It was at that juncture that Paul Hammer tossed a rock at an attic window of the shingle-framed guest house Nicole had pointed out to Jesse's father when showing him around the estate the first time he was here.

Glass shattered noisily in the afternoon stillness and the three ran again for cover in the woods. There was a flurry of wings, as from a dozen trees nearby flocks of starlings and robins ascended in a wild flutter.

"Let's go!" Hammer whispered after the last sliver of glass had slid from the roof of the guest house and landed on the gravel path below.

They hastened along the row of oak trees, firmly convinced that LL's fortress-like headquarters at present harbored no one but the billionaire and his last remaining business associates. In the distance they took note of a man, obviously the bodyguard, his gun drawn, making a dash across a lawn and heading for the guest house, away from them, as another car, a Lincoln Continental, was taking off for Rosedale's forest exit. There were only two automobiles left when the seekers of retribution safely reached the main building. Nevertheless, they knew that they faced one more obstacle: Luckstone's servants.

33

"Stop gawking at everything!" Hammer warned Kurt and Irene in an impatient whisper after the three made their entrance to the Gothic hall where barely two weeks earlier the imperious Louis Luckstone was introduced to him. "You know what to do. Especially be on the lookout for the staff!"

They listened for the sound of men's voices in the interior of the mammoth castle and moved stealthily toward the distant murmur of the conversation. They tiptoed through a number of rooms, luxurious, spacious, expensively and expertly furnished rooms, elegantly laid out—a library, living room, movie theater—until they came to a wrought-iron reinforced oak door which stood slightly ajar.

Hammer gestured to his two conspirators to halt, then make a detour. Judging from the sound of the voices, Luckstone was in the room with the open door. But instead of entering, Hammer closed the oak door now very slowly, cautiously, turned the key soundlessly in the lock, and put it into his pocket. Shushing his two puzzled companions, he led the way through another room in order to reach the large glass-domed greenhouse adjoining the mansion. The only entrance to this hothouse was from the outside, so the trio slipped once more out of the main building, making sure they were not detected, sped around the Executive Wing to its rear and filed through the open door into the stupendous solarium.

After the brisk snap of the fall weather outside, the warm humid air inside was a welcome change. The atmosphere was rich with the fragrance of greenness, of loamy dark earth and chlorophyll. To their astonishment, an explosion of color welcomed them; a savage jungle of fire-red sophronitis orchids criss-crossed beds of snowy-white cattleyas, and sea-green Himalayan mountain clematis climbed up gnarled tree trunks bursting with violet flowers.

Still guided by Hammer, the three weaved their way in a crouch under the drooping branches of tall Chinese wisteria shrubs and around a small pond aswarm with Veiltail goldfish and sprinkled with white petals from a flowering rosebush. They halted, then quickly ducked behind a broad-leafed walnut tree and were given additional cover by large fern fronds fanning out before them across the marble-alternating flagstone floor. Not twenty yards away, they made out the postern leading into the Executive Mansion, and from there two subdued voices could be heard clearly.

They had found Louis Luckstone!

Irene squeezed Kurt's hand. At long last! The object of their hunt was within sight. He was addressing his top aide. John Shadow sat prissily upright at an immense mahogany table taking notes on a yellow legal pad. A dozen long-stemmed goblets and several ashtrays filled with discarded cigar and cigarette butts were scattered across the table.

Luckstone snapped out a stream of instructions to his confidant, standing beneath a gigantic pair of antlers mounted high overhead on a granite wall. For the most part, though, the tremendous conference room boasted dark, varnished tongue-and-groove oak paneling and bookshelves lined with leather-bound volumes and rare, exquisite porcelain and glass figurines and archaeological finds. On the extreme left the three just made out an open bay window. Several black leather club chairs with mosaic inlaid smoking tables by their sides dotted the parquetry floor and the deep-pile Persian carpet near an unlit fireplace. Altogether a room of Wagnerian proportions that proved to be a fitting annex to the Valhalla-vaulted hothouse.

"You know what to do!" Hammer whispered as they crouched behind the leafy protection of a Tartarian honeysuckle bush loaded with clusters of berries. Both Kurt, who had donned a pair of sunglasses, and Irene nodded "Don't go back on your word now, Irene. Remember your gun *isn't* loaded. The magazine is empty. You and Kurt keep them covered while I make sure the window is locked. . . . Ready?"

Irene took a deep breath, and the three intruders rose in unison. Irene stepped forward, pulled the postern wide open and Hammer burst into the conference room while Kurt remained by the door, aiming his Luger at John Shadow and Louis Luckstone.

The two men spun around, speechless, staring incredulously at the strange trio, at Hammer rushing for the bay window leading into the garden, at the tall man in sunglasses pointing a pistol at them, and at the elderly woman by his side.

"One false move and you'll get it!" Kurt barked in English, training the Luger at Luckstone's brow.

"What is this? Where's Grasser?" demanded a shaken Louis Luckstone.

Shadow had leaped to his feet and, in the process, kicked over his chair. With one hand he righted it, never taking his eyes off the invaders. "Is this a robbery?" he blurted out. "Who are you? Terrorists?"

Hammer had locked the garden door meanwhile and returned to his two cohorts. Only now did Luckstone recognize him.

"For God's sake, it's you!" he exclaimed, puzzled as well as relieved. "What's this supposed to mean, Hammer?"

Instead of an answer, it was Irene who stepped forward, resting her good hand on the back support of one of the black easy chairs.

"You don't remember me, do you . . . Mr. Gl . . . Luckstone?"

The billionaire furrowed his brow, totally disregarding the old woman. "What're you after, Hammer? And why did you bring that character with a gun in here?"

"Put the gun away!" Hammer said in an aside. "For the time being. And you two, don't do anything you might regret. My friend here is a killer. A very experienced killer."

The two executives visibly sighed with relief as Kurt replaced the Luger in his breast pocket. It did not escape their notice, and was not meant to, that his hand remained inside his jacket, just in case.

"What the hell are you trying to pull, Hammer?" Luckstone repeated, more annoyed now than startled. "What d'you want from me? And what did you do with my bodyguard?"

"He's taken care of," said Hammer. "Don't worry about him!"

"What about Shadow? At least let *him* go!"

"Nobody leaves! Let him hear what we have to say. Soon the whole world will know anyway."

"What the devil are you talking about? Now look, if it's money you're after, I'll . . . Nicki promised to cut you in . . . I think . . . on the new shopping mall, the. . . ."

A terrible crash spun everybody around. Glass was shattering on the parquetry floor behind them, and the five saw a burly middle-aged man with a rose in his lapel hammer the butt of his revolver against the glass pane, punching it through the locked bay window into the conference room—Luckstone's bodyguard, Grasser.

Without wasting a second, Kurt pulled out his 9 mm. Luger '08 and strode across the conference room, boldly sticking the gun's muzzle against Luckstone's temple.

"You raise your gun, Mister, I'll blow his brains out!" he shouted at Grasser.

The latter had succeeded in opening the window through the jagged hole in the pane and planting one foot inside the room, when he froze. His pistol pointed down at the window sill. A confused frown scrunched up his brow.

"You better do as he says, Grasser," LL addressed the bodyguard, much calmer already, then turned back to the greenhouse where Hammer had posted himself near an Irish yew, his hand in his breast pocket.

"We're all armed," Hammer warned, "and you better realize that we mean business. Okay, Grasser, drop the weapon on the floor!"

Reluctantly, with an apprehensive look at his employer, Grasser placed his Mauser delicately on the floor.

"Right—into the room!" Kurt's voice of command brooked no

contradiction. He was back in his element, a man of power backed by the barrel of a gun, moving closer by the moment to the fruition of a forty-year dream of revenge. He secured his sunglasses on the ridge of his nose. "Next to Luckstone! Quickly now, or I'll pull the trigger."

The guard lifted his other foot awkwardly into the room and walked, self-consciously, hands upraised, around the conference table until he came to stand between Luckstone and Shadow.

"We'll take care of your servants the same way, if they interfere," Hammer cautioned the billionaire. "Butlers, the kitchen help, whatever."

"Don't worry. Except for the switchboard, I gave them the rest of the day off, once the conference was over." Luckstone's voice had become a mixture of studied boredom and condescension as he stole a glance in the direction of the heavy oak door, which Hammer had already locked from the outside. "Just tell me: is it money you're after?"

"Don't move—stay where you are, Luckstone," Irene said. She had noticed the magnate's furtive look. She picked up the bodyguard's Mauser and slid it away from her, down the slick greenhouse marble floor, then dug into her purse, produced the .45 caliber Colt automatic Kurt had lent her. She aimed it, as planned, with her right hand at Luckstone.

"We're not joking," she said tremulously, repelled by the touch of the cold, heavy firearm, unloaded as it was, but cognizant of the fact that she had to play her part in this ugly drama of confrontation against a man who respected force and power more than anything else. "We've waited too long for this moment to let anybody interfere."

"For Pete's sake, you too?" Luckstone growled. "Do you realize that breaking into this house, all of you brandishing guns, threatening our lives, makes you liable to prosecution? I could have you all arrested and charged with. . . ."

"Believe me, LL," Hammer broke calmly into Luckstone's threat, "that when this is over, the last thing you'll want to do is to get the police involved."

"And I have a feeling," Irene seconded Hammer, still shakily, "that your friends here may not want to have anything to do with you either after they've heard why we're here."

"Well, in this case, let me remind *you*, Mr. Hammer, that I own the ad company you work for. It strikes me as a terrible mistake for you to sacrifice your livelihood, your pension, for the sake of some misguided joke. Or perhaps you'd prefer your son losing his position as head of the Neurological Rehabilitation Center in a couple of years just because of . . . well, this scene."

A smile of wonderment creased Hammer's face. "Always the man of power, Mr. Luckstone. Pulling strings non-stop. Cutting people off their life-support systems. But don't think for a moment that those threats haven't crossed my mind. And they don't make a bit of difference."

"It must be wonderful to be so sure of yourself, Mr. Hammer. So, for the last time I ask you, *please*, why are you here?"

The smile on Hammer's face was replaced by a business-like expression. "You're right—I'm not being fair. After all, why should you recognize *us*, if I only recognized you from your laugh—and the missing tip of your thumb?"

All eyes turned to Luckstone's hands resting on the back of an armchair. The tip of his left thumb was missing indeed. In a seemingly casual manner, Luckstone bunched up his hands, hiding both thumbs.

"Mr. Hammer." For the first time his voice betrayed signs of unsteadiness. "Let's get to the point! What's your game?"

"I assure you we didn't travel thousands of miles to play games with you, LL. Take a good look at this woman. Have you ever seen her before?"

This time all eyes focused on Irene. Luckstone gazed hard at her.

"Sorry, I can't recall any acquaintance of mine with a crippled hand."

"Crippled hand!" Irene cried out. "You mean crippled life. And do you know who crippled it?"

"How could I? We've never met before, ma'am."

"You didn't call me ma'am in 1944. No, not in '44, when you crippled me."

All of a sudden Luckstone's face twitched uncontrollably—a rapid series of expressions—despite his attempts at presenting a calm façade. His eyes glazed over behind his thick spectacles as everybody stared at him.

"Surprised to see me, Herr Glückstein?" Irene mocked the visibly bewildered man, savoring his German name as it rolled off her tongue. "Still don't remember? In Auschwitz, *Herr Oberkapo* Glückstein, where you strutted around with your weapon, your piano leg, and ordered me to have sex with you? In Birkenau? Near one of the gas chambers under the newly erected orchestra stand? You were never starved into impotence in the death camps, were you, *Baldwin*? You always got enough to eat—the leftovers from the SS officers' mess hall."

Her throat was contracting with anguish as memories crowded in on her. She saw the man in front of her sway. "You knew very well I couldn't let you touch me—I belonged to one of the top SS men. But no—you paid no heed. So you struck me in the back of my skull with that piano leg when I refused you, and when I hit the ground you kept on clubbing me, with all your might, and you smashed my shoulder. You completely shattered the bones of my shoulder, you crumbled them, Glückstein!" she shouted, pounding the table with the hand that held the gun. "It took seven major operations after the war before the doctors finally gave up on it as a lost cause, Herr Glückstein!" Irene's voice rose to a high-pitched shriek of anger, of frustration, of utter despair.

"Because of you I've gone through a life of agony, of unending, unbearable pain. My left arm withered away until it looks like a matchstick. It's dead! Dead, yet even now the shooting pains won't stop. Not even at this very moment! But you wouldn't know about that, Baldwin, would you? Not with all your fancy trees and helicopters and limousines and bodyguards. You wouldn't want to be reminded of how you clubbed a weak, defenseless woman, sixteen, eighteen, twenty times into the ground with that piano leg."

"Oh my God!"

The exclamation came not from Luckstone, but from John Shadow as he gaped from the tortured face of the woman to the man he had served, unquestioningly, for decades.

"No! You're making a mistake, dear lady," Luckstone at last muttered in a rush of words, his hands again gripping the leather chair, this time for support. "It's not true, you must believe me, I never struck anybody. Others did, but not me."

"You forget one thing, Glückstein," Irene said harshly. "There are witnesses. They can attest to what I say."

"Witnesses?"

"Look around, Baldwin! Why do you think Paul Hammer brought *him* along?" she asked, pointing uneasily with the gun to Kurt Frank. "He and Paul are my witnesses."

"But wait a minute!" Grasser the bodyguard spoke up for the first time before Luckstone had a chance to take a closer look at Frank. "You're not making any sense. Hitler didn't pick Jews to be SS guards. And Mr. Luckstone is Jewish."

"I'm Jewish too, young man," Irene quickly cut in before Luckstone had a chance to reply. Two dots of rose flushed her wrinkled cheeks.

"And your Mr. Luckstone wasn't an SS guard. He was a kapo—a prisoner who cooperated with the Nazis in running the camps—a trusty, an accomplice."

"Right! To save my own life!" Luckstone had found his voice again and punched the air emphatically with his fists. "But you can't judge the madness, the violence of Auschwitz, by the standards of a peacetime world!"

"We're not here to sit in judgment of anybody, but to see that you confront *your* past, Mr. Luckstone. And the public will confront it too."

"Then tell me what the hell makes *you* so smug, so superior?" Luckstone suddenly shouted at his accuser, totally indifferent to the gun Kurt was still aiming at his head. "I've lived all my life with my past and I've tried to make amends for it. How did you repent for your sins, old woman? At least I've paid my debt to society by giving away millions to the poor and the sick."

"Millions," Hammer snapped, "that you're no more likely to miss than I would a dime."

But Luckstone did not seem to have heard. He kept glaring at his female inquisitor. Then he shook his head.

"I don't understand," he said darkly. "I saw you being shot. You're an imposter, ma'am. Because the woman on the ground was shot. I saw it with my own eyes. Her name was . . . yes, Irene Fischmann."

"Ah!" Irene exclaimed, for the first time seeing her former torturer squirm before her. "You do remember then. You saw me shot by Karl Ludwig."

"You are well informed, I admit. But you are not Kurt Frank's mistress. I saw her shot, saw her body lying dead. I saw it with my own eyes; you are bluffing."

"My name is listed among the dead of Auschwitz, that's true," Irene said. She seemed to grow in stature as she confronted her befuddled tormentor. "And you saw me shot. True again. But I'm no imposter. I was very much alive after the war. I was one of the witnesses at the trials of Höss and Stangl, the commandants of Auschwitz and Treblinka. You can verify this by checking the court records, the transcripts, and the newspapers of nineteen hundred. . . ."

"But I saw you being killed," Luckstone persisted dully.

"And you saw everything leading up to that too, didn't you, in the morning?"

34

The rollcall was at 4 A.M. It had been snowing heavily the night before, and now sharp gusts blew flurries of flakes across the dismal Appellplatz. *An hour later, in the wintery gloom of dawn, the first names would be called out: the 5 A.M. selections for the gas chambers in Birkenau. But already the air stank of roasted human flesh.*

Voices were muffled in the howling wind as the prisoners ran out of the toilet barracks and stood in endless lines, shivering, ankle-deep, in the early November snow.

Everything in the Auschwitz camps was done on the double, and the Sonderkommandos, which included Irene Fischmann, prepared for another busy day of throwing corpses onto the Totenwagen *and the iron racks which rolled ceaselessly into the crematoria. Some of the bodies were not even entirely lifeless yet.* Those prisoners—Mussulmans—*who were too sick, too cold, too old, too weak to rise from the frozen ground where they had collapsed, also were flung unceremoniously onto the* Totenwagen *with the fully dead to be burned, alive, in one of the fifteen crematoria.*

Irene was blue from the cold, the easterly gale knifing into her. Today, the wind had teeth. Her striped uniform hardly protected her, and certainly not the emblem with the red triangle and the yellow line running across it that had been sewn on her jacket. This morning Rachela, a young gypsy girl dressed in rags, helped her toss the bodies up onto the cart. Nearby a Ukrainian guard kept a wary eye on both of them.

Suddenly the guard was approached by a woman SS officer, the dreaded Scharführerin *Schmidt, who whispered something into his ear.* The next second, the husky guard swung around, to Irene and Rachela, and pulled out his Luger pistol.

He shouted something unintelligible in broken German and pointed at Rachela's stained, tattered prison garb. Blood showed on her ripped pants. She was menstruating.

"Dirty gypsy swine!" the guard yelled. He aimed the gun at the 15-year-old girl and squeezed the trigger.

Bits of the girl's brain splattered into Irene's face, a shower of hot, wet, white, red tissue.

Irene wheeled away, about to retch.

"Throw her on cart!" screamed the guard. "Prisoners to be clean. Good camp, this."

The German SS woman Frau *Schmidt* and the Ukrainian guard turned away, grinning and rubbing their gloved hands in the numbing, debilitating cold, set on finding new victims. Irene knew that stalling for only one second meant instant death. The girl who only seconds earlier had helped her handle the emaciated bodies, now herself landed, warm, soft and plump, next to the frozen corpses. Tears stung Irene's eyes; early in the morning she had helped Rachela try to find burdock leaves to stuff into her vagina to block the bleeding. Most female inmates had stopped menstruating, but not Rachela and Irene, being part of the Sonderkommando *team and receiving better scraps of food. And both knew how particular the Germans were about the aesthetics of bodily functions.*

Irene walked faster now to generate a semblance of warmth. It had started to snow again, a squall of flakes, with the temperature hovering between twenty and thirty degrees below zero. The winter of 1944-45 was unbelievably grim. People dropped everywhere from the unceasing cold, from starvation and sickness. They were drugged with exhaustion. The fifteen crematoria were working at full capacity day and night, belching thick smoke and dyeing the heaven a bloody red during the starless hours of the night and black during the day.

While Irene loaded her cart with corpses, a cadaverous woman nearby in zebra-striped pajamas held up her hands, feebly cupping them to catch a few snow flakes. Hauptscharführer *Moll, manager of that part of the camp, immediately came running up the ramp and zeroed in on the female inmate. Moll was well-known as a brute, an unpredictable monster who had made the barbarous business of murder his life's work. Small and stocky, with a glass eye and freckles, his sadism, his lust to kill, was seemingly unquenchable.*

"What the hell do you think you're doing?" he demanded fiercely, his hand already on his pistol as he reached the B2C Women's Camp. "Starting a snowball fight?"

The skeletal, blue-skinned woman stared vacantly at the member of the master race, shaking her head. Her eye sockets were craters of blood. She was almost blind. "To drink it," she said in a hoarse whisper.

"Drink snow?" Moll roared, removing the gun from his holster. "Our water isn't good enough for you, you Jew-cunt? Ungrateful bitch!"

The muzzle of the firearm slammed into her head and the bullet sprayed her skull, blood, mushy brain, in all directions.

Irene closed her eyes briefly, trying to block from her mind the madness she had just witnessed, then glanced upwards in abject despair at the leaden sky. To her surprise she noticed at precisely that moment, high above her, a gaggle of white geese streaming southward in a long, loose V-formation, swiftly straining against the icy wind, as if to escape in a hurry the monstrous stench of death and gloom below. It occurred to Irene that it was the first time she had ever been aware of a bird, a living creature other than a human or a rat, near this or any of the other death camps, as though even those geese could sense the horrendous insanity of murder under their spread wings. And she envied them, their freedom, their peaceful nature, as they vanished one by one, far away in the pastel haze of smoke and hoary sky.

"Irene!"

She spun around, not sure whether to pick up the body of the woman who had wanted to slake her thirst with melted snow instead of her own urine and the contaminated water dripping from rusty pipes, or whether to obey the command of the deafening voice behind her.

It was Glückstein; he had been shipped, with her, to Sobibor, then to Auschwitz II-Birkenau as a Sonderkommando Oberkapo, when Treblinka was closed down in the fall of 1943.

"Come with me!" he ordered, clutching his ever-present piano leg.

"I think Moll wants me to put the body. . . ."

"Moll is gone. Besides, they're already stripping her."

Indeed, like a flock of vultures, a dozen inmates were hurling themselves upon the emaciated corpse and ripping the prison garb off her for their own use, and her soup and urine pot as well.

"I can't," protested Irene. "Kurt told me to operate the Totenwagen today and then to join the Scheiss Kommando."

"My orders come from higher quarters," he thundered. "Don't waste any more time! When you're finished with my job you can complete your other assignments."

There was nothing else she could do. She trailed after Glückstein as he strode briskly across the compound to the hospital. Like many kapos and members of the Sonderkommando, both Glückstein and Irene carried passes that enabled them to traverse freely from one compound of the city-sized concentration camp to another. This included the much-favored Kanada Kommando Camp where the belongings of the millions of murdered prisoners were sorted and readied for shipment to Germany. Nevertheless, in spite of the "privileged" status they enjoyed, their relationship to Sturmbannführer Kurt Frank was a closely guarded secret known only to a few of the Treblinka survivors. Headquartered in Auschwitz's old main camp was the inquisitional branch of the secret police, and this department of the Gestapo spied even in death camps on prisoners, guards, and SS alike, to prevent unauthorized contact between the staff and the inmates; it would have regarded Kurt's connection with Paul Hammer, Irene Fischmann and Ludwig Glückstein with the sternest disapproval. Their recommendation would certainly be that Sturmbannführer *Kurt Frank be sent to the Russian front and the three prisoners gassed.*

Oberkapo *Glückstein had access to some of the facilities in the sick bay of Block 12, the "Infection Hospital." He marched straight into the terminal ward where the patients, dying of medically inflicted SS experiments as well as spotted fever, measles, dysentery, scarlet fever, diphtheria, were lying in their own excrement, with as many as six patients sharing one blood-soaked blanket. Lice were crawling all over them. Rats scurried brazenly across the room, jumped on beds, tore at the bits of flesh that still hung from the bones of the skeletal patients as they lay, helpless, defenseless, on their rotten cots, being eaten alive.*

Glückstein pulled one of the cleaner blankets from half a dozen unprotesting, dying patients and stumped out again.

Next he headed for Crematorium 5, one of the larger, more efficient termination centers, which had the capacity to burn up to 2,000 corpses a day in each of its three ultra-modern ovens. Close-by they could hear the wailing, the sobbing of people, many of whom had been standing naked for hours in the lung-searing cold, outside the "Death Waiting Room," the dreaded Block 25, waiting in line to be gassed.

In the distance the strains of the Blue Danube *waltz could be heard, played by the women's orchestra to keep the death candidates entertained and as calm as possible. Guarding the endless queues of those waiting to be exterminated were a dozen snarling Doberman pinschers and German shepherds straining at the leashes of the SS men. Whenever one of the more recalcitrant prisoners was on the verge of rebelling or keeling over, the dogs immediately yapped at their exposed genitals, and the inmates hurriedly took their places back in line.*

As Glückstein and Irene passed a long column of prisoners, a young Polish boy suddenly realized, as he tried to move forward in the long line to the gas chamber, that his legs would not budge from the place where he was standing. An SS guard not far away yelled at him to keep moving but not even threats seemed to work; he simply could not move one leg in front of the other.

SS Oberscharführer Muhsfeld, who was in charge of Crematorium 2, happened to pass by on his way to supervise the ovens and immediately tried to yank the boy out of line with both hands, but to his amazement could not dislodge him either. Having waited for seven hours, barefoot, in sub-zero temperatures, the youngster's feet had frozen within a solid block of ice, right into the rain puddle where he had been standing.

Infuriated at being made to look like a fool, Muhsfeld ordered one of the SS men to unleash his dog and pointed his crop at the sobbing child. The German shepherd at once lunged for the boy's genitals, and in one ferocious mouthful ripped the penis and testicles out of the eight-year-old's groin. A wild bestial scream blasted out of the child's throat. The blood flowed from him, as though from an open faucet, onto his ice-embedded feet. But the cry lasted only for a matter of seconds. Because an instant later the dog, crazed by the taste of blood, leaped at the child's throat and tore out his jugular.

Weeping women walked quietly around the dying youngster who simply collapsed in his own puddle of blood, audibly breaking one of his ankles as he fell, while Muhsfeld continued on his way to Crematorium 2, humming along with the melody played by the women's orchestra.

Glückstein hardly paid any attention to this commonplace spectacle. He pulled impatiently at Irene's wrist, dragging her alongside him to the new music bandstand where another Strauss waltz by the women inmates was getting under way.

"Under the platform!" Glückstein ordered.

"What?"

"I said under there. Hurry up now!"

"But why?"

"Are you that stupid? I'm a man, you a woman. Figure it out for yourself."

Love. Lust. Rape. Old principles tumbled helter-skelter through Irene's mind, mingled with the now-familiar taste of blood and execution. The hard kick of her pulse pounded under her jawbone. "You know I can't," she whispered. "Kurt would kill me. And you too."

"He'll never know." He slung the blanket over his shoulder, then tightened his hand around her arm, like iron pincers.

"Someone will see us, Baldwin. Let go! I told you I won't!"

"He's an SS man. We're Jews. Are you going to deny a fellow Jew the only pleasure he can have here when you offer it to that Nazi swine?"

Irene swallowed hard and glanced around, terrified. "Let go! They're watching us. . . . Why don't you go to the Kapo Brothel?"

"Because I want you. You remind me of my wife. Now don't make me mad, Irene!"

She wrenched free of him, turned and hurried away. But Glückstein was taller, stronger, faster, and caught up with her near a mountain of rusty chamber pots that had been used by inmates as soup containers. He grabbed her by the wrist.

"Let go I said," Irene shouted, more frightened than angry, and once more wrested free. "Do you want us both to go to The Showers?"

"You bitch! Come back!" Three long steps, and he grasped her arm.

"Have you gone crazy?" The flat of her palm smashed into his face.

"I'm going to report you. To Kurt himself. That'll be the end of you!"

"Oh no, you won't!" He pressed the words through clenched teeth. "Or do you want me to tell him that I saw you screw Paul Hammer here, yesterday?"

"You bastard! You've been spying on me. You really do want me dead!"

And like a demon possessed, she lunged at his throat, clawing, kicking, biting, scratching his face. Suddenly he jumped back, out of her reach, eyes blazing maniacally, and swung out with the piano leg he was carrying. The first blow struck her in the back of her shaved head.

Something inside her brain exploded. Semiconscious, yet hearing him roar with rage in the far, far distance, she spilled forward limply, sprawling into the snow.

"What's going on here, Kapo?" a voice boomed through the desolate landscape.

It was SS Sturmbannführer Karl Ludwig. He approached swiftly, but Glückstein was totally immersed, blindly encapsulated in his own world of hate, loneliness, rejection, and releasing his unbearable frustration with the piano leg, raining blow after blow on the prostrate woman.

"Stop it!" the SS man shouted. "Step back, Glückstein! You have no business in this part of the camp. I'll finish her off."

Karl Ludwig's authoritarian voice pierced Glückstein's unbridled rage. He hauled off once more, but then moved back a couple of steps, perspiring wildly from the exertion of bringing the massive wooden weight down on his hapless victim again and again.

The SS officer knelt on the freshly fallen snow and rolled Irene over on her back. Something cracked inside her, like an old wooden plank breaking under a heavy footstep. An animal shriek unleashed itself from the depths of Irene's consciousness and echoed through the frosty dawn. She opened her eyes, saw the SS man's emotionless face, above him the black clouds belching out of a crematorium stack. Even in her agony she thought of the soft warm body of 15-year-old Rachela, already being pushed up as smoke through the chimney into the indifferent sky and coming down on the living as flaky grey soot.

From a thousand miles away she heard Karl Ludwig's whisper as he bent over her, and the death agonies emptied her bladder reflexively.

"Open your eyes!" The words came in tiny nebulous gasps through his tight lips and bounced off her eardrum. "When I fire my gun, shut your eyes, and lie motionless. I've got only blanks."

He looked up at Oberkapo Glückstein, who was standing slightly aside, still out of breath. The blanket had slid off his shoulder into the snow.

"She's almost dead," Karl Ludwig said, standing up. "I'll finish her off. Move back now!"

Karl Ludwig swiftly unholstered his pistol, and it was at that very moment that Kiwe, newly promoted to Sturmscharführer, strolled past the odd trio on his way to supervise the excavations for pits to burn additional corpses. He stopped short, surprised by the scene evolving before his eyes. Karl Ludwig now aimed his gun at the rapidly heaving figure of Irene Fischmann and squeezed the trigger three times. At once the body on the ground stopped breathing, twitched once more, then lay absolutely still. Karl replaced his pistol and led Glückstein by his elbow across the road to Compound B2E, the gypsy camp.

Kiwe merely shrugged and headed for the adjacent excavation site. The pits were to be strictly regulation—each 150 meters long, 8 meters wide and 2½ meters deep. Four hundred inmates were laboring on them day and night lately, using shovels, bricks, cement, trowels to add a number of drainage pans. Paul Hammer was one of the laborers working on the enlargement of these ditch designs, scooping earth out of the hole with his spade when he too, like Kiwe, became aware of the bone-chilling scene being played out less than thirty meters away.

Tears sprang to Paul's eyes. The kindhearted woman who had introduced him to the pleasures of sex, who had occasionally let him make love with her since then in Treblinka's Hair Storage Room and the Shoe Depot in Auschwitz while Kurt was away on leave in Zurich, lay murdered in the snow now, her bones shattered—and the man who had killed his mother was responsible, at least in part. Soon Irene, too, would be burned in the very hole he was helping to dig and sculpt. The drainage channels he worked on were to serve as a riverbed for the stream of liquified human fat which would result when approximately two thousand bodies were stacked in layers of three crosswise in each excavation pit and being cremated.

How much Paul preferred his old job in Birkenau's goldsmith workshop, set up in the annex of Crematorium 3. The extracted gold teeth of the corpses were soaked in hydrochloric acid to cleanse them of the remnants of human flesh and bone, then melted in graphite molds with a blowtorch and, for the benefit of the SS, shaped into newly designed pieces of jewelry. How often Irene had tried them on before Paul was to hand them over to the SS guards. Even after this jewelry production, more than twenty pounds of gold were shipped out of Birkenau every day to Hitler's Reichsbank.

But instead, Paul had to work most nights now with the 45-man-strong Ash and Pulverization teams, using buckets to scoop up rivers of human fat that had collected in the earthen drainage pans and pouring it back, with oil, over the burning bodies to expedite their cremation. Somehow, perversely, it reminded Paul of the evenings he had watched his mother baste their annual Christmas goose with ladlefuls of goose fat.

The liquid human fat and lymph poured on the fire shot the flames up househigh, causing the corpses to boil and sizzle and spit. It started with books—the Nazis at the beginning burned books—and they ended up burning bodies. Blisters would rise on their victims' naked skins, then pop. Bellies would strain upward, split open like overripe fruit and expose the entrails of tens of thousands of inmates; their bowels and bladders—visible to all—would bubble furiously, not unlike pork sausages in a frying pan, and mount their own chest cavities, as if the dead—and Irene would soon be among them!—actually performed a danse macabre *for the benefit of their slayers in afterlife*. Other internal organs, lungs, kidneys, would be shifting, bursting, literally exploding with a bang. Finally, their faces would start to glow, to twitch, melt, then suddenly disintegrate—faces, kissed and loved in the morning, became dripping blobs of wax by lunchtime.

Tears rolled down young Paul's face like drops of quicksilver as his trembling hands perfected the drainage pan where the dissolved remains of Irene Fischmann's frail human flesh would soon flow.

35

"A lie! All of it a lie!" shouted Luckstone, trying to block out the memory of the past. Pearls of sweat ran down the sides of his temples. "Irene is dead! Karl Ludwig did *not* use blanks! I saw him with my own eyes a week later when he killed an old German Jew wearing the Iron Cross of the First World War."

"You won't give in, will you?" Irene was shaking all over, her face damp with exertion from reliving the impressions of her harrowing past. "Nothing ever is your fault. You have no morals, no scruples—you never did!"

"Don't you tell me what I have or don't have! With me, it was a question of survival, not scruples. And besides, Karl Ludwig *volunteered* to kill the old Jew."

"Yes, he did," Irene shouted back. "Höss challenged Karl to prove his loyalty to the *Führer* when somebody ratted on Karl, yes ratted on him that I'd been seen alive after he allegedly shot me."

"Kiwe gave Karl away." Hammer's explanation was meant for Irene as well as Kurt and Luckstone. "To *Kommandant* Höss. That's how Kiwe got his next promotion. After he had observed Karl executing Irene, he was sure, like you, she was dead. While I was digging the human fat drain in the excavation pit, I overheard him remark to *Standartenführer* Fritsch, who supervised part of that operation, that he was glad Kurt's Jewish mistress was finally dead. Not just because another uppity Jew was eliminated, but to get even with Kurt for having had fifteen-year-old Luzie killed in Treblinka."

"Kiwe was the worst bastard of all," muttered Luckstone.

"From him I'd expect such senseless brutality," Irene said belligerently. Her eyes were bright with the fever of hate, her cheeks flushed. "But not from a fellow prisoner like you. You started it all, Glückstein, when you tried to rape me. And when Kiwe bumped into me accidentally a week or two later, he knew that Karl Ludwig had never shot me, that his gun contained nothing but blanks."

"Didn't he try to seize you?" Luckstone asked anxiously.

"Of course he did, but I managed to get lost in the work detail nearby and make my getaway to Bunker Five. I knew Karl was on duty there. I had to warn him that he might get reported by Kiwe. And that's just what happened. Kiwe informed on Karl to Höss himself. It was then that Karl replaced his blanks with live ammunition. Höss called him on the carpet, he testified after the war, but Karl claimed that Kiwe must have mistaken another prisoner for me since I had been cremated and was listed as dead. Naturally, Höss wasn't satisfied. And you know what happened next, Glückstein, don't you?" Her voice had become shrill. "I asked: don't you?"

LL moistened his lips with the tip of his tongue and blinked nervously. "Do you have to shout like that, my dear lady? Can't we sit down at least and discuss this in a civil manner?"

"In a civil manner!" Irene uttered a brittle laugh and slammed the barrel of her Colt on the shiny surface of the table. At once, a deep indentation appeared in the wood under the pistol's steel rim. "You of all people have the temerity to pass yourself off as being civil, or civilized? You who instigated this tragedy?"

The veins in Luckstone's temples bulged like blue worms and his frightened eyes swept to Irene's revolver.

"Your gun . . . it could go off if you aren't careful. Please!"

"Are you frightened, Baldwin, of the .45?" she said scornfully, aiming it again at her fearful captive. "You weren't that scared of a weapon when witnessing the scene where *Kommandant* Höss compelled Karl Ludwig to shoot a prisoner with the same gun he had used on me. Oh yes, Luckstone, he did shoot the hunchbacked old Jew who had won the Iron Cross in the First World War, but it was something for which he could never forgive Kiwe, even though a prisoner killed Kiwe shortly afterwards."

"But that old German Jew—he would have been gassed minutes later anyway," Luckstone said miserably.

"My God, don't you understand?" cried the exasperated woman. "That's not the point. Karl had become a murderer at long last. All his carefully laid plans to enter the death camps to help the inmates were demolished at that moment. Killing that old Jew devastated him for years, Glückstein. And you were the one who, indirectly, provoked him to do it."

Luckstone cast his eyes down and said nothing. Everybody was staring at him. Irene waited a few moments longer, but when the silence persisted and no words of compassion, of remorse, were forthcoming, an unspoken anger dormant for over forty years suddenly erupted within and drove her to bang the gun pitilessly on the table, leaving an even deeper depression in the wood.

"What is it, Mr. Billionaire? Cat got your tongue?"

Luckstone finally aimed his eyes at her, a look of hurt on his face.

"The table," he whispered reproachfully. "It's brand-new and. . . ."

"The table?" Irene ranted. "We're talking about life, the life and death of an old man, the danger of Karl Ludwig almost caught red-handed by the Nazis, and you are worried about this damn table!" And for emphasis she battered the gleaming surface several times more with the tip of the Colt's barrel, leaving the mahogany pockmarked with notches and circles. "That's what I think of your table," she shouted. "How can you be worried about dead wood just when I'm through telling you that Kiwe was about to hunt me down, to kill me if fate and Karl Ludwig hadn't stepped in and intervened? Don't talk to me of inanimate objects when I speak of life!"

Luckstone took a deep, tremulous breath. "I'm sorry,"—his voice was husky, contrite, but began to reveal some of his intrinsically hardy nature again—"I am glad, Irene, truly glad that the Nazis didn't catch you—that you got out alive."

"And no thanks to you, either," Irene shot back. She was still flushed with excitement and fighting hard not to let her emotions deprive her of the common sense needed to express herself clearly. "Though sometimes I've felt that death would have been better by far than the agonies I've had to endure since the war. All I could do was curse, curse 'em! God, how I cursed them! Hitler, Kiwe, Höss. But you too, I cursed you to hell with them for what you did to me, to so many. Even to Karl Ludwig . . . I remember him and me standing near the Toy Appropriation Chamber that evening. The sky was orange from the flames of the crematoria. Ashes were falling as usual from the sky, day and night, and I was . . . oh God, I was in such agony, Luckstone—as I am at this very moment—with the shoulder you had shattered. But I had to keep busy; either that or it would have meant the oven for me. So, with the arm I could still use I shoveled the droppings of the dysentery-riddled inmates into a wheelbarrow. At the same time I also kept a wary eye on two German SS men nearby, Boger and Kaduk. Jesus! If you ever wanted to see two homicidal maniacs on a rampage, then all you had to do was to watch that duo.

"I glanced up at Karl Ludwig. He had averted his eyes from them. I think he could no longer bear to watch these two cutthroat mutants; they were using female prisoners, especially young girls, for what they laughingly referred to as their Sunday treats: they jammed the barrels of their carbines up the women's vaginas, then fired a salvo of bullets into them and let them die in agony in the snow. Those two killers happened to be the favorites of *Obersturmbannführer* Mulka, the brutal aide to Höss—and that may interest *you* particularly, Luckstone, so that you don't think you're all alone: for most of the rest of their lives after the war Boger worked as a bookkeeper in Stuttgart, Kaduk became a male nurse in West Berlin, and Mulka a rich coffee importer in Hamburg. Anyhow, when Boger and Kaduk finally passed the Toy Chamber and moved on to look for new wretched prey, Karl lit up a cigarette, and from behind the hollow of his hands shielding the lighted match from the raw wind I heard him mutter to me, 'This morning I killed my first victim.' He looked briefly in the direction of the two shrieking SS guards and dropped his hands. 'Tomorrow,' he mumbled, 'tomorrow I'll be just like them!' It was the last time I ever saw Karl in camp. The next day he vanished from Auschwitz. *Sturmbannführer* Karl Ludwig had gone AWOL. He didn't surface again till well after the war. And you, Baldwin—I repeat—you were the one who had forced him to commit that murder!"

"As God is my witness, I knew nothing about that," LL defended himself forcefully. The veins were throbbing visibly in his temples now. "And if your friend Mr. Hammer had brought Karl Ludwig down here as well, he'd have. . . ."

"You know perfectly well," Hammer interrupted, "that it's impossible for Karl to be here. Don't play innocent with us now!"

"How do you expect me to know about Ludwig's private life? And tell your goon here to put away his gun. We're all unarmed, so. . . . Look, all I know is that Karl Ludwig would have set the record straight if he'd come along with you. Once I'd have explained my side of the story to him, he'd be the first to understand."

"But he *can't* understand, Baldwin," spat Hammer. "You know perfectly well you had him killed."

"I had him *what*? What the hell are you talking about?" Luckstone pounded his fist on the armchair. "I've never had anybody killed, not after the war—least of all a fine human being like Karl."

"You had him killed just last week, liar."

"Last week! You're crazy. I didn't even know where. . . ."

"Don't lie to me, Glückstein! You knew he could reveal the truth about you. He had seen you as kapo in three camps."

"Last week! You must be a raving lunatic! I don't even know where he lives."

"Oh, sure! You didn't personally go out and kill him. A rich bastard like you has thugs to do such dirty jobs for him. They didn't even mean to kill Karl. The bomb they attached to the starter of my rented car was meant for me. But they miscalc. . . ."

"Wait! Wait! Wait! You're babbling like a madman. What bomb? And why in God's name would I want to kill you?"

"Why are you still playing innocent? Or don't you recall what happened when we met a couple of weeks ago?"

"Recall what? That you weren't very polite? Or not too happy about Jesse marrying Nicki? Do you mean to say I would want a man dead because of that?"

"No, Luckstone. You wanted me dead because you knew I had

recognized you as the man who murdered my mother in Treblinka!"

A hush fell over the onlookers in this fierce shouting match. Everybody except John Shadow stared unblinkingly at the accuser and accused. Shadow alone averted his eyes, peering hard at the yellow pad, uncomfortably conscious of the fact that he himself was involved—even if only remotely—in at least one murder tied to the past.

"I what?" gasped Louis Luckstone.

"You heard me. You clubbed my mother to death the day we arrived in Treblinka. February 1943, remember? I told you about it when we first met. You realized that I was a danger to you, that I could spread this part of your past to the public, and you did everything in your power to have me silenced."

Again all eyes fixed on the perspiring billionaire.

"This is crazy, absolutely crazy," he muttered. "I don't have to go on listening to this pack of lies. And you can tell your gangster friend here that I'm not afraid of his gun."

He spun around, away from Kurt who was momentarily left at a loss, and headed for the door. Seething with anger, yet shaky at seeing a buried part of his well-guarded past come to light, he needed to break out of the confines of the room. He tried to yank the door open. It did not yield.

He wheeled on Hammer, infuriated. "We're locked in!" he shouted.

"You're not going anywhere!" Kurt snapped. He had recovered his presence of mind and motioned with his pistol to have him return to his former place. Seeing his exit barred and feeling more than a bit foolish, Luckstone sheepishly moved back next to Grasser.

"You never mentioned a word about this to me when we first met, Hammer," Luckstone said unsteadily. "And let me tell you that a person who can't clearly remember what happened a week or two ago can hardly be held accountable for mixing things up that purportedly occurred more than forty years ago."

"I'm afraid you're wrong, Herr Glückstein," Hammer said, each syllable clear and emphatic. The hour of reckoning finally was at hand.

"I remember exactly how you. . . ."

"Well, you better think again. Because this time I have a witness who can verify that you didn't speak about this to me."

"Oh? And who's that?"

"Your son. He was with us all the time. Go ahead—ask him!"

Hammer slapped his forehead, in disgust with himself. "How stupid of me! You *are* right! I apologize, Luckstone. I didn't bring it up in your presence, after all. It was outside in the garden after you had retired. I described the entire foul scene, in detail. All of your viciousness."

"And Jesse was present?"

"Of course. With this man," Hammer said, indicating John Shadow, who stubbornly refused to look up from his legal pad.

"John!" The word rang out like a name being read out on the *Appellplatz* for the selection of prisoners to be gassed.

The executive assistant looked up, thoroughly shaken. "LL?"

"Just a second, Luckstone," Hammer cut in. "I even came to blows with Mr. Shadow because of one of his insensitive remarks. In fact, it was Jesse and the guy from the White House who pulled us apart."

Luckstone turned to his assistant, his voice overflowing with righteous indignation.

"How come you never told me about this, John?"

The magnate's confidant drew himself upright. "It was a private argument, LL, and there was no reason to burden you with it. As far as I was concerned, it was over and done with."

"He told you about his mother?"

"Yes. But I didn't believe him."

"Then why, Mr. Shadow, did you have us tailed all the way to Karl Ludwig?" demanded Paul Hammer.

"I did nothing of the sort," Shadow said resentfully. "I never had anyone tailed."

"What about the bomb in the car, Mr. Shadow?" Hammer grew increasingly agitated. "What about the bomb in my kitchen that killed my fiancée?"

"John! You?" Luckstone gasped. "Involved in this?"

"I swear I . . . LL." The beleaguered aide did not know which way to turn. "I had nothing to do with any of this. I don't have any hoodlums at my command. The truth is, LL, Mr. Hammer, I forgot all about the incident in the garden after you left."

Luckstone nodded gravely and turned back to Hammer.

"Have you got any further reports on your fiancée's death?"

"Only that Scotland Yard found traces of an explosive device in my kitchen after she was killed."

"Dreadful. I remember now. Jesse brought it up one night recently. I'm sorry, Hammer . . . John!"

"LL?"

"What about Josh? Josh Hamilton! I want the truth, John. Did you discuss this matter with Josh after Mr. Hammer and Jesse left?"

Blood rushed to John Shadow's face, darkening it. His sweaty hands tightly gripped the pencil he had held ever since the breakin.

His voice was shaky. "Vaguely, LL. I do recall talking about it." He cleared his throat. "I was angry about the bloody nose Hammer gave me, so I didn't pay too much attention to what Josh had to say."

"Well, try to remember."

"I'm sorry, LL, I really can't."

"Don't lie to me, damn it! I won't tolerate it! I've always trusted you. Now, what did Josh say?"

"Well, I don't recall exactly; he was a bit vague and. . . ." The pencil snapped in his hands. He looked up alarmed, aware that all eyes were trained on him. "I think he said something about Hammer proving to be a nuisance."

"Ah!" Hammer exclaimed. "We're finally getting somewhere."

"He had no right to take matters into his own hands," Luckstone observed tightly, "matters that were none of his concern."

"LL, they *were* the White House's concern . . . at least that's what Josh said." Suddenly Shadow seemed to have total recall of the discussion near the Rose of Sharon bush. "It would reflect on the President if word got around about your responsibility in the death of Hammer's mother. Also it might result in another Watergate scandal, he said, with the President's friend and adviser—a Jew moreover—portrayed as some kind of war criminal. And then Josh wanted to know how it would look to have the Chief Executive come down here for the opening ceremony of Luckstone City. But most of all he hated to think what might happen to the funds your companies had earmarked for the Presidential campaign, if any of this became public."

"Then why in hell didn't you tell me what he was after?"

"LL, I swear I didn't know what he had in mind."

"You certainly had enough common sense to come to me with his fears, his thoughts. You heard what happened to Karl Ludwig and to Hammer's fiancée. You should have spoken up when Jesse first raised the issue."

"LL, let's be fair here," Shadow had recovered some of his suave urbanity now that he felt reasonably sure that the finger of guilt pointed at Josh Hamilton, not himself. "There is no absolute proof that those deaths can be attributed to Josh."

"Of course not, damn you! Do you imagine, his men, probably CIA, were going to leave clues all over the godforsaken place?"

"We're talking about more than two murders," Hammer interjected. "All together, there have been four attempts on my life. Surely even you can't chalk them all up to coincidence."

And Hammer briefly summarized the experience he had with Danielle in the Cotswold Hills and, a few days ago, the fire in Kurt's basement room in Kaisersdorf. At the same time he elaborated on the death of Karl Ludwig and the fact that the London gas company had no records of ever sending any repairmen to his flat. And that the Jewish tenant in Kurt's building was away in Paris.

"Hitmen," Luckstone said in a conclusive tone of voice. "The typical work of hitmen."

"Right," Hammer agreed grimly. "*Your* hitmen!"

Luckstone's head whipped around to his accuser, eyes blazing with anger. "Don't you dare blame me for these murders! This time I'm *not* guilty! Not of *those* crimes!" he shouted, beside himself, and shaking his fist at Hammer. "I had nothing to do with it, and if I had known about this plan I would have done anything in my power to prevent it. But I knew about none of this because he didn't inform. . . ."

Suddenly the torrent of words came to a dead stop. Luckstone's head swerved around to John Shadow who had been following the angry outburst of the two men in stunned silence. The aide blinked nervously and unconsciously twirled the broken pencil stubs in his hands as he felt the full force of Luckstone's wrath descend upon him.

"You. . . ." The financier struggled for words. "You could have prevented this, Shadow," he roared. "You could have saved the lives of these people if you had only opened your mouth."

"LL . . . I. . . . What could I . . . Honestly, LL. . . ." Shadow stammered, breathing quickly and turning deep crimson.

"Because of you, two innocent people have been murdered," Luckstone thundered at his hapless aide. "You could have mentioned your fears to me, but you chose to remain silent. You could have saved two lives by speaking up, but instead you did nothing. Goddamnit, Shadow, you had it all figured out! *Didn't* you? . . . You thought you were in the clear yourself, not connected with murder, just like the good little Germans under Hitler who shut their eyes to the concentration camp massacres. You knew what Josh had up his sleeve just like the Germans knew what happened in the camps since 1933. But like them, again, you did not want to get involved. Shadow!" Luckstone bellowed with his gargantuan voice. "You really wanted Hammer to die, didn't you? Didn't you?"

"LL," Shadow stuttered as his jowls began to tremble like glazed jello. "I swear I didn't know what Josh planned to do. All I. . . ."

"All you did was to keep your mouth shut, you moron!" Luckstone stormed. "And now they blame these murders on me. Do you know what you have done, Shadow? Destroyed me. Yes destroyed me! For four endless decades I've tried to make amends for the horrors I was forced to commit in the camps. For forty years I've tried to help the sick, the rejected, miserable people of the world in order to make my own life livable. And then you come along and ruin it all with your cowardice. You coward—you miserable coward! I don't want you around any more. Do you hear? I can't trust a coward like you. For thirty-five years you have betrayed me! Shadow you are finished! Two weeks severance pay is too good for trash like you, but I. . . ."

"What're you talking about?" Shadow raised his voice in a high-pitched crescendo of hysteria and bewilderment. "You can't . . . you can't do this to me! I've worked for you day and night for over. . . ."

"For thirty-five years," the billionaire continued for him, rampantly. "And all this time you have stabbed me in the back!"

"I have *not*!" Shadow's scream matched the fire-red glow of his face. "I did it to protect you. I swear, LL. I've served you faithfully, selflessly, day and night, for over thirty-five years, and you have no reason, no right to dismiss me like this. I even stood by you when my son asked me to choose between you and him. You have no right to do this to me, I'm telling you, to toss me aside like this, as if I were a piece of garbage."

"That's what you are!" roared the billionaire. "Garbage! And don't you dare tell me what I can or can *not* do. You're no longer working for me, Mr. Shadow. That's final!"

It was more than Shadow could take. The challenge hurled at him by Luckstone seemed to have the opposite effect of the one intended; it put starch into his backbone. He had nothing to lose. A towering fury, at seeing his lifetime service so ruthlessly trampled upon, replaced his former subservience. He stood up and confronted Louis Luckstone.

"I'm sorry . . . but I refuse to leave," he stated flatly. "There's nothing you can do about it. You hear? Nothing! Nothing!" He had calmed down somewhat, but was still breathing heavily and defiantly stuck out his chin toward his employer. "I know too much. You can't get rid of me that easily, LL. I won't let you! I'll simply stay. I know too many secrets about your corporations. I know all about your killings in camp, as a kapo—*they're* the witnesses!—and I know. . . ."

"You have the nerve to blackmail *me*?" The enraged financier screamed. "You scum!"

He lunged forward, fastened both hands on his former assistant's chest, picked him up in an outburst of titanic strength and hurled him backwards with a mighty shove, propelling him off his feet into a collision with the wall. John Shadow slumped, dazed, to the floor and sat there in a motionless heap.

"Get out of here, you wretched bastard!" Luckstone yelled. "Get out and stay out! And don't expect to work for any corporation, in this country or abroad. Believe me, Shadow, I'll give them all one hell of a reference when they ask about you!"

"No! He's going to stay!" Kurt's commanding voice rang out. "Let him hear what we've got to say about the man he's served so selflessly."

Luckstone was panting now, his face ashen, with a shiny film of sweat on it. He glared at Shadow, as though seeing a cockroach on the floor.

"It's his last day with me, anyway," he said with difficulty, suddenly short of breath. "What I want to do now when I'm calmed down a bit . . . is to call Josh Hamilton at the White House and tell him . . . to have his men lay off you." He turned back to Hammer. "To stop any further action against you."

Kurt shot a quizzical glance in the direction of Hammer, who nodded. The billionaire shut his eyes briefly, then lifted the receiver and dialed the number that gave him direct access to the White House aide's desk.

Hamilton himself answered the phone. In as few words as possible Luckstone summed up what he had just learned, but, as expected, the White House aide denied any implication in these vile deeds. However, when Luckstone brought up the man in the red woolen stocking cap spotted by Hammer, there was stunned silence at the other end of the line. Luckstone warned Hamilton that if any further attempt were made on Paul Hammer's life, the entire sordid scheme would be reported by him personally to the "Chief" and to the news media.

Luckstone slammed the receiver on the phone and collapsed into the nearest armchair, rubbing his eyes. He looked drained. His eyes were red when he looked up and focused on Paul Hammer.

"Who are you? I honestly don't recall your face."

"Does the name Michelangelo mean anything to you . . . Baldwin?"

"Michel . . . oh! The boy artist—of course! You were . . . how old?"

"Fourteen."

"You painted the clock on Treblinka's railway station. It was always six o'clock, wasn't it? Or was it three o'clock? And you planted the forget-me-nots around the SS mess hall and designed jewelry from the gold teeth Irene had to extract for the guards."

"How well you remember," Hammer said, slowly moving from one end of the conference room to the other, fingering objects here and there. "Then you will recall the day I arrived with my family."

"The day you arrived?" Luckstone mumbled. "No . . . no, I don't."

"Do I have to remind you of the way *Kommandant* Stangl ordered me to draw a sketch of him and then of his adjutant? And when my mother interfered, saying that I shouldn't show off with my temper, you came swooping down on her like a vulture and struck her in the back with your piano leg, killing her on the spot. It was the blackest moment of my life, Glückstein," Hammer said.

He was shaking all over. "I swore that if I ever got out of that hell and met up with you, I'd avenge my mother's murder, somehow. But you probably don't even remember them, all your murders. After all, it was just an hour or two later that you were told by Kurt Frank to get rid of Luzie, the blond girl who Kiwe had his eyes on. So you clubbed *her* to death in the *Lazarett*. At least she fell into the fire and was cremated right away. Not my mother, though. They dragged her, like a dead cow, by her legs down to Camp Two, where they pulled the marriage ring from her finger and asked me the next day to melt it down and use the gold for a swastika pendant one of the SS men wanted for his Polish whore. I touched that ring, Baldwin, the ring I had kissed a million times whenever my lips brushed my mother's hand, and I wept. But you wouldn't remember that day, would you, Glückstein? Not when you murdered dozens and dozens of your fellow inmates over the next two years. . . . Come on, at least have the decency to look at me!"

Total stillness met this outpouring of torturous reminiscences. Even Grasser, the bodyguard, stared aghast at his employer.

"I said: look at me!" Hammer stormed once more at the battered, old man, as if to squeeze the last of the toxic past, like pus, out of his bursting heart. "Even now, Luckstone, at this very second, I still remember—over the stretch of all those decades—the *eau de Cologne* scent of my mother's skin as she tucked me into bed in Munich and kissed me good night, her soft cheeks against mine; only you, Baldwin, you alone were the one who had added the taste of blood to this beautiful memory, and you murdered part of me too!"

"I didn't . . . I didn't mean to kill her," at last came the broken reply from the armchair, "just to push her back in line."

"But you did kill her. You broke her neck. You broke Luzie's neck. You were trying to break Irene's neck. Of course, these were all accidents, weren't they?" Hammer waited for a reply, but there was none. "Come on, answer me! I asked you if. . . ."

The shrill ring of the telephone cut into Hammer's tirade. Every eye flew to the gleaming white phone on the buffet, then back to Luckstone.

"Pick it up!" Hammer ordered. "One false word and he'll blow your brains out."

"It's only the switchboard," Luckstone said feebly.

"Tell them you don't want to be disturbed for the rest of the day."

Luckstone picked up the receiver with a trembling hand and after listening for a minute mumbled a few words about having Kuwait call back tomorrow and then relayed Hammer's instruction not to pass on any more calls for the remainder of the day and to tell the staff to stay clear of the Executive Mansion later that evening. Suddenly he felt utterly spent by the events of the afternoon; he slumped back in his chair.

The ramrod-stiff imperiousness and self-confidence that had sustained the lord of the manor for decades was crumbling at last. As he glanced up at his merciless prosecutor, tears began to glisten behind his horn-rimmed spectacles and run down his cheeks.

"The SS had marked almost the entire transport for death," he said huskily. "Thirty minutes later she'd have been dead."

"That's not the point, damn you!" Hammer shouted. "That's the way Karl Ludwig had to rationalize it for the rest of his life after shooting the hunchbacked old Jew. Every second of life counts, you bastard."

"She would have died anyway," Luckstone repeated dully.

"But why at the hand of a Jew?" Hammer screamed. "From one of those Aryan Hitler fanatics you'd expect this horror. They were only too happy to mutilate and kill. But why a Jew?"

"It was an accident," Luckstone said miserably, clutching his hands in his lap.

"Like the blows to my shoulder?" Irene asked bitterly. "My life ruined by an accident?"

The conference room burst with the deafening sound of silence.

36

"And what about *my* life?" Kurt Frank suddenly spoke up, his voice rumbling with suppressed anger.

Luckstone's head whisked around, astonishment replacing the deeply etched pain of reliving the terrible past he hoped had died.

"You too? I killed. . . ?"

"You betrayed me. I saved your life a thousand times. Without me you'd be ashes, Glückstein."

"Your voice." For the first time since the break-in, Luckstone concentrated hard on the stooped colossus in sunglasses. A deep frown engraved itself on the tycoon's brow as the mystery of the elderly man's identity fell away layer by layer. "Your voice," he muttered again. "Could it. . . . No, yours is hoarser . . . deeper."

Luckstone rose slowly from the armchair, took two, three steps backward, then stopped behind the chair, gaping at what appeared to be a hallucination. He was silent for a very long time.

"That's right, Ludi," Kurt said, removing his sunglasses and slipping them into his jacket pocket. "I'm alive. I'm free."

"You . . .You. . . ." A tremor raced through Luckstone's large frame.

The next second every muscle, every sinew in the body of the seventy-year-old magnate tautened, like a bow-string too tightly drawn. Something inside his body seemed to snap. A moment later his hands reached forward, his body flew through the air, lunging at the former SS officer's throat. The sound of his cry curdled the blood of the startled onlookers—an inhuman shriek of rage. Caught off guard, they watched in horror as the butt of Kurt's pistol smashed into Luckstone's face—with such force that LL fell back with a shout of pain, tripping over the arm support of the easy chair behind him and flopping clumsily into its seat.

"Again! You did it again!" Kurt bellowed, waving the firearm in Luckstone's face. "You virtually had me killed forty years ago. Now you're doing it again!"

Luckstone's glasses lay askew over his nose. He righted them and peered up through swollen eyes. "You. . . . It's you! . . . Of all people. . . . *He's* the one who turned me into the monster you despise," Luckstone suddenly yelled, totally unconcerned about the danger of Kurt's gun going off in his face. He addressed the shocked group around him. "*He* alone is responsible for it all."

"I saved your life," Kurt bellowed back, gesticulating wildly with his pistol. "I saved his life. I never touched him. I saved the life of his daughter. Or have you already forgotten, Mr. Luckstone? I saved your Inge. For almost three years I kept her in my room, all through Treblinka, Sobibor and Auschwitz. No harm ever came to her—no one could touch her. I could have sent her to The Showers but wouldn't"

"Because you were after my money," the financier fumed. "Not for any love of Inge."

"But I did love her. And it was *my* money. Irene, Paul, tell him; let them all hear whose money it was."

"Excuse me for asking." There was a clattering sound as, like an unwieldy beast, Shadow raised himself awkwardly from his inconspicuous position on the floor. His head was a balloon of unbearable pain and it surged in deep waves through his body. His voice came out thinly and shakily, not resolutely as he had intended it to be. "What money? Prisoners had money in death camps?"

Luckstone turned toward his questioner, glared at him full of loathing, and turned back without a word to his nemesis, Kurt Frank.

"Sir," Irene explained quietly, in agony herself, "they're talking about postwar money. This man here is Kurt Frank. He was the Deputy Commandant at the extermination camp of Treblinka, and at the end its chief."

"Jesus Christ!" Grasser muttered under his breath. "An SS officer?"

"That's right," Hammer elaborated. "Killing, hanging, gassing, whatever—to him the Hitler period was the good old days. He never denied his guilt."

"And he's free? Free to walk the streets?" Grasser was plainly perplexed.

"He has paid his debt to society, the authorities say. He spent thirty-eight years in jail, most of it in solitary confinement."

"Maybe he's free but as guilty as ever," Luckstone said bitterly. "None of us are without guilt. But he's the guiltiest. And you were his whore, Irene. Making love to this monster for two years is nothing to be proud of. You have no right to single me out. Kurt Frank, you, me—we're *all* guilty!"

"Not *equally* guilty, though, Glückstein," Irene said grimly. "But it's true: there's more to Hitler's death camps than the skeletons the world knows from newsreels. I make no bones about. . . ." Irene stopped abruptly and pinched her eyes closed. "Oh my God!" She gulped for air. "The pain!" She began to tremble violently. The .45 Colt dropped out of her hand, landing noisily on the mahogany table, and she grabbed for something inside her pocket. "Water," she whispered as her right hand plopped a large red pill into her mouth. "Some water . . . please!"

Luckstone looked down at her disdainfully. "You come barging in here, Irene, threatening me, and now I'm supposed to wine and dine you?"

"Get her some water, damn you!" screamed Hammer, outraged. "You're not in Auschwitz now playing kapo. The *water!*"

"Here!" Shadow had rallied enough to find the moral and physical strength to pour Irene a glass of Perrier on a sideboard buffet. He shoved the wet glass hastily across the table, spilling some of the water, and she took two, three desperate swallows, then sank back on her chair, her face a mask of wax, and picked up the pistol.

"I admit it," she gasped out the words. "To stay alive, I pulled the rings off the gassed inmates, and—yes—most of the jewelry went to the Reich Property Office, but the biggest baubles were skimmed off the top of the buckets, by me, for Kurt. . . . Those were some of my sins, my crimes. . . .But then *you*, you took over, Glückstein. You can't hide this fact . . . and your other crimes were far grimmer!"

The industrialist regarded the group of listeners morosely. "No good denying it now that it's all out in the open," he said. "And it's true, Kurt and I were best friends once, like brothers. We. . . ." He stopped abruptly and gazed at the tortured figure of the old woman with the gun. "Are you all right, Irene?" But she did not react one way or another, simply stared at her tormentor. "I'm sorry . . .about my behavior just now . . . as I am sorry about so many things I've done in my life. . . . But what could I do? . . . What could *you* do, Irene? Or Paul Hammer. Survival in that hell had nothing to do with decency or morals. . . . So I killed those who were doomed to die anyway, and in return Kurt kept *me* alive."

"Tell them why," Kurt prodded his former captive. "Go on!"

"Please. . . ."

"No, *you* do it." Kurt demanded. "Tell them!"

Luckstone rubbed his eyes under his glasses and heaved a deep sigh of resignation. "When Kurt's suitcases were jam-packed with jewels, gold, diamonds and silver, even cutlery," LL spoke slowly, as if each bit of recollection caused him great pain, "and he got his leave every three months, he went to my uncle in Zurich. Uncle Harry was a financier, a banker, who promised to store it all in my name for the postwar period. Kurt had a stake in keeping me alive, so he could collect half the fortune Uncle Harry was stashing away for me."

"Holy smoke!" Grasser blurted out in astonishment.

"Yes." Kurt nodded gravely. "That's what it boiled down to—smoke! Our agreement went up in smoke. He cheated me out of my share after the war. And I still don't understand why!" Kurt's voice brimmed with indignation and anger. "When I kept you and Inge alive, at the risk of my own life."

"I'm not accountable to you for anything," Luckstone shot back. "I've been trying to atone for my sins for forty long years. But you. . . . Even *today* you show no compassion, no mercy. You are *still* driven by greed and hatred. A murderer without a conscience!"

"I *paid* for my crimes," the ex-SS officer exploded. "While you ended up in a palace! You were *never* deprived of the luxury you always knew. With all your acts of penitence you *never* felt pain. Never! I should have killed you that last day in Auschwitz! At least I would have been spared your stabbing me in the back."

"Well, you didn't. Because without me you wouldn't even have made it into Uncle Harry's office in Switzerland after the war."

"And without me your daughter would have been cremated," Kurt Frank snapped back, "even as late as January the eighteenth 1945."

"The eighteenth? . . . Why that particular date?" Grasser asked, mesmerized by the violent exchange of words between the two erstwhile comrades.

"Because it was the day the Nazis, and Ludi and Inge and I retreated from Auschwitz," Kurt explained glumly. "One crematorium was still in operation that day, so his daughter *could* have been fed to its flames. But we were all driven by fear, the fear of discovery of what we had done, and we escaped. Even our precious billionaire here."

"I told you the past is dead for me," Luckstone said irritably.

"But not for us," John Shadow protested, feeling increasingly confident now that he had adjusted to the notion that he was free at long last. "I think we're entitled to know what sort of man is so saintly that suddenly he feels he can't tolerate even a wretched sinner like me under his roof."

"Shadow is right," Hammer agreed. "If you've got a different version of the past, Luckstone, you'd better tell us now. That way our stories won't clash when we call the reporters tonight and give 'em *our* version!"

"Reporters!" Luckstone blanched and clutched at his heart. "Why do you want to do that? Call the media."

"To let the world know the *real* Louis Luckstone."

"You can't do this to me, Hammer." LL sounded genuinely alarmed now. "I won't let you!"

"Oh yes you will! And don't think you can stop us," Hammer warned, "because my attorney will be informed that we are here. You've always been a danger to us."

"Your attorney! Why? You think I'm going to have you bumped off, or something? Like in gangster movies?"

"You have been an executioner before," Kurt took up the verbal onslaught. "So we've come prepared for all eventualities. Jesse will get a registered letter tomorrow with instructions to forward Paul's enclosed list of accusations against you to his lawyer—provided, of course, Jesse doesn't hear from us in the next three days."

"You needn't have bothered," Luckstone said wearily. "Murder is no longer part of my life. . . . All right, Kurt, go ahead. I can't bear to talk about those last days of the war. You tell them."

Completely unabashed, Kurt Frank selected some refreshment from the buffet behind him. "I remember it like it was yesterday," he said, munching noisily on a handful of grapes. "January eighteen 1945. We had taken two new suits out of the Clothing Acquisition Hall and changed in the gas chamber where *Frau Lagerführerin* Mandel and the SS woman Irmgard Grese kept their rabbits in hutches. We. . . ."

"Rabbits in a gas chamber?" John Shadow shook his head skeptically.

"Yes, Mr. Shadow. Except for Crematorium Five, none of the gas chambers and ovens had been in operation since late in November '44, after Himmler got in touch with the Allies and told us to lay off." Luckstone winced at the mention of this reminder, but the others appeared to be virtually hypnotized by the ghoulish details dug up from the war criminal's memory.

"Remember, Ludi, how the SS rounded up tens of thousands of inmates while we were leaving and how they marched them hundreds of miles through the deep snow to Buchenwald and others to the Mauthausen concentration camp, in Austria, where *Kommandant* Ziereis had most of the survivors shot at once?"

But a glacial silence met this historical footnote once more.

"Soon after, on January twenty-second, the Russians liberated a relatively deserted Auschwitz. Anyway, after that Thursday the eighteenth, we crisscrossed Europe for about three months, always on the lookout not to be caught by the Red Army or the Gestapo. But finally we made it. To Italy, to Lake Como. That was early in May 1945." Kurt halted his narration for a short breather, grabbed a Golden Delicious apple from the sideboard and took a huge bite out of it. "So, the day after we reached the lake we decided on crossing the border into Switzerland, at Chiasso. We had dinner in Como that night—right?—on an open-air dining terrace, and during espresso you said you'd call your uncle in Zurich to tell him we were safe, that you were alive and we'd be at his bank in a day or two to claim our wealth. We were so happy we had survived the war and were together again, like brothers. Only I didn't realize at the time that you hadn't called your Uncle Harry at all but the Military Police stationed nearby. You told them that if they were interested in catching the last commandant of the Treblinka extermination camp, all they had to do was to pick him up after midnight in Room Twelve of Como's finest hotel, the old Albergo Metropole-Suisse. And they did. At midnight. You weren't even in the hotel when they arrested me. You didn't even have the courage to face me at your hour of betrayal. It was the last time I saw you, at dinner in that hotel. You and the millions of dollars I had to kiss good-bye."

"*Whose* millions?" shouted Luckstone. He had become more and more agitated while listening to Kurt. Once again he rose awkwardly out of his chair. "That money wasn't yours or the Reich's property by a long shot. It wasn't. . . ."

"Nor yours, you bastard!"

"Nor mine, right!" exploded LL. The two former friends faced each other like old bucks squaring off for the fight of their lives. "Did you really think I gave you away to the police just to enrich myself with the loot of Hitler's murdered victims? Did you? Then you're sicker than I thought. Because ever since the day my family was put to death, *Herr Sturmbannführer*, I vowed to bring you, all you mass murderers to justice one day, and that was the main reason I handed you over to the authorities. But to put your filthy mind at rest," Luckstone drove at his torturer contemptuously, "I gave it away, all of the plundered wealth, over the years. More than six buckets of it, twenty-five million dollars worth. I gave every penny away to the poor, the starving, the sick, many times over since that day on Lago di Como. I had invested it well. Oh, I admit I double-crossed you, Kurt, with the grimmest pleasure. Without scruples or guilt feelings, any more than you had scruples or guilt feelings when killing thousands of prisoners."

Luckstone stopped briefly to sip from Irene's glass of Perrier.

"And hard as you may try to put me before the bar of justice, you can't convict me of a single offense today."

"Try you perhaps, but not convict—true!" seconded Paul Hammer. "It's so easy to brainwash yourself into believing that you acted irrationally in irrational times, that you really were a hell of a guy but committed those crimes under pressure—and, of course, only to save your own skin."

"How the hell would *you* know about what goes on in my mind?" Luckstone stormed back. "You know nothing of the torture I'm going through. Even today. Of the fire inside me, you swine!"

"Sounds familiar, Baldwin, you calling us swine," Hammer said cynically. "The good old days, huh?"

"Yes, damn it, I killed. But I killed not to *be* killed." The room filled with his virulent bitterness. "Not to have my daughter killed. She was everything to me. Everything I had left."

"So was my mother!" Hammer overshouted him.

"And *my* family," Irene spat at the ex-kapo. "All gassed."

"That's why we're here: to make you face the consequences of your actions, Luckstone," Hammer said firmly. "For forty years you've lived behind a smoke screen; now let the public that loves you know who you really are."

"All right, go ahead!" Luckstone screamed. "Tell 'em! Tell 'em everything. And don't forget any details! I'll come along and help remind you. Not just the list of *my* crimes. Let 'em hear about what happened *after* I was welcomed to Treblinka in 1942. Some of the crimes, *Herr Sturmbannführer*, for which you have *not* been tried yet."

"Ludi!"

"Are you afraid, *Herr* SS officer? Why not give *me* a chance, for once, with *my* story? And *then* let 'em judge me!"

37

On arrival in Treblinka the filthy, starved, stupefyingly exhausted prisoners were immediately sent to The Showers, also known as The Factory, to be gassed. In Auschwitz

II-Birkenau, the children transported from Theresienstadt received priority and also were gassed or drowned immediately. But some of the tiny tots in Treblinka received special treatment.

Inge Glückstein's brown hair fluttered in the breeze as she walked between the towering SS man and her father. They rounded the corner of the Textile Storage and Bakery Building and walked down Kurt Seidel Strasse. By the time they had come to an agreement about the best way to convert the looted jewelry into hard cash in Zurich, they had reached the Roll Call Square.

At the far end of it, near the fake ticket window of the station, they observed half a dozen SS men milling around a few of the youngest children from Glückstein's transport.

"Look, Papa!" Inge suddenly cried out and pointed to the group in the distance. "Over there! Klaus!"

Glückstein had spotted him too. It would have been hard to miss him. His three-year-old son was wearing a tiny sailor's suit with a marine cap sporting a long black ribbon that hung halfway down the back of his navy-blue uniform. Inge tugged at her father's hand and the three quickened their step.

"Thank God, he's alive," Glückstein sighed. "Kurt, you've got to hide him too."

"No!" the Commandant's adjutant said sharply. "Stop!"

He grabbed Glückstein's elbow, then came to a halt behind the huge coal pile near the entrance of the Station and Roll Call Square.

"Can I play with Klaus, Papa?" Inge lifted her chocolate-smeared face to her father.

"Can she?" Glückstein turned meekly to Kurt Frank.

"No! Don't move. Just watch them!"

The curt, uncompromising reply drew Glückstein up short. All of them now peered around the corner of the mountain of coal and watched the congregation of burly SS men and the children in their soiled Sunday clothes walking about aimlessly, so it seemed.

"Those women," Glückstein furrowed his brow, "off to the side of the SS officers, aren't they from the trainload too?"

Kurt nodded. "They'll be the housekeepers and concubines of the officers. They're the mothers and sisters of the kids."

"What is it all for? What on earth are they doing now?"

Two medium-sized military trucks slowly, ominously, approached the small crowd and backed up, stopping with their rear axles facing each other, about ten meters away from the children. The drivers did not get out. They kept the motors running. The sun had vanished; it had become bitterly cold and everybody was blowing into their hands and stamping the ground with their feet. The blue had seeped out of the sky and left an overcast heavy with snow as fitful dark clouds sailed swiftly across the landscape.

"What the hell do they intend. . . ?"

Glückstein felt Kurt's hand tightening its grip on his elbow. He raised the collar of his jacket absently to protect himself against the raw wind and rubbed his stubbly chin as he watched, at first with apprehension, then with a growing sense of horror, when a couple of SS men fastened an iron-link chain around each of the ankles of a four-year-old girl who was wearing a corn-blue bonnet and matching coat. Next, they hooked the other ends of the chains to the rear bumpers of the two trucks and stepped back.

"Kurt, they aren't. . . ."

A snappy command from one of the SS officers crackled across the wide square. At once, blueish fumes billowed from the exhaust pipes of the two trucks and enveloped the puzzled child in its clouds.

One of the young women close-by rushed forward, thrusting out her arms to her daughter, but an SS guard grabbed her by the sleeve and yanked her back brusquely, screaming at her.

The next second both trucks jumped, leaping forward at thirty or forty kilometers an hour. The loose chains straightened, pulled up, tightened. The girl's body literally flew two or three meters up into the air and the tautened chains ripped her legs from her body, splitting it up the middle, guillotining the helpless little torso in two as if a meat cleaver had come down hard through the middle of her.

A blood-curdling shriek soared across the square as the girl's legs snapped, were torn out of their joints, her pelvis. They came off the rest of her body, and part of the young torso dangled unsymmetrically from each of the chains. Long unwinding entrails plopped out of the child's lower trunk and blood poured out of her onto the cobblestoned ground. The blue bonnet that, moments earlier, had slanted coquetishly askew on the smiling girl's chestnut hair now sloshed forlornly, like a drifting sailboat, on the wet red cobblestones among her bowels and intestines. But she still was not dead. She was screaming horrendously, an unending, mind-piercing scream that shrilled through the desolate morning. Cries and unrepressed sobbing of the female onlookers mingled like a Greek chorus in the background, and the mother who had borne, nurtured and formed the fetus for nine long months of creation under her breasts, hurled herself on the bloody remains of her young daughter as the trucks braked to a halt. One of the guards immediately rushed forward and dragged the sobbing woman, her clothing dripping with the girl's blood, from her daughter, or rather the part of her daughter to which the screaming head still was attached. The mother struggled with the guard, but with all his strength he still had great difficulty restraining her. Then, suddenly, he withdrew the pistol from his holster, aimed it at the mutilated four-year-old, fired, and literally blew her brains out.

At this signal, two zebra-striped, pajama-clad kapos came bolting out of the Reception Camp pushing two wheelbarrows, unfastened the lumps of flesh and bones from the chains, dumping the two half-carcasses into their wooden carts, and wheeled them off on the double.

Glückstein lifted Inge in his arms. She was whimpering softly, not quite sure what to make of this distant scene of insane horror. He pressed her face gently down into his shoulder. Tears dribbled down his unshaven cheeks as he turned to Kurt. Any spoken questions appeared redundant.

"It's to keep the women in line," Sturmbannführer Kurt Frank remarked idly. "To let them know the same punishment will be meted out to them as to their children, their little brothers and sisters, if they don't toe the line, our line. And the same thing Ludi, is going to happen to Inge if you don't play along with me."

"To Inge? I thought you said she. . . ."

"She'll be with me as long as you help me with the jewels, and do your job as a kapo in getting rid of the scum that arrives here every day by the thousands."

"What do you mean, get rid?"

"Kill them."

"I already told you I can't kill. I simply won't!"

"You'll learn. Just consider the alternative. You and Inge both will meet the same fate . . . as Klaus is going to now!"

"What?"

Panic, abhorrence, madness raged in Glückstein's eyes. He spun around, staring, stricken with terror, across the huge cobblestoned square. Even Inge was startled by her father's exclamation and looked in the direction of the children and SS men in the distance.

"He's next," Kurt announced stonily.

Glückstein gaped at his captor and let Inge down on the pavement.

"You don't mean. . . ?" Anguish choked the question in midsentence.

"C'mon, you've got eyes in your head. They're chaining him to the

trucks."
"No!"
Like a crazed bull let out of its pen, Glückstein burst from behind the pile of coal. Danger was forgotten, the fear of death, of torture, non-existent, as he raced across the station square, Inge trailing behind him. At the other end, the drama about to unravel came to a dead stop. Everybody looked up, dumbfounded at the sight of a solitary inmate running toward them, pursued by a small girl and the second-in-command of the extermination camp. One of the SS men at once raised his carbine and took aim at the obviously escaping prisoner.

"Don't shoot!" screamed Kurt, trying to keep up with the demented father. "Put that gun down, Miete!"

The guard lowered his rifle, and the group of Waffen SS *waited in amused silence, expecting Kurt to catch up with the fleeing inmate and meting out his own version of the "final solution."*

Nobody paid any attention to the little girl tagging behind them, way behind, stumbling and falling and crying for her papa to slow down. Finally, she shouted her brother's name, and Klaus skipped around and hopped up and down with the sheer joy of seeing the people he loved most and wanted to hug, the chains all the while clattering noisily around his ankles.

Out of breath, Glückstein dropped to his knees, flung his arms around the small boy in the navy outfit, smothering him with kisses, sobbing, his tears wetting the cold, downy cheeks of the child.

Kurt was totally exhausted from running. Chest heaving, he leaned forward with his hands on his kneecaps, trying to catch his breath after reaching them.

Unterscharführer *Miete, one of the most remorseless bullies and killers in the camp, stepped forward and cocked back the safety catch of his rifle.*

"Want me to finish them off, Herr Sturmbannführer?*"*

Kurt looked up, his heart hammering away painfully. "No! He's my kapo. My personal kapo. I'll decide what to do with him."

"Jawohl, Herr Sturmbannführer." Miete clicked his heels.

"Glückstein!" Kurt shouted, still out of breath, but the father did not seem to hear; he simply hugged the crying, hungry child and whispered soothing words into his ear. "Glückstein, I'm addressing you. Stand up!"

The command echoed back and forth in the wind across the mammoth square and finally penetrated Glückstein's conscious. Slowly, the new inmate got to his feet but still held on to his son's tiny hands.

"Glückstein, I don't want you to have any misapprehension about the value of life among prisoners here. All of you count for nothing. We're the law here, and what we say will be carried out. You obey me, or you and your two children will die now! Verstanden?"

Glückstein stared hard through his tears at his former friend, aware that there was no escape from fate, and that Kurt, indeed, was master over life and death here. The new kapo nodded wordlessly.

"You address me as Herr Sturmbannführer," snapped Kurt.

"Yes, Herr St. . . ."

"To test your loyalty as my new kapo, you will carry out your first order this instant."

"Jawohl, Herr Sturmbannführer."

"You will receive a gun with one bullet in it and you will shoot your son."

Chuckles rippled through the cold morning as the SS officers watched Glückstein intensely.

The latter stood absolutely still, petrified. He could only shake his head. His eyes again overflowed with tears. Klaus tugged at his coat and began to grimace as if he, too, were about to start crying.

"No . . . no, Kurt, I'm his father," Glückstein said brokenly. "Anything . . . I'll do anything, but don't ask me to. . . ."

Kurt's fist smashed into Glückstein's face.

"Kurt? Did you call me Kurt, you Jew-bastard?" His powerful voice bounced off the square's surrounding buildings. "I told you to address me as Herr Sturmbannführer." The laughter among the SS men now subsided; they were anxious to miss none of the evolving drama. Only the wind could be heard howling across the spacious station plaza. "I'm talking to you, Jew-prick. How are you going to address me?"

Blood dripped out of Glückstein's nose. He sniffled and wiped it with the back of his hand. "Herr St. . . Herr Sturmbannführer."

"Correct. All right, Miete—your Schmeisser, not the rifle."

Miete stepped forward and handed the gun to Kurt. There were six slugs in the revolver. Five were emptied into Kurt's hand. One lone bullet remained in the pistol.

"No tricks now or all three of you will die. Take this gun and put a bullet between his eyes. You obey, and you and your daughter will live."

Kurt grabbed Glückstein's right hand and slapped the Schmeisser into it. Glückstein stared at the firearm as if it were an object of an indecipherable nature, then shook his head. His lips began to quiver, and he looked up.

"Why?"

"Because I say so."

"I can't, Ku . . . Herr Sturmbannführer. My wife, my parents, you've already wiped them out, and now you want. . . . Have mercy on me! Please!" he sobbed. "Don't ask the impossible of me . . . killing my own. . . ."

"The impossible?" screamed Kurt. "In this camp nothing is impossible. My orders will be carried out!"

More sobs broke from Glückstein's lips. He dropped again on his knees and embraced his son tightly, burying his face in Klaus's cap.

"Papa, don't cry." It was Inge who had reached the two and was wrapping her arms around her father and brother, completely out of breath.

"Herr Sturmbannführer," Miete addressed Kurt Frank.

"Shut up! . . . All right, Sau-Jude, what is it going to be? Death for all three of you? Or are you going to obey my order?"

Slowly the tear-streaked face peeked up from the four little arms encircling their father.

"Death, Herr Sturmbannführer," came the choked up reply. Glückstein again burst into tears. The guards kept watching the scene in tense silence, saying nothing. The group of female prisoners in the background stood riveted, like statuary, shivering, hungry, fearful it would be their turn next.

"Again?" Kurt demanded angrily.

"I don't care what you do. Kill us. Kill my son. But don't expect me to do it."

Like an audience at a tennis match, all eyes swerved back to Kurt Frank now. The SS colossus towered over his prey.

"So you refuse to obey my order."

"Herr Sturmbannführer . . . I have nothing to lose. We're as good as dead anyway."

"All right, you asked for it. The gun."

Blinded by tears, Glückstein stood up and handed the pistol back to the uniformed barbarian.

"Jew-coward that won't obey orders must be taught a lesson, and I'm going to teach you a lesson you won't forget. Ever!"

With this, Kurt removed another Sarotti bar of chocolate from his pocket, tore off its wrappings and broke off a piece. Squatting down in front of Klaus, he held the morsel of food out to the three-year-old boy. Famished beyond description, the child broke away from his father and snatched the candy out of Kurt's hand. Having gone without food for two days, he stuffed it into his mouth and wolfed it down greedily.

"You want some more?" asked Kurt.

The child nodded wordlessly, licking the sticky remnants off his stubby, little fingers.

"All right, Klaus, do you see this?" Kurt pointed to the Schmeisser in his hand, and the boy again nodded. "You see, Klaus, there is some milk chocolate in this barrel. Now if you want more candy, all you have to do is to put the barrel here into your mouth and then hold it like this and squeeze the trigger. Do you want to try it?"

Before the little boy had an opportunity to react to this offer, Glückstein's voice bellowed out, "No! You can't do this. Not to a child!"

He was about to step forward and pull his son away from Kurt when two SS men pounced on him and pinned both arms behind his back. A third officer, Miete, grabbed Inge by the scruff of her neck, yanking her back with such brutality that her head collided with the stock of his carbine and she started crying.

"You see, Jew-scum," Kurt said matter-of-factly, still holding the Schmeisser. "There's no evading the issue. The boy's got to go. I'm doing you a big favor in letting him go as painlessly as possible. All you've got to do now is watch."

"I won't! I won't! Let go!" Like a madman struggling to free himself, he tossed and twisted in the grip of the two SS men, but it was no use. "Kurt, kill me," he screamed. "Anything, but don't let me. . . ."

"Shut his fat Jew-yap!" Sturmbannführer Frank's voice thundered over Glückstein's.

A leather-gloved fist immediately crashed into the prisoner's mouth. Blood poured from both nostrils this time and from a split lip onto his coat's lapels. His sobs became hysterical, a choking jabber of pleas and tears. He spat out more blood and a tooth, then pinched his eyes shut as Inge started to cry bitterly. She had wrested free of the SS guard who held her, ran to her father and buried her face in his coat.

But Miete would have none of this. He dashed after her, roughly jerked her head back by her hair and barked at her, "Stop bawling, you kike! Stop it, I say, and watch your yid brother!"

"And you too, Glückstein," Kurt snapped at her father as Inge continued whimpering. "Watch him!"

He rose to his feet and handed Klaus the weapon.

"No! Please, Kurt!"

"Shut up! And stop shutting your eyes! . . . Perschke!" he shouted to one of the SS men pinning Glückstein's arms behind his back. "Keep his eyelids open!" While the other SS guards held both of Glückstein's arms up by their wrists, Perschke immediately grabbed the two eyelids with both hands and pulled them up savagely so that Glückstein was compelled to watch the imminent suicide of his small son.

Kurt guided the barrel of the Schmeisser pistol into Klaus's mouth and placed the child's hands carefully around the butt of the gun. The youngster at once started chewing the barrel.

"No! Don't chew it. The candy is far inside," Kurt reminded him amicably. "It will only get into your mouth if you squeeze this trigger. Now will you pull on this?"

The pint-sized boy nodded soundlessly, eagerly, intent on concentrating on the enormous task ahead and its sweet reward at the other end.

The pistol was heavy, very heavy, all metal, and colder than a snowball, and Klaus's little arms, tired from lack of nourishment, sagged. His hands were so small that they had difficulty reaching around the Schmeisser's stock and encircling the trigger with his two tiny thumbs. But the child knew that the prize was worth the effort. He was so hungry, and by pulling the trigger, lots of chocolate would pop into his mouth.

He did not understand why his papa was crying and the tall men clasping his hands behind his back, and why Inge was sobbing and keeping her eyes closed tightly. She was always such a funny, laughing girl and hugging him, even when she let him pinch her nose, and now this big soldier was making her cry. He'd ask her why after he had eaten the sweets. Ah, it wasn't so difficult. The trigger began to yield and move back. To make sure he would get lots of candy he shoved the barrel deeply into his mouth. There! And the tall men in uniform liked what he was doing. They kept laughing, applauding, cheering him on. Good, the trigger was almost all the way back now and with one last, big effort he could. . . .

The gun leaped out of his hands. A blinding flash. The entire top half of the child's head blew off. Sideways. Bone. Brain. Eyes. Nose. Blood. Splattering on Kurt Frank's uniform. He jumped back, furiously brushing the skullcap's remains from his tunic, but large gobs of blood and slimy ropes of brain clung tenaciously to his sleeves.

Roars of laughter burst out of the SS men, then more wild applause. When the unconsolable screams of the child's father threatened to dampen their amusement, one of the guards whipped out his firearm, leaped at the hysterical man and mercilessly pounded his face with its butt until he was silent.

Sturmbannführer *Kurt Frank* advanced on the profusely bleeding prisoner and wiped the barrel of the Schmeisser on Glückstein's coat.

"*A bit of your flesh and blood, Papa, so you won't forget your yid of a son—and stop that jabbering!*" he commanded, disgust exacerbating the contempt in his voice. "*Listen to me, Jew-filth! Listen I said.*" And he yanked up Glückstein's head by his hair. "*You saw what happened to the little vermin. If you don't do as told, we'll have you watch the same thing happening to Inge. That clear?*"

"*God! God!*" Ludwig Glückstein wailed, the tears blinding him as he looked up at his tormentor. "*Where is God? Why does He allow this to happen?*"

A clenched bony fist flew into Glückstein's face. Fresh blood poured down his chin onto his soiled overcoat.

"*You're calling on God, Jew-pig?*" the SS officer roared at his captive. "*God has nothing to do with this. He doesn't live in this camp. God only gives you life and death. What lies in between is up to us. And you. Only the strong survive. And you've proven yourself to be weak. A coward. Now clean up! Tomorrow you kill your first Jew, kapo!*"

38

As Luckstone finished his tale, there was silence in the beautifully furnished room, broken only by Irene's muffled weeping.

"Perhaps now you'll understand why I turned into what you call a monster, a killer," Luckstone said hoarsely, the lines in his face stern, severe, showing no emotions, not even hatred. "Why I became so eager to please Kurt. Yes, I learned how to kill all right . . . kill to keep my daughter alive, to spare her a death like Klaus's. I suppose after a while people are capable of getting used to anything, any excess, except having the will to put an end to it. Even so," he shrugged fatalistically, "before I was able to kill others I first had to kill my own true feelings. I had to sever the link that ties human emotions to what went on around me. What else *could* I do?" He glanced at his audience, but their eyes avoided his.

"The alternative would have been madness. Or death, with no outsider ever being the wiser for it. Besides, the Nazis didn't want to leave any witnesses behind, anybody who could create a world different from Hitler's. Even rebellion didn't uproot him; his accusers simply wriggled from piano wires and meat hooks into oblivion. And I had no intention of being among the forgotten heroes. Murder was my only gateway to life, Irene—and so I killed, killed indiscriminately the living dead to right the monstrousness of the Holocaust after the war. I never asked who my victims were—Jews, Christians, young or old. Neither did the SS. Oh sure, the German SS hated the Jews. But that wasn't why they killed so ferociously. Their real motivation was to keep their records untarnished and avoid being sent to the Russian front. To be pure and innocent in the eyes of their superiors meant far more to them than to be pure and innocent in the eyes of some abstract concept, such as world opinion, or conscience. No argument about it, it dehumanized them, all of us, but that was of secondary importance. The main concern was our careers, our lives, and the knowledge that we could only be safe by anticipating the will of our superiors. I desperately tried to anticipate Kurt's orders, he in turn tried to anticipate *Kommandant* Stangl's orders, even though he hated, sometimes even challenged him; Stangl tried to anticipate Globocnik's orders, Globocnik tried to keep Himmler happy, and Himmler tried to anticipate the will of the *Führer*. Our world had become topsy-turvy. The chain of command did not work from the top down. It was reversed. Orders from above became almost superfluous because they were superseded by our own eager initiative from below. The twentieth century Dark Age of the Barbarian was complete.

"To please Kurt, Irene became his mistress, his housekeeper and later handled the jewelry end of the business, with me, pulling the rings off the fingers of the gassed inmates, and both of us saw to it that they were delivered safely to Kurt's office."

"Something occurs to me just now," Kurt Frank cut into LL's train of dusted off memories. "Himmler had appointed a German lawyer, Konrad Morgen, at about that time, to investigate widespread corruption among the SS troops in Nazi concentration camps. He even came to see Stangl, but he never found out about our scheme. Thank God!"

"It would have meant instant death, even for Kurt," Luckstone agreed, nodding emphatically. "But things worked in our favor. Kurt knew the jewelry would be secure in Zurich, so he treated me well. I always wrote Uncle Harry a brief note to convince him I was alive, and Inge added a few lines too. Kurt even took pictures of her playing with some dolls. Irene had taken them from children who were gassed. As I said, our operation went smoothly. It had to, or we'd all have ended up in The Factory and someone else taken our place. Hammer is right, though. I killed his mother. Not because she was his mother, or Jewish, or Aryan, but to show my superiors that their trust in me was not misplaced. And to save the life of my darling daughter."

"Finally!" shouted Paul Hammer. "At long last you admit it! That you had been dehumanized enough to murder my mother."

"Yes, yes, yes, damn you; yours and a dozen like her!" screamed the enraged billionaire, rising to his full height. "And you would have done the same if you'd have known that your mother might be ripped apart by two trucks. I make no excuses for it, Hammer. I no longer can. I was one of them. Dehumanized. That is the major tragedy of totalitarianism: that bestiality is not only ordered from above, but that it is executed spontaneously by the rank and file. Of that I, too, stand accused. Go ahead—broadcast it to the world for all I care! At the same time, though, don't you play the smug, sanctimonious victim whose innocent nature is crying out for revenge. Because you, too, though only a boy at the time, were guilty."

"Me! Me guilty?" Paul Hammer banged his fist on the table. "How in hell can you say that I'm also guilty? I never killed a soul in my life."

"No? Are you sure, Michelangelo?" taunted the ever more confident financier, now that he was free of the burden to hide the truth. "Do I have to remind you of 1943? The summer of '43?"

"What in the name of God are you talking about?"

"Ah, so you have a short memory too, Herr Hammer?" Luckstone burst into a sly grin. "Think again! Forty years ago, Kurt and his gang of cutthroats kept us busy, didn't they? We sorted out millions of pieces of clothing, books, razors, toys, kitchenware, so that the Nazi soldiers at the front were well cared for and their German families back home also could be supplied with what the SS had plundered. And when you and Irene weren't busy stealing valuables for Kurt Frank and the Third Reich, or converting some of the gold into jewelry for the guards and their families. . . ."

"Those were orders I was given!" Hammer turned purple with indignation. "I never stole a ring from a dead prisoner. The SS brought the jewelry to my goldsmith workshop and left instructions what they wanted done with it—mostly swastika pendants. How dare you insinuate that I was involved in your wretched acts! I was just a workman."

"Wrong, Herr Hammer!" A glint of triumph shone behind Luckstone's spectacles as he helped himself to a peach and bit lustily into it. "Perhaps you have forgotten your guilt, the way I've tried to block out mine for the last four decades. But late in the summer of 1943, there was a period when no transports arrived in Treblinka for almost four weeks. We were all in the same boat and getting increasingly nervous. The *Goldjuden* and *Hofjuden*, the carpenters, shoemakers, tailors suddenly found themselves without a job. There were no inmates to be gassed, no coats and suits and toys and pots and pans to sort out, no jewelry to be fused or gold to be annealed. That chore had been completed five days after the last transport arrived. There were no executions, no whippings, no sports events.

"In fact, Kiwe was already debating whether to open up the gas chambers just for you inmates in the goldsmith workshop, since there was no jewelry left to work on. But Kurt overruled him because he knew that the goldsmiths were too valuable to be eliminated just yet. Still, all our rations were reduced to two dry slices of bread a day and a cup of water. Even the SS guards were scared that there would be no more transports and no need for them in camp.

"They thought they'd be sent to the Eastern front to fight the Russians. Everybody frantically sought ways to keep busy, because we guessed that the time was at hand to gas the whole bloody lot of us, you, me, Irene, all the work-Jews, in Camp One and Two. Almost a thousand of us. I even remember you, Paul Hammer; you wangled a job feeding the exotic birds near Stangl's old billets. Then I saw you planting new flowers—forget-me-nots also—around the SS officers' munition depot, even repainting the Treblinka sign at the railroad station, rebaptizing the town Obermaïdan. And some of us worked on an offshoot of the *Ansiedler Strasse*, lengthening the Road to Heaven by a hundred and fifty meters." For a moment LL dried his sticky fingers on a damask table napkin.

"And right plumb in the middle of that hiatus, in July '43—a week or two before the prematurely triggered prisoner revolt—Himmler transferred Stangl to Italy and Kurt became Treblinka's last *Kommandant*. He had saved our lives for obvious reasons, but even he did not know whether to exterminate all the work-Jews now, the *Kommando Totenjuden*, and the rest of us. Moreover, by July '43 more than eight hundred thousand gassed Jews that were buried in mass graves had been excavated by us on Himmler's order, and the makeshift crematoria had burned all of them, so now there was nothing left to do. As a last resort, Kurt told us to decorate a guard house in medieval style and reconstruct the old barracks in the architectural style of the Middle Ages, hoping that Obermaïdan would come to look like a fortress of Teutonic knights. A place of history and putrefied madness! Remember?"

Irene nodded, recalling the insane horror only too well.

"Then one stifling hot summer day," Luckstone continued, "SS man Otto Horn lit up the 'Roasts,' the crematoria. The thirteen gas chambers that could kill up to twenty-four thousand inmates a day were readied, and Kurt ordered the kapos and *Kommando Arbeitsjuden* assembled on the *Sortierungsplatz*. Kurt Frank was there, as were Kiwe, Miete, Mentz, Münzberger, Horn, Gretter, Petzinger, Karl Ludwig. There were big grins on their faces, as if they could hardly wait to see trained personnel like us, our bodies, turn yellow from the carbon monoxide of the gas chambers and then go up in a roar of flames on the Roasts."

LL stopped for a second to wipe his mouth with the napkin.

"This was it, we whispered to each other. Remember, Irene? You were crying. And you too, Paul Hammer. A fourteen-year-old boy, and not even a Jew. We were herded to the entrance of the Tube, the Road to Heaven, that led to the gas chambers, and the SS officers encircled us. There was no way of escaping. We knew we were finished. And it was then that Kurt made the announcement: there were new convoys on the way carrying twenty-four thousand Bulgarians, with the first train scheduled to arrive early next morning. And do you recall what we did, all of us, including you, Herr Paul Hammer, and you Irene, and me, when we heard that news? Well . . . *do* you remember?"

Nothing but deadly silence followed the question.

"We cheered! Damn you, we cheered! We shouted Hurrah! And when the SS saw us cheering, they burst into even wider grins, and they shook our hands and asked us to join them in a drink. Or do you deny any of this?"

Nobody uttered a word of contradiction, or even moved. Remembrances had chilled the blood of the listeners, and stamped their faces in cast-iron guilt.

"They realized that we had become like them," the billionaire continued darkly, "baptized in the fire of death and destruction. They had some schnaps with them, and we toasted the arrival of the new transports, with the SS guards, and we got drunk together. Yes, you too, Hammer. We passed the bottles and drank from them; right at the entrance of The Tube to the gas chambers we squatted, and then we embraced—are you listening?—you and I *embraced* the only time in our lives! You, Paul Hammer, actually hugged your mother's murderer. And then we embraced the SS men, we were so happy, and loved them for not being gassed by them. And would you believe it, they hugged us back, and we sang the *Horst Wessel Song* together and *Deutschland, Deutschland über Alles*."

Paul Hammer did not move; he was absolutely transfixed, rigid, with shame, with humiliation. "Whoever battles with monsters," he muttered, "had better see that it does not turn him into a monster. Nietzsche said so a century ago."

"And he must have had you in mind, Herr Hammer," Louis Luckstone thundered, "When it was *you*, yes you yourself, who asked that bastard Kiwe if we could assist in driving the Bulgarians with whips into the gas chambers next day. Maybe it was the schnaps talking, the gratitude of being kept alive, but it's no good denying you didn't make the suggestion. You see, even Irene remembers. Look at her nodding. Kiwe, of course, agreed on the spot, and that's exactly what we did, Herr Hammer. Join the devil in his handiwork. Killing gratuitously. Kiwe insisted that all of us work-Jews participate in this woeful spectacle. Eight huge convoys of twenty-four thousand fat Bulgarians lugging suitcases crammed with the finest sausages and cakes and candied fruits. You were drunk with power, Herr Hammer, grateful to be spared their miserable fate, and goddamnit we whipped the poor bastards into The Showers."

Far away a bell chimed five times, deep mournful sounds.

"It took a week to cremate them after that—men, women and children—because they were so fat.

"And I even pretended not to see you, Herr Hammer, when you were ordered to help Irene in the Sorting Barracks with unpacking and collating the Bulgarians' clothing, their toys, medicines. You two were alone, and you were busy screwing among the suitcases, Herr Paul Righteousness Hammer, and don't bother to deny it! I'm sorry, Kurt, but your faithful mistress liked to shop around once in a while for another piece of meat. Though she steadfastly refused to have anything to do with me."

"Is this true, Irene?" Kurt Frank's voice trembled with reproach, betrayal.

"You were the one who ordered me to have sex with her," Hammer snapped angrily at the ex-SS man. "Just don't give us that holier-than-thou attitude now!"

"It's not the sex that bothers me here, Hammer, but the timing!"

Luckstone drove on relentlessly. "First kicking the Bulgarians, stripped of their clothing, into the gas chambers, and then, as the icing of the cake, to fuck your favorite woman on mountains of suits and dresses still warm from the bodies going up in smoke outside the window."

Paul Hammer slumped on a chair, next to Irene, and both of them cast their eyes down on the guns in their laps. Retribution was stone-dead.

"No, I make no excuses for myself," the tired industrialist concluded. "I can't any more. But tell me, Herr Hammer, how are you going to explain away your Treblinka behavior when addressing the media tonight? As a temporary excess of youthful zeal? Or will you admit that the brutes had turned many of us into depraved beasts, like themselves?" He paused long enough for a reply, but when none was forthcoming he faced Hammer directly. "No, sir, make no mistake about it: none of us here is among the unsung heroes of the war, like your parents and the White Rose group they belonged to. And don't entertain the idea that we can count ourselves among such exalted heroes as the Danes and Raoul Wallenberg and Eric Erickson and Sigrid Lund and the Countess Maria von Maltzan or the Schindlers and Kolbes and Korczaks and Wirkusses and the Swedish church in Berlin. Because we can't. We don't belong in their class. Indeed, the sooner we realize what unmitigated bastards we were the better for all of us. We had become Nietzsche's monsters. And you, Herr Hammer, you have opened this can of worms yourself and they're crawling all over you too now!"

39

Silence was the only answer as bit by bit the serpents shed their skins of guilt, and let the past lie there, discarded, bleeding, for all to see in the modern elegance of the conference room.

There just seemed to be no adequate response to this flailing, furious assault, no boomerang of retaliation. And when no counter-charge was in the offing, no defense voiced, Luckstone began prodding again, more calmly now that his initial passion had passed.

"As you can see, you're as guilty as I am, every one of you," he said broodingly. "We're all in the same boat. We all stand condemned. Just keep this in mind, you're as rotten as I am, Paul Hammer, give or take a degree or two. In fact, maybe more so. Nobody forced you to hug Kiwe, or to volunteer to drive the Bulgarians with whips into The Factory. You did it gratuitously, of your own free will. I was blackmailed into killing the inmates. You and Irene. . . ."

"Just shut up now, Glückstein!" Hammer suddenly flared at the astonished financier. "Don't you twist everything around as if I were the black pariah and Irene the despised outcast while you're just an innocent victim of circumstances. I warn you, Luckstone, don't push your luck! You've had nothing but good fortune since leaving Auschwitz, while we had to struggle and claw our way out of the gutter. Even your daughter Inge was saved."

"Don't you bring up my daughter, you son of a bitch!" Luckstone exploded with a ferocity that made the others wince. In a completely unexpected fit of fury, he swept ashtrays, tumblers and ledgers from the table onto the floor and rose to his full height. "How dare you even mention my daughter, you lump of shit! What do you know about Inge? Nothing! Absolutely nothing!"

"I know what everyone knows: that she's Nicole's mother," Hammer shot back, slightly startled by the vehemence of the billionaire's outburst.

"You know nothing! Nothing! She was all I had in the world, you ignoramus, and all you know about her is that Kurt kept his side of the bargain and did not kill her. He *had* to keep his word. Because if he hadn't, I would have forced him to send me up the chimney. I would have had nothing left to live for. She alone gave me the courage to endure the monstrosities in the camps, and without me Kurt would not. . . ." Luckstone stopped in mid-sentence and glared at his bodyguard. "What the hell do you think *you're* doing?"

Listening intently, Grasser had lit up a cigarette and was exhaling a long jet of smoke. He stared at his employer, utterly flabbergasted.

"Put that goddamn cigarette out!" rampaged the tycoon. "I gave you no permission to smoke. From now on *no*body'll smoke in my presence again—ever! Do you hear? The smoke of the crematoria was enough to last me *ten* lifetimes. It *still* burns in my nostrils. Put it out I said!"

Flinching at this new burst of ill temper, the bodyguard at once dropped his Chesterfield and nervously stubbed it out in one of the ashtrays on the floor.

"All right." Luckstone was perspiring freely now and seemed to have difficulty calming down. "Now then—Kurt Frank was *forced* to take care of us, of Inge and me, forced especially to see that I wasn't included in the selections for gassing. The promise of reward, of riches after the war, gave him enough reason to keep me and Inge alive. The fear of death, of Inge being tortured, put me on the devil's side. And there you have it in a nutshell," he sighed. "Fear and reward, the ever-present incentives serving as the spur for all human activity. Yours, mine, Kurt's. And Kurt was right in what he said earlier about the day we fled Auschwitz. But he didn't tell you everything. With regard to Inge." He mopped his brow with his handkerchief.

"Kurt had swiped two suits and an SS uniform in the camp, and extra dresses for Inge," the financier continued. "But wherever we went after that, mingling with the refugees streaming west, the Russian planes bombed us, all over East Prussia, and only in late winter, in February 1945, we crossed into Germany proper. Kurt reported at once to a Nazi aid station, near Frankfurt an der Oder, and was given a couple of parcels of garments and food. I remember unpacking them in the shelter where we were holing up, and as we unwrapped them we realized that they were the very articles Paul and Irene and I had packed eighteen months earlier, after the fat Bulgarians were gassed in Treblinka. But there they were: the salamis, and cookies in jars. Only that the Ruskies didn't give us much peace to enjoy our feast. Again we were bombed out." He shut his eyes momentarily as if to block out the horror of the blood-soaked past.

"But you survived," whispered Irene.

"What?" LL startled, peered at her. "Yes . . . And no," he said. "We slept in barns, foraged for food on farms, but were always on the lookout for the Gestapo, not to be caught by them. Or by the Russians. The war was drawing to a close, and at the end of April we slipped overnight across the Austrian border into Italy. By that time we had thrown away the SS uniforms and were wearing civilian clothes only."

"But why go to Italy?" asked Hammer. "I thought you wanted to reach Switzerland."

"It was impossible to cross the Swiss border from German soil. Our plan was to enter Switzerland, unnoticed, from the Italian side, at Chiasso, near Lake Como where only a few days earlier Mussolini had been shot with his mistress. But Como was swarming with Allied soldiers at that time, so we could travel only when it was dark." Luckstone took a deep breath. "And then it happened."

"What?"

"One night, while crossing a large railroad yard, Inge tripped over some tracks. It was pitch-black. We couldn't see a thing, only heard the sound of an approaching train. Kurt and I called her name, dozens of times; the noise of the locomotive became so loud that she didn't hear us, or maybe she had panicked in the dark. Her shouts became more frantic, she was calling for us, but we couldn't see her. It was still wartime, and the locomotive headlights were almost totally blacked out." LL paused briefly, barely aware that Irene was covering her eyes.

"The train struck her at full speed." Luckstone's voice sounded flat, lifeless. "It never noticed the tiny obstruction, simply ran over her small body time after time as the rows of wheels severed her legs. We had no idea she had been hit and continued calling her name over and over after the train had passed. But there was no reply, only the wind moaning in the telegraph wires overhead and our own steps crunching on the gravel, the coke between the railroad ties. I was in a frenzy, running around in the dark shouting her name. An hour or two later the sun rose over the endless iron tracks. It was then that we spotted her, about a hundred yards away, in a pool of blood, her two legs sheared off just above her kneecaps." Tears rolled down LL's cheeks as he paused briefly.

"Like a broken doll she lay in the cold dawn of an Italian railroad switchyard, and we raced across the tracks and knelt at either side of her and stared down at the little corpse. It was the end of the world for me. I started sobbing, and as I looked up noted tears in Kurt's eyes—the only time I ever saw him cry.

"He bent over her mouth, put his ear to her heart and shook his head. Only the whites of her eyes showed, staring blankly at the fog above us. Tears were blinding me. I was paralyzed with grief. To have lost her hours after crossing to safety was incomprehensible to me, especially when she had lived through three concentration camps. Somewhere, far away, a shot rang out. I remember it echoing back and forth endlessly among the columns of boxcars, like the dying beat of a heart.

"Kurt then picked up her two legs, I her cold body, and we carried her, without exchanging a word, across the railroad yard, around the waiting freight trains, into a wood nearby and there, outside Como, we buried her with our bare hands between two tall cypresses at five o'clock in the morning.

"I had nothing left to live for. My life was meaningless without Inge.

My entire family was gone now, wiped out. It was the punishment God meted out to me for my atrocities in the camps.

"For about a week we traversed Northern Italy, like gypsies, sleeping in woods, cattle cars, gardens, vineyards, talking only about Inge until, almost as if by catharsis, we had burned the worst of our grief out of our hearts." He wiped his tears away with his truncated thumb.

"Then we heard, in May, that Hitler was dead, the war over, and we decided to start a new life, finally to claim the valuables stored in Zurich. That evening we strolled down the via Bellinzona into Como, rented two rooms in the Albergo Metropole-Suisse and—well, you know the rest from Kurt, how he was arrested around midnight after I alerted the Military Police. I watched him being taken away by the uniformed officers from across the street in a dark doorway, and I wept. I never loved a boy as much as Kurt. I never hated a man as much as Kurt. All I knew was that I had to make amends for my sins, and that could only be done by obtaining an enormous amount of wealth. Wealth meant power, and power meant the ability to pay my debt to society. I made my fortune and paid out hundreds of millions of dollars to soothe the horrendous wounds I helped to inflict on the world—to soothe my own wounds.

"A year later I married and my second wife had a son—Peter, who became the father of Nicole in 1965. It helped a little to have a family again, but it all turned ugly once more when . . . first my wife left me for another man, and a few years later Peter was killed, with his wife, in a plane crash. Then their son Eric, Nicole's twin . . . decapitated. . . . And now I ask myself: who'll be next?" Luckstone's face shivered in an uncontrollable spasm of tics and twitches. "Why is it, Lord . . . why is it that all those I love must die?"

Nobody moved or spoke.

Memories, steeped in unbearable pain, submerged Luckstone's listeners. Not even Grasser was exempt. Like lightning, an event—mired in the psychological mud of four endless decades—suddenly flashed through his conscious: how his best buddy, Pfc. Terson, was killed near Bataan when the Japanese tied him up inside a canvas bag with two starving animals—a cat and a dog—and then hurled all three of them off a cliff into a river, hoping that Terson would be scratched beyond his endurance by the crazed animals before drowning.

Paul Hammer's remembrance, on the other hand, anchored thousands of miles to the west, on the ice-bound plains of Auschwitz: here, ambulances with large red crosses painted on their sides constantly crisscrossed the various camp sections but never picked up a single dying prisoner to take him or her to a hospital; instead, the ambulances were used exclusively for transporting cartons of poison gas pellets.

Bataan, Auschwitz, Hiroshima—it had long become apparent to everyone present that World War Two had not simply killed man; it had killed the very essence of what it meant to be human.

PART FOUR: THE FINAL RESOLUTION

40

"Those were dark, blood-stained days." Luckstone gulped for air and slumped back into his chair. "It was an insane world . . . horrible . . .violent . . . different from ours. . . ."

The sound of a gun clattering noisily on the mahogany table drew everyone's attention to Irene. She looked up at Luckstone, massaging her wizened hand.

"For forty years I had wanted to kill you, Glückstein," she said haltingly. "And now that I have the automatic and listened to you I can't. And I don't know why."

"And I don't know what is worse," Hammer observed grimly, laying down his weapon. "To hate you and to make this hatred the focal point of my life. Or no longer to hate you and feel cheated, empty. . . . My darling mother . . . unavenged . . . dear God!" His voice broke. "Not hating you any more, Luckstone, does it mean I'm betraying her?"

"No!" Luckstone shook his head vehemently. "No mother wants her child to go through life, seething with hatred. I can't ask your forgiveness, Hammer; I don't deserve it. By all means, go to the press and report me. Even so, I feel at peace now. For the first time in my life. You tell them your story, Hammer. I'll tell them mine. Only let me—and please don't think I'm attempting to bribe you—let me make life more comfortable, for you and Irene. It's the only way I know to ease my conscience, the only weapon I have to atone for my crimes. Don't misunderstand me; I want you to do what you have to do, regardless."

Hammer narrowed his eyes, perplexed. "What are you talking about?"

"I'm going to set up an annuity so that every year, for as long as you will live, and Irene, you'll each receive a check of one hundred thousand dollars."

"One hundred. . . ." Irene's jaws slackened. She even stopped massaging her dead arm.

"I'll also see to it that you'll get the finest medical treatment, Irene. I wish I could undo that horrible, unforgivable scene in Birkenau and give you back the full use of your arm, but. . . ."

"Don't, Luckstone, I beg of you," Irene broke in softly. "I know you mean well. But I don't want your money."

"What!" This time it was the financier's turn to look puzzled. "Why the devil not? What are you saying?"

"Whether I live in a palace or my own little attic, I'll still be in pain. My body is shattered, my life, my spirit are broken. Every waking minute I'm in agony, even now, regardless of whether I'm surrounded by riches or not, and I just want to be left alone and go home to my room and. . . ."

She could not continue speaking and lowered her head.

"Irene, you must allow me to make the last few years of your life as painless as humanly possible," Luckstone said somberly and approached her. "No more shopping for you, no more cooking, no cleaning. You'll have maids to do this for you. There is no other way I can be absolved from my sins, in God's eyes, no other way I can make amends for what I did to you. Don't go on punishing me! Allow me to help you, Irene, make life easier for you. Or I'll be very unhappy. Please, woman, help me!"

Irene lifted her wet eyes up to her tortured benefactor and swallowed hard. She closed them again as though ashamed of surrendering to his plea, and nodded wordlessly.

"Thank you," Louis Luckstone whispered.

"Okay, so they receive something," Kurt Frank cried out indignantly. "But what do *I* get for saving your life and that of Inge?"

Luckstone's head whipped toward the stooping, old man, still holding his pistol.

"You? You must be joking, Kurt. You only kept me alive to claim your ill-gotten wealth."

"Wealth that you used to. . . ."

"To return a thousandfold, as you well know. But don't expect me to reward the killer of my family, of Klaus, of my fellow-prisoners, Jews, gypsies, Christians, anti-Nazis."

"I *paid* for my crimes. I spent thirty-eight years in a dank cellar."

"But to this day you feel no compassion, like Karl Ludwig did. Him, yes, if he were still alive I'd give a million dollars in a minute because he at least showed true love. He was a hero—far braver than I could ever be. But you only reveal greed. Miserable, unending greed. Even today."

"You mean I come three thousand miles and I get nothing? Not one token of gratitude for saving you?"

"I don't hate you, Kurt. God knows why I suddenly can't hate the man who played that cruel trick on my Klaus, on countless thousands of others. But don't expect me to stab my family in the back now and pay you restitution for not murdering my daughter and me as well."

"Then nobody gets the money! Nobody!" Kurt screamed. "I *have* paid for my crimes. Why should *I* be singled out all my life? Why should I continue living forever in a cellar while you and these two live a life of leisure?" Suddenly the gun gleamed in his hand as he stepped back. It's not fair!" he shouted. "I've suffered enough—more than enough! I won't take any more of this!"

His hand whipped up, aligned the gunsight with Luckstone's brow, released the hammer, the safety-catch. Terror rooted everybody to the ground as Kurt squeezed the trigger. Even before Luckstone could duck behind a raised elbow, an explosion rocked the room.

The pistol jumped out of Kurt's hand and blood splattered all over the table. Hammer and Irene spun around, toward the greenhouse from which the sound of the gunshot had come.

Nicole was standing under a huge Chinese wisteria shrub, the smoking firearm aimed at the group.

"My hand!" Kurt shrieked. "She smashed my hand!"

His right hand, as if by magic, had been converted into a crimson collage of mangled tendons and bones. "Why?" he howled. "I never did you any harm. Why did you. . . ."

"For shattering a child's skull, you scum-bag!. . . No!" Nicole screamed, swinging the bodyguard's Mauser she had picked up off the floor toward her grandfather. "Stay where you are! Don't come any closer. Anybody! You too."

"Child! Darling Nicki!" Luckstone was about to rush around the table, but came to a stop when he saw that she was pointing the weapon at his heart. "I only want. . . ."

"Don't move, Grandfather! Any of you!"

Wet mascara streaks were lining the milky pallor of her cheeks. It gave them the appearance of the shadows of prison bars on pale skin.

"Don't pick up that gun, Irene! Nor you, Paul! And stop moaning like an idiot, Kurt Frank!" Her voice was suddenly bloodless, icy. "Nobody move! I'm serious."

"But, child, you saved my life," her grandfather exclaimed in exasperation. "All I want is to be by your side."

"I said stand back, Gramps. I mean it!"

"But why? What's gotten into you, doll?"

"Into *me*?" she cried out. "You've got the nerve to ask what's gotten into me, when it's *you*, you who's brought this on yourself."

"Me?. . . Oh, I see!" Luckstone glanced around him, confronting the faces of those who had shared the dark days of death and madness with him. "You were eavesdropping."

"I came through the greenhouse to warn you. But then I heard everything, every word since Grasser crashed through the window. . . . Grandfather, you meant everything to me. Everything! And now. . . . Just tell me how—because of you—I can ever love *any*one again!"

"But, Nicki, dear girl. . . ." And he started toward her.

"No—stop, Grandfather!" The tone of her voice had become undisguisedly threatening. "You deceived me. You of all people the most depraved killer!"

"You're upset, child. And I don't blame you. I. . . ."

"Don't come any closer! I warn you. And that animal next to you—let him bleed to death!"

"Miss, you understood nothing," Kurt said, grimacing with pain.

"Don't speak to me about understanding, you dog!" she snapped. "A real hero, killing kids! You'll pay for it, so help me God, you'll pay for this for the rest of your life!"

"Then you're no better than he is," Hammer observed glumly. "Believe me it requires no great sacrifice to give away part of your fortune when you're rich and happy, but you're not really after justice here, Nicole. What you want is to start the blood flowing again. Eternal revenge! It's so much easier than to accept facts for what they are, or to show a spirit of charity when it counts most, some tolera. . . ."

"I don't need a lecture on compassion, Paul Hammer," Nicole sliced in fiercely. "Least of all from you! Save it for the boys and girls you helped drive into the gas ovens. You've forfeited your right to live too."

"Okay, then play executioner!" Hammer's raised voice could not conceal his frustration, his anger. "Go ahead—play concentration camp guard!"

"A great idea, Herr Hammer." She tossed back her hair and stared hard at her challenger. "I'd love to play your captor. Someone to teach you a lesson you won't forget in a hurry."

She raised the gun quickly, then, with both hands, aimed it with an excruciating sense of precision at her prospective father-in-law, and pulled back the thick, cocking hammer.

"Nicole!" Jesse's father cried out aghast, diving under the table.

The young woman whisked the Mauser sharply to the left of the wall shelves. Four, five shots rang out deafeningly in rapid succession. The slugs smacked into the paneling, well away from the paralyzed group, splintering the wood and tearing chunks of mortar, behind it, out of the wall.

"Have you gone mad?" screamed Luckstone. "Destroying my house."

Nicole moved slowly from the Chinese wisteria but came to a halt already a few steps later. "Be grateful it's only the house." She still aimed the gun at her six prisoners. "None of you really have paid your dues. In my opinion *all* of you should have perished in Treblinka!"

"You're only condemning yourself, young lady; or don't you realize that your threats make you the cruellest of us here?" her grandfather said bitterly. "And the most destructive. You even lack the compassion, the forgiveness, of Paul and Irene."

"Compassion!" She spat out the word with contempt. "When did any of you show compassion forty years ago?"

"We lived in insane times, Nicole." Hammer had risen from the floor and leaned weakly against the conference table. "You have no right to judge your grandfather. Or me. Any of us."

"Your kind let the world go insane, Herr Hammer."

"That's a lie, and you know it," he hurled back at her. "My parents died fighting Hitler."

"And I, too, would have fought him, right from the outset," she exclaimed shrilly. "I never compromise, Hammer. Not when faced with evil. That's why I feel I *have* the right to judge you!"

She jerked up the Mauser again. But even before she could pull the trigger, the door leading into the garden slammed into a trellis, far in the back of her. At once Nicole wheeled around. Through the drooping branches and fern fronds, she made out Jesse Hammer hurrying into the glasshouse.

The distraught woman pointed the gun at his head. "Over there!" she shouted. "Into the room!"

Jesse rooted to the ground near a lime tree, an expression of utter bewilderment etched on his face. Behind Nicole, arraigned as in the docks of a mass trial, stood the stone-rigid sextet of figures with their strange, grim faces. One man was bleeding profusely; a window was completely shattered, the wall paneling splintered, while the Persian carpet was littered with ashtrays, glasses and ledger books. But most shocking of all was his fiancée, training a gun at him, her face a demented mask of black lines, the eyes burning insanely with hatred.

"What's going on here?" Jesse's words hovered between incredulity and shock. "What's this with the gun? And that man—why's he bleeding?"

"She's gone mad," Kurt croaked out, holding up the pitifully bleeding stump of what ten minutes earlier had been a hand. "Someone help me. Please! The woman is mad."

"Yes, of course I'm mad," Nicole cried caustically, stepping out of Jesse's way so he could pass. "You always said just one more disaster and I'd flip out. Well, I guess now it's *my* turn."

"Nicki, I don't know what went on here, but I think you better. . . ."

"No, *you* better move. Now! Come on! In there, with the others. Or so help me God I'll squeeze the trigger."

"You better join us, Jesse," Paul Hammer spoke up. "She isn't fooling. She shot him already."

"For God's sake, what's gotten into you?"

"Move!" Nicole ordered sharply.

Keeping a wary eye on the weapon, Jesse at last uprooted himself from the spot near the American linden and stepped rapidly across the greenhouse interior toward the others.

"Would someone mind telling me what this is all about?" he asked. Fear of the gun going off kept his eyes glued to its barrel.

"I know everything about grandfather, that's what," Nicole declared simply when Jesse was about to shoulder his way past her.

Then, abruptly, without another word of explanation and only an arm's length away from her fiancé, Nicole raised the gun, lightning-quick, to her temple. Her forefinger coiled around the trigger. And squeezed it.

Jesse froze, stock-still. There was an audible gasp from the horrified onlookers, followed immediately by a sickening metallic click as the pistol's hammer locked into place. It had struck an empty chamber.

"Bang!" she said softly.

She grabbed the Mauser by the barrel, reached for Jesse's hand and slapped the weapon into it.

"See?" She smiled knowingly. "Empty!"

The unexpectedness of this swift display of melodrama, followed immediately by her peace gesture, startled Jesse, leaving him momentarily numb, speechless. An instant later his fingers closed around the Mauser and he slipped the gun into his jacket.

"Why, Nick?" he whispered. "What did you hope to achieve by this madness?"

To the amazement of the onlookers, Nicole turned unconcernedly from her lover, broke a small twig laden with pink blossoms off a Japanese cherry tree and impaled it expertly in her long hair. The obstinacy had drained out of her face, the crazed fire died down in her eyes, and she turned back to her fiancé.

"Your father is right, Jesse," she said calmly. "I did shoot Kurt Frank."

He gave her a perplexed look. "Who?" A fraction of a second later he understood.

Jesse rushed through the greenhouse, around the ink-black goldfish pond, and headed for the wounded man who was a total stranger to him. It took him only a few seconds' examination to reach a decision.

"I'm going to take him to the hospital," he announced, then glanced uneasily at Nicole. "And you're pleased with yourself, obviously."

"Jesse." Hammer caught his son's attention. "Nicole shot a gun out of this man's hand. Otherwise her grandfather would have been killed."

"You did?" Jesse's expression changed at once to astonishment, mingled perhaps with a tinge of admiration, as he regarded his fiancée once more. But only for a moment. Because the next second his head snapped around to Louis Luckstone. "Thank God, you're safe, LL. I don't know what I would have done if. . . ." He left the sentence wisely unfinished.

"Thank you, my boy." Luckstone beamed, visibly flattered and relieved that the worst of the danger had passed. "Your sentiments are appreciated." A new frown, however, replaced the smile almost immediately. "I think, though, you better take Kurt to the clinic now."

"No! Wait—just a second!" Nicole's voice was deceptively coquettish as she addressed Jesse once again. "You thought I couldn't handle your secret, Jess, the really heavy news about my grandfather's past—that I'd flip, have a nervous breakdown. Didn't you? . . . Well, you can see for yourself how wrong you were—can't you?—even with all my fireworks. . . . But you'll admit there's one question that *still* remains unanswered. Correct me if I'm mistaken. Or don't you agree that we're all curious to learn how our three uninvited guests now intend to cope with their new lives? Like, for instance, are you, Paul and Irene, going to carry out your threat and reveal the truth about LL to the news media, as you had planned? Or are you backing out of it?"

"Heavens, I thought we had all that settled," Luckstone growled.

"No—let them speak for themselves!" Nicole's eyes swept from Irene, who was quietly kneading her dead fingers, to Paul Hammer, who kept staring at the folded hands in his lap. "It's the money, isn't it?" she taunted, after giving them half a minute to reply. "For a hundred grand a year hush money it's easy to let bygones be bygones. Or am I wrong? After all, what's a murdered family? Or a broken body? Right?"

"Its *not* hush money, Nicole!" her grandfather objected incisively. "If Irene and Paul change their minds and decide to give me away to the authorities, whatever, they'd still get their annuity."

"I'm sure they would. Otherwise the question they'll have to bear in their hearts for the rest of their lives is: what price justice now?"

"Not if they temper justice with mercy and understanding."

"Grandfather, surely you mean: Not if they temper justice with the promise of money! Or am I interpreting your silence incorrectly, Paul Hammer?"

"Why don't you leave him alone?" Luckstone drove at her angrily. "I think he has suffered enough, a whole lifetime. Now I'm trying to make up for it. And certainly your metaphysical hogwash doesn't work very well when applied to life."

"And I should have thought that it is precisely the metaphysics of what we know of honor and honesty that will set us on the right course, Herr Glückstein," Nicole flung back at her grandfather. "Or we'll all end up—right here in this conference room—exactly like the Germans did in the Thirties and Forties, when we let the Leader seduce and corrupt us so we can legally do what our baser instincts drive us to do."

"You're right, Nicole," Paul Hammer spoke up once more. "Nothing is harder in life than to make the right choice. None of us here are perfect—then or now. I don't know what to say . . . except maybe . . . that perhaps there is a bit of Hitler in all of us."

"Paul's right, we're all guilty," the financier observed swiftly, but with conviction. "Which only goes to prove what I've always maintained—that, whatever else it did, World War Two has changed the meaning of morality, that in fact Hitler's aberrations are at the heart of what ails mankind even today."

"My oh my, aren't we profound this afternoon, Mr. Luckstone!" Nicole commented dryly, trying to secure the pink blossoms in her hair. "As if it were a revelation of sorts that goodness and evil have always lived side by side in man. But you still haven't answered my question, Paul. . . . Irene. Now that LL has given you the green light to act in accordance with your conscience, are you going to dispense justice and report him to the media? Or has the money erased all your memories?"

"For crying out loud, what are you trying to prove, Nicole?" The alarm in Luckstone's voice now was apparent to everyone. "Don't you realize that even though they no longer wish me ill I will *always* be condemned—*all* of us are condemned, regardless—to live with the guilt of our sins, with the crimes we committed in the past? Isn't that enough punishment?" But only silence, an unspoken, unforgiving defiance met her grandfather's new appeal. "Why are you so vengeful all of a sudden, Nicole? God knows, we're aware of your streak of cruelty, but. . . ."

"Living up to one's principles of honesty is not cruelty except to the guilty," her shrill voice broke into his defense. "Or do you seriously believe that by waving your own sense of guilt before my eyes you're automatically absolved of all responsibilities for your crimes?"

"But why strike back at the one person who's supported you and loved you selflessly throughout your whole life?" he pleaded, more contrite now. "I gave you everything you wanted. I've never harmed you, Nicole, never!"

"You betrayed me long before I was born." Nicole's voice again was icy, unyielding. "A mass killer in my family, posing as a saint, as the fount of all my aspirations, my love, is more than I can stomach. Those German shepherds should have ripped your balls out!"

Luckstone shuddered. "You're sick, girl! Insane! Out of control!"

"Oh sure, twist it! All of you are innocent and *I'm* a loony—right?" She uttered a bitter laugh, her eyes thin slits of provocation. "That's what you try to make me out to be. That's what you want them to believe. That I *am* mad!"

41

"Nick, why don't you cool it?" Jesse Hammer reminded his fiancée of his presence as Grasser quickly stepped forward and pocketed the two discarded guns. "In all fairness, I think you're overreacting."

"Overreacting!" Nicole cried out incredulously. "Are *you* crazy, Jesse? You may be brilliant, but you're an idiot too. You *never* take a stand! My lifelong idol is suddenly revealed as a mass murderer of helpless women and children, and you have the nerve to tell me I'm overreacting? You better take a refresher course in psychology, Mr. Hammer, if you think a calm reaction to this scene is normal."

"And you better take a good look at yourself, Miss Luckstone," Jesse said as barely suppressed anger turned his face fiery scarlet. "Because this overreaction is quickly assuming the symptoms of one of your old hysterical outbursts. Or should I say a nervous breakdown?"

"I knew you'd finally come up with that tripe."

"It's *not* tripe!" Jesse raised his voice to an unfamiliarly, stridently high pitch. "And I think your grandfather has been remarkably patient with you, considering."

"Considering what?" she challenged him brazenly. "That I may unmask him as a killer?"

"No, considering that he has done his best for forty years to atone for his sins, to help millions of the world's unfortunate, and those like me who can help countless others."

"Thank you, my boy," the billionaire chuckled and nodded in a gesture of friendship at his future son-in-law. "You've said it a thousand times better than I ever could."

"Of course, *you'd* lap that up! You found a new satellite, Grandfather. You two make me want to barf." Nicole spat on the floor. "You, Jesse, allying yourself with a self-confessed war criminal for filthy lucre against the woman you allegedly love—it's disgusting! A toady—that's what you've become—a toady out for his pot of gold!"

"It's *you* who's disgusting!" Jesse's body was trembling with revulsion, at this unexpected assault on him by his beloved. "To even suspect I'd stoop to that level. You're only debasing yourself."

"Sure, while you're the knight in shining armor defending the rich thug."

"You're getting hysterical again, Nicole. You claim that you can cope with life, even the ugly side of it. But you're becoming even more vengeful than these three victims of uncontrollable circumstances. *You*'ve slept on a bed of fluffy white petals all your life, Nicole, but *they*'re climbing out of a bloodbath. And still they can go beyond the drive for revenge. Only *you* can't. God, I just wonder what kind of a concentration camp guard *you* would have made if you had been in your grandfather's shoes."

"How dare you!" Nicole's hand darted up to the branch of a nearby wisteria vine. It broke off in her fist and racemes of white, purple and rose blossoms showered on the marble floor. "I have never murdered anyone. *They* have—all of them. And you dare accuse me of having the potential to be a kapo—even an Ilse Koch! And what about you, Jesse Hammer? I've trusted you with everything, with all my secrets, but you never returned that trust. You knew about LL, but held out on me. Well, Jesse Hammer, I wouldn't want you to be saddled with a woman you think has the makings of a Bitch of Buchenwald. The engagement is off! Here, take this! I won't need it any more."

She hurled the wisteria branch on the floor, pulled the engagement ring off her finger and threw it at the stunned congregation. The diamond skipped off the long table onto the deep Persian carpet and rolled ignominiously under the buffet. Jesse lowered his eyes, his face a mask of stone.

"You behave like a child, Nicole," Luckstone said, after waiting a few seconds. "Giving all this up: a man who's kind, patient, intelligent. The dream house that's nearly ready. A life of culture and ease. And for what? It's something strange in your nature that's making you do this, something demented, and I don't like it."

"Grandfather, what someone like you likes or does not like is completely irrelevant to me. I wouldn't expect you to understand not compromising on matters of principles involving truth and justice, even if it hurts the accuser." Deep contempt burned in the implacable, steely eyes she trained on her benefactor. "Now that I come to think of it there are some war criminals who *have* paid for their crimes. So they are *not* beyond salvation." And she turned imperiously from her startled grandfather to the former concentration camp SS officer.

"Kurt Frank, come over here! I want to speak to you!" The command was peremptory and brooked no contradiction.

"What?" The old man, once master over life and death, glanced around helplessly, confused, his arm still bent upward at the elbow in a futile attempt to stop the trickle of blood.

"I said, come here!"

Everybody looked at Kurt in surprise, not knowing what to expect, as the stooping leviathan struggled out of the armchair. He limped tiredly around the conference table and stepped through the sea-green portal into the glasshouse.

"I'm taking him to the clinic," she announced firmly. "I'll have him fixed up. I shot him and it's my responsibility to see he's looked after."

"And then?" demanded Paul Hammer.

"Then? Maybe *he* has the courage to tell the world about all of you. But since apparently I can no longer depend on those who claim to love me, I will just have to attend to those who can't disillusion me—people like Kurt. The ones the rest of the world hates and despises."

"Despises for a good reason," LL ripped into her speechmaking. "They senselessly slaughtered innocent people and feel no remorse. Playing Major Barbara may be all right with Paul and Irene, Nicole, but not with him. I won't allow you to splurge my millions on garbage like Kurt."

"You won't?" Nicole strode past Kurt toward her grandfather in scathing, cold fury. "What are you going to do about it? Disown me? Have Josh Hamilton call out his assassins to exterminate me?"

"Don't get paranoid now!" Luckstone's lips were pinched into a thin, colorless line. "I'm afraid you're forcing my hand, Nicole. It's your own doing. I have warned you. Because what I intend to do, my dear, is to have Jesse commit you to the Rehabilitation Center until you have come to your senses."

"You mean until I agree with *you*! Don't you?"

"The people in this room are witnesses to the fact that you're not fit to handle the millions entrusted to your care. But most tragic of all, it's only too plain you're heading for a nervous breakdown again."

"I see." Nicole confronted her grandfather, unflinching. Not a flicker of an eyelash betrayed her innermost turmoil. "That's what it boils down to. I don't see things your way and off I go the funny farm. Mustn't stir things up for the Big Man." For an instant she seemed almost to marvel at her grandfather's attitude. A slight smile softened her hard, pale features as she shook her head in disbelief. "Odd—but doesn't it occur to you that this is exactly what the Russians do when *they* face people with a mind of their own? They pack 'em off to psychiatric wards."

"A smart woman, Ludi!" Kurt cut in with a cackle. "She may have wounded me, but your granddaughter *is* smart." He turned to Nicole and pronounced each syllable with painful exactitude despite his growing weakness. "What do I have to lose, Miss Nicole? I'll be happy to come along with you, *and* testify as an eyewitness, if that's what you want. And I thank you for offering to take care of me, thank you most kindly."

"Now wait, wait, wait!" Luckstone raised his voice in alarm. "Just remember that you've come all the way from Europe to settle a score with *me*, Kurt, *not* with my granddaughter, and don't you forget it! Because *I* don't." The words tumbled in a wild frenzied rush from his lips. "And the more I think about it the more I realize that you're right. You *did* save my life, and that of my daughter—I can't deny that—without you I wouldn't even be here. So I *must* learn to shut my eyes to some of those awful chapters in the camps. People there committed unspeakable crimes under duress. I make no bones about it. I should know. I'm the living proof of that."

"What the hell are you driving at, Grandfather?" Nicole demanded, eyeing him suspiciously.

"Simply that if Paul and Irene find it in their hearts to forgive me for what I did to them, my dear girl, then the least I can do is to show Kurt that the past *must* be buried once and for all and a new beginning be made. Therefore. . . ."

"I asked you what your game is, Grandfather," Nicole insisted.

"Pardon me for speaking, Nicole, while you're interrupting. Perhaps you can tell me, what is the good of nations being able to make up if individuals can't? Didn't the United States help its ex-enemies after the war? Then what is wrong, I ask you, if I want to prove today that there must be no more ill will between Kurt and me, *ever*! And that that is why I have decided to support him, like Irene and Paul, with an annuity, too, of a hundred thousand dollars, so that we can. . . ."

"The same old story!" Nicole broke in angrily, seeing the light at last. "You intend to buy him off like all your other cronies."

". . . . so that we can bury the hatchet," Luckstone overshouted her. "Forever. That is, of course, if this arrangement is satisfactory to Kurt."

Again the war criminal became the focus of everyone's attention. The throbbing pain at the end of his wrist's splintered stump suddenly turned into a matter of secondary importance. The blood dripping through his sleeve onto the marble floor was forgotten. Forty years of feeling victimized, swindled, vanished as if by a magician's wand. The old man stood transfixed, gaping at his closest friend, his foremost betrayer.

"Ludi!" Kurt's voice was husky. He visibly groped for words to express his most private sentiments, the aching vacuum of greed all of a sudden filled, filled to overflowing—but he couldn't. He never got the chance.

Because at that moment Nicole spun around to her grandfather, yelling, "I should have let him pump the slug into your brain, you monster!" She was in the grip of a torrential rage. "Buying his loyalty with your pilfered goods, like you bought *all* your associates, your kings and sheiks and presidents. But not me, Glückstein. Do you hear? You can't buy *me* off!"

Her eyes flitted about wildly, like those of a woman deranged, until they lighted on the wall in the conference room, on the bookshelves, which held scores of matchless leatherbound volumes—rare editions, museum pieces, worth a king's ransom.

"Don't trifle with me, Nicole," Luckstone threatened. "I warn you!"

But she did not seem to hear him. Her eyes were trained on dozens of intricately fashioned art objects between the books, amongst them some crystal and porcelain figurines, each an exquisite treasure from Meissen or Limoges or Boehm.

The realization of what her next step would be had an amazingly tranquilizing effect on her. The target of her objective was in sight. Once more she reverted to her previous state of deceptive cool, and her entire manner became more composed. Her mind carefully weighed the strategy on which she was about to embark as she approached, with studied casualness, the priceless treasures posited on the shelves. She picked up the lone Steuben glass figurine of a swan and examined it seemingly in deep thought. Everybody watched her curiously.

"Nobody claims that you're a Nazi, Grandfather," she said in an uncharacteristically restrained voice as if none of the foregoing had taken place. "Or that you bear the same guilt for the Holocaust that must be borne by your German masters. You, too, are a victim. But since you have never really felt any pain for abetting their crimes, incurred any losses, allow me at least to play the role of your conscience."

"What *are* you driveling about?" Luckstone upbraided her. "Playing my conscience, indeed! What *I* see is a girl who's downright spiteful. And put that glass sculpture back on the shelf!"

"Grandfather, I am *not* spiteful." Nicole's slightly condescending attitude remained undaunted, but her figure grew rigid as though bracing itself for an impending attack. "Kurt Frank saved your life, but you can't deny that fear corrupted you, the fear of death."

"Perhaps you would rather that I had not been corrupted and gone to my death instead, meekly, like six million other Jews?"

"On second thought, no—I wouldn't. But now it is *you* who is corrupting Paul Hammer and the others."

"It is *not* corruption, Nicole," Luckstone protested strenuously. "I checked on Paul Hammer when I heard that you were going to marry Jesse and there was no mention anywhere of any pension coming to him for his years in the camps. And Irene's restitution no doubt amounts to a mere pittance. All I want today is to help them. Can't you get this through your thick skull? Now, for the last time, please put back that swan!"

"You still don't understand," his grandchild replied, completely unfazed. "That it is the fear of the world hearing the truth about you more than anything, more than wishing Paul and Irene well, that goads you to dangle the riches before their eyes, just the way Kurt Frank offered you the reward of riches decades ago."

"Life he promised me," the financier shouted. "That's what impelled me to play along with him. I would have been a fool not to comply with his plan. But it was *not* for riches."

"I believe you," she said in a tone of utter reasonableness. Somehow the delicate glass figure of the swan in her hands seemed to take on the essence of life, because she cuddled it in her arms now and stroked its exquisitely curved, long neck. "But you see, Grandfather, you and I are Jews—non-practicing ones, admittedly—but still Jews. An ethical people. And we don't lack the courage to accept the responsibility for our actions. Do we?"

"Damn you!" Luckstone blew up, seeing that his granddaughter was trying to come to terms with his guilt by persuading him to see things her way in taking the spiritual rather than belligerent route. "What do you want of me? *I* didn't instigate the Holocaust. *He* did. *His* ilk." And he leveled an accusing finger at Kurt. "Nicole, the *goyim* kill and mutilate by the millions and you go out hunting for a Jew so you can hang him in public. You are the worst of the lot here. An anti-Semitic Jew."

Nicole's gaze did not waver, it did not stray. It remained on her grandfather's face, calm and unafraid. Luckstone was the first of the two to cast his eyes down. But only momentarily.

"What about him then?" he yelled at her, embittered, gesturing with his head toward Hammer. "Paul also whipped some of the arrivals into the gas chambers. He admitted it. Are you going to inform on him too?"

Nicole cocked a surprised eyebrow. Her jaws squared, but she did not glance in the direction of Paul Hammer or her fiancé.

"If Jesse has any character," she said softly, "he will see to it that justice is done."

"Nicki!" Jesse's exclamation plainly revealed that her harpoon had struck home—the blood she had drawn. "My father was fourteen years old. A child. A child wanting to live. His parents had already sacrificed their lives in the fight against Hitler. What more do you want?"

"A clean slate, Jesse."

"Not a clean slate, woman, but blind, stupid, vengeful justice," thundered her grandfather. "And you achieve nothing by it except the destruction of reputations, of the lives of people who through no fault of their own were suckered into this horrible dilemma. Just as Paul said, you have no right to judge us. You weren't there, Nicole."

"True, I wasn't." She nodded and lowered her eyes to the swan in her hands. "But you're wrong, Grandfather. I *have* a right to judge you . . . since apparently nobody else will. . . . You see, justice may be stupid and blind, but it does entail *some* hurt and loss."

The last word had barely left Nicole's lips when, in sharp contrast to her tranquil outward behavior, she suddenly hauled back with her right arm and with all her might flung the fragile glass figure of the swan at her grandfather. It missed him by the merest fraction of an inch and shattered against the enormous red-brick fireplace. Splinters flew in all directions, showers of transparent needles. Without even glancing up to see if it had hit its target, Nicole grabbed another piece of statuary, a Roman general's head, and threw it, too, across the conference room, and then another, and another, grabbing gigantic glazed seashells, Nile-green jade statuettes, Grecian vases, Etruscan artifacts, whatever came to hand first, and scattering them at the amazed onlookers.

"Blood money!" she shouted. "Murderer's money!"

They ran for cover under this barrage—all except Luckstone. He ducked right and left to avoid the objects crashing, shattering and bursting around him. Sharp shivers exploded like shrapnel. A few more seconds of that—and he leaped forward, barrelling into Nicole with his shoulder, knocking her violently to the ground.

He immediately fell to the floor beside her, placed one of his knees on her chest and, packing all his force into his hands, slapped her face. Hard. The smacks rained down on her briskly, stingingly, their sound ringing through the conference room.

"What's wrong with you, Nicole? You're destroying my home, damn you!" he screamed as first his left, then his right palm came crashing down on her burning red cheeks. "You don't deserve to live among us, you little bitch!"

Her head twisted sideways under his blows. "Go ahead—kill me!" she shrieked. "I'll never be your prisoner at the Center!"

Her arms thrashed and flailed about frantically, against him, after the first shock of his assault; her legs were in the grip of quick spastic jerks as she tried to kick him off her. Suddenly a long jagged splinter—the swan's neck of the Steuben glass figure—appeared in her hand, and she jabbed the long pointed end of the glass at her left wrist, screaming, "I don't want to live, you bastard. I don't want to live in your world of killers!"

Her grandfather's fist swept up and struck. Struck hard. He did not even realize it—he had knocked the fragment of glass out of her hand, barely managing to deflect its fatal blow. But the sleeve of her dress had ripped, her skin ruptured—the puncture of a gash far below her wrist—dyeing the turquoise silk tatter dark sodden red.

Around them the others rose and approached cautiously, not realizing what had happened, yet unwilling to interfere with the industrialist's attempts to bring his granddaughter to her senses. Seconds passed, then a few more, but still the barrage of blows did not cease. It was only then that the viewers realized, with horror, that the openhanded slaps had become crushing blows with his clenched fists. Luckstone had stopped his explosive shouting—he was simply beating the young woman senseless. A stream of crimson began to flow from her nostrils. Her lip split under the unremitting onslaught. She tried to cry out, to make some protest, but the bulk of her grandfather's body and the ferocity of his punches left her helpless to resist.

Jesse rushed forward, visibly alarmed by Luckstone's murderous tantrum. He grabbed the maddened old man by the shoulder, trying to pull him off her. Someone came to Jesse's aid. But Luckstone was in the spine-chilling grip of a blind rage. He twisted free of his captors without difficulty. Jesse lost his balance, fell back and tripped over a chair. The industrialist instantly hurled himself upon his young victim with renewed vigor, smashing both fists brutally into her face. Nicole's pale skin, the long blond tresses of her hair, the parquetry floor dyed wine-red with her blood.

The incensed voices of John Shadow and Grasser rent the air over the new outburst of their employer as he exploded once more in a black and thunderous storm of demented howls, but it was his avengers, Paul

Hammer and Irene Fischmann, who at long last felt that here, finally, was the moment to act boldly. The two plunged—undismayed and heedless of all consequences—into the fiendish melee, colliding head-on with the septuagenarian gone amok. Using every last ounce of their remaining strength, they hauled the berserk man off the girl's battered body and yanked him away from her.

"Are you starting it all over again?" shouted Paul Hammer. "Killing! Like in Treblinka!"

Luckstone slumped in a daze against the buffet behind him, gasping for air, eyes fixed glassily on his two assailants.

"How could you!" Irene cried out, pain twisting her face as she grabbed her emaciated forearm and rubbed it wildly. "You would have killed her. Like you almost killed me in Auschwitz."

The billionaire scowled at her. "You're crazy, woman."

"No, *you're* the one who's crazy. It's like a demon in you. A demon! Always killing! And you expect me to take money from such a man? Never! Do you hear? Just let me live my life out alone in my little room and I'll be a thousand times happier than with. . . ."

A paroxysm of sobs burst out of her frail body and cut her accusation in half. She turned away quickly and hid her face in her gnarled right hand.

"My money isn't good enough for you?" Luckstone roared at her, righting himself. He was bathed in a film of cold sweat but seemed to have recovered sufficiently to fly into a new rampaging fit and vent his anger, his frustration, at being rebuffed by Irene. "Is that what you're saying? . . . Answer me, woman!"

Irene turned around slowly. "Are you still ordering me around, Glückstein?"

"My name is Luckstone, Irene Fischmann," he screamed. "Not Glückstein. You address me with respect! As Mr. Luckstone!"

Irene stared at her old tormentor through a veil of tears, barely aware of Jesse leaning over Nicole cleaning up her mauled, swollen face.

"You have shattered my body, Mr. Luckstone," she said between gasps for breath. "You have shattered my spirit. Forty years ago, and again today. Now you're doing it to your granddaughter. And you want me to accept money from such a monster?"

A cluster of muscles knotted Luckstone's cheeks and contorted his face with a barely controlled fury. "All right," he said through clenched jaws. "Have it your way. Go back to your attic! Starve for all I care, and play the eternal victim!"

The fragile, little woman lowered her eyes, saying nothing. There was only a hopeless, sparrow-like flutter of her good arm. Tears would no longer do.

42

Purple clouds swam inside Nicole's head. Hands grasped her under the armpits and firmly raised her up off the floor. But her legs were numb, lifeless, like wet spaghetti; she went limp and flopped forward against somebody—a man. *Eau de Cologne* flooded her mind, and she slowly, painfully, unglued her eyes, gazing in a stupor at the face of . . . her lover.

She wanted to speak, to cry, but no sound came out. The pain in her mouth became unbearable, ballooning explosively to a screeching crescendo directly behind her eyeballs.

Everywhere, on all sides, a fuzzy blur of voices engulfed her; a humming of mad, shifting tones reverberated in her ears, and it grew and grew and grew. Her mouth filled with blood and she spat it out, and part of two teeth, against Jesse's chest, smutching the grey suit he wore. Immediately she felt his arms encircling her and his hands gently stroking the ropes of her hair, sticky with her own blood.

"Steady, darling," the reassuring voice penetrated the miasma of pain, and she braced against her fiancé.

"How could you, LL?" Jesse's reproachful voice suddenly rang in her ear as he turned to Louis Luckstone. "It's one thing disagreeing with her, castigating her, but you nearly killed the girl."

"And you're ready to defend her?" the immediate countercharge uncoiled like a viper. "Defend this crazy, little bitch? Christ!" He bunched his fists angrily. "Don't you even realize yet that she's been playing you for a sucker ever since you two first met?"

The taunting tone in his voice did not escape Jesse, or the others.

"That's a lot of bull, and you know it!" Jesse retorted heatedly, still protecting the young woman's shaking body in his embrace. "She behaved foolishly, unreasonably today—I agree with that completely. But Nicole has never deceived me, and it's no use you trying to drive a wedge between us." A short, raucous laugh of ridicule from Luckstone was the sole response to this deeply felt defense. "But much more important, I will not stand by idly and see Nicki—*any* woman—abused and mistreated. And if this means my having to give up the directorship at the Center, then that's just too bad. But from now on she'll have *me* by her side, no matter what!"

"No matter what?" The magnate cynically arched his eyebrows.

"You heard!" Jesse stood his ground. "I realize that I love Nicki even more than before. So let me tell you in front of these people that her happiness means more to me than any top position in your institution. And if you want me to leave I'll do so right now. With Nicki!"

"Are you finished, Dr. Hammer?" Luckstone was breathing heavily, rocking back and forth on the balls of his heels, digesting, so it seemed, the impact and import of Jesse's ultimatum. But then, quite unexpectedly, a faint smile lightened his strained, glacial countenance. "Well, Jesse Hammer," he said, "in this case I think it might be wise to let you in on a little secret about this woman you adore so much . . . and explain why I said that she's been playing you for a sucker almost since she first went into therapy with you."

Nicole's arms instantly tightened around Jesse's neck as though she was afraid of the next verbal assault her grandfather was about to discharge on her and the unsuspecting group of eavesdroppers.

"I don't think that anything you can say about Nicki can shock me, LL."

"Well, perhaps you'll change your mind if I tell you that this darling little girl in your arms *has* deceived you, consistently, *has* lied to you, and that the disclosure *will* shock you."

Nicole swung around, out of Jesse's embrace, crying out a word. Her voice was thick, the word—grandfather—came out awkwardly, as though her tongue was leaden, pumped full of Novocaine. Tears shone in her swollen eyes as she retreated, shakily, out into the greenhouse. Here she held on to the branch of the Japanese cherry tree for support. "Grandfather!" she said again, more plaintively, clearer, and shook her head in silent entreaty.

Jesse's gaze swept in a turmoil of confusion and sudden doubt from his fiancée to her grandfather.

"What on earth are you talking about?" he demanded. "How *could* she have deceived me?"

Luckstone let an even wider smile break through his triumphant expression.

"Remember how she swore to you that Eric, her twin brother, was killed while they were vacationing in Mexico?"

"Of course. So what?"

"So—it's a lie, one big goddamn lie! She knew she could get away with it, fooling you, your saintly profession. The truth is they were on their way to an abortionist while living with me in Mexico. Oh yes, Dr. Hammer, an abortionist! Nicole was pregnant, by her own brother. They'd had an incestuous relationship since they were thirteen, she confessed to me later, and. . . ."

"What!" Jesse wheeled around to Nicole, his features twisted with betrayal. "Is this true, Nicole? Is any of what he says true?"

A sob shook her body; the teardrops were rolling down uncontrollably, mingling with the blood, the bruises, the puffed nose, making a clownish blur of her former beauty.

"Jesse." The word came out in an almost unintelligible whimper. She extended both arms to him. "Jesse. . . . I. . . ."

"Answer me, woman!" he pressed her, revulsion already knotting his stomach.

A wave of fatigue, of helplessness, a surging, overwhelming pain in her skull overcame Nicole then and there, and her legs buckled. She folded up on the marble path, kneeling forward, her forehead touching the floor, sobbing, sobbing so inconsolably, so stricken with grief, with betrayal, that the onlookers were rendered speechless. Visible shivers ran along the knobby vertebrae of her arched spine under the shimmering silk of her dress, and she inched away from him.

"Why?" Jesse exploded into the desperate stillness, broken only by the muffled sobs of the woman who was suddenly a stranger to him. "Why did you lie to me? I could have helped you, Nicole—not the music, but *I* could have helped you. Why wouldn't you let me?" He advanced a few steps and towered over her like an avenging god. "I pleaded for the truth, month after month. Six lousy months! Nicole . . . I'm speaking to you! Why couldn't you trust me? Answer me!" He stopped haranguing for a few brief seconds, waiting just long enough to let her defend herself. She was crying softly now, unprotesting, her head still buried in her arms. "So it *is* true what your grandfather said. . . . And then you have the nerve to accuse me of not trusting you when you have *always* lied to me. My God, Nicole, don't you realize what you have done? You have made a fool of me! As a psychiatrist! As a man! Your husband-to-be!"

She raised herself then, kneeling in the soft green moss under the cherry tree, and stared through the blinding stream of tears at her lover, saying nothing, only shaking her head wordlessly. Her swollen lips were moving but no words formed on them.

Jesse turned to the victorious figure of Louis Luckstone. "I'm sorry, LL. I had no idea. The official reports never mentioned. . . ."

"Of course they don't," Luckstone dismissed this new objection with a magnanimous wave of the hand. He stepped forward and quickly grasped Jesse's right hand in both of his. "I had that detail removed," he explained, "to protect Nicole. Some Mexican officials are very easy to bribe, really."

"I don't know what to say, sir. I'm just. . . ."

"Forget it, my boy." Luckstone bestowed his most gracious smile on the young doctor. "And I don't hold the fact that you were ready to give up on your promising future for the love of my granddaughter against you at all. I value loyalty, Jesse, I admire it. It shows strength of character. That's why I am doubly determined to see that you *will* take over the Center in a couple of years."

Jesse swallowed hard, unable to fathom how far he could trust the present mood of Louis Luckstone.

"Thank you," he said in an almost inaudible whisper.

"Perhaps all of us have said things this afternoon we didn't really mean in the heat of batt . . . of arguing." Luckstone's voice had regained its old bounce, was steadfast once more, undefeated, in contrast to the other participants in the drama. "I am convinced, though," he continued, "that by the time you head the Center, Jesse, Nicole will have benefited greatly from the therapy and be free to enjoy life as we all wish her to enjoy it."

Jesse knew there and then that only one thing was worse than being too closely allied to Louis Luckstone, and that was *not* being closely allied to him.

Hesitating a few seconds longer, the psychiatrist cast his eyes down and cupped the billionaire's hands with his own. Both men shook on their unwritten contract.

43

"Kurt! . . . Kurt, please!"

Nicole's unexpectedly strong exclamation one more time drew everybody's attention to the girl kneeling in the moss. She was holding both arms out before her and extending them to the injured concentration camp officer.

Kurt Frank felt his face burn as he was torn by his reborn loyalty to Louis Luckstone and the pathetic female who had offered to come to his aid when he stood alone and despised.

"What do you want?" he asked shakily.

"I'll help you." The words came out of the battered woman with enormous effort—a thread of verbal anguish compounded by the fear of ostracism. "As I promised. No strings attached. . . . I won't let you down . . . ever."

All eyes turned toward the wounded war criminal. Kurt sized up the group nervously, and paused for a brief painful moment, almost apologetically, on the noncommittal face of his benefactor. Finally he shuffled down the flagstone path between the thick, luxuriant vegetation and with his good left hand grabbed the outstretched hands of the young woman.

He planted a respectful dry kiss on the skin that was grainy with soil and caked with blood, then straightened up stiffly.

"I thank you most kindly, Miss Nicole, for the offer," he said in his deep rumbling voice, emphasizing each syllable as if to soften the impact of the message with the sincerity of his feelings. "But you must understand, Ludi and I always were like brothers. Even in the camps. I can't desert him now, for the few years we have left on earth. . . . Perhaps . . . perhaps it's for the best, Miss Nicole, for you . . . for all of us, if you take a little rest in . . . well, you know where."

And he disengaged himself swiftly from her desperate clasp, from the eyes pleading, that held him in thrall of the memory of a million victims being led up The Tube to the gas chambers. He turned quickly, avoiding the glances of the others.

Luckstone at once dropped Jesse's hands and strode toward his former friend and tormentor. When he was within arm's reach of him he drew the ex-*Sturmbannführer* close and without further ado hugged him in a brotherly embrace. Momentarily taken off guard, Kurt stood petrified, unyielding as an oak, and gingerly tapped Luckstone's backside with his good hand.

They were standing in a pool of blood under the white blossoms of a dogwood tree and remained frozen in this ungainly bear hug when Kurt suddenly exclaimed, "The blood!"

"What?" Luckstone pulled back, alarmed.

"The blood from my wounded hand is dirtying your suit."

"Oh." A smile of relief wreathed the financier's face. "*Your* blood! . . . Remember the last time we embraced like this, Kurt? . . . Outside Como. Blood then stained our suits too. Inge's blood."

"Jesus, yes—you're right." A deep frown wrinkled Kurt's brow. "She'd be in her fifties now."

"But what would she've thought of you once she learned the truth?" Nicole's words lacked vigor, and her voice came out devoid of all impact, in the stuffed-head-cold tone of a woman who had sobbed heartrendingly. "Probably have cursed both of you to eternal hell—back to Treblinka!"

"My dear Nicole," her grandfather said with a grand show of patience, gazing calmly down at her. "Don't you realize that your own cruel words convict you of not being fit to live among peaceful people?"

"Like you?" The tortured girl spat blood on the floor. "How strange this *Waffen SS* language sounds coming from you, Grandfather. I'm sorry I destroyed the purity of your perfect little society here!"

No one uttered a sound. Only stillness met her outraged cynicism. She tried to rise from the floor, but merely managed to hobble a few paces on her knees, then fell back against the trunk of a lemon tree, utterly weakened.

"For Chrissakes, can't you see it, you fools!" she cried out with a final outburst of energy. "That you're repeating it all over."

A downcast Irene Fischmann raised her head. "Repeating what?"

"Playing Nietzsche's monsters—kapos to my grandfather's Camp *Kommandant*. A man who won't . . . who still can't expiate his culpability in what he did in the past and is doing to you now."

"But he *is* expiating," Paul Hammer remonstrated feebly, avoiding the girl's eyes. "He *is* paying reparations for the sins he committed."

"Like Johann Tetzel's sinners with their absolutions and indulgences five hundred years ago!" Contempt defied the weakness in Nicole's voice and strengthened it. "You behave as if there were no absolute moral truth, Paul. Rationalizing everything with excuses. . . . Are you that blind, all of you, you can't recognize that even today you still play the part of the good, silent Germans of the nineteen-thirties?" A shudder passed through her young ravaged body. "Why is it that human beings always create their own Auschwitzes? Hell—here I am, the *innocent* new arrival being sent to the death house, and all you can do is nod in agreement." Exhausted again, she slumped back against the lemon tree.

"With all due respect, Miss Nicole, but the point *isn't* innocence," Kurt Frank interjected politely, holding his mangled lower arm steady.

"It's strength. And the weak have always had to pay for the good of the strong. Survival of the fittest."

"That's a lie!" thundered a voice from the back of the conference room. "They pay for being weak—outnumbered!" A chair was upset somewhere, toppling with a loud crash on the floor. "Can't you see?" shouted John Shadow. "You're killing the girl with this mockery of justice! Have you no eyes, you bullies, no conscience?"

Everyone had turned in amazement to observe Luckstone's former aide walking energetically past the stunned congregation and charging into the hothouse.

"You're coming with me, Nicole," he announced in a tone of absolute determination, and helped the girl to her feet. "We are no longer wanted here . . . either of us. . . . Can you manage?" She nodded wordlessly, a tiny, astonished smile twisting her swollen lips. "Don't worry, I'll look after you—especially now that I've got no career left."

Tears came anew out of Nicole's puffed up eyes and converted her clownishly streaked skin into a wash of pink, black and claret. "Oh John . . . John," she whispered. "Thank you." She raised his hand to her lips and kissed the tips of his fingers.

"Shadow!"

Luckstone's commanding voice boomed through the glasshouse, startling his former confidant.

"Don't listen to him!" Nicole whispered. Fear was already distorting her grateful, trusting expression.

"Let's go," he muttered, careful not to turn around to Luckstone as he guided her slowly, cautiously, by the elbow, down the marble path that led out of the greenhouse. "Let those cowards find another victim to gang up on."

"John Shadow, I am addressing you," the tycoon raised a voice well-versed in the art of command.

Shadow could no longer control himself. He wheeled on his former master. His eyes burned with an insatiable furor.

"I don't give a *damn* whether you address me or not!" he flung back, the pent-up anger of the afternoon's humiliation and of three decades finally boiling over. "I'm finished being your lackey. Do you understand?" The words rushed out in a burst of wrath. "I've given you *everything* for decades and that's the thanks I get: you boot me out. I tried to protect you, to save your reputation, but you step on me, as you did on Frau Fischmann. Well, let me tell you, Herr Glückstein, the times are gone when I've got to quake every time you throw one of your tantrums. Because now I *am* free. Do you hear? Free! And Nicki is coming with me. She's an adult, and we're going to walk out of here, *together*, and there's not a damn thing in the world you can do about it!"

For a shocked second, Louis Luckstone stared at his former assistant, not trusting his ears, then burst out laughing.

"Did you hear that, all of you? Did you? The liberated slave spitting at his master!" He walked around the conference table. "What's gotten into you all of a sudden, John? So meek for thirty-five years and now playing Goliath."

"Don't you even remember?" Shadow snapped back. "You not only attacked me physically; you swore you'd ruin me. You fired me."

"Fired you?" The billionaire shook his head in apparent disbelief and glanced around, as though trying to have everyone join in his little private joke. Instead, a dead hush met his pretense of wonderment. For a fraction of a second, LL winced with embarrassment, then, like a man used to go on the offensive, he approached the abused woman and her indignant champion, extending his arms, palms upward, in a gesture of warmth, reconciliation and friendship. Even so, he wisely stopped a few steps short of them.

"Why do you take everything so seriously, John?" Luckstone addressed Shadow in his most ingratiating voice. "In all those years with me you should have learned *some*thing about the way I treat crises. Goodness gracious! Here I felt I was betrayed by you, so my first reaction was to fire you. Hell, you've fired secretaries just for being late twice in a row." A wide, gold-toothed smile again broke through the sternness of his features. "I'm sorry, John. I truly am. I was wrong for losing my temper. But you've got to look at it from my angle too. Two innocent lives butchered because of your silence. That's unforgivable! Yet even so I'm willing to let bygones be bygones, tragic as their loss is to all of us. And I'll say it again, John, if—at the height of my anger—I questioned your character and lost my head, I want to apologize. In fact, right in front of these witnesses, I'll ask you for your forgiveness."

"You what?" Shadow asked skeptically.

"You heard. I am asking you to forgive me. It was inexcusable of me to attack you like that."

"And your granddaughter? You almost killed her, LL."

"But we're talking about you now, aren't we?" Luckstone turned around to the astounded audience and managed to elicit a few halfhearted nods of agreement from them. "There, you see! They *want* you to join the team again. It's not a question of forgetting, John, but forgiving, and don't tell me that you're less capable of forgiveness than these fellow sufferers from my past. Come on—after all our years together I think I know you well enough to describe you as a *Mensch*, a friend who doesn't harbor a grudge."

Shadow dropped Nicole's hand and stared at Luckstone in total confusion. "You still call me your friend? After what happened here?"

"As God . . . and my friends here are my witnesses. John, let me put all my cards on the table. Without you, I couldn't go on. I mean it. I need you. I'm not afraid of admitting it in front of these people. *And* I know I can depend on you that word of what happened here this afternoon won't leave this house, ever." He waited expectantly, but was insistent on forcing an answer from Shadow. "Right?"

"I don't know . . . LL, I just don't know . . . the way you hurt me," Shadow said, wavering already in his determination to take Nicole out of her grandfather's grasp.

"Let's not forget about our long partnership, John, shall we? After all, we've been together thirty-five years. The Luckstone-Shadow team, that's what they call us. . . . Listen, John, I hadn't brought this up before, but a famous writer approached me a month ago that he was interested in collaborating with me on my autobiography, and surely you'd like to be included in it, wouldn't you? After all, your contribution to my conglomerate is priceless, indispensable. We were talking about it just the other day with Jesse, remember? How you were the one to suggest that we shatter the American-company mold, promote only the talented, *not* our friends, and give our work force huge economic benefits. Engenders loyalty and pride in their work, you said. My God, you don't want me to edit all this out of the book, John, as well as our friendship, our team spirit, do you? And that's another thing: I was using that term—the Luckstone-Shadow team—only a couple of weeks ago while discussing the Luckstone City ground-breaking with the President. He wasn't even surprised when I mentioned to him . . . well, I wasn't going to tell you this just yet, but under the circumstances. . . . You see, John, I've decided that the large Mall in the center of the new town will be named after you. So our names are linked forever! It was supposed to be a surprise, John, but . . . well you know." He stopped for a matter of seconds to let the surprise of his message sink in. "What do you say? . . . Are we still partners then? Still friends?"

"Don't!" It wasn't Shadow rejecting the generous offer, but Nicole's imploring voice. "Don't, Grandfather! Leave me one friend!"

She turned away from Shadow, dejectedly, resting her forehead against the slender trunk of the blooming lemon tree.

"Be honest now! What can she offer you, John?" the billionaire drove his point home relentlessly. "Besides, hasn't she betrayed you enough?"

"What d'you mean: betrayed me?" Shadow looked at him blankly. "Nicki has never been treacherous."

"Hasn't she?" Scorn, pure scorn registered on Luckstone's face. "Your son knew the secret. About the incest. Yet she kicked him out. Out of her house, her life, when he needed her most, when she could have saved him. Don't you realize David may have died because of her—her rejection? Jesus Christ! If you did know, John, what exactly *is* it you are after? To live with that memory in the flesh right beside you? The killer of your son! Is that what you want?"

"Gramps!" Nicole's body shook helplessly in the spasm of a new crying fit as the hopelessness of her situation became a reality. She was all spent, deserted by everyone. "Why. . . . God, why are you killing me, Gramps?"

"Come on, John!" Luckstone guardedly approached his aide. "Nobody is killing Nicki. We all want the best for her. But she does need help. Even her psychiatrist agrees to that. And she *will* get the best treatment available from medical science, I promise you that. But she's sick, and she *must* be cured—you realize that, don't you?"

A wave of sympathy came over Shadow as he gazed in silence at the pitiful sight of the girl cringing against the lemon tree. "Yes," he whispered.

Luckstone immediately snatched his aide's hands. "That's why I respect you, John," he said firmly, holding both hands warmly in his. "You *always* are a man of decision. She'll stay at the Center. Under Jesse's personal care. And I promise you that she won't be alone. She will be surrounded by friends—new friends, old friends. In fact, Jesse,"—LL turned to the psychiatrist he still recognized as his prospective grandson-in-law—"I want you to requisition an entire floor in the new wing at the Center. A suite of rooms for Nicki, and one for Kurt with his hand, and of course appropriate accommodations for Irene Fischmann. Even if she's stubborn about being helped, I still want the doctors to take a look at her arm. And I want all this done by tonight."

"It'll be arranged, LL."

"I depend on you, Jesse. Get in touch with the chief at the Interferon Labs; tell them we need a team of top surgeons to treat Nicki and the rest. Is that clear?"

"I'll see to it right away. . . . Hey, Nick—look out!"

Nicole was sliding down alongside the lemon tree; she slumped in a heap on the bed of moss, twisting her face away from everyone. Jesse cast a questioning glance in Luckstone's direction and, seeing the billionaire give a slight nod of consent, hurried past him and raised his granddaughter up gently under her arms.

"You know what to do, Jesse," Luckstone said. "Take good care of her!"

Jesse draped one of Nicole's arms over his shoulders and slung his left arm around her slender waist.

Her breath came in short, shallow gasps as she repeated brokenly over and over, "Why . . . oh God, why. . . ?"

"We all love you," Jesse said in a tender murmur. "Nicki, I love you. I'm sorry . . . I lost my temper with you."

She lifted her head with a Herculean effort, her great pain visible to all, and through the blinding wash of tears made out the silent, frozen faces staring after her as Jesse shepherded her out.

"Nicki!"

Jesse and his fiancée stopped under the walnut tree and turned around to her grandfather. "Regarding the new Concert Center in Luckstone City"—his voice echoed through the hothouse—"weeks ago I gave instructions to the architects that it be named after you. That's my special gift for you. Now go along, children!"

But Nicole did not move. She stared incredulously at the man who was sealing her fate, the door to her future.

"Don't, Grandfather, don't you bribe *me*!" she said at last. "Everyone, but not me. And you know what you can *do* with your Concert Center!"

"Nicki!" John Shadow looked aghast after the unhappy young woman. "Turning down this magnanimous offer! You *must* be out of your mind!"

Nicole nodded sadly. "Maybe I am, John. Perhaps the just, the idealists of this world *are* insane." Her voice was thick and her eyes again clouded with tears. "I no longer know what it was, outrage . . . events . . . or madness, that snapped my mind. . . . But one thing I know: I won't leave the Center again, ever."

A stillness of guilt and shame weighed heavily upon everyone in the oppressive heat of the greenhouse. Fear and promises had converted Rosedale into a thorny haven.

As the young couple slowly, painfully, weaved its way along the path overhung with dark fronds, Luckstone quickly urged Kurt Frank, who was nearly in a state of shock from the loss of blood, to join them, so that he and Irene Fischmann, too, could be accommodated immediately in the new medical wing of the Rehabilitation Center. There, Kurt could be treated at once for his wound.

"John!" Luckstone pulled Shadow aside and, placing a hand on his shoulder, spoke to him in a subdued voice. "You better help Jesse out. You have the experience. I leave it to you to get hold of the surgeons. See that everybody has the best food and keep me informed how Nicki's adjusting to everything."

"Okay. Will do, LL." Shadow nodded officiously, his old obliging self again, and followed the others out into the garden.

"You too, Paul." LL turned to Paul Hammer who was the last of the uninvited guests left behind at the Executive Mansion. "They're your friends and I want you to stay with them, look after them for the first few days at least."

"I'd love to, but it's impossible," Hammer said apologetically. "I must be back at my job on. . . ."

"Nonsense! Your place is with your friends, Paul, right here!" Luckstone interrupted him sharply. "You're no longer with Elwin, Boyd and Cohn. I'll contact Gustafson in London about it tonight. You have your hundred thousand annuity, and you know you can come to me for anything else you need. Jesse tells me you love to paint. So now you have the rest of your life to follow your vocation."

Hammer met Luckstone's eyes resolutely, then nodded. "Thank you, LL."

He was about to pass the billionaire when the latter stopped him.

"That fiancée of yours," he said, frowning. "The one who was killed so tragically—what was her name?"

A puzzled look darkened Hammer's features. "Danielle Brulle."

"I intend to name a street in her honor in my new city. And, of course, the same goes for Karl Ludwig. And your parents. Especially your mother. None of them must be forgotten, especially in death."

For a few seconds Paul Hammer could not move. He swallowed hard. Instinctively, his hands reached out for his former torturer's.

"Thank you . . . thank you from the bottom of my heart, LL, for this kind gesture."

"And the streets leading to the main plaza will bear the names of Klaus and Inge Glückstein. And my wife's, my parents'."

"Yes, LL. . . . That *will* make a fitting tribute to our lost loved ones." And, curiously, Hammer recalled Thomas Mann's words that no man's thoughts be ruled by death.

The two men regarded each other silently for a few more moments, encircled by white, pink and blue hydrangea shrubs, when all of a sudden a change came over Paul Hammer. He pulled his hand out of his donor's with quite unbecoming brusqueness. An expression of doubt, even dismay, entered his eyes, and he lowered them guiltily.

"Anything wrong?" Luckstone asked, already on guard.

Hammer gazed up at the billionaire. "No, of course not." But his frown deepened. "Yes, I think there is, LL. . . . It's silly perhaps, but . . . to tell the truth, I *am* worried."

"You are? About what?"

"I don't quite know how to say this . . . but now that the others are gone, I think I better speak out on it."

"I don't understand. Speak out on what?" Luckstone eyed him suspiciously.

"Something that's been bothering me the last few minutes, LL."

"Well, out with it then."

"It's almost impossible to put into words. But when you attacked Nicole, I . . . well, there were those eyes of yours, the same cold, brutal expression I remember from the time you killed my mother. And then. . . . "

"But that's ridiculous, Hammer!" the financier protested. "All I. . . ."

"No, let me finish, please! It's not you personally I'm afraid of; it's the uncertainty that despite all your good deeds, your offer of the annuity, you may suddenly decide to turn against me, against Irene, when we least expect it, and put *us* out of the way the way you're doing now with Nicole."

"Nonsense. She'll be out soon."

"Just tell me how can I ever be sure if there isn't some sniper lurking behind a tree taking a shot at me, or a bomb has been planted in my car, in my stove. We know so much about each other now that I'm a danger to you—I admit it!—as you're one to me. There's no getting away from this fact. And when I saw you almost kill your own flesh and blood this afternoon, I thought what chance do *we* have—total strangers—if something displeases you about *us*? . . . God, I wish I didn't have to say any of this. I'm sorry, LL, I just no longer know what to do."

"You mean you don't believe me, that I'm serious about wishing you well, you and Irene, to atone for the crimes of my past?"

"Oh I do, I do. But what if you suddenly become as fearful of us as we are of you now? Fear can turn anyone into a coward . . . or a killer, as you well know. Maybe I should just disappear, not even accept your money."

The two men stared at each other for a long time. Grasser had followed Hammer's impassioned outburst in silence and gazed at his shoes, immobile, at a deferential distance.

"In other words," Luckstone said at last with a deep sigh, "we're back on Square One. You're still the committed crusader and may even go to the press and tell them about me. Is that it?"

Hammer's eyes fixed on Luckstone's, unflinching. "Don't put me on the spot, LL. Please! I only. . . ."

"No, sir. It's *you* who's putting *me* on the spot. And I demand an answer. I think, considering my life is at stake, I'm entitled to one."

"I don't think so . . . I no longer know," Hammer said miserably, and his shoulders sloped from fatigue, from sheer emotional exhaustion. "I'm tired, LL . . . and, like Irene, I just want to be left alone."

"Well, maybe you should have considered all this before breaking in here." Luckstone shrugged his shoulders and started cleaning his spectacles with his handkerchief. "Anyway, if that's what's bothering you I'll be only too happy to oblige and leave you alone . . . provided you leave *me* alone. I'll give you my word on that."

"Yes." Hammer nodded gravely, knowing that he could *never* be sure if Lucksotne would stick to his promise. "Your word."

"Fine. That's settled then. We won't interfere in each other's lives. Okay?" He smiled down at the distraught art director of Elwin, Boyd & Cohn, but his eyes were cold, suspicious. "I think," he said, feigning casualness, "you better follow Jesse and the rest to the Rehabilitation Center. They may be worried about what happened to you."

"Yes." Hammer felt beaten, unavenged. "Of course, you're right."

Their eyes met once more, briefly, but even though only an arm's length separated the two men, an unbridgeable gulf seemed to open up between them, then Hammer turned abruptly to leave the greenhouse and hurried after his wounded, unhappy friends. Once outside, he strolled pensively across a lawn and approached his rented car, which was still parked in front of Nicole's Music Salon, but his steps now were hesitant, shaky.

It occurred to Paul Hammer that he felt twenty years older than he had early that morning when setting out for Rosedale with Kurt and Irene.

44

When they finally were alone, Louis Luckstone turned rapidly to his bodyguard, who had watched the rise and fall of the tide of battle, for the most part in stunned silence.

"I could have been killed, you damn fool!" Luckstone exploded with unexpected vehemence. "What the hell do you think I hired you for?"

Grasser stared in disbelief at his employer. "Mr. Luckstone," he said, trying to sound steady and purposeful as he entered the glasshouse. "I had no way of knowing where the intruders were hiding out. I've pointed it out to you before, sir. The grounds are too large for one man to cover."

Luckstone adjusted his cleaned glasses on the bridge of his nose and glared at this man who had failed him, totally disregarding the logic of the protest. "First these goddamn maniacs from the past try to destroy me, and then that crazy granddaugther of mine with that insane fixation on absolute justice goes berserk. All because of *your* incompetence!"

"I resent that, sir. If we had had more bodyguards. . . ."

"Don't you raise your voice at me, you lame-brain!" Luckstone thundered. "And I don't give a good goddamn what you resent!" He glowered at Grasser and angrily kicked at one of the *objets d'art*—the nose of the Roman bust—which was destroyed in the wild melee. "Well, maybe you're right," he reflected after a minute of deliberation. "I do need more protection. Ironic, though, isn't it? One of the great philanthropists of modern times needing the tightest security—it's laughable! Still,"—he shrugged—"I guess it's cheaper than having to. . . ." He left the thought wisely unspoken, his countenance grim and unyielding, then nodded in businesslike fashion at his bodyguard. "All right, Grasser, make the necessary arrangements. Hire twelve men. The best sharpshooters. And some watchdogs. You'll be in charge of everything. That clear?"

"Thank you, sir. You can depend on me."

"Good. And tell Shadow to have someone design uniforms for the men. Simple dark uniforms, dignified ones, nothing ostentatious. Shadow will know what I want—he's good at that kind of bullshit assignment."

"Very well, sir."

"Then, for tonight, right after dinner, I want you to come along with me to the Rehabilitation Center, with your gun."

"Of course, sir. It's here somewhere in the glasshouse." His eyes were already searching for it.

"I know, damn it! . . . Unless Jesse's got it. . . . But I've got to keep an eye on them, make sure that these troublemakers are well taken care of and keep their mouths shut." Another bothersome thought passed through his turbulent mind. "I also want the Center to get rid of the Baldwin . . . have it replaced by a Steinway."

Luckstone was about to enter the conference room when he changed his mind once more. "Grasser," he called after the hastily departing bodyguard.

"Sir?" Grasser stopped at the greenhouse exit, knitting his brow apprehensively.

"On your way out, tell the switchboard to get me the Kuwait office. Now! I've got to catch up on business. Wasted the whole goddamn afternoon."

45

Louis Luckstone watched Grasser cross the lawn, then headed himself for his study to check the messages received on the teletype machine. He gripped the silver-plated doorknob of the conference room and pulled, but to his amazement the door would not open.

"Damn!"

Paul Hammer had never returned the key! LL had forgotten to ask him for it. Hammer spelled trouble, bad trouble. The committed crusader—that's what he was. A man with a conscience.

Deeply in thought, Luckstone traced his steps back through the conference room and the greenhouse and walked out into the garden to reach the front of the Executive Mansion. The shadows of the blue spruces had lengthened considerably with the setting sun and cast elongated daggers across the darkening lawn. It had grown unexpectedly cool. There was a nip in the air, and Luckstone shivered.

He entered his headquarters and glanced at the roll of telex messages from all over the world, inquiries and transactions dealing with gold, oil, coal, electronics, stocks and bonds, but somehow his mind could not focus on the statistics and fiscal verbiage spewing from the fiercely chattering apparatus. Even so, he returned the call to Kuwait.

But LL's thoughts dwelled exclusively on Paul Hammer, on his fickleness and undependability to keep his mouth shut, in spite of the fact that he had been offered what any other mortal would have considered the answer to his lifelong prayers: retirement, leisure, and financial security to pursue his every dream. Now this damn conscience of his was going to ruin it all, including, perhaps, the financier's own future. Evidently Hammer still fantasized that Luckstone was going to revert to the brutal behavioral stage of his death camp practices; he actually thought that the assault on his granddaughter had snapped LL's mind back to the dark, blood-drenched days of playing kapo in Treblinka and Auschwitz. Damn it, Hammer was a fool to boot!

No, Luckstone could not allow his laboriously built-up corporate empire to be torpedoed by letting an absolute nobody—the little common man with an atrophied ego—ride roughshod over him and start an avalanche of cannonballs rolling in his direction and, possibly, drag people like Irene Fischmann and John Shadow and Nicki along with him until this unreasonable fire culminated in the total destruction of Luckstone's good name, his autocratic command. Hammer meant trouble, serious, incorrigible trouble!

Plainly, none of this had anything to do with being a Christian or Jew, a German or American. The road Hammer took was blind, unpacified revenge; all to rectify an alleged wrong. It always drove humans needlessly, endlessly, into the cul-de-sac of torture chambers—creating new holocausts.

Louis Luckstone realized that Paul Hammer had never fully comprehended Goethe's dictum that with only the slightest shift in a man's character, there was no crime that he was incapable of committing. Moreover, LL felt that Hammer had not made a single attempt in his life to redeem himself by good deeds, only by feelings of retribution. In short, Jesse's father had learned nothing in a lifetime of trials and tribulations, the industrialist brooded. *And* Hammer stood condemned by his own words that he was a danger to the financier. Let him be hoisted then by his own petard.

Paul Hammer had to be stopped at all costs!

And yet—on second thought, LL reflected, wasn't he himself a danger to Hammer too? Weren't we all, in the last resort, hostages to each other?

Louis Luckstone dropped his eyelids, like a visor, but an instant later realized that there was no need to feel pangs of guilt over his secret ponderings . . . and he glanced at his watch. It was almost seven o'clock. Time for supper. Yet he was not the least bit hungry. He'd give the afternoon visitors another ten minutes, to make sure they had all arrived and settled in the new wing of the Rehabilitation Center, then get in touch with Jesse. Suddenly he wondered how much he could rely on Paul Hammer's son, where *his* loyalties lay when it came to the nitty-gritty.

The billionaire collapsed in the swivel chair in his mammoth office, his fingers nervously drumming the monumental walnut desk.

Soon he'd know if Jesse would pass the ultimate test and be on his side or that of his enemies. In any event, he wanted this main point cleared up before making his personal appearance at the Center later that night.

46

Slowly, LL picked up the receiver. His eyes feverishly scanned a page in his private telephone book. He pressed the numbered push buttons on the underside of the receiver, the uncertainty of the conversation's outcome knotting his stomach into a ball.

He had to let it ring about a dozen times before Jesse Hammer answered the telephone, out of breath.

Yes, everything was all right at the Center. The patients had been shown to their private accommodations—the priority units—and seemed reasonably happy, considering everything. No, Jesse's father was not around. At this moment he was upstairs with Nicole, and when Jesse had left the two they were involved in a rather conspiratorial, whispering conversation, which oddly enough seemed to put Nicole very much at ease.

Hell—it flashed through Luckstone's mind—Hammer is already working on his granddaughter—as if she needed a great deal of persuasion to come over to his side.

LL knew he had to strike now, fast, before any extraneous business threatened to interfere with his plan. He came straight to the point, telling Jesse what had transpired after everybody except for Paul Hammer had left Rosedale.

"Oh no!" exclaimed the psychiatrist. "I thought most of these problems had been ironed out. As a matter of fact," he added quickly, "just before Kurt Frank passed out in the car he told me that he and Dad and Irene had accepted your money offer and were prepared to forget all about that awful mission of theirs." A short stretch of silence underscored the mental confusion at Jesse's end of the line. Then: "LL, there must be something we can do about this . . . together."

We—together!

Luckstone heaved a sigh of relief. Jesse saw his own fate inextricably linked to that of the tycoon's.

"We will, my boy. I'm just as upset about these new developments as you are. First my own flesh and blood turned against me and *she* had to be committed. And now it's *your* father."

"I warned him once before, LL, when he attacked Shadow, two weeks ago, that he's as wild as any of the patients at the Center, that he also could be committed one day."

"I'm afraid, Jesse, you're right. He *is* a dangerous man. Completely irrational. A tragic consequence of what the Nazis did to him. You know, he actually sent you a letter, Kurt told me, that you're supposed to forward to his attorney."

"A letter?"

"In case anything happened to him. It lists all the grisly things that occurred in Treblinka. And to cap it, he's still blaming me in the letter for the murders of his fiancée and Karl Ludwig."

"And you can assure me, you had nothing to do with this, LL?"

"Of course not! I even proved it to him that Josh Hamilton was behind it. In fact, in your father's presence I called Josh and ordered him to cease with this ghastly plot at once. I didn't even learn about it till this afternoon. Yet he still holds me responsible."

"That is paranoia, LL. Almost schizoid."

"I'm sorry, but I've got to agree with you, my boy. And if your father's letter ever gets to see the light of day, we're finished, you and I. With me out of the way, you wouldn't stand a chance of getting the directorship of the Center. You know, the old entrenched doctors wouldn't let you."

"Well, it *won't* see the light of day, LL," came Jesse's determined reply. "I'm going to destroy the letter. That's an outrage, after what you intend to do for him."

"Not just the annuity, Jesse. I even informed him I'd name streets after him and his mother, your grandmother and your grandfather. In Luckstone City. But it all seems to fall on deaf ears. He's set on destroying us."

"Malicious I call it. I've never known him to be so destructive. Sorry, LL, but I think I better keep him here for a while. With the rest. For observation."

Luckstone slumped back into his chair. A world-heavy load dropped from his shoulders. His eyes lit upon a bowl of apples imported from France. He grabbed one of them off his desk and bit eagerly into it.

"You're the doctor; you know best, my boy," he said. "But give him comfortable quarters. The best treatment. Even if he's got to be locked up. Indefinitely. I'll make all the other arrangements regarding the termination of his job."

"You can depend on me, LL. He'll get a good room, barred windows, however; but with a beautiful view of the maple forest. After all, he's my father."

"Great. And look after the others too. How are they taking it so far?"

"Pretty well. A surgeon is already working on Kurt and another's examining Irene. I put them up in adjoining units."

"Good. They deserve each other. They always did." Luckstone took another hefty bite out of the juicy apple. "You're a good boy, Jesse, the best. I think you deserve something too. . . . Tell me, do you remember my speaking about the children's hospital I'm going to build in Luckstone City?"

"Of course, sir."

"Well, I've decided to name it after you," he said, munching heartily on the apple. "What do you say? The Jesse Hammer Children's Clinic."

The pause at the other end could not conceal the pride, the ecstasy Jesse felt at hearing this awesome news, of seeing his own name engraved in granite, perhaps for centuries to come. Jesse Hammer as good as immortalized at the age of thirty!

"Thank you, LL," at last came the husky response. "I'll always be indebted to you for that!"

"As long as you know what to do, son. Use that psychological method of yours. Change their minds, quickly. Nicole's and your father's. They're not to be released until they think exactly as we do."

"I know my duty, LL."

"Good. Then act on it!"

Louis Luckstone slammed the receiver into its base.

_____ . . . _____